The Maelstrom

Matthew Barnes

Copyright © 2012 Matthew Barnes

All rights reserved.

ISBN-10: **1477645896**

ISBN-13: **978-1477645895**

FOR ISOBEL

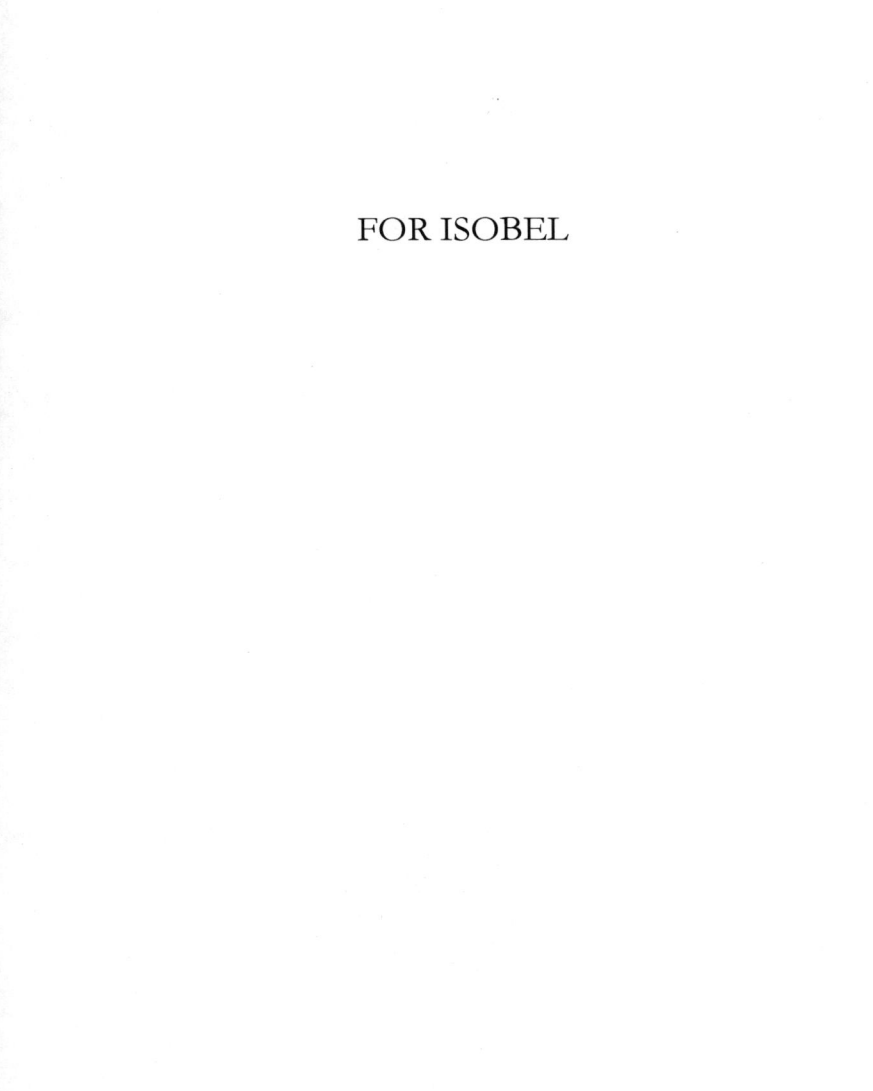

ACKNOWLEDGMENTS

I would just like to thank all of my friends for their support and encouragement over the years but in particular, to Staff Nurse Clare Verrall for her time in getting me started. Without her knowledge I would never have found the confidence to begin. Inexpressible thanks must go to my editor, friend and butt kicker, Kate Eglinton for reining me in. To my parents for always being there. And to my partner, Dawn, for her constant love and support throughout. Thank you all.

Chapter One

Five Months Ago

From the shadows *He* watched, motionless, feeling nothing from a black and wizened heart that had been dead since the moment of *His* creation. Unseen, *He* observed with intrigue as the paramedics unloaded Nicholas Howell's shattered body from the back of the ambulance and rushed his gurney into the hospital. *He* knew that time was no longer a luxury Nick could afford and so, patiently, *He* waited for the last of the dying man's life force to ebb away. Once gone, then would be *His* time to strike.

'Hold the doors, please.'

With his head restrained, Nick opened his eyes for the briefest of seconds only to be blinded by the harsh glare of strip lights as they soared overhead; blocks of white interrupted by shadow.

'How long has it been since his last arrest?'

'Seven minutes.'

'Daniel, we need a theatre prepped and ready, please.'

Nick began to gag as his mouth filled with blood coughing out torrents that fell back upon him smattering his face and running down the side of his neck soaking his hair and collar.

'Damn it, he's choking. Move him on his side ... try to keep his mouth open.'

Nick's cheek was pushed against the cold plastic of the gurney and his mouth drained of blood. The oxygen flowed again but, unable to prevent his coughing, spits of blood were projected at the corridor wall.

The rooms along the corridor sped by, and each time Nick's gurney rushed by an open door he snatched a glimpse of the unlit quarters inside. Through the first he saw an empty chair at the back of the room before the sight was replaced by the chipped surface of the corridor wall. Another doorway sped by containing nothing but darkness, then once again the blank corridor wall. Another empty room with an identical chair flitted by. Then through the next open door, Nick saw *Him.*

Half dead and paralysed by fear, Nick's eyes widened but the doorway disappeared from view.

Nick felt a hand press against his shoulder as he struggled to speak. 'We need to hurry.'

The rushing team passed a closed door, followed by another and then another but when the gurney travelled by the next open one, Nick again saw the monster half masked in shadow staring back at him with unmistakable hatred in its eyes. He wanted to scream but his broken jaw refused to work and his blood stained tongue was numb.

As quickly as the dark angel had appeared, *He* was gone again.

With a resonant bang, the gurney clattered through a set of swing doors and Nick felt his entire body wrack with pain as the impact vibrated across its metal frame. In that instant, his vision blacked out.

'How did you escape?'

Nick's eyes flashed open again to see a shrouded figure looming above him, the eyes just visible above the surgical mask.

'Okay ready, on my mark, one, and two ...'

Nick felt his body rise as countless hands transferred him from the gurney to an operating table.

'R.T.A, massive loss of blood, cranial collapse-'

'Do we have a name?'

'There was a wallet in his jeans. No drivers licence but the name on his bank card says Nicholas Howell.

Records are doing a search on him now.'

'Excellent. Good evening, Nicholas. Pleased to meet you. Right then, I think we need to get those shards out of his brain for starters.'

'BP's 115 over 83. Pulse 146 and rising.'

'Okay, we need to work fast. What was the eta on those records? We need a blood type.'

'Soon as. Blood's been notified.'

'Damn, this thing is really wedged in here.'

'Steady.'

'BP's dropping.'

'Damn it. Could somebody please get me a line in? Come on, people.'

Hacking out more blood, Nick's vision turned crimson and his screams filled the theatre as he squeezed his eyes tight to cope with the pain.

'*How did you escape?!*' a voice yelled, its words emanating from behind Nick's eyelids.

'Ah ... doh ... unersand ...' he mumbled, coughing out more blood.

'It's all right Nick, we've got you. Surinder, we could do with some sedation about now, please.'

Whether it was the effect of the drugs or just that the end was so near, Nick began to no longer feel pain, and any fears for his own mortality which may have been there before disappeared as he lay beneath the complete mercy of the surgeon's knife. As his face was cleaned of blood, and against his will, Nick's eyes closed and he drifted off into darkness.

Suspended in the emptiness of his mind, a voice echoed out a low and hideous laughter. '*Oh Hesamuel, you are full of surprises aren't you? But there was only ever to be one outcome. There will be no cage for you this time. I shall take extreme pleasure in displaying you as my trophy; a warning to all others of the retribution for defiance.*'

Releasing a triumphant roar, the angel punctured a hole into Nick's chest with *His* powerful talons and cleaved his soul from his body.

Everyone around the operating table flinched back as Nick's unconscious body arched upward, convulsing wildly before slamming back to the table, motionless. The entire crew stood silent, unsure as to what had just happened. The ominous drone of Nick's heart rate monitor filled the room.

'VF! We're not losing this one, not today.'

A defibrillator was wheeled alongside the table from the back of the room.

'Charging ...'

'Clear!'

Nick's body rose and fell back to the table as the electrical current surged into his heart. Still nothing happened.

'Charging ...'

'Clear!'

Thud, back to the table.

'Dr James, you can only try this one more time. His body won't take any more.'

Gripping the paddles with determination, the surgeon stared at his colleagues. 'Clear.'

Thump.

'We got him, he's back!'

'Okay, that's more like it.'

'Wait. Look at his vitals.'

Placing the paddles back into the cradle, the surgeon made his way around the table to gain a better look at the monitors. 'All right, we've done a good job but he's not out of the woods just yet. Don't worry, Nick, you're not going anywhere.'

The surgeon and his team went to work on piecing back together Nick's body while in the furthest shadows of the room an unseen presence watched and waited with all

The Maelstrom

the time in the world.

Chapter Two

Present Day

'Good morning, Nick,' said a soothing calm voice. 'How are you feeling today?' It was a voice he did not recognize. Where was he? In his confused state he could not be sure of anything other than that he was in bed. Though he found it hard on his spine there was nothing he could do, his body being far too weak. Outside, in the distance, he could just make out the wail of a siren. Perhaps it was a police car, maybe an ambulance. He neither knew nor cared. It was someone else's problem.

Ever so slowly, Nick opened his eyes causing blinding white light to pierce through stabbing pain into the backs of his eyeballs. Snapping them shut again, he wanted to cry out but his inflamed throat failed him. Instead, the noise came out as a rasping sigh.

'Careful now, take your time,' the voice said as two strong hands rested him back into a more relaxed position. 'Nurse, could you bring me some water, please.'

The hands left him.

'Now, just a moment,' the voice said to Nick, then to someone else, 'make a note. Eye-opening, three. Vocal response, two.'

Nick was then told to open his eyes again. With caution, he did so and was grateful to find the curtains now closed. Through crusted eyes he tried to make out the man stood beside him, but before he had time to properly register, another face blurred into his field of vision.

'Here, drink some of this,' a pretty nurse said, offering a beaker of water to his dry lips.

Taking the first mouthful, he swilled it around

enjoying its refreshing coolness before losing control of his actions and spewing it out across the bed sheets. Though some of the water had managed to trickle down his throat and sooth a fraction of the soreness he still could not find his voice to speak.

Emitting a feeble croak, Nick gazed up from his bed at the broad black man dressed in a beige check shirt and light beige trousers. Reaching down into his right-hand pocket, the man's deep brown hand produced a set of car keys and, selecting one, used it to force pressure onto Nick's fingernail. As Nick flinched, the man smiled.

'Motor response, four. Hi,' he said, sounding pleased. 'My name is Dr. Collins. You've been our guest for a while. How are you feeling?'

Nick's look of confusion was answer enough.

'You are in hospital, Nick. You were in a really nasty accident.'

The nurse leaned over and whispered something to the doctor. Collins gave a small nod.

'Nick,' the doctor continued. 'The reason for you not being able to talk or move that well is because you are at a very delicate stage of your awakening.'

What was this man talking about? Why was he here?

'Your parents will be along soon, and I know they will be overjoyed to see you.'

Nick just managed to register what the doctor was saying. He had a family? But why could he not remember? What was happening to him?

'Please Nick, I need you to remain calm,' Collins said, lowering him back down even though the slight raising of his left shoulder was all he could manage. 'There, that's better.'

Lying in his broken state, Nick inhaled to hold back his tears and calm his already strained nerves. The bed sheet was left with the slightest of indentations where his frail hand tried to grip without success.

'There is nothing to worry about; I can assure you of that. You are in safe hands,' the doctor said. 'The staff and I are here to make sure that you are properly cared for.'

Although the statement was true, it was still far too early to predict how Nick would respond to his new environment, but Collins knew that he must project an air of optimism for the patient's sake. Taking a chair from the corner of the room, he seated himself next to the bed. 'I can imagine how traumatic this must be for you, Nick, but I assure you the worst is over with. All you have to do now is rest and allow us to help you get back on your feet and home to your family.'

This brought a weak smile to Nick's face.

'I need to be honest with you, Nick. It is essential that you know the truth, and it's important that you're clear about everything.' Collins leaned closer trying to decide on the most diplomatic route. 'From what we know of your records, you were hit by a car which failed to stop in time. The impact was severe and you shattered the windscreen, which is why you ended up with us.'

Nick remained motionless, staring at the impressions his toes made at the end of the bed.

'I won't lie; you were in a pretty bad state. I'm telling you this so that there can be no misunderstandings. I want you to be under no illusions because things may get difficult before they get better. I want you to know that you can always rely on me to be frank and honest with you. And so, you suffered three broken ribs. The bones in the upper section of your left leg were shattered needing extensive reconstruction, and you also suffered a broken collar bone.' Collins took a deep breath. 'Worst of all was the blow you took to the head. Parts of your cerebrum were damaged which caused you to go into a coma, but luckily none of the limbic sys…'

The doctor's voice faded away. *Coma?*

The Maelstrom

Collins could see that Nick was becoming agitated. 'Nick, please try to stay calm,' he said. Collins had always found it hard talking to patients, making them aware of their predicament. The look of initial confusion followed by stunned shock was always the same and always made him uncomfortable.

Nick's mind went deeper into shock. *A coma?* How long had he been asleep? His heart pounded as he struggled to keep pace with what the doctor was telling him. How long had it been?

There was a pause.

'Your awakening came as quite a nice surprise to us all, and you have been conscious now for about four weeks. You won't remember much because of the medication though, it does take some time to work its way out of your system. So, until then, you may feel drowsy or sluggish. That's normal.' The doctor lowered his head knowing what Nick was really waiting for. 'It's been five months, Nick. You've been gone for five months.'

Five months. Five months. Five months.

Nick just kept repeating it over and over again in his mind, trying to grasp the enormity of it; unable to comprehend that one moment he was… was… (Damn it!) Then in the blink of an eye, nearly half a year had been stolen from him. Without caution or consent he had been ripped away into a desolate place where even memory was a void. Sinking, suffocating, as every last living thought was peeled away until he too became nothing.

'Nick, are you all right?' the doctor asked, squeezing Nick's shoulder in an attempt to break his trance. The last thing Collins wanted was for this to be a temporary reprieve. It was the best news he had received all morning. 'Nick?'

Blinking, Nick gave his reply. 'Hm.'

'Good,' Collins said. 'I'm sure you will do a lot of thinking over the coming days, but as I said, the worst is over with so all you have to worry about now is get plenty of rest and getting well again.'

Nick just stared at the doctor with a half-baked expression, his jaw lax. The scars across his face had healed into thick faded lines, pulling at his left eye where the scar tissue had become taut. A thick disfigurement had formed around the lower part of his septum which raised his lip giving him an Elvis type grin, another traversed up into his hairline.

'Nurse,' Collins said, 'could you get me some more water, please.'

The nurse, who had waited in dutiful silence, leaned across Nick again with another half-filled beaker.

Nick tried to sip but ended up coughing it back out again. Without a fuss, the nurse mopped up the spillage to save Nick's embarrassment, and then tried again with more success.

'That's better,' she said with a smile.

'We're going to leave you for a while now, Nick,' Collins said, 'but don't worry; we'll be monitoring you from up there.'

Nick followed Collins's finger to the cold lens of a discreet surveillance camera clamped in the far corner of the room.

'I'm also going to call your parents. I know they will be overjoyed to hear the good news.'

Collins stood. 'Everything must seem very scary right now but believe me things can only get better from here on in.'

Nick's eyes were a mixture of terror and hope as his comprehension of the events unfolding around him was still too difficult for his damaged brain to grasp.

'A nurse will return later to do a few more tests on you. In the mean time, as I said, try to get some rest.'

Nick managed a slight nod and, happy with his work, Collins left the room followed by the nurse.

The Maelstrom

Today was promising to be a good day.

Chapter Three

Nick watched Collins exit through the door and out of sight. Laid there, staring at the magnolia walls, his thoughts were on fire. This could not be happening. It was impossible! Though it was difficult to recollect details, he could still remember how in the past he had experienced dreams so vivid that on waking he would have sworn them to be real.

That must be what's happening now, Nick thought. It was a frightening, realistic nightmare.

Suddenly, the memory of a crowded room consumed his mind. The people appeared moody, on edge, and drunk. Nick could feel himself smiling at them. There was no sound, just a multitude of faces sweeping faster and faster before his eyes; too fast and too many to count. Then the image was gone and his mind was still again.

After a while a creeping pain began to pinch the back of his eyeballs, an ache that started at the centre of what was left of his brain then catapulted to the front of his skull threatening to shatter the bone. He neglected to tell Collins before because it had hardly been noticeable but as the agonising seconds ticked by all Nick wanted to do was curl up and die. Desperate to rub his throbbing forehead, he lifted his shaking hand but dropped it again without success. If this was a dream, then now would be a good time to wake up. But as his struggle continued, Nick became more aware of his situation. He prayed for it not to be real. It couldn't be. Things like this never happened to you. It was always the guy on T.V. or the friend of a friend, never to you!

The doctor had said something about an accident but, try as he might, Nick could not remember a thing about it. Where was Collins, that bastard? How could he just feed him half a story and expect him to be content? He should be here, now, telling Nick how this was not real, not happening, nothing but a sick joke. It had to be!

Nick's chest heaved as his despair finally broke and tears spotted his pyjama shirt. He began to think of his mother but could only recall a rough outline to her face. The frustration only fuelled his anguish further. He began to remember how it had felt to hold her hand as child, the coarseness of her chapped skin, her touch ice cold against the warmth of his own. He remembered the aroma of her shampoo, the straggling ends of her wet hair that would rake dark wet trails down the fabric of her dressing-gown, and her smile, her beautiful reassuring smile. What he would not give to see that smile just one more time.

The feed tube inserted up Nick's nose was beginning to irritate. It would have been so easy to pull it out had he the strength to reach, but as his quivering arm still refused to move. Nick took three more attempts then gave up, the exhaustion too much for his frail body.

His head continued to pound.

For God's sake, all I want to do is scratch my fucking nose!

As the pain continued to pulverize his skull, Nick could do nothing but stare at the camera in the top corner of the room and hope that someone would notice him. His tears came with added fervour. For the first time, and it would not be the last, he began to wish he had never woken up.

Nick heard a noise. The door began to open and his saturated eyes managed to see a fraction of the world beyond. The corridor was a pale blue. There was a whiteboard on the opposite wall covered in red ink but the words were like a foreign language to him. Wanting to wipe the embarrassment from his face he tried to raise his hand again but again the fatigue made it impossible.

'Hello,' said a middle aged nurse with flame red hair. 'How are feeling?'

Nick turned away to hide his tears, the tracheotomy tube in his neck tugging as he did so. She was older than the one who had accompanied Collins.

'I was just up the corridor and heard you were awake so I had to come and say hi,' she said.

Nick watched her from the corner of his eye, scared and confused by her familiarity. She was a nurse; he had figured that much from the uniform, but what was her connection to him? Was his mother a nurse? No, somehow he knew that this woman was not his mother. So who was she? Just then, a young male nurse entered the room pushing a large wooden cabinet on wheels. Nick's attention remained on the woman though as she combed her fingers through his hair to tidy him up.

'How are you feeling?' she said.

Nick stayed silent and stared.

'My name's Maureen,' she said as if in response. 'I'm the ward sister. Have you been crying? Here, let me deal with that for you.'

As Maureen took a sterile wipe from the wooden chest, Nick dropped his gaze, unable to protest, and just stared at the bed sheets as she cleaned his face like a child. Meanwhile, the male nurse had been busy rummaging through his box of tricks and produced a fluid filled syringe.

'There, that's better,' Maureen said, binning the screwed up wipe at the foot of his bed. 'You know, you're a very lucky young man.'

But Nick ignored her, his full attention now focused on the syringe being flicked and cleared of bubbles by the male nurse.

'You must have someone watching over you,' Maureen continued, moving further down the bed, pulling back the sheets to take hold of his leg. Nick's eyes flitted from her to the syringe. As she gripped his calf, Maureen proceeded to raise it pushing his knee into his chest and then back again. 'You know, like a guardian angel.'

With each movement, Nick could feel the tug of the catheter tube inserted in his bladder without understanding what it was or why it was there. The male nurse approached and Nick's eyes widened.

The syringe was inserted into the cannula on the back of Nick's hand where the intravenous line invaded his body, and he mumbled his displeasure. The drug entered his system without pain and he instantly relaxed.

'Is he all there then?' the male nurse asked.

'I don't know,' Maureen replied, moving to the other leg to carry on with Nick's exercises. 'I hope so. His family has been through enough now.'

The male nurse hummed in agreement.

As the drug took effect, Nick fought to remain conscious. His headache had softened, but he needed to work hard on staying focused. Everything around him was fading to a blur, swimming and twisting in an ocean of tranquility.

Snapping her fingers in front of his face, Maureen dragged Nick's attention back to the room. 'Hey there, are you still with us?' she coaxed. 'Nick?'

Like a warning dog, Nick gave a low growl of acknowledgement. The male nurse had now disappeared leaving Nick and Maureen alone for her to pull and twist him as she pleased. No matter how hard he tried, Nick could not suppress his paranoia.

'We'll have you up and walking in no time,' Maureen said. 'What do you think to that?'

Nick did not reply. His attention was now caught on a thread-vein that shocked across the white of her left eyeball like a petrified tree reaching for her cornea sky; such beautiful colour from such imperfection. As the drug's effect intensified, Nick became more immersed in the varying features of her face and no longer heard her words.

How simple everything seemed, how perfect in the undulating chaos. He could have happily lost himself within the complexities of her face, to peruse every blemish and acne scar that painted a picture so unique it was priceless. That was, of course, if she would for just one minute stop yanking his limbs like a rag doll.

Please, just let go of me, he thought. Please, stop interfering with me. Please, just leave me the fuck alone!

Nick's mind screamed for calm, but his voice remained silent, trapped like a prisoner in his unresponsive body. He began to weep again as the cortisones in his system played havoc with his already damaged brain. Why was this happening? Why?

'You can hear what I'm saying, can't you,' Maureen said. She lowered his leg to the bed. 'Nick, you're going to be fine. You're in the best hospital in the county, and you have me to help you. We'll make sure that you get out of this all right. There's nothing for you to worry about.'

Nick closed his eyes and exhaled. If only this was a dream, if only. His heart sank deeper, his damaged mind unable to understand what was happening to him. Why would his body not work? All he wanted was for her to leave but instead of allowing him solitude she took hold of his arm and continued with her labours. With one hand on his elbow and the other on his wrist she pushed his arm across his face and back again. Arm to face, arm to face. Nick watched his hand as it rocked to and fro above his head like a swinging pendulum ticking off the seconds, minutes, and hours he would spend in this place incapacitated and helpless. Time was running out, his time was running out. He had so much to do. Important things, if only he could remember what they were.

Is this what it's like to be crazy?

Perhaps that was the answer. He had gone completely insane.

Maureen lowered his arm and moved to the other

side of the bed. 'Amy will be here soon, and then you'll be fine.'

Here was a new name. Amy.

She must have read his body language because she looked at him surprised. 'Amy is your girlfriend, Nick.'

He had a girlfriend? He had a girlfriend but no idea what she looked like, and as for feelings, his heart as well as his mind was empty. Were they close or had it just been a fling? They must have been in love. Why else would she wait five months?

'You have a picture. Would you like to see it?' Maureen said.

Crouching beside the bed, Maureen searched through his cabinet. 'Here we go.'

Nick stared in awe as though falling in love all over again. Maureen just smiled as she held the portrait for him. Even though pain burned through every muscle in his arm, Nick reached to touch the glass. She was so beautiful. The photograph had been taken outdoors. It was a bright summer's day. However, the thing which shone the most was not the sun but the two smiling faces, happy and in love. Staring at the portrait, Nick felt more alone than ever.

'You don't remember do you?' Maureen whispered.

Nick was so tired of this. He had only been properly aware now for all of what, twenty minutes and already he was wishing…

'Look, I'm sure as soon as Amy gets here things will start to come back. Get the ball rolling again,' she tried.

But Nick had stopped listening.

'Come on; lift up for me if you can.'

Maureen slipped her arms round Nick's head and back and, with a heave of strength which belied her frame, managed to prop him up to give him a better view of his surroundings. Nick closed his eyes though, longing for the world to just disappear and leave him to rot in peace. His wish was denied.

'I'm not going to preach but if you want some advice from a woman who knows, when Amy arrives don't let her know you forgot.'

Looking back at the photo which Maureen had placed on the bedside cabinet, Nick lost himself within its scene, and in that split second caught a glimpse of his deformed reflection on the glass in the frame.

Oh my God, he thought. That's me?

Then he looked at the picture again, at his old self with Amy, and changed his mind. I wish it was me.

Chapter Four

As a child, Nick had been afraid of the dark. Who knew what monsters lurked in the shadows, inside the cupboard, under the bed. How many unseen demons waited for you to fall asleep before venturing from their dark havens to sample your fear and your flesh? Now, as Nick stood alone in the dark he was not just scared, he was terrified. The back of his neck shivered as every hair stood on end, reaching out in an effort to sense the evil that stalked him. The surrounding air was not just a black emptiness, but substantial as if the darkness itself was his fear manifested into a throbbing depravity that engulfed his body and his senses. In this place, he felt neither pain nor fatigue, not like he had back in that prison they called a hospital, just fear, yet not of what the dark may be hiding but of the blackness itself.

Nick could hear tiny imp like whispers buzz around his head and his attention darted from left to right, up and down, to try and catch where the murmurs might originate but everywhere was black. Even when he raised his hand and touched his own face he saw nothing.

'Where am I?' Nick shouted.

But his question went unanswered, and the frantic whispers continued to harass him. Not even an echo came back for reassurance. It was as though the darkness absorbed every piece of light and sound, smothering it, killing it; everything but those ominous whispers.

'Who are you?' he yelled.

As if in reply, silence fell all around him. Only then did he realise just how foolish his question had been. From nowhere, a clawed hand gripped the top of his skull puncturing his scalp and forehead. Warm blood trickled down his face tasting sour upon his trembling lips. When the pressure on his head became too intense his legs gave way, but instead of falling Nick just hung, swaying like a useless puppet.

'I knew that you would not have the strength to follow it through to the end. Did you honestly believe that you could hide from me forever?'

It was a deep, gravelly, voice as dark and empty as the void surrounding him. Nick went rigid with fear, his heart pounding in sheer terror as a deluge of coldness swept over his skin.

'Help me. Please God, help me.'

'You place too much faith in a god who leaves you to suffer. Your god cannot help you now.'

'Please don't, please. Leave me alone!'

Again, the blackness absorbed his sound. Breathing became difficult. His throat felt tight.

'But Hesamuel, there is so much I want to show you.'

Nick was shot forward through the blackness with the talons still clamped to his head. If it had not been for the immense exhilaration he would not have believed he was moving at all. The feeling was amazing, as if all of his senses had been focused into one colossal power the size of a pinprick that shot through the very essence of reality, the hum of static electricity tingling within him.

In the distance, Nick could see a point of light that intensified the closer he came, and all around him the whispers continued their deliberations chattering away with added fervour. As the power being used to project him flowed through his insignificant body, Nick felt invincible. And through the force of that power he had gone from being terrified to fearless. Still there was the light; what a wonderful light. As it expanded in size he saw what appeared to be the downward view of an oak tree, green and full, with a sea of grass flowing all around it.

And in an instant, they were there.

No, Nick was there, alone. He doubled over, still reeling from the experience. His body felt heavy and real again. Nick winced at the puncture wounds left by his attacker and searched the open grassland for his assailant but he was nowhere to be seen. It did not take him long though to realise why he had been brought here, to this place. His lips parted in horror as his brain fought to accept the scene before him.

As a child, Nick had loved trees, especially the great oak at the bottom of his grandfather's garden. He remembered the old man's pride when summer rose to full bloom and the garden became a picture of perfection. To the right of the central lawn surrounded by a carefully laid border of shrubs and flowers was an ornate rockery that encompassed a crystal clear pond where Nick had sat for hours gazing at the fish beneath its cool flat surface, daydreaming of submerged adventures with the carp that would brush and nibble his fingers as he dragged them back and forth across the water. That was nothing though in comparison to the adventures that were to be had in the branches of his grandfather's oak tree. With a good imagination and the thrill of being so high off the ground, Nick and his rucksack army played the most exciting games because up there he was king, in control and free from the world below. He was happy, and that was all it had taken; an afternoon of innocent play that he would remember for the rest of his life.

The tree which loomed before him like a macabre shrine was a far and distant cry from those fond childhood memories. Staggering forward in shock, Nick's legs trembled as he wandered amid the tree's rotten fruit which hung lifeless by their necks. Too many to count, he had no idea how many bodies were swinging here but the branches seemed to be jammed, their faces and necks black and swollen. The taut ropes creaked and every so often Nick was harassed by overfed horseflies. Fear gripped his throat as if he too were up there among the suspended congregation. What could justify such an act?

Suddenly, he flinched in surprise as a cold grey foot brushed against his shoulder.

It was a girl, no more than eight years old. What had happened here? Nick saw that she could have been beautiful with a sweet face that was certain to have one day blossomed into a graceful beauty. But now, wearing her death mask of black and purple bruising, she would never have the chance.

The girl's white tunic was heavily stained with blood from the crusted wounds around her neck, and the stench of her flesh nauseating. What sort of monster could torture a child so young? He reached up and cupped her face stroking her cheek with his thumb.

'Poor baby,' he said, 'you poor baby.'

Her eyes snapped open.

Nick sprang backwards, banging against the bodies behind him before losing his balance and hitting the ground.

Using what was left of her worn and bloodied fingers, the girl clawed at the rope around her neck as it squeezed tighter draining what little life she had left. 'Help ... me!' she gagged.

As her eyes bulged, her body buckled and twisted in the noose.

She's still alive, Nick thought. She's still alive! Get up, you idiot!

Springing to his feet, Nick barged the bodies aside to reach her leaving them swinging like carcasses in an abattoir. 'Hold on!'

When she caught sight of Nick charging towards her, she reached out for him to save her. Nick went straight for the legs scooping her up above his head, but it was to no avail. The noose had been tied in a slipknot and was still squeezing the last ounces of her life. Quickly realising his mistake, he searched around in a panicked frenzy, desperate for any way to save the poor child. He looked at the trunk and adjoining branch she was attached to, but it would take too long to climb. She would be dead before he even got halfway. Then, Nick saw his only option. Leaping as high as he could, he heaved himself up onto the shoulders of a fat man hanging beside her with no thought as to how the aggressor could have overpowered such a brute because as he climbed the girl's thrashings were becoming weaker.

Nick grabbed the supporting branch but adding his own weight to the limb proved to be too much. With a creaking snap the limb gave way and Nick, the girl and the fat man crashed to the dirt in a heap. As Nick dragged himself off the ground, the pain wracking his body was the last thing on his mind.

The girl had vanished. Where was she?

Nick stared at the rancid tangle of arms and legs, then grabbed hold of the huge man that had borne his weight and rolled him to one side. Beneath in a crumpled mess, he found what remained of the poor girl.

She was dead.

Nick dropped to his knees and beheld the lifeless chaos sprawled like a stain against the lush grass that played and danced in the breeze.

'No!' he screamed as the agony of his failure tore deep.

He stroked her face, pushing aside clumps of matted hair to expose her dirty skin.

Suddenly, a monstrous hand grabbed him from behind filling him with indescribable pain as though his whole being was on fire.

'Tell me Hesamuel; are you ready for the pain?'

The door to his hospital room flew open and three nurses rushed in.

'Quick, grab him!' Maureen ordered rushing to the opposite side of the bed. 'Grab him!'

Chapter Five

If there was one thing George Howell hated more than his job it was hospitals. The sterilised solemnity as people whispered their hushed conversations for fear of being too loud. How very British. The pain and suffering that went on behind closed doors, closed eyes, closed minds, and the all-knowing consultants who seemed so confident in their opinions. That was the part which scared him the most. If he was having a bad day an order would probably be forgotten or mislaid; no big deal as far as George was concerned. It was something that could be easily rectified. However, if *they* were feeling the strain of work or the pressures of a stressed mind then people died, and that was what really scared him. The life of his eldest son was in their hands, these so called specialists. Both his parents had lost their lives in this building; one of a heart attack, the other by contracting a superbug while recovering from a bowel cancer operation. He could still remember the night of Nick's accident as if it was yesterday. The memory would take time to heal of course but deep down George knew it was a night that would haunt him for the rest of his life.

'George, get the phone,' Janet said, her voice muffled by the pillow.

'Humph?' he replied, emerging from a bizarre dream.

'George, the phone's ringing.' This time she was more insistent and tugged as his pyjama shirt as the constant ringing drilled her nerves.

'For God's sake, what time is it?' George spat in annoyance. He knew that the coming day was going to be bad so the longer he managed to sleep the better.

'I don't know,' Janet replied.

Huffing, George fumbled for the elusive bedside lamp switch. 'For fuck's sake,' he mumbled as he knocked his glass of water to the carpet. Locating the switch and allowing his eyes the moment they needed to adjust, George stared down at the mess as it soaked into the carpet, spreading a moist dark patch. He lifted his watch from the bedside cabinet. The phone continued to ring.

'Quarter past two!'

'George, you'll wake Andrew.'

'I don't believe this. You get the bloody phone. It'll only be your son, pissed again.'

'He's yours as well.'

But George had had enough. Tugging the sheets back over, he settled back down and reached for the light switch.

'I don't believe you sometimes,' Janet said. She sat up and swung her legs out of the bed. Whoever was on the phone was persistent, but then a two mile hike with a belly full of beer could do that to a person. Still, she could not help but feel just a little concerned. Through a half opened eye, George watched her silhouetted figure slump out of the bedroom. He knew he was not doing himself any favours, but right now he found it hard to care. Nick may have been his son but if he continued like on this the time would soon come for him to either shape up or ship out. After all, his girlfriend had her own place now. He could go there. He spent most of his time there anyway until he needed his clothes washing. He would not have minded, but this was not the first time Nick had called in the dead of night drunk and begging a lift home. George being the dutiful father had turned out without question in rain and snow. But just lately conditions at work had been getting tense. The bosses had done a shake up with a new intake of younger, fresher recruits, and even though ageism was supposed to be a thing of the past his career prospects looked grim. And to top it all off his bladder was playing Niagara again adding to his frustrations. No, tonight Nick could walk. Wouldn't do him any harm, might even make him appreciate people a bit more.

The phone continued to ring.

As Janet passed the door to Andrew's bedroom his pale and bleary head poked out. 'Mum, what's going on?' he croaked, squinting at the light.

'It's all right baby, it's only Nick. Go back to bed.' Without another word, Andrew closed his eyes then closed the door.

The phone continued to ring.

'All right, I'm coming.'

Turning on to his back, George stared at the ceiling. Why could his son not have a normal job like everybody else? Be a proper nine-to-fiver like him? Were they supposed to just carry him for the rest of his life? Nick would need to learn to stand on his own two feet without the support of Janet or himself, or else what? Become a dreamer achieving nothing and live with his parents? George decided that it was time to put his foot down. But despite his best efforts paternal guilt nagged him that no-one deserved a two mile hike at this time in the morning, and besides, he knew that if he refused to help Janet would make his life hell.

'Damn it.' Throwing back the covers with a huff, George dropped his leg off the bed.

The ringing stopped, and that was when it came. It was a noise George would never forget, a noise which would haunt his nightmares for weeks to come. At first there was silence, like the calm before the storm, and then there was the scream. George was pulling on his slippers when his head jerked up, his eyes turning to golf balls.

'Janet?'

Suddenly, there was the sound of something

breaking.

'Janet!' he cried.

Bolting from the bed, George rushed down the stairs, hardly touching the steps as he flew. 'What's wrong, what's happened?'

Slumped against the front door amongst the remains of the telephone table, Janet sat motionless and whimpered incoherently. George grabbed her by the arms and repeated his question. 'What's happened?'

'Ni... N... N... Ni,' she stuttered, swallowing back tears as she tried to get the word out. Then with a final scream that threatened to tear the world apart she cried out in agony unable to stop her grief.

Oh God, George thought. Not my boy, no, not my boy.

A bead of sweat trickled down the contour of George's temple.

'Where is he, Jan? Where is he?' George cried, shaking her to break the shock.

'Dad?' a voice said drifting down from the top of the stairs. 'What's happening?'

Oh Christ, Andrew, he thought and then said, 'Andrew, call your Aunt Jane. Jan, where is he?'

'Th ... the.'

'Jan.'

'Hospital.'

George sprinted for his overcoat that he always left slung over the carver chair at the head of the kitchen table. It was a habit Janet hated, but right now he did not care.

'Mum, what's happening?'

'I've got to go,' George called from the kitchen. 'Call your Aunt Jane. Get her round here!'

'Mum, what's going on?'

It was a night he would never forget.

* * *

The door to the private consultation room opened

and Dr Collins' beaming face greeted George and Janet's expectant stares. When they received the call this morning both had decided it best that Andrew remained at school, just in case.

Their intense anticipation was something Collins had experienced often in these situations but would never allow himself to participate. Perhaps if he was to sample a modicum of the anguish they endured he might feel closer to the poor souls he dealt with everyday. But he knew that the first step to ruin was to care too much. He did find it difficult to stay remote but knew that if he got too close to every patient he encountered the hurt would drive him insane and so, like the professional he was, he kept his distance.

'Excellent news!' Collins said. 'Okay, time to put my official hat on. Mr. Howell, Mrs Howell. I'm pleased inform you that approximately an hour ago we gained a positive response from Nick.'

Grabbing hold of her husband's hand, Janet burst into tears. 'It's all right,' George said, his own eyes beginning to well. 'Doctor, can we see him, please?'

'Well now, that was what I wanted to talk to you about.'

'Why, what's wrong with him?' Janet asked.

Both of them sat trapped in their silent hell hanging on the doctor's every word.

Taking his seat, Collins continued.

'Nothing, he's doing fine,' he said. 'Obviously, you already know the history of his condition but as far as developments are concerned I now think that we are in the best position yet to make some serious progress.'

'You mean now he's awake,' George said.

'Now that he's *aware*,' Collins said. 'You see, while he's been asleep we've had obvious limitations to the degree of research afforded to us.'

'That's fine, but what about our boy,' George said.

'Yes, when can we see him?' Janet added.

'You can see him now, but there are just a few things I wanted to discuss with you first.'

'How do you mean?' George asked.

'Well,' Collins said leaning in close. 'When Nick first awoke we performed some initial tests on him. It's what we call the Glasgow Coma Scale. They test for things such as movement, vocal response and so on.'

The two parents listened.

'Nick's initial results showed a relatively poor level of awareness but today we received quite a good response considering the type of injuries he suffered. At the moment he only seems to respond to voice and pain stimuli which, in itself, are good but what we should really be aiming for is spontaneous action independent of any stimuli whatsoever. Nick's motor responses are localized, which is good. When pressure is applied to a certain part of the body he feels the pain and withdraws the offended area, a normal reaction for any person. This shows that his nervous system is functioning and that all the wires are properly connected, so to speak. Now, the only problem that seems to be showing at present is his vocal response. At the moment he seems limited to sounds only rather than any form of speech. They may come in groans or cries, but do not expect any words for a long time yet. Of course, his rate of development will largely depend on the amount of brain damage suffered.'

They both sat in silence. For five long months they had dreamt of this day and now it was upon them the finality of it all still seemed such a long way off. But then, as long as they got their son back, even just a small part of him, maybe they still had a chance of salvaging some form of life again instead of the constant feeling of emptiness as the waiting continued.

'A coma patient is a very fragile thing,' the doctor continued, 'especially with regards to their perception of reality. Nick will suffer from nightmares and possible hallucinations. The strength of the disturbances of course depends upon each individual case and that, as yet, needs to be determined. His grip on reality may become strained. Nick's only requirement right now, now more than ever, is love and support. He needs to feel hope, that no matter what, there will always be someone here that loves him.'

'Well of course we love him,' Janet said. 'What kind of parents do you think we are?'

'No, I'm sorry, you're misunderstanding me. I am sure you love your son very much, nobody is suggesting any other, but what I'm trying to say is that even the smallest disturbance can sometimes set off the greatest catastrophe.'

'I'm not following,' George said. 'Is there something wrong with Nick? What are you implying?'

'No, please don't take this the wrong way. What you must understand is that, for Nick, our five months have been like an afternoon nap. He has had no real sense of time since the accident so try to imagine how cheated and displaced he must be feeling after finding out that he has lost nearly half a year of his life. In an instant, everything he has ever held faith in has been thrown out the window. His reality stopped five months ago while ours continued to exist. Now he has been thrown back to the lions, so to speak, completely stripped of armour. He is alone, he is afraid, and he needs your help and devotion in order to prevent him from losing his sense of reality altogether.'

George leaned in closer. 'Are you trying to tell us that Nick thinks he's in a dream? That we're not real?'

'Perhaps, in a sense, I suppose. As he possesses no firm grip on reality yet, he has been left in a highly weakened position. What we must do is convince him that our reality, the real world, is where he belongs before he starts clinging to others. I've seen some cases in my time believe me; men and women who were convinced that they came from the past, the future, from outer space. Some had become so detached that they started to imagine their dreams were the real world and that life as we know it was fiction.'

'It's that easy for our son to go mad?' Janet asked.

'In his present condition it could be very easy for Nick to lose his way. That is why it is vital for us to give him a reality he will want to cling to. We must love him, gain his trust, and above all, give him hope.'

'That Samson boy has got a lot to answer for,' George said trying to quell his venom for Janet's sake. Had it not been for Mark Samson's enjoyment of other people's vehicles none of this would have happened, but there was no point in dwelling, the past could not be changed.

'Samson. That was the driver I suppose?' Collins asked.

'Hmm,' George replied. 'Anyway, forget that waste of space. Tell us about our son.'

'Of course. Before we can start any real treatment we must first determine how many of Nick's functions have been damaged then we can begin with his medica-'

'Hold on. Are you saying that he could be a vegetable?' Janet asked.

'Mrs. Howell, please. I think that is completely the wrong term to use and besides, Nick has made a remarkable start.'

'I'm sorry,' Janet said. 'We're very grateful for all you've done but, he's not just another one of your statistics. You talk about love and hope but how can we be sure that all of your staff realise that as well.'

'Mrs. Howell, I can safely vouch that all of the staff here are fully trained to deal with the situation so, please, relax. You have nothing to worry about; he is in the finest hands.'

That was easy for him to say. This was her baby they were talking about, her own flesh and blood. No matter what they thought, neither George nor Collins would ever understand how it felt to be a mother. To have

The Maelstrom

that intense feeling of anxiety waiting for the first movement, the first kick. They would never know how hard it had been giving up the cigarettes, or not being able to take one single drink for nine months. Cravings that expectant mothers were not supposed to have. The occasional resentment that your body was no longer yours alone, and the overwhelming knowledge that within you slept a living, growing, person who could one day be great, revered even. Within the smallest of spaces was situated the stuff of gods, the power to create life. As men, they could never appreciate that.

Ignoring the conversation, Janet stared out through the venetian blinds into the ward. Her son was out there, fifth door along at the end. She could see the closed door to his room from where she sat, but could not hear through the sound proof glass of the consultation room. She could not hear her son screaming. George and the doctor's conversation became a distant blurb as her attention focussed upon Nick's door; watching as uniformed figures flashed past her, disappearing into his room. As she stood, reaching for the door handle, her eyes fixed on her son's now open door, she went unaware of his cries of distress. The handle turned, the door opened.

'Nick?' she said. Her hesitant step became a stride, which in turn became a sprint. 'Nick!'

By the time she was halfway down the corridor, George and the doctor were also on their feet.

'Mrs. Howell, wait!' Collins exclaimed. 'Please, wait!'

But he had been left ignored. As she gaped through the open entrance, Janet watched on in horror at what was more of a wild animal than a human being thrashing about on Nick's bed.

'Grab him!' one of the nurses cried as the other two pounced on his chest and shoulders.

Nick screamed out in a low, guttural, voice freezing

Janet to the spot. This was not her son, it couldn't be.

'Keep hold of him, Nathan,' Maureen called as she began siphoning a sedative into a syringe. 'Just a little longer.'

Nick screamed again as he saw the perceived weapon in her hand. No matter what, they were not bringing that thing anywhere near him!

With a primeval yell, Nick heaved his body, lifting the two nurses away from the bed.

'Bloody hell,' Nathan proclaimed.

'Be careful with him!' Collins ordered barging his way past Janet as George joined her at the door.

Adding his extra weight to the struggle, Collins and the nurses finally managed to pin Nick to the bed.

'Maureen, quickly please,' the doctor urged. His face flushed under the strain.

In a distressed frenzy, Nick tried for another heave but the combined weight was too much. All they would allow was neck movement, and that was limited. Resigning to the burden, Nick gave in and Maureen forced the syringe into the cannula on the back of his hand. George and Janet stood aghast as they watched the determined nurse infiltrate their son's restrained body. Nick's whole upper arm was suddenly filled with intense burning as though it was being torn apart by a thousand razorblades. Nick's arm flicked loose, hammering Sarah in the jaw. With his eyes clenched tight, he did not see her as she spun against the wall before hitting the hard linoleum floor.

Raising his leaden head, Nick gazed across the room as the light of consciousness slipped further into gloom, and beside the open door he just managed to register the shape of a woman. Her features were a blur, but her eyes shone through like emerald lanterns, crying out to be seen. For the first time in five months Nick looked into the eyes of his mother.

Using unintelligible words, Nick tried to reach for

her before his head sank to the pillow.

Janet looked on in fear. That's my son, she thought. That's my Nick.

Sarah lifted herself off the ground, her jaw throbbing. She would bruise tomorrow.

Knocking Collins aside, Janet pushed her way through to embrace her son. Was this what was meant by the best care? She recognised the force had been necessary, but this was Nick, her baby, her flesh and blood. For five long months she had developed an image of how this moment would be. It should have been like a movie, tearful hugs and an overflow of 'I love you's'. Not this mess. With her arm wrapped round him, she pulled Nick closer to her chest and could feel his saliva dribble down the back of her hand as he stared out into open space, a zombie. The staff decided to make a discreet exit leaving the Howells to their re-union. George stood behind her and touched her shoulder.

'I love you, little Nicky,' she whispered, gently rocking him to sleep. But no reply was given as Nick slipped into unconsciousness.

Chapter Six

It was so pleasant in this place. Nick felt safe and free from the bondage of his inhibited existence. It seemed that only in his dreams was he truly free; standing here under the shade of the great oak tree, its lush green canopy over-hanging like a protective shield against the beauty of the cloudless sky. The air was still and void of noise as though time had frozen and granted him this perfect moment in time to enjoy its magnificence. All he could see for miles around were fields of rolling green interrupted by patches of forest, and a river in the distance. The hanging bodies were gone leaving not a single trace of the massacre he had witnessed before. Even the branch that had snapped beneath his weight was replaced and whole again. Nick stared at the patch of earth where he and the murdered child had fallen. It was green, unsullied. For all its beauty though, the surrounding scene felt like a lie. Standing beneath the shade of the great oak tree, Nick scanned the distant hills and wondered where he was.

'Should it matter?' said a gentle, comforting voice which seemed to emanate all around him. Nick looked around in surprise and listened for a long time but nothing more was said.

Moving cautiously from beneath the tree into the open where the sun was brightest, Nick noticed that even with a lack of shade the temperature did not change. With nothing better to occupy his mind, he decided it was time to explore so he set off in the direction of the river.

'I should stay away from there if I were you,' the voice said.

Nick stopped, gaining comfort from the voice's melodic tones.

'Why?' he asked, raising his face to the sky as if it might help him to be heard.

'It is a place of danger.'

'Oh. Where are you?' Nick asked, looking all around but seeing no-one.

'Should it matter?' said the voice again. 'I am, and that is all that matters.'

'So why won't you show yourself then?' Nick asked.

'You sleepers are always so dependent on what you can see, what you can touch.'

'Am I dreaming?'

'Yes,' the voice replied, and that was when Nick saw him. In the distance stood a solitary figure, a dot on the glistening horizon just large enough for him to see. At first Nick did not move, deciding instead to just wait and assess the situation. As time passed by, the mounting anxiety inside his chest became too much and he set off in the direction of the figure. Making his way across the fields, which seemed to stretch forever, he noticed how each individual blade of grass stood to attention in impossibly perfect symmetry, proud and solid. The surrounding foliage also held itself static and frozen. All that seemed to exist in this land of stationary charm was Nick and the distant figure that looked no closer now than when he had first set off. Nick stopped again to study the terrain between them, convinced that he had gained no ground, but found to his surprise that the great oak had also become a mere blip over his shoulder.

'Come to me, Nick,' the voice said. 'Do not delay.'

'I'm trying,' he said.

Nick set off again, striding across the landscape without breaking a sweat as only a dream could allow. Yet, just as before, the further he travelled the further away the figure seemed to be.

'Why can't I reach you!?'

'Come to me, Nick. What are you waiting for?' the voice replied, still calm and in control.

'I'm trying,' he called, 'but you're just too far away.'

'You have not even begun to try yet. Free your mind, Nick. Come to me.'

Nick stood still feeling confused and on the brink of giving it up as absurd. Free his mind? What was that supposed to mean? He knew this was a dream yet, just as in the hospital, he was not the one in control here. With a thought he should be able to imagine himself anywhere, but the lone figure still seemed so far away. Then something changed as the air became charged and the picture-perfect scene around him rippled like waves on water.

'Nick,' the voice called. 'Come to me, Nick, right now.'

He could feel the urgency, but was still powerless to follow the order through. 'You're too far away!'

'I'm only as far as you want me to be, Nick. Come now.'

The ground beneath Nick's feet began to tremble, knocking him off balance like a drunken tramp stumbling along a crowded pavement. 'What's going on?'

'Nick, please, come to me!'

'I can't. What's going on?'

Fearing for his safety, Nick tried to make a dash towards the dot on the horizon, but before he could complete a single step he was caught.

Two mangled hands spat from the earth, snatching Nick's ankles from under him so fast that no amount of reactions could have prevented him from smacking his face into the dirt. With the wind knocked clean from him, the hands began to drag him backwards and down, down into the earth.

Nick cried out for help but despite his pleas the mysterious lone figure remained silent as if in fear of being detected himself. By now Nick was submerged to his knees and sinking fast.

Falling backwards, clawing at the dirt, he tried in desperation to prevent his burial, but it was no good. As his body sank deeper and deeper, Nick felt his chest compress beneath the weight of the soil. There was no escape. All he could do was resign his struggling body to the bowels of the cloying earth and fight for one final gasp of life. The last thing he saw as his screaming mouth choked with dirt was the silent dot on the horizon that could do nothing but watch as the top of Nick's head disappeared beneath the gritty ocean of green and brown until the scene was still once more, betraying not one scrap of evidence that Nick had ever been there.

It was night, and Nick found himself in a dark place with rain beating down upon his fragile body as he lay abandoned in a pool of mud that soaked his clothes and skin, his wails of agony drowned out by the crash of thunder that boomed all around. Weighed down by his water-logged clothes, Nick needed all his strength to heave himself from the quagmire, his forearms remaining submerged beneath the water as he tried to focus through the rain. He needed to find shelter before he sank into the ground again. Through the torrent his vision was limited but, whether due to fate or just plain luck he recognised the outline of a large building. Deciding it to be his only option Nick stood to his feet and waded his way toward the structure. It was an old farmhouse with a rickety wooden porch, windows that had been blacked-out, and roof tiles that rippled as if alive as the rain danced across them. If anyone had ever lived here they were long gone leaving the building to fend for itself against the elements. The floorboards of the veranda were soaked, creaking noisily beneath Nick's step, but at least the unstable porch allowed a slight reprieve from the never ending deluge. Rusting chains hung and swayed where a swing-bench had once been. Nick found the black and rotten door ajar, and from within could see a dim flickering light.

The creaking door revealed a single room; a motel room. As the rain trickled through the broken canopy above, the water fell upon him ran down the back of his neck. Unsure of whether to enter or run for his life, Nick remained where he was and just stared through the open doorway. In the centre of the room was a double bed next to which stood a low cabinet and lamp from where the token light originated. A vanity dresser with a large wall-hung mirror was positioned at the foot of the bed. Reaching around the doorframe, Nick located the light switch and flooded the room with a harsh glare as the single hanging bulb crackled to life. After his eyes had adjusted, Nick could see the walls were a dark peach. The closed curtains on the opposite side of the room looked nicotine stained and dirty. Something about this place filled him with unease. This was a place of darkness. Nick could feel its essence seeping from the walls. Evil lived here.

'Hesamuel,' a dry raspy voice whispered, like dead leaves from a corpse's throat. 'Step inside, Hesamuel. Come in from the rain.'

Still afraid, yet desperate to get out of the storm, Nick stepped over the threshold pressing a dirty big footprint into the thread-worn carpet.

'Hello?' he called. 'Is anyone in here?'

In the nearest corner of the room was a wardrobe which had been previously blocked from view. 'Hello?' Nick called again, waiting for the unit to open or rattle or do something, anything that would betray the location of the voice, yet the wardrobe remained still.

Taking another step into the room, Nick was bathed in warmth as the temperature rapidly changed.

'Hello Hesamuel. I've been waiting for you.'

'Where are you?' he asked, still staring at the wardrobe.

'Come in Hesamuel, make yourself comfortable,' the voice continued. 'Rest your bones and sleep a while.'

Nick glanced at the inviting bed before turning to look at the mirror, and was surprised to see not a reflection, but a hollow flat blackness instead.

'Come closer, Hesamuel. I will protect you.'

Nick stared deeper into the darkness, its density appearing to stretch beyond the simple walls of the room it occupied as if he could climb right into the frame just like Alice and fall into its hollow chasm. From the darkness, a shape began to form. At first it was unrecognisable, a confusion of shades interlacing one another struggling to catch a pattern. But when it did find form, the dark mass began to take the appearance of something human until Nick found himself standing before a black carbon copy of himself, its surface oily and smooth. Twisting his head to the left, the image followed suit. To the right and again the reflection kept pace with perfect symmetry. It was not until Nick stuck out his tongue that the creepy mimic stopped and, instead of copying him, smiled. Feeling foolish, Nick retracted his tongue.

'What are you?' Nick said.

'Do you like the room?' the face enquired. 'It holds a special meaning.'

Nick sat back onto the edge of the bed and continued to study the mysterious face.

'It's nice,' he lied. 'Why does it have a *special meaning* though?'

'All places have a special meaning to some-one whether it is a favourite spot in the park or just a comfortable chair.'

'Is this yours?'

'No,' the face replied. 'My special place exists now only in memory, a very long time ago. What about you, where is yours?'

'Erm well... I don't really...'

'Of course you do. Everybody does. You just have to think about it.'

Nick stood and thought a while of what it was like to be young again, innocent and carefree, but he could hardly remember anymore.

'I... when I was young there was a railway embankment that ran along the bottom of our street. Behind it was a river.'

As more of the memory came flooding back, Nick focussed even harder, eager to regain as much of the lost information as possible.

'My granddad, he used to go fishing there. He was a great fisherman; he'd won trophies that he kept in a display cabinet in his living-room. But he died when I was young,' he said, saddening at the memory. 'I remember there being a set of lock-gates to the river beneath the train track. On sunny days I would sit down there and watch the birds dive under to catch fish. It was peaceful; yeah, I really used to love it down there. Wow, I haven't thought about that place in years.'

'Sounds nice,' the face said, staring at him from the blackness.

'Yes, it was... so whose place was this then?' Nick asked, looking around the room again.

'This special place once belonged to a man called Jeremiah Fleming. It is quite a famous monument. Lots of people travel to visit this room every year.'

Nick hummed. 'I don't think I've ever heard of him. What was he famous for?'

'He was a murderer.'

Nick stared at the face, a cold fear working its way beneath his skin.

'This room is where he would bring his victims before performing a very painful and horrible surgery upon them; on the bed behind you in fact.'

Nick looked at the pristine bed-sheets feeling a

dread well up inside him as he tried to prevent the gruesome images from entering his mind.

'They were all beautiful women. In their prime,' the face continued. 'Tight, slender figures. Perfect skin. Truly delicious creatures, which is what he had always wanted to be. You see, he was a poor effeminate soul trapped within the body of a man in nineteen fifties Louisiana and the jealousy he felt, the raging hate toward every beautiful woman that passed him by, drove him insane.'

Nick remained silent not wanting to hear any more, yet powerless to quiet the voice in the mirror.

'Mary King had been the first; you never forget your first. It had been a messy business, pure carnage. But it was on that first outing that Jeremiah discovered a taste for his new found craft. And through time and diligent practice he honed his skill becoming more artistic in his endeavours. Using a surgeon's scalpel he would carefully remove the victim's face and scalp, and then stretch it over his own head and parade around this room like a fool in a vain attempt to emulate their beauty, admiring himself in this mirror. He would rob these poor souls of their identity in order to feel attractive, and then he would defile and mutilate their bodies beyond all recognition in envy of their voluptuousness; a form he could never possess.'

'Why didn't he just have a sex change?' Nick asked, 'why all the killing?'

'In the fifties there was no such thing as *a sex change*. People were too busy rebuilding the world after the devastation of the Second World War. Even to this day, those of the Cosm are still not aware to the true extent of how many women fell beneath his knife. Jeremiah was a master of his art.'

'He sounds like a maniac.'

The face smiled at him serenely.

'Well, you will be able to found out for yourself. He should be back ... any moment.'

As soon as he heard the words, Nick realized what was happening now, why he had been brought here. He had to get out, fast. Bolting for the door he wrenched at the handle but it was frozen solid. He thought of the window. The face in the mirror followed Nick with mild amusement as he dashed across to the other side of the room, throwing back the curtains to reveal the sickening sight of a solid brick wall where glass should have been. Tightening his white knuckled fists around the fabric of the curtains his heart sank. He was trapped, and from behind he could feel the oily face grinning in his direction, its eyes boring into the back of his skull.

'There is a way of escape, Hesamuel.'

Nick turned to face the mirror.

'Climb into the frame and join me. Allow me to protect you. Touch the darkness.'

Nick's veins ran cold with terror. Outside, he heard the sound of a car pulling up as tyres crunched over wet gravel, and the thud of a door being slammed. With the window bricked up and the door an immovable object his options were zero and his time was out. Stepping towards the mirror with an outstretched hand, Nick touched the darkness. Lightning struck within his mind as a horde of horrific images flashed through, images of pain and mutilation just as the voice had described. The images of every woman Jeremiah had ever murdered raged through his mind like an unstoppable force soaking his brain with blood and rotting flesh. Nick yanked back his hand grabbing it close to his chest as if burned, his features etched with agony. Outside, he heard the sound of another car door being slammed followed by a scraping, dragging noise getting closer and closer to the door. In a blind panic, searching for any means of escape other than the demonic mirror and seeing none, Nick took the only option left. Wrenching open the wardrobe doors he bundled himself inside and closed the doors behind him, settling himself down into the confined space while trying not to put any pressure on the panels and give away his position. Concealed in the darkness, he crouched with no other senses but hearing and fear, and swallowed back gulps of air in a desperate attempt to quiet his pounding heart. In the room outside, the door was unlocked and all six foot seven of Jeremiah stomped inside dragging behind him an unconscious woman, throwing her onto the bed like a discarded toy before closing the door. Externally, he was a beast of a man with hands like shovels and straggly, greasy black hair that matched the colour of the fluff protruding from his nose. Internally, he was as black as the deepest chasms of Hell. Hunkered down in the pitch black, Nick listened as Jeremiah slid the top drawer of the vanity unit open.

Without warning, Nick's face was assaulted by a hot stench. Pinching his nose, he strived not to vomit and for a moment there was reprieve, but no sooner had Nick gained a fresh intake of breath than the hot stench returned again in a fresh wave of filth. Something was in the wardrobe with him, breathing on him, yet trapped as he was Nick was powerless to act.

'In the top drawer of the dresser is where he keeps his knives,' the foul voice whispered. 'He has selected the scalpel to remove the woman's face.'

Nick could feel his hunched up legs begin to quake.

'This is lady number three; quite early on in his career, but by no means the bloodiest.'

Nick wanted the voice to shut up, for the nightmare to stop, yet still it continued.

'At the moment she is still unconscious, but wait and see. She soon won't be.'

'Be quiet, he'll hear you,' Nick pleaded.

'Her name is Emma. She was a real-estate agent, not a very good one. She should have stuck to waiting tables. It was with her that Jeremiah started to develop his technique. First he will insert the blade into the fleshy underbelly of her jaw, slicing it from back to front.'

From outside the wardrobe, Nick could hear a low moaning sound as the woman began to feel the pain of Jeremiah's blade and was starting to come round.

'Now he is slicing the skin from the back of the incision all the way up to her earlobe before tracing it round the back of her head to join with a similar cut on the other side.'

Nick expected to hear morbid squelching noises yet everything was silent. That was until the screaming started. Emma had regained consciousness to find herself lying in a pool of her own blood that pumped freely from around her face, enveloping her world in blinding white pain. Though she screamed to the heavens for all she was worth, the pain had already taken her far beyond anything normal into a state of shock and, straddled across her struggling torso, Jeremiah looked down on her with the black eyes of a shark, emotionless and void of mercy.

'Make me beautiful,' he pleaded, massaging her face and scalp to make the skin more pliable. She tried to form words but failed. The scalpel's first incision had sliced the underside of her tongue, severing the muscle and causing her mouth to fill with blood. It flowed down the back of her throat, choking her screams and staining her perfect teeth.

'She's now grabbing at his shirt pleading for him to stop,' the voice continued. Nick's body shook with fear. Beyond his clasped eyelids the half-screaming, half-groaning sounds of the dying woman filled the claustrophobic confines of his tiny wooden prison.

'Make him stop,' Nick begged. 'Aren't there any neighbours to hear this? Can't they make him stop?'

The reply given was cold and flat. 'In Jeremiah's avichi, there are no neighbours, only his personal private pain. His sentence for a life of depravity within the Cosm, condemned for eternity to relive every murder one after the other. The trouble with Jeremiah though is that he enjoys it.'

Nick released a whimper before realizing what he had done and clasped a hand to his mouth.

'The skin is now loose enough for him to slip the carving knife beneath its surface and ease it away from her skull.'

From the other side of the wardrobe door, Nick heard a sucking squelch as muscle tore from bone and the woman's skin started to peel away. His stomach clenched at the sound of every tear, her voice fading to a semi-conscious whimper as she clung hopelessly to some remnant of life. But her blood was almost entirely drained, having been soaked into the mattress beneath her and Jeremiah's sweaty clothes. Coming up next was the part Jeremiah enjoyed the most because it required a delicate touch, a need for precision so as not to rip the skin. The greatest conundrum for Jeremiah had always been the eyelids. He had overcome this problem by simply snipping them away with scissors, not wanting to tear the skin at the crow's feet. Then, with a quick sucking pop, the woman's sticky death mask came clean off and Jeremiah held it out before him twisting it from side to side, enjoying the stir it produced in his loins.

Nick scrunched himself into a ball, quaking, summoning every store of strength he possessed to prevent a combination of the evil outside and the foul stench of the voice inside from making him gag. Jeremiah left the woman's, faceless, twitching body to its own devices while he moved over to the mirror to sample his prize.

'She is not quite dead yet, but the agony has sent her body into shock. He is now trying on her face.'

Standing before the mirror, his despised cock hard with anticipation, Jeremiah's eyes were clamped tight like a child ready to receive an eagerly awaited birthday present;

his hands trembling as the room began to develop a surreal haze. With the flaccid tissue stretched over his larger head, the gore still warm from the previous owner's body heat, and the taste of her blood metallic on his lips, it smelled sickly sweet like infected urine smothering his head.

'Make me beautiful,' he pleaded.

His eyes opened and a broad wound stained grin emerged from beneath the disembodied face as Jeremiah beheld himself in all his horrific glory.

'I am beautiful,' he sighed, stroking the stolen skin. Through the baggy red holes where her sparkling eyes used to be, he watched himself transform into the beauty he so longed to be. For this brief moment, he was the pretty woman all the men glanced at from the corner of their eyes, too afraid of her perfection to look at directly. He was the elusive fox that men wanted to bed and would mentally undress fantasising each delicious movement; his curvy thighs, his full sumptuous breasts that blotched pink under the intense heat of passion as their hot sweaty bodies rose above his prone and waiting figure. Their lips hungrily kissing the inside of his smooth thighs higher and higher until they reached...

Jeremiah shuddered with delight.

'He certainly was a creature of purity, completely unashamed of his depravity and cruelty towards women. He wanted their sex so badly and hated them all the more deeply because of it,' the voice hissed. 'You're afraid aren't you? I can feel you trembling. You should be.'

Nick could not hear Jeremiah as he turned to look at the dead hunk of meat on the bloodied bed, could not sense his confusion as he caught sight of a strange mark on the carpet that should not have been there.

In the darkness of the wardrobe, the voice transformed into something darker, more evil.

'Dear Hesamuel. In your hurry to find a place to hide you forgot one tiny detail.'

The Maelstrom

Due to the stretched skin covering his head, a good portion of Jeremiah's view was obstructed. He crouched down to the stained carpet to get a closer look before readjusting his mask. Bending even further, he saw what appeared to be ... but it couldn't be, not here. How on earth could something like that get in here?

'Remember the rain and the mud, Hesamuel?'

Somehow, and God knows how, but somehow during the distraction of his work, Jeremiah had missed a nasty patch of muddy churned up grass on the carpet, a dirty great footprint followed by another and another... leading into the closet. His gaze followed their trail until his dark, baggy, black eyes fell upon the large wooden doors. Someone was here. Someone had breached his domain and broken the pattern of things. Someone had invaded *his* territory. Swinging round with violent speed, Jeremiah snatched the carving knife from the vanity unit and rushed towards the wardrobe unafraid as to what he may find. This was his domain, his private pleasure. Anyone who dared to enter without his consent would learn a quick and sharp lesson in etiquette. As his mother had constantly reminded him, manners cost nothing. He remembered the way he had been forced to be polite to the slobbering inbreeds that would accompany her home from the bar where she worked every night, just to make sure she got home safely you understand. It was not until he was seven years old that he understood, that he realised why they were still there in the morning, shuffling uncomfortably at the breakfast table while he eyed them, wondering how long this one would last. It was always the same pathetic excuse, always the same lie. It was not until Jeremiah was older still that he realized when a man said 'I don't think I'm ready for this kind of commitment' it actually meant, 'You're a good lay, baby. Just a shame about the kid'. Dave, Mike, Bobby, Steve, Randy, Josh, Pete, Hank, blah blah blah. Jeremiah would lie beneath the sheets in his darkened room, unable to prevent himself from hearing the panting cries of his mother, picturing her naked body riding yet another faceless meat sack, a morph that would evaporate as soon as the sun came up. At a very young age, he had learned the invaluable power of making people feel uncomfortable, wary of him.

But right now his mind was set upon another type of intruder. Never, since Jeremiah's *arrival* had there been a change to the monotony of his repetitive existence, just the same women one after the other. Maybe, just maybe, if there was a way in, there might be a way out. Something other than this stale existence, with fresh meat to sample rather than the regurgitated whores he was forced to consume on a never ending rotation. He grabbed the wardrobe door with his blood-stained hand and yanked it wide.

Beneath Jeremiah's powerful stare, Nick trembled, his face tucked into his knees looking pathetic, small and vulnerable.

'How'd you get in here, boy!?' Jeremiah bellowed with a voice that was barely human, the knife in his hand quivering with intent.

Nick was speechless with fear, trying even harder to make himself as small and insignificant as possible.

'Look at me when I'm talkin, you piece o shit!'

Terrified, Nick raised his head to face his captor and screamed at the sight of the dead woman's face stretched across a madman's head, his black eyes glinting through the ragged holes where hers used to be, her blood matted hair hanging about his shoulders. Nick screamed until his throat tore and his blood boiled, praying to anyone that would listen to be heard, but in Hell everyone screamed and no-one listened.

'*Welcome to my world, Hesamuel,*' the invisible voice hissed. '*It's all just a matter of time, and I have eternity.*'

Chapter Seven

Although she had been offered a bed of her own, Janet had chosen to stay with Nick throughout the night. For her it was too reminiscent of the weeks that had followed the accident, yet this time there was a significant difference which shredded the malevolent cloud that had hung over their family for far too long. In the morning, when the birds sang and the sun arose, so would Nick. Stroking his hair, Janet caressed his face with her eyes. What were his dreams, his aspirations? There was so much about her son she did not know, parts of his heart she would never see, and life was far too short to waste the time they had together in polite silences. At the end of the day, after all the frustrations of their mundane lives which seem so important at the time, the most important thing, the only thing, was family. Janet felt that over the years they had, as a family, lost that sense of connection. Christmas's and birthdays never seemed quite the same compared to when the children had been younger. The anticipation as they would tear like maniacs at the brightly coloured wrapping paper, then joy at their beaming faces as they clasped the gifts against their tiny chests. It was only by remembering moments such as those that Janet was reminded what being a family was all about; sharing the good times as well as the bad. Being the rock, yet not being too proud to ask for help. She would never leave him again, would never allow him to be hurt again.

It was a quarter-to-six in the morning. Nick had slept for over nineteen hours and Janet was anxious about what was to greet her once he awoke. Images from the previous day were still heavy on her mind. She had never seen her son behave like that and it scared her. George left not long after the incident to check on Andrew, or so he had said, but she was not stupid. She knew her husband and could see his horror despite his attempts to mask it. Nick was disorientated and confused, that was all. She had to be strong, for herself, for the family, but more so for Nick.

Janet watched nervously as Nick's eyes opened.

'Hello my baby,' she spoke, stroking his hair, feeling the jagged edges of her bitten down fingernails snag at his locks. As if in pain, Nick recoiled from her jerking his head away, releasing a squeaking cry as his retracted neck muscles fought against the movement. Janet tried to remain strong as he trembled at her presence.

'Nick, it's me,' she pleaded. 'It's mummy.'

He knew this woman. Still, her proximity terrified him but as he looked around he noticed there were no knives or blood. Yes, the blood was gone. He looked back to her again.

The sudden image of a faceless corpse sprawled across a blood soaked bed flashed into Nick's mind. Janet's heart sank as he screwed his eyes tight and struggled like an infant refusing to behave. Eventually, he calmed, opening his eyes again to see her face.

'It's me, Nick. It's mum.'

He stared at her offered hand, then back to her pleading eyes.

Mum.

Another image flashed into his head. It was pain; intense stinging pain. Rubble and building materials were strewn all around, and a recently laid dirt road. Half constructed homes were spaced out in a line behind him. By his side was a young boy, no older than himself, laughing and throwing stones found on the road at the clear blue sky. Nick was laughing too. Not far off was a small hill of dirt with a formation of old steel drums upon it, arranged like a defensive fortress. Hiding inside one of the drums was another boy who threw stones back at them, but they always fell short. Partnering the boy in the drum was a much older boy who stood proud and unafraid on the mud hill and, together with Nick and his friend Leigh they all laughed having fun in the summer heat. Nick threw his stone and watched as it soared high toward the sun before plummeting back down kicking up dust clouds in the dirt. Then, Nick watched as the older boy lifted a piece of shattered brick, testing its weight in his hand before hurling it with all his strength. Both Nick and Leigh watched it soar high into the perfect blue sky, getting ready to dodge its descent, but Nick got blinded by the sun and in that moments distraction the missile came crashing down on his head. Doubling over in agony, he could hear the cries of concern from his friends, realizing their game had taken a devastating turn. He felt hands grasping his body but wriggled free, running away as fast as he could; keeping his head bowed low the entire time. With his eyes to the uneven pavement, Nick knew exactly where he was going, his impetus fuelled on by the sight of his own blood splattering the concrete. Like a programmed machine his feet pounded one in front of the other, his cries of pain and shock alerting all who saw him. That was his intent; to alert, but not just anyone. The only one who truly cared, the only one who could make it all better, make the pain go away. With her arms and a kiss she could halt the coming tides, dispel the foulest of dreams.

    Nick opened his eyes and gazed deep into his mother's expectant face. He wanted to cry, to speak her name, to be able to remember the person he knew he had once loved and depended upon like no other. His eyes welled with tears. His hand quaked but still he could not find the strength to touch her so she made the move for him.

    Scooping him into her arms, Janet squeezed until it hurt. Nick released a small timid cry.

    'I'm sorry my love, I didn't mean to hurt you,' she

said, her own face red and moist with tears of relief. 'I've missed you so much. We've all missed you so much. I thought I'd lost you, I thought I'd lost my baby.'

She pulled him into her chest again but Nick hung limply, unable to return her embrace, and just stared at the ceiling with his head lolled over to one side.

The photo, it was gone!

Where had the photo of the two people gone? Where was the beautiful girl with the beaming smile that he had wanted to kiss, and the man the nurse had said was him yet who he envied with all his being? Where was that damned photo?

The screaming and shouting from the day before had not been kind to Nick's already damaged throat and Janet found it hard coping with how feeble he appeared.

'He will not be the same Nick,' Collins's portentous words echoed inside her mind.

'I know my darling, it's all right, I'm here,' she said, combing his hair again with her fingers. 'Your dad was here earlier, but he's at home right now taking care of Andrew. He'll be back soon though, don't worry. How are you feeling? You won't believe how worried we've all been.'

Instead of trying to remember who Andrew was Nick was more concerned about where his photo had gone. Where was it?

'Everything's going to be just fine now,' Janet said, holding Nick's head to her chest so he could feel the rhythmic beat of her heart, just like when he was a babe. 'No-one's ever going to hurt you again.'

But her words were wasted on Nick as his mind began to wander and the images of the now fading dream still fought to remain, overriding his concern about the missing photo. There had been screaming and darkness so intense he could touch it. And there had been the voice; that damnable, wretched, voice. What was happening to him?

The Maelstrom

When Nick re-focussed his attention back on his mother he found her studying him with a worried expression. At any moment she expected him to simply snap out of whatever cruel joke he was playing and become normal again, to start talking so he could tell her just how much they had all been missed, that he was ready when she was to go home. Nick eyed her with suspicion. For months she had re-enacted this moment, playing it over and over in her mind, the hugs, the kisses; each time perfecting her speech so when the moment arrived it would be exquisite, memorable. It had been one of the few things which had kept her strong. The waiting and the hope that one day soon Nick would wake up with the same exuberance she remembered and that life would carry on as normal again. But this was not a perfect world, or a just one. Janet stared into his searching eyes, desperate to see some semblance of the son she had lost, but found a frightened, frowning stranger. He was in there; she knew it, somewhere, fighting for his freedom.

He had to be.

Janet leaned forward and kissed his head.

'Welcome back, Nicky,' she whispered.

Janet's car keys chinked on the kitchen worktop as they skidded to a halt against the wall tiles. It felt so good to be home again, back within the familiarity of her surroundings.

Leaning against the units, she arched her back, drawing the tension from her muscles, feeling it seep from her aching bones. During the night she had hardly slept a wink having focussed all her attention on Nick. Drugged to the eyeballs, his face had looked so peaceful. It reminded her of his infant days when his perception of the world had been as fresh as his complexion, before he had learned to listen and form opinions of his own, to have a will of his own and fight against her every step of the way. If she had only known then what she knew now, how things could have been different? Wrapped in a bubble of lies and self-denial, they could have pretended what a wonderful place the world really was. Maybe then this would never have happened. They would still be whole, a happy healthy family without the torture of waiting and the endless sleepless nights. God, she was tired.

Massaging the back of her neck, Janet sighed as the tension oozed out, not just from the strain of her sleepless night but the whole tormenting affair. For five long months they had survived on hospital food, T.V. dinners and hope. Only once in all that time had Janet attempted to prepare a proper meal, but it had not been the same without Nick. It only reminded them of just how much they had lost.

Five months.

The way he had lost that time was incomprehensible to her. She could not begin to imagine how terrified he must be, lying alone in bed, not fully understanding what was unfolding around him. The thing which upset her most was that even though Nick was back, inside she still felt no different; the emptiness remained, dragging her deeper into depression. She needed a shower, not only to clear the grime of the previous day but also the cobwebs in her mind. Maybe then she would start to think straight.

Like a battle weary soldier, she slumped up the stairs.

In their bedroom was a tall full-length mirror. Letting her clothes drop where she stood, Janet stared into the other world where her naked body looked sagging and used. Twisting her torso she examined her hipline with exaggerated criticism, repulsed by the hint of flab that clung there; nothing like the lithe sexy days of her youth. With her hourglass figure, Janet had been the first in her school year to need a bra, and didn't the boys just love it. It was such a long time ago. For months she had been held in respected envy by her classmates with their flat cotton vests but, because she was different, Janet considered herself freakish and found games lessons a tortuous time of embarrassment. She could feel the sideways glances from her classmates, and hear the sordid comments from some of the more confident boys.

As Janet stared at the reflection of her now drooping breasts, she decided to give herself a break and moved to the bathroom. Turning on the valve, she tested the water with the back of her hand before stepping in. As the heat glided over her tired skin, she could feel the stress seep from her body, washing down the drain with the rest of the grunge. It felt so good to just stand beneath the cascade and let something else do the work for a change. Though it only seemed a short while she spent the next twenty minutes in that position until the heat of the water turned her skin numb. Then, towelling herself dry, Janet wrapped herself in a robe and went back down to the kitchen. Flicking the kettle on, her thoughts turned to their youngest son, Andrew. Adjusting to life without Nick had been so hard for him, not having his brother there to playfully torment him. And although he had hated his brother's constant jibes, life felt abnormal without them. Bursting with sorrow, the house still felt empty without Nick. Consumed by her thoughts, the silence was suddenly broken by the click of the kettle coming to boil. All Janet could think about was whether or not George had told Andrew of Nick's awakening yet? She hoped so. The idea of having to watch his expression darken even further would only break her heart.

Spooning coffee from a jar, she dumped the granules into her favourite mug, a Christmas present from Andrew.

Just as she began to pour the boiling water she stopped as the back door opened and George stepped through, still wearing the same clothes from yesterday. He was unshaven, his hair a mess, and he stank like a damp dog. Where had he been? She had neither seen nor heard from him since Nick's episode yesterday and a plethora of conclusions sprang to mind. She knew the sight of Nick's violent outburst had disturbed him and was so afraid of it dredging up the bad memories which, as a family, they had tried so hard to bury. Again, the question of whether or not Andrew had been told was yet to be answered.

Not wanting to make conversation, George hung his head and left the kitchen moving into the living-room. Pausing for a moment to gather her thoughts, Janet eventually followed but held back in the doorway as if waiting to be admitted. The silence came as a lifesaver to them both, rescuing them from the need for useless conversation which neither really wanted, and besides she needed the time to restrain her anger.

Sat on the sofa with his hands clasped upon his lap, George stared into the hearth. Using a transparent excuse, he had escaped from the hospital in total shock. How could Nick have been that way, after all their waiting, all their suffering?

'I'm sorry,' he whispered.

Not knowing what to say, Janet sat beside him unintentionally mimicking his pose. He stank of dried sweat and old booze, and ... Was that cigarettes she could smell? He had promised months ago that he had given up. But then she considered that perhaps she might be doing him an injustice. The damning odour on his clothes could have easily just been the remnants of whichever bar he had been beating himself up in. Despite everything, Janet still wanted to believe in him.

'I didn't know what to do?' George said. 'It was just ...'

Janet remained silent leaving his words to hang.

'Do you remember how we used to talk,' he continued. 'How we used to tell each other how things would be when he woke up? Life could go back to normal we said, didn't we? That wasn't normal, Janet. He's not normal.'

'He's our son.'

George fell into a shameful silence.

'I spoke to Dr Collins after you left,' Janet continued. 'He told me that Nick's got the potential to make a substantial recovery...'

'But will he ever be our Nick?' he interrupted.

'He *is* our Nick, you ... you stupid man.'

Janet's head slumped forward causing her long damp hair to hide her face, while her shoulders quivered in sorrow. The loneliness that had been fighting to consume her was finally taking its toll.

'I needed you, George. *We* needed you, but you weren't there. You didn't even have the decency to tell me where you'd gone. And what about Andrew? Has he been on his own all night? Did you even think to come home and tell him that his brother was conscious or were you just too busy getting pissed? And smoking? I thought you'd given that up, or is that just another lie as well?'

Snapping from his lethargy George went on the defensive. 'I never lied to you once. It just took me by surprise ...'

'Surprise? Took *you* by surprise did it? Well what the fucking hell do you think it did to me, you selfish bastard!' Janet shouted.

George was about to retaliate but instead hung his head again in shame remembering how, at the time, getting wasted seemed like the only way of blocking out the pain. It *had* occurred to him that Janet would need him there to unload her grief, to analyse the situation, to pick at it and pull it apart until there was nothing left but a logical understanding, but that was just one process too many he couldn't handle any more. His confidante went by the name of Jack Daniels who filled his head with delusions until the pain was nothing but a staggering blur, the room a spinning fairground ride. Before walking through the door, even before dragging himself off the sofa where the landlord had left him to sleep for the night, George had known that he had once again disappointed everyone he swore to protect.

At eight o'clock this morning, he had been rudely awakened by the clattering of empty beer kegs being loaded outside and decided that it might have been a good idea to go home. Janet had been wrong about Andrew though. Before falling foul of his all day binge, George had actually found the decency to call Janet's sister, Jane, and ask if she would mind taking care of Andrew for the evening, using Nick's awakening as the excuse. Of course, he had neglected to mention that he wasn't planning on being there himself to support Janet, but at the time that was just a minor detail.

'So, does he know then?' she asked.

'I... I don't know. I asked your sister to take care of him.'

'What? You dumped him on Jane so you could sod off down the pub? You'd better be joking. What kind of a father are you? You were never like this before. What's happened to you?'

'Look!' he shouted, grabbing her by the shoulders. 'I didn't know what to do, all right! This is tearing me apart and I don't know what to do! I feel so powerless and, and... useless and frustrated. I love you all so much. I just wish I knew what the answer was to end all this.'

'You love us, do you? And I suppose you tried to find your answer in the bottom of the bottle you were nursing all night then? Did you find it? Well? No, of course you didn't? And another thing, where did you stay last night? Find a better offer did you?' she spat, wriggling free from his hold.

'No ... No! I would never do that to you. I slept on Dave's sofa, honest. You have to believe me.'

'I'm not sure what to believe anymore. We needed you and you weren't there. If this is the way that you're going to deal with this situation then I think it's for the best if you just stay away from the hospital.'

'You can't say that. He's my son too you know,' he said.

'The doctor said that Nick needs stability, and that means a father who won't be getting pissed at every opportunity.'

Janet stood to leave.

'Where are you going?' he asked.

'I'm going to get dressed, and then I'm going to find out exactly what Jane's told Andrew. He's bound to be wondering what the hell's going on. In the meantime, you can take a long hard look at yourself and decide just what role you intend to play in this family.'

'Janet, I'm sorry.'

But it was too late; she had already left the room and was making her way upstairs. George had really messed up this time. He had to make things better. He had not waited all this time just to let an idiotic mistake ruin everything they had fought so hard to retain. He needed to get freshened up, get a shower and a shave, and start to try and make things right again. Janet was right; Nick was the main concern here. George had had his moment of self-pity. Now was the time to step up, time for constructive action, and he knew exactly where to start.

Chapter Eight

As the morning sun gently warmed the earth, its light filtered through the bedroom curtains casting rays upon the glistening naked bodies of two people making love. As they moved and caressed, enjoying the touch, the taste, the sensation of the other's skin, the sunlight projected their ever-changing shadows across the room, the flames of passion raging higher, covering their bodies with sweat. All was forgotten but the sex and the wild fire racing through their souls and their groins, swelling, consuming every part of their being as the frenzied apex was reached and they cried out in ecstasy.

Resting together in the afterglow, she kissed his clammy jaw.

'Good morning to you too,' he said, basking in the warmth flowing through his body.

The woman gave a naughty sigh before breathing; 'that was amazing.'

The man's self-satisfied grin widened as she rested her head on his toned chest.

'Do you have any plans today?' she asked, circling his nipple with her finger.

'Working baby,' he sighed. 'Why, what were you thinking?'

'Nothing in particular, it's just that I've got the day off so thought it would be nice to spend it together.'

'Amy, you know I'd love to, but I have to go. It's more than my job's worth to get caught. Maybe some other time, hey?'

'Yeah, no problem,' she said. 'I suppose I could go into town, do some shopping… and there's plenty of jobs around here for me to do.'

'There you go then, you'll be fine.'

'Maybe we could meet up for lunch?' she asked seductively, *lunch* meaning back to hers for a sport fuck.

'Sounds good to me,' he said, smiling.

'Good, you know it'll be worth it,' she said, pressing her lips against his chin before sliding off the bed.

Resting his hands behind his head, he watched Amy's naked buttocks sway from side to side as she headed into the en suite, closing the door behind her. With a stretch and a yawn he snuggled into his pillow and thought about the day ahead. He would arrive at work by the usual time and check his Facebook page before ploughing into what he was being paid for, hopefully leaving himself a good fifteen minutes before lunch for coffee and a chat with the sexy brunette in reception with the sparkling eyes and nice tits. Teenagers were great, so full of the wonders of the world, easy meat, and if there was one thing Simmo loved more than anything it was hedging his bets. If things turned sour with one *relationship* you could be certain that the next would not be far behind. His addiction to sex had always been the reason why the majority of his liaisons never lasted longer than a month, two at a push if they were worth it, and seeing as Amy had been a month and a half now his fingers were getting itchy, and so was his dick for that matter. Simmo's last conquest had left him with a bit more than a tear and a goodbye kiss, but nothing a regular visit to the clinic every so often couldn't put right. At the age of thirty-four all his friends were either married or living with someone, but not Simmo. He had kept himself in good shape and was still living the dream baby, and loving every minute of it.

The bathroom door opened and Amy emerged from the foggy mist, clean and refreshed wearing his Manchester United shirt and a pair of white cotton panties, a toothbrush poking from the corner of her mouth.

'God, you're sexy. Come here,' he said with a

devil's grin, staring at the indents of her nipples through the fabric of his beloved football shirt. 'Have I ever told you how good you look in a Man U strip?'

'You're so cheesy,' she said, positioning herself into his arms with a smile.

'Ha, yeah, but you love it. You know, I don't have to be at work for at least another hour yet. That gives us plenty of time for a quickie.'

'Oh, that's romantic,' Amy said. 'Seeing as you put it like that, hmm, that'll be a no then.'

'Aw, baby. You know I'll make it good for you.'

'You're terrible,' she said with hungry eyes and a cheeky smile.

As she leaned in to kiss him, the phone in the hall began to ring. Giving him a dry lipped peck, Amy skipped off to answer it. As she bounded away Simmo tried to playfully grab her but missed, and so stretched back onto the crumpled sheets. Life certainly was sweet.

After a while, Amy returned in silence, her mind cart-wheeling with the message she had just received.

'Who was that?' Simmo asked.

'Just Pippa,' Amy replied without missing a beat.

'She all right?'

'Yeah... she just called to see what I was up to today.'

'It's alright for some,' he groaned. Amy started pulling on her jeans. 'You're getting dressed?'

'Afraid so, lots to do.'

'Don't. Come on, come back to bed.'

'You'll live,' Amy replied, popping the final button of her jeans in place.

'Is everything okay?'

Amy gave him a sideways glance as she sifted through her wardrobe for a suitable top. 'Of course it is. What makes you ask that?'

'Well, you've gone weird all of a sudden. You sure

you're okay?'

'I'm fine, really.'

'It's just that I thought, you know, we were going to ...'

'Is that all you think about? I just don't feel like it anymore.'

'All right, now seriously, what's wrong with you?' Simmo asked.

Without a word, Amy removed his football shirt and replaced it with a blouse. 'Why does there always have to be a reason?'

Simmo was about to reply but Amy disappeared back into the bathroom closing the door behind her. Dumbstruck, he was left sitting on the bed with his legs spread and his erection unsure. Looking down between his hairy legs, Simmo huffed and, unabashed by his own nakedness, pushed himself off the bed and went into the bathroom. With her face up close to the steam smeared mirror, Amy was applying her moisturiser before the foundation went on.

'What's going on?' Simmo asked.

'I'm doing my make-up,' Amy replied, her eyes squarely fixed upon her smudged reflection.

'I can see that. Now what's going on *here*? One second you're well up for it, then the phone rings and you go all weird on me.'

'You're imagining things. I told you why. Just accept it.'

'I beg your pardon? Who the hell are you all of a sudden, and who exactly was on the phone? It's obvious this is what it's all about.'

'I told you, it was Pippa,' Amy said, wiping her hands on a towel before screwing the cap back on the jar of cream.

'Right, so why don't I believe you then? Come on, Amy, give me some credit. I know it wasn't Pippa, so who was it?'

'Simmo, it *was* Pippa, and besides do I need a reason not to have sex with you?'

'Don't try and turn this back on me, and now you come to mention it, under these circumstances, yes, you do need a reason. You turn from hot to cold in the blink of an eye, talk to me like crap, and then expect me not to wonder why? What was that phone call about?'

'Shopping,' Amy sighed, dropping her gaze to the basin.

Simmo had not been dealing with the female species for this long without realising that a shouting match never solved anything. Perhaps he did revolve his life around sex but so what? That was who he was. Why should he have to fight his own nature just please another? Because that was how relationships worked. There needed to be compromise for any relationship to survive, which was probably why he hated them so much. Nevertheless, he hated seeing her like this more.

'Okay, let's just slow down a minute. Please, let's just calm it can we? Are you all right? Who was that?' he asked with genuine concern.

'I ... I can't talk about it right now,' she said, refusing to make eye contact. 'I think its best... I'd like you to leave.'

'What? Amy, come on. I'm here for you. What's going on?'

She paused. 'Maybe later. I just need to be alone right now. That's all I can give you. Please, just leave.'

'So it wasn't Pippa then?'

Amy stayed silent.

'Fine, I'll go. If you don't feel you can talk to me then I guess there's nothing I can do about it.'

'Trying to make me feel guilty isn't going to change my mind, Simmo. Now please, just go before we really start to fight,' she said.

Simmo went back into the bedroom slamming the door behind him. What the hell had just happened in there? Usually, with the first whiff of trouble would be his rapid departure, but this time he felt different. Jesus Christ, was he actually feeling something for her? The brunette in reception, the multitude of pretty faces he had arranged in his mind became redundant because for the first time in his life *he* had been rejected. Was it love or just the twang of pride on his jilted ego? As he got dressed, the strange sensation plaguing his senses bothered him greatly. Why had he even entered the bathroom in the first place? By God, he *was* feeling something for her. All he wanted was to go back into that room and hold her, and yet after the way she had spurned him, despite any growing sentiments, his pride would not allow it to happen and so he just stared at the door. Eventually, he put on his jacket and left.

From behind the bathroom door, Amy had listened to Simmo getting dressed, waiting for the slamming of the front door to confirm his departure before re-emerging. The first thing she did was head back to the telephone punching in the numbers with erratic speed, her actions too quick for the dialler to register. She tried again, slower this time. It rang, she waited.

'Hello, 350036,' a cheery female voice said.

'Pippa?'

'No, sorry, it's her mum. Is that you, Amy?'

'Err, yes. Is Pippa there please?'

'Of course, darlin. How are you keepin anyway, is everythin all right?'

'Not bad,' said Amy, trying hard to swallow back her tears.

'Good. An how's that new man of yours? I hope he's treatin you well.'

Amy paused, realizing just how awful she had been to Simmo. 'He's... great.'

'Good, cause if he's not he'll have me to answer

to,' she said, her raucous laughter bellowing down the phone. 'You know that you're both more than welcome to drop by whenever you want. I haven't seen you in ages.'

'Yep, definitely,' Amy said, her voice straining. 'I'd like that.'

'Well then, make it soon. I'll just go n fetch Pippa for you.'

'Thank you.'

Amy sighed as she listened to the sound of the woman's footsteps echo down the hall, diminishing the further she went. Moments later the footsteps returned carrying a different voice.

'Yo.'

'Pippa,' Amy said, her tears beginning to well. 'I've made a huge mistake.'

'Amy, what's wrong?'

'It's Simmo ... no, it's everything.'

'What's the bastard done? Has he cheated on you?'

'No, no, it's nothing like that.'

As her tears began to flow, Pippa's voice darkened with apprehensive dread. 'Amy, what's happened? Please, tell me what's wrong. Oh God, you're not pregnant are you?'

'Nick's awake,' she said, her voice trembling.

'Fuck.' There was a pause. 'When did you find out?'

'Just now ... Simmo was here ...'

'And?'

'I don't know; things got confusing. Pippa, I was awful. What am I going to do?'

'Don't go anywhere, I'm coming round,' Pippa replied.

'But what about your work?'

'Ah, sod them. I hate the job anyway. Besides, you're my best friend; do you think I'm going to leave you alone at a time like this?'

Amy gave a tiny smile. 'Only if you're sure.'

'Course I am. Get the kettle on, I'll be round in a minute.'

As the phone went dead, Amy's life collapsed around her, suffocating her until she could take no more. With the telephone clasped in her hand she slid down the wall, wailing in confusion and remorse, the cool plastic of the handset becoming slick with sweat in her palm. She wanted to let go, that was all she had ever wanted, but even now she could still not bring herself to do it. After all this time, she had not let go.

Twenty minutes later, Amy heard the thunderous roar of Pippa's 78 Beetle pull up below her second-storey window. She watched through the dirty glass as Pippa's curly ginger head appeared from the car, hearing the crunch of the car door as she slammed it closed. Pippa entered the building using the spare key Amy had given her for emergencies, and headed for the elevator. Outside, the world was alive with colours of sky blue and leaf green, of the shining cars and reflective screens, of all the colours of the spectrum merging in chaotic harmony. Yet through Amy's eyes the world appeared dirty, dull, and soulless.

The front door shook beneath the force of Pippa's knocking before she unlocked the door herself anyway. Amy shuffled into the hall and was greeted with a hug.

'I came as quickly as I could. How are you?'

'I've been better. Come on inside so I can close the door,' Amy said, peering over Pippa's shoulder, conscious of the neighbours and their gossiping.

Pippa went into the small kitchen, heading straight for the biscuit tin but coming away disappointed at the scattering of crumbs rattling about in the bottom.

'Sorry, I haven't had time to go shopping this week,' Amy said.

'It doesn't matter. I've got to cut down anyway. I don't know what it is with me at the minute but I only have to look at something sweet and gain ten pounds.'

'Hmm ...'

'Yeah, well ... Nick, hey?' Pippa said.

'The doctors said he was lost, the damage irreversible.'

'I know.'

'So what's going on?' Amy asked, searching for anything that would take away the burning guilt of her betrayal.

Pippa gave her a blank expression, unable to provide the answers Amy needed.

'I loved him so much,' she continued.

'I know,' Pippa repeated, killing the conversation, leaving nothing but a hollow silence for Amy, an awkward silence for her. 'Who called you?'

'George, Nick's dad ... He sounded embarrassed, said that he thought I should know.'

'That was good of him. I bet his mum wouldn't have done that.'

'I don't know. She's never been the reasonable type has she?' Amy said. 'Anyway, if she chooses not to like me there's nothing I can do about it. Too be honest, I don't even care what she thinks any more. I'm sick to death of trying to please that woman.'

'You can choose your friends ... Still, what did she expect? It's not as if you were married or anything.'

'I should've waited though. God, what have I done?' Amy said.

'Hey, now don't you start that, you've done nothing wrong. What, did she expect you to become a nun for the rest of your life? Life has to go on Amy, and besides he probably won't even remember you. Remember what the doctor said? He's probably a vegetable for all you know.'

'Pippa.'

'I'm trying to make you see sense. You're not psychic and you can't live your life on a dream. You have to do what's right for you, which is exactly what you did, yes?'

'I suppose so,' Amy agreed.

'I know so. After all the shit I've seen you go through over this I should know.'

Pippa looked Amy in the eye.

'You know there's only one way to sort this, don't you? You'll just have to go and see him. You're obviously not going to rest until you do, and I think we both know it's what you want.'

'Am I that obvious?'

'Seriously, it doesn't take a genius, and besides, that's why I'm your best friend,' she said, wrapping her arm around Amy's shoulder. 'Go and make yourself presentable. You look like crap. And don't be too long about it.'

With a hesitant smile, Amy went into the bedroom to put the finishing touches to her hair and wipe the tear stains from her face, leaving her friend to make herself a drink. Opening the refrigerator, Pippa took out the carton of milk and recoiled in disgust as she sniffed the neck.

'Nice,' she gagged. 'Your milk's off!'

'I know!' Amy called back. 'There's some squash in the cupboard!'

Placing the milk carton back in the fridge, Pippa went through the cupboards one by one until she found a bottle of orange cordial, but before she had time to get a glass Amy was back and ready to leave.

'Come on, let's go,' she said. Her dark hair had been tied back into a ponytail and the puffy circles beneath her eyes were beginning to fade.

'You sure you're ready for this?' Pippa asked.

'I have to do this. I've got to get it out my system.'

'Yes ... but do you still love him?'

Amy fell silent.

'Come on,' Pippa said. 'Let's go.'

Nervously squeezing the wings of her Beetle

through the raised barrier of the hospital car park, Pippa found the nearest available space and parked the car. Thanks to the heat exchangers seizing open, the interior of the car was baking and carried a bizarre aroma of pinecones. Reaching into the backseat for a magazine, Pippa got comfortable.

'Are you ready?' she asked.

Amy could feel her heart pounding, her stomach doing cartwheels. 'I feel sick,' she said. 'Do you mind if we just sit here for a while?'

'Take all the time you want, I've got a date with Jonny Depp,' Pippa smiled, waving her magazine.

'Do you think I'm doing the right thing coming here? I mean, do you think it would be easier on everyone if I just stayed away?'

Pippa placed the magazine on her lap. 'You've come this far, don't back out now. Just go up there, look him in the eye and see how you feel. You've got to do this. If not for your sanity, then do it for mine!'

Amy gave a small laugh realising just how ridiculous she was acting. 'I'm sorry, you're right. What's wrong with me, for God's sake? I'll just walk straight up there, say hello, and ask him how he's feeling. Do my duty, and then come back out again.'

'That a girl,' Pippa said. 'Off you go then.'

'Yep,' Amy said, not moving.

'Well?'

Amy remained in her seat, staring at the dashboard with a doleful expression.

'Get out of the bloody car.'

Exhaling, Amy heaved the car door open and stepped onto the tarmac. The crisp morning air bit at her cheeks and in the distance a flock of starlings twittered at the passing cars. Crunching the door closed, she made her way across the car park, stuffing her hands into her coat pockets. Ahead, towered the massive shimmering structure of the hospital where she had spent the majority of her time, and coming back almost felt like returning home.

Passing a line of ambulances, she headed for the main entrance which was littered with huddled groups busy in their quiet chatter, circled round drifting plumes of cigarette smoke like conspirators; each consumed by their own problems, dealing with them in the only way they knew how, by forming a smoking circle. Is that how she had appeared to the outside world all those months ago? Not wanting to be intrusive, Amy's gaze didn't linger on them for long and she scuttled past, through the sliding doors to the reception desk directly ahead. From behind the desk, a smartly dressed fifty-something woman took one look at her before returning back to her computer screen.

'Good morning?' Amy said.

'Good morning dear, how can I help,' the woman said without removing her eyes from the screen, her fingers dancing across the keyboard in a practiced motion.

'I was wondering if you could tell me which ward Nicholas Howell is on, please?'

'Of course,' the woman said, briefly making eye contact before turning back to the computer screen again. 'How are you spelling that?'

Amy gave her the spelling and waited while the woman checked the information. 'He's on ICU; that's Intensive Care.'

'Thanks,' Amy said motioning to go.

'I don't know if you're aware, but the ward has been re-located from floor two to floor six. They're having new windows put in. It should all be sign-posted when you get up there.'

'Oh, right. Thanks,' Amy said. She then made her way towards the elevators at the very back of the foyer.

Seeing the newsagents, Amy realised it would be a nice gesture to buy Nick a card. The one she chose was vivid blue with the picture of a cartoon giraffe on the cover, cheerful and nondescript. Above its head was written 'Chin Up!' in a stylized child like scrawl. Inside the card she wrote a simple message.

> Dear Nick,
> Get well soon.
> 'Chin Up!'
> Love Amy /xxx

With the card in hand, Amy stood in front of the elevator doors and waited. The ride up was nerve-racking. Entering the sixth floor, she was confronted with a tapestry of makeshift signs informing her that the ear, nose and throat clinic had also been re-located while the renovations were taking place. Both wards were sectioned off from the main corridor by electronically sealed security doors. Amy pressed the call button to the one marked ICU. It wasn't long before a voice spoke over the intercom.

'Good morning, can I help?'

'Erm ... hello,' Amy said. 'I was wondering if I could see Nicholas Howell, please.'

'Are you a relative?'

'No, I'm his... I'm just a friend.'

'I'm sorry but only close family are allowed to visit at the moment.'

'But ...' Amy hesitated for a second. 'I'm his girlfriend.'

Those words felt so strange coming from her lips as if she had lost the right to use them anymore, and her cheeks burned with the lie.

'I'm sorry, but without the consent of Nick or his parents I'm not allowed to let you in. Sorry.'

'That's fine. Why don't you just ask Nick then? I'm sure he'll want to see me.'

'I'm sorry, but you'll have to get permission from a

member of his family.'

The intercom went dead; the conversation was over.

Damn it, she thought.

Unable to do any more, and saddened at being denied after coming so close, Amy turned to leave. At the elevator doors, Amy inwardly fumed at the jobs-worth on the other end of the intercom. What did they expect her to do for God's sake, kill him? Her thoughts were suddenly stopped dead as the bell pinged, the doors parted, and there stood Janet re-arranging the hem of her coat. The space between them was electric with confrontation, the silence deafening. Neither said a word, both just staring in disbelief that the long overdue clash, that neither really wanted, had finally come to a head. They had not spoken since Janet had found out through gossip about Amy's new love interest. As far as she was concerned the girl was disconnected from the loop, and they were better off for it.

'What are *you* doing here?' Janet asked, making it sound more like an accusation than a question.

Amy stood in stunned silence, the hostilities overwhelming her.

'I ... I heard about Nick's recovery and just ...'

'You just what, thought you'd come and say hi? Where did you hear that from then?'

'I ...' Damn, she really didn't want to drop George in it but what else could she say? 'I just wanted to see how he was, that's all.'

'Why? Why now, after all this time? You left him, remember? Do you really think he'll want to see you once he finds out about your new *boyfriend*?'

Amy's downcast eyes focussed on her own shuffling feet. Janet was speaking sense but still, seeing Nick again was something that she needed to do not only for him but for her as well. Janet was a stubborn arse though. She would not be interested in Amy's reasons and who could blame her? She was only thinking of her son's happiness, and Amy knew without a shadow of a doubt that when left to Janet no amount of selfish reasons were ever going to get her through those doors.

'Look, he doesn't need to know, I would only be in there for five minutes.'

'Not likely. Stay away from this ward and away from my son before you cause him even more distress than he's already in. You're not needed around here anymore.'

'He's in distress? Why's he in distress? How is he? At least tell me that,' Amy pleaded.

'Amy, just go and never come back,' Janet said. 'We are his family and that's all Nick needs right now, not a head full of confusion from someone he's only known for five minutes of his life. Now if you don't mind, I'm going to see my son.'

Amy was left in muted sorrow as Janet barged her way past to speak golden words of passage into the intercom, the door clicking to give her access. Hanging in the waiting mouth of the elevator, Amy squeezed her eyes shut trying to suppress her tears. Janet was right, why had she come here? What had she hoped to expect as a greeting? Their relationship was in the past now and that was precisely where she should have left it, but she couldn't. Something deep inside was gnawing at her conscience, and even though she felt they had this unfinished business hanging between them, she found it impossible not to recognise her continued presence doing more harm than good. Stepping back into the elevator, Amy finally allowed her tears to come as the doors closed and the corridor to the ICU vanished from sight.

Below, the foyer was bustling, the influx of hospital traffic picking up pace, filling the coffee shop with worried and complacent faces alike. The air was heavy with the welcoming aroma of freshly ground coffee and Amy would have gladly enjoyed a cup, but she knew now that coming here was a mistake. With her head bowed she powered her way toward the main doors, but was stopped by George calling out to her from the crowd. For a brief moment she just stared vacantly in his direction until she caught his face.

'How are you?' he said. 'You were in a world of your own there, weren't you? I'm so pleased you could make it. Have you seen him yet?'

'No, no I haven't. They wouldn't let me through; family only, but it's okay.'

'Of course,' George said. 'I should have arranged it with them sooner. Sorry about that. I didn't realise you were going to arrive this early. It's alright though, come with me and I'll sort a pass for you, then you can come and go as you please.'

'No, I don't think that would be a good idea.'

'Oh ... you've changed your mind?' George asked.

'No, not at all,' Amy quickly replied. 'It's just that...'

'I know, it's been a while, and I realise how much the accident affected you so I can understand you wanting to try and move on. It was probably wrong of me to call and stir things up again.'

'No, that's not what I mean. I...'

'Are you all right?' George asked, glancing over at the coffee shop. 'Do you fancy a sit down? If you need to talk you know that you can always rely on me and Janet.'

Amy gave him a weak smile. Though she knew the truth only too well, it appeared that George did not, unless he was just being polite. Perhaps it would be best for everyone if things were just left alone. After all, she was supposed to be with Simmo now. An hour ago they had been having sex and now here she was in the hospital trying to see her ex. Where was her brain? What possible good was she hoping to achieve by all this?

'George, I know that you meant well but I really think that coming here was huge mistake. I met Janet coming out of the lift and she was not pleased to see me, at all.'

'What?'

'Look, she doesn't want me anywhere near Nick, and to be honest I think that it's probably for the best. When you called me this morning I was so ... I don't know... shaken like you wouldn't believe, but now I'm here... it's all in the past for me now. I've already moved on and I think it would be wrong of me to open up old wounds, not only for myself but also for Nick. I'm so sorry.'

George felt awkward and embarrassed. 'No, I'm the one who should be sorry. It was wrong of me to upset you again after all this time.'

'Please, don't get me wrong. I'm really glad that you called. I'm glad to know that things are finally going to change for you all but, I think what Nick and I had was a long time ago now and... I don't know what else to say. I'm sorry.'

'That's all right, I understand. Please, don't worry. Look, I'd better get upstairs.'

'Yes, of course.'

'Thanks for being honest. I really appreciate it,' he said.

'No problem. I really do hope everything turns out well for you all,' Amy said, ready to leave. 'Good luck.'

'You too,' George said with a sympathetic smile.

With nothing left to say, they both turned and went their separate ways, George to the elevators and Amy to rescue Pippa from her boredom. As she walked out the hospital entrance, she decided that the next stop would be the pub. To hell with the time of day; she needed a drink and couldn't see Pippa arguing with that one.

Chapter Nine

After saying good morning to the nurses for the second time today, Janet headed straight for Nick's room, seething over the idea that Amy thought she could just waltz right back into their lives as if nothing had happened. Before entering the room, she paused for breath to regain her composure and subdue her anger. It must have been George who had contacted Amy. What the hell was he thinking?

Well, it was safe to say that he had not heard the last of this. For the first month after the accident, Amy had been inseparable from Nick holding a bedside vigil every night. Together, Janet and Amy had supported each other through the initial shock. Janet had come closer to her than most married couples, discovering Amy's most intimate thoughts of Nick, and finding comfort in sharing her own. They had become sisters in mourning; sometimes laughing, sometimes crying, but most of the time just sitting in silence, prisoners of their shared sorrow. Eventually, for Janet, it came to a point where her brain ceased to function and she would just stare aimlessly into space, the act of simply being in the same room as Nick enough to satisfy her longing for him. However, for Amy the endless days and nights of hope and misery became too much to bear. Deep down, Janet not only felt as though Amy had abandoned Nick, but had also left her to suffer alone. Hardly visiting at all, George was following his own path of destruction and so without Amy, without her sister in mourning, she had been left as destitute as the day Nick had been taken from them. It had not happened straight away. At first, although her visits were still regular they became shorter in length. Then less frequent. Every day became every second day, turning into every few days until eventually, nothing. Not until today.

Taking a deep breath to purge her mind of Amy, Janet entered Nick's room to find a nurse, Sarah, exercising his arm back and forth across his face.

'Good morning,' Janet said, laying her handbag on the bed by Nick's feet. 'How's my boy today?'

Nick's look of frustration soon turned to delight at the sight of his mother, but as his smile widened a line of saliva escaped his mouth, sliding down his chin. The nightmare from the night before was already forgotten by his damaged mind.

'Ahh,' he said in a drawn out, simple greeting.

'Morning,' Sarah said between breaths of exertion. 'Good day?'

Janet considered the question. 'So far so good. When did your day start then?'

'Don't ask. Try six o'clock. You get used to it. It just means that you don't get much of a life in the week, but who needs one of those when I've got this hunky stud to look after, hey Nick?'

Nick curled his lip in mild disdain.

'Suite yourself,' Sarah said.

'Now Nick, don't be rude,' Janet gently scolded.

Nick just grumbled and lowered his head.

'It's all right,' Sarah said. 'I'm used to it. Well, I have something that will please you.'

Janet's interest piqued while Nick continued to grumble.

'I was talking to Dr Collins and he said he's been chatting to Nick's physio. Nick's now considered to be off the danger list so, maybe even today, we're going to be removing the feed tubes.'

'That's brilliant news,' Janet said. 'Nick, did you hear that? It looks like you might be having some of your tubes out today. Isn't that great?'

Nick just huffed as Sarah began to work his other arm, but Janet ignored him, thrilled that at last they were gaining some headway.

'Is the doctor around?' she asked, needing to hear the words from him too for reassurance.

'He's in his office, I think,' Sarah replied.

'Lovely, I'll just have a quick word. Nick, I'm just popping out but I'll be back in a minute, okay?' Though her words were wasted on him, she had to try and keep up the pretence of normality for his sake.

Making her way to Collins's office, Janet passed the beds of the critical or dying, the quiet sound of beeping machines filling the ward as they worked like busy bees monitoring and supporting the lives of their patients. The sight of all those needles and tubes really used to get to her, as well as that incessant beeping. Even in her dreams she could hear its monotonous tone. This deep into the ward, hardly a word was spoken; the look of concentration on the nurses faces speaking volumes. Idle chitchat was not welcome here and so she silently made her way past the beds to knock at Collins's door.

'Come,' his voice called from within. Seeing Janet enter, his entire demeanour changed. 'Hello Janet, please take a seat. Is George not with you?'

'He's downstairs locking the car. He shouldn't be too long.'

'Right,' Collins said, sensing some of her residual tension. 'Well, I have some great news.'

'I know,' Janet interrupted with excitement. 'Sarah just told me, about the feed tubes.'

Collins's smile broadened. 'Oh, that's good. I think with his current state of awareness, the tubes are causing more harm to his psychological wellbeing than good, and according to the physio's examination he should be capable of taking fluids orally now anyway. I don't know if you've noticed the bleeding around his nose? That's irritation. He'll be sedated to keep the trauma to a minimum so don't worry about a thing.'

Janet shifted in her seat.

'Seriously, don't worry; it's not a complicated procedure. It's just that with Nick's state of mind I feel that putting him to sleep while we do it will be more beneficial to everyone and greatly reduce his anxiety, that's all.'

'Yes, yes of course, whatever you think is best,' she said. For a moment, Janet found herself transported back to the old days of operation after operation, but this time was different; this time there was a light at the end of the tunnel. 'I just want Nick to be as comfortable and stress free as possible.'

'And that he will, which is why I would like you and George to be present in the preparation room when we put him to sleep. I want him to be surrounded by friendly faces.'

Just then, George entered the room, out of breath. Janet ignored him and Collins could not help but notice the coldness between them. This was not good.

'Hello George,' Collins said, rising from his seat to shake his hand. 'I was just explaining the good news to Janet.'

'What's that then?' he asked, accepting Collins's hand.

'They're taking out Nick's feed tubes and they want both of us to be present,' she said with a hint of dryness, still clearly angry with his act of treachery.

George took the statement for what it was, pretending to ignore her veiled threat of a later confrontation. 'Really? Well, that's great. When do you think that might happen, doctor?'

Collins went through it all again for George's benefit before going on to explain the procedure. Nick would be sedated and then the tubes would simply be dragged out and dumped into the waste. Though being a

The Maelstrom

relatively simple task, for the uninitiated it could often come across as more traumatic than it actually was, and the last thing the staff needed was the hassle of intervening parents. Completely out of the way would have been a much better option but Collins needed to keep them involved and give them a sign of progression, anything to soften blow that if Nick's mental state did not improve then he would remain that way for the rest of his natural life. It was a discussion for later that Collins could happily do without.

Chapter Ten

'Hello Hesamuel.'

Nick froze as a familiar dread gripped the length of his spine.

'You will have to forgive me as I am not accustomed to the social niceties you sleepers perform in the Cosm. Would you care for drink?'

It was the same voice that had tormented him inside the confines of Jeremiah's closet. As Nick's eyes opened, he saw a grotesque and obese, acne scarred woman stood behind the filthiest bacteria riddled bar he had ever seen. The beer pumps were coated with a layer of mould as were the optic bottles along the back shelf. Climbing up the walls and across the bar, masses of huge black cockroaches clambered over one another, dragging light streaks of muck through the carpet of fungus. They came from the cracks and the drains, anywhere that would accommodate them, making a beeline for the obese barmaid's legs, disappearing up into the folds of her ragged dress.

'He asked you a fucking question!' she spat, leaning over the counter and sinking her flabby fist into the rot covered bar. Exposing her decaying teeth with a meaningful glare, Nick thought she would rather grind a glass into his face than fill it for him.

'No thanks… thank you,' he replied, his body pivoting away from her as the stench of her fat unclean body infected his nostrils with the promise of disease.

'Do not mind her,' the voice said, *'she becomes highly… irritable. It is the mives, but then you must all bear your crosses sooner or later. There is only so much darkness a soul can produce until the Light refuses it entry.'*

Nick looked at the woman again, unsure as to what

the mysterious speaker meant by 'mives', but the truth was soon revealed in all its putrid glory. Peeling back the shoulder of her loosely hung dress, the woman exposed her bruised dead skin and displayed one of her breasts that hung like a flabby sack of fat, veined and redundant. Its surface looked alive. Needing to strain his eyes in the murky light, Nick whipped his head away as he was assaulted with the reality of her condition. Covered in tiny creatures, the woman was being slowly eaten alive as they crabbed across her skin, leisurely feasting on her, mating on her, multiplying on her. Eventually there would be nothing left but the soul, and that would be when the real pain started. In his revulsion Nick tried to pull back, but was stopped by an intense pain that clamped the back of his head and neck holding him fast. With the woman's depravity being aired for all to see, the room became polluted even more with the stench of her decay.

My God, how she stank.

Nick became aware of something moving behind him. During his moment of revulsion he had managed to grab a quick glance backwards before the crippling pain took hold, and in that moment he saw the figure of a man standing against the far wall.

'You have nothing to fear from mives. They are her punishment for crimes committed within the Cosm.'

Nick found himself being unconcerned with his aggressor's words, instead becoming consumed with the need to finally put a face to the voice. Despite the burning pain raging down his spine, he twisted his head backward again bringing more of the room into view.

Just a little more, he thought.

In the shadows behind him were brown stained walls, dry and cracked and crawling with insidious cockroaches. Then, just as Nick thought he could take no more, there *He* was. Without warning, the pain in his spine increased and Nick's head was snapped forward again, leaving his heart pounding as the most ferocious fear crippled his ability to flee, and gripped his throat making it impossible to scream. He should not have looked back; he should not have looked back.

The voice roared in anger. *'If you had the slightest comprehension of who I am, you would not dare to cast your eyes upon me.'*

Indescribable pain engulfed Nick's body, his vocal cords rupturing with a deafening scream as he crumpled beneath the pressure of the agony. Falling to the floorboards he lay quaking with terror, his eyes shut against the presence of something sinister close beside his ear.

'What do you want? What have I done?'

'You saw, but that is nothing new. What intrigues me is how you managed to escape. I don't think even you know how you did it, do you? That is why you tried to hide from me in the River, but I knew you would not last for long. There is something different about you.'

Nick squeezed his eyes tighter, clamping his ears with his hands to prevent the words that flowed like poison. 'I don't know what you're talking about.'

'Of course you do.'

'No! I don't!' Nick's yell erupted from him like a meteor, echoing off the walls, bouncing the panicked cockroaches to the floor and shattering the scum-covered mirror behind the bar, careening as though the very fear coursing through his veins had taken on a metaphysical form to destroy that which gave it strength. Nick sensed the dark entity pull back.

'You do know, you just don't remember yet,' the voice said. *'You truly are an enigma, Hesamuel. Do you know how many of your kind have witnessed what you have seen and escaped?'*

'You're not real,' Nick whispered, his throat choking on the detritus and filth.

Staring down at Nick in mild amusement, the owner of the voice experimented with a chuckle.

'You're in my head. You're only a dream.'

'*Maybe I am,*' the voice said, '*but on the other hand, what if I'm not? What would happen if the pathetic existence that you call Life, being crippled and useless, was the dream; what then?*'

'You're in my head.'

'*You sleepers are all the same. Your blindness makes you weak. Your petty fears for your own mortality unfounded and still you refuse to believe. Yet, why should I tell you what you already know?*

The irony of your kind is that you already know the truth but waste your entire lives trying to deny it for fear of going mad, running around like children mortally afraid of not conforming to the conventional thinking of the time or location. How truly pathetic a species you are, like sheep, all of you. Do you think you are insane, Hesamuel? Can you feel the grains of reality slowly slipping through your fingers, or are you still convinced that this is nothing but a dream?'

Nick sank into submission. Why was this happening to him? All he wanted was to dream of freedom and girls and escape from the prison of his ruined body. Only in his dreams would it be possible for him to break away from the torture of his living hell, and even now he was denied that tiny pleasure.

'*How pathetic,*' the voice continued. '*To think you possess so much power and knowledge, and all you can think of are your petty earthly pleasures. Well, Hesamuel, if that is what you desire ...*'

Everything disappeared. Not just the voice, but the darkened room, the bar, and the obese woman with her rancid flesh. All of it, gone.

Nick found himself transported to an unfamiliar cobbled street outside a terrace of medieval style houses made of timber and dirt. One gnarled and twisted building in particular commanded his attention. In the blink of an eye, daylight had been replaced with night like an oil slick across the sky, the only illumination coming from the watchful eye of the moon and the open doorway of the misshapen house which was surrounded by a crowd of drunken revellers. Even from this distance, Nick could hear the faint thumping of dance music emanating from the doorway, and it completely felt out of place.

'Hey Nick, where have you been?' a ginger haired man shouted from the crowd, not much older than himself.

'I'm not quite sure,' Nick replied making his way over, already forgetting that he was in a dream, running with the new fantasy, but still feeling the remnants of the nightmare experience. 'Have I missed much?'

'Nah, everything's been pretty tame so far,' the man replied, handing Nick a beer.

Hesamuel; why was the voice calling him by that name? It meant nothing, but then as quickly as the thought had come it was gone again like smoke on the wind and he fell back into the role-play of the dream.

'So where's the action then?' Nick jibed as though he and the party reveller had been bosom buddies since birth.

'Ha, go on inside, Tahira will show you the goodies,' the man slurred, his drunken grin brimming with lecherous promise.

'I might just do that,' Nick said, stepping through the door into the dimly lit corridor, the blaring music enveloping him in a blanket of bass.

Four strides in and Nick was surrounded by activity in what was an ordinary looking kitchen where he was greeted with a hot, sensuous, kiss. Now, this dream he liked. As the deliverer of the kiss moved away into focus, Nick could hardly believe his eyes; she was gorgeous, and as he caressed the shape of her voluptuous breasts with his eyes travelling down to her tight flat stomach, she playfully giggled at the idea of him mentally undressing her, masterfully clicking off each of the buttons to her waist-tied denim shirt one by one.

'Do you like what you see, cowboy?' she invited,

gazing at Nick with dirty eyes, rhythmically grinding her supple hips against the fabric of his jeans. With ease Nick popped open one of the buttons to her shirt and slipped his hand inside cupping a plentiful amount of her bosom, teasing her nipple with his thumb.

'Yes I do,' he said, moving in for another kiss. She thrust her tongue into his mouth kissing with such passion that Nick was brought to immediate attention. Reaching around to grip his buttocks, the girl pulled herself hard against him continuing to grind his throbbing cock against her own pulsing groin. He kissed her even harder, relishing thoughts of the delights to come. Sighing with pleasure, Nick came up for air as she worked her way lower, nibbling and sucking at his neck, his skin tingling with ecstasy. Nick pulled away her shirt letting it fall to the floor exposing her huge breasts in all their sumptuous glory. Despite the people around them he could no longer fight the urges raging through his body. Bending low, he curled his tongue around her nipple teasing and sucking, provoking the girl to new heights of pleasure.

'Fuck me now,' she breathed into his ear, nibbling at the lobe. 'Fuck me hard.' Reaching down into his jeans, she vigorously ran her clasped fist up and down the length of his hard shaft. Nick arched and gasped with enjoyment.

But before he could oblige it was too late as every muscle in his body stiffened and he came, smearing his shorts and the girl's hand with his sticky juice. Grinning, she pulled out her hand to admire the milky mess on her hand.

'Did I do that?' Nick watched her raise it to her mouth to lick it off, swallowing deeply, gratefully. Even the people around them were not enough to prevent her from sliding her fingers all the way in, sucking off the remainder of his cum.

Whatever pleasure Nick gained from the brief encounter was short lived as his moment of gratification became shattered by a blood curdling scream. From the murky darkness of the corridor that led to front of the house, a spiral staircase appeared which had not been there before. Somewhere at the top of the metallic steps, inhuman cries of pain were beckoning for Nick to follow. As he stared at the shadowy steps, he found it hard to ignore the cum-eating vixen draped across him, but the screams were so horrible and yet so familiar, they called to him like an old memory. Drawing on his soul and his senses they begged to be heard, to be acknowledged. And again, everything changed.

The noise of the party disappeared as an icy wind howled through the building, and the room became empty. *He* was back, the voice had returned. Nick was beginning to wonder whether his mysterious stalker had even left. Perhaps *He* had just been mingling with the crowd, leering as the beautiful woman had finished Nick in the middle of the room; or maybe, like the foul barmaid this temptress was nothing more than another of his denizens sent to play and confuse him further. Were his dreams really that out of control? Everything just seemed too weird, too dark, and the fact that he was able to rationalise about it all was stranger still. Dreams were supposed to be fragmented scenarios without true sense or reason. But then, if that was true, how was it he was able to distinguish between the two states so easily?

As the dying screams beckoned, Nick knew that he must follow.

'Don't go,' the girl moaned, curling her tongue around her thumb to suck in what remained.

'I have to see where that cry is coming from. Someone may need help.'

'But we were having so much fun,' she begged, staring at him with puppy dog eyes, slipping her hand back inside the top of his still open jeans.

Nick pulled away, trying hard not to fall into her seductive gaze. With a massive effort, he removed her hand

and re-zipped his jeans. Snapping his belt tight against his stomach, the woman sighed at the sound, and he headed for the staircase. Had Nick looked back he would have caught a fleeting glimpse of her before she evaporated into twisting starlets; nothing but another illusion.

With the foot of the spiral staircase consumed in darkness, Nick felt alone and exposed as though some unseen force was watching, waiting, ready to pounce at the slightest movement but he continued.

The screaming stopped.

His eyes wide with fear and adrenaline pumping through his veins, Nick ascended the creaking steps, interrupting the gloom that hovered like a dirty mist over the floor above. At the top was a man sprawled across the landing surrounded by hundreds of burning candles, the melted wax flowing across the floor like lava creating an outline around his damaged body. His head was slumped at an impossible angle against a polished mahogany dresser, and he wore nothing but a green bath robe and a look of bewildered terror. In places, patches of hair and skin had been torn from his scalp and the sticky gore that remained glistened in the candlelight. Although the man's body was still, his eyes followed Nick's every move as a dour smile began to spread across his face.

'Are you all right?' Nick asked.

'I don't believe it,' the man said in quiet exclamation, staring at Nick in a maniacal way that unnerved him.

Without understanding why, Nick could feel the man was not looking *at* him but inside him, deep inside, past all the flesh and bone to his soul. 'You don't know how good it is to see you again, pilgrim. You look like crap. How's *life* been treating you?'

'I'm sorry, do we know each other?'

The man ignored Nick's question. 'You know, I thought long and hard about what you did. I've never seen anyone do that before, didn't know it was possible; no-one did! Ha! I tell you what though, it gave me hope, gave a lot of us hope; and I tried... I tried so hard. I concentrated long and hard, I folded myself away from my cell, shut out the whole dark place and thought long and hard about *you*. Then eventually, it came to me! I don't know how it happened, but damn! A whole explosion of possibilities came to me! It was like a massive floodgate opening and the whole lot just came pouring in, and now here I am. I'm free! You set me free, and I don't mind telling you it's good to see you again. There are still the others though; that's why you're here, right? We've got to save the others!'

'I'm sorry but I have no idea what you're talking about,' Nick said. 'Who are you?'

'No, of course, damn it you're still asleep!' The man turned his head away in sorrow as a tear of frustration fell upon his cheek. 'I can't... no, I won't tell you anything more. It's forbidden.'

'What?' Nick exclaimed. 'If you know something then you have to tell me what's going on.'

The man looked up again, his eyes softer this time.

'Nicholas Howell, you may not understand what I am about to tell you but you must remember it when you leave this place. We are all just microscopic parts of a much larger picture, yet more rests on your shoulders than you could possibly imagine. You are important and must survive for the journey home. You must be strong, the strongest of us all, to save us all. No matter what games *He* plays or how many illusions *He* throws in your path you must remain strong. If not then all is lost. I know it's vague, pilgrim but everything depends on you, and if I tell you anything more in your present condition you will never make it home.'

'What are you talking about? This is no ordinary dream is it?'

'Are any dreams ordinary?'

'I don't understand; you have to tell me more.'

'I cannot tell you any more than you already know. It would be pointless and dangerous. One thing I can tell you is that the monster tormenting you is very real. *He* is without mercy or regret. I would tell you *His* name but if I uttered the word even once *He* would find us and torture us both, not even for sport because that would require an emotion; just because *He* can. *He* feels nothing. *He* is a vacuum, a being of true evil. Be vigilant and trust nothing, Nick; not your eyes or your ears, only your heart. Everything can be manipulated, but you are the Messenger, do not lose your way. Promise me that you will stay true.'

Nick crouched beside the struggling man. 'Wait, what is this place, why are we here?'

'I cannot say.'

'But you've got to; I need to know the truth.'

'I'm sorry ... I cannot say. You have to find the reasons for yourself, pilgrim. You have to search deep within yourself to discover the truth, just as you taught me to do; or else everything that you have endured will be for nothing and the darkness will endure. Even in its most complicated form the answer is so simple, but I cannot say for the law prohibits it. You already know the truth. Just believe.'

Nick gave a sigh of resignation, finally accepting that he was going to gain nothing further from the man. 'At least tell me *His* name. What's in a name?'

'Did you not listen to a word I just said?'

Though abashed, Nick remained stubborn and for what seemed like an age the man just stared at him seeming to bathe in his aura and, as Nick gazed deeper into the man's eyes unable to break the bond between them, he felt love. Not the lustful, selfish, egotistical kind that drives sleepers insane with jealousy and insecurity but a warm and unconditional type of love that made him feel secure and trusted filling him with the promise of a faraway place. The man began to weep and smiled at Nick as though accepting a fate he feared yet knew to be inevitable. Recognising the man's look of acceptance, Nick's heart filled with shame and he wanted to stop him from answering his selfish question but before he had the chance it was already too late.

'*His* name is *Abaddon*.'

Without warning an immense boom echoed through the building, shaking the floor and walls like an earthquake, forcing the lit candles to sway and topple. Losing balance, Nick tumbled backwards, conscious of the staircase behind him, just managing to steady himself before toppling over the edge.

'*He* is here.'

'Abaddon?'

Another enormous boom rippled through the fabric of the reality surrounding them and the man clutched at Nick's shirt pulling him closer until they were nose to nose.

'*He's* found us! You have to get out of here. Don't let *Him* catch-'

But before he could finish his sentence the man's head jerked back at an unnatural angle as something sharp and vicious rippled beneath his bathrobe. All Nick could see was the green fabric bubble ferociously as a crimson patchwork of blood spread across his torso. The man let out a final agonising cry for help... and then there was calm.

'It is coming... the Awakening ... is upon us... be... strong.'

Suddenly, the man's eyes bulged in pain as blood bubbled from his lips. All Nick could do was watch in horror as a bulge of flesh stretched out from the side of the man's neck before ripping open and a sinewy creature with needle sharp teeth burst out leaving a baggy hole of meat where the man's throat had been. The monster leapt at him pinning his body to the floor beneath its solid muscular weight, sniffing the sweat on his skin with its deformed and twisted nose. Raising its head high, the beast howled with bloodlust before leaping off Nick's chest and bounding down the stairs, scoring strips of metal from the steps with its claws. Without hesitation this time, Nick sprang to his feet, his heart and temples pounding as he prepared to flee in the opposite direction. But Nick froze. The monster had stopped just short of the final step and was turning, baring back its lethal blood-stained jaws, presenting them in all their menacing glory.

Nick's petrified eyes widened. The beast once again raised its head releasing another howl of fury, splintering Nick's nerves to the quick. In a vain attempt at protection, he threw his arm across his face when the beast leapt high, but the blow never came. Nick peeked out from beneath his arm and just managed to glimpse the monster's raw behind as it squeeze itself through the keyhole of the front door. As it vanished from sight, Nick half expected to hear a ridiculous cartoon pop signifying its retreat, but there was nothing but a cold blank silence and a dead man at his feet.

'Hello? You're still here then?' a sickly-sweet voice called up from the kitchen below, dripping with innuendo and manipulation.

The nymph had returned. Feeling displaced, Nick backed away from the dead man's corpse and descended the staircase. From the corridor, he could see her leaning seductively against the kitchen units sipping coke from a glass stained with dried cum and faded lip-gloss.

Trust nothing but your heart.

'All right,' Nick said, sticking his face into hers. 'What the hell's going on? Who was that man up there and what the fuck was that thing?'

'Oh poppet,' she mewed, turning her head away from him to take another sip of her drink while at the same time caressing one of her nipples through the fabric of her shirt. 'Wouldn't he tell you anything? That must be *so* frustrating for you.' She took another sip from the crusty glass. 'Perhaps I could take your mind off it?'

She giggled and her provocative manner repulsed him.

'What the fuck is going on!' he shouted, grabbing her by the shoulders, squeezing and shaking. 'No more games, tell me!'

As if his grip meant nothing, she threw back her head in laughter.

'You're so tense. Are you sure that there's *nothing* I can do to relax you?' she said reaching for his crotch.

Nick threw her to the floor in frustration where she landed hard, giggling, enjoying the roughness.

Another loud boom rattled through the house.

'Oh dear,' she said. 'You're in trouble now.'

Nick turned to see the front door shake as something big, very big, pounded at the panels outside. As the banging continued the door began to splinter beneath the relentless barrage. Nick made a run for the stairs.

Just as he reached the bottom step he had to fling himself to the ground as a mangled bloodied fist exploded through the central panel of the door sending shards of splintered wood spinning into the corridor and kitchen. In a panicked frenzy, Nick scrambled up the stairs on all fours with his heart in his throat.

But reaching the top, he was stopped in his tracks as his hand pressed into the dead man's blood that covered the top step with gore. It had not been the blood which had stopped his progress though. There was simply nowhere left to go. There was no landing, or walls or ceiling. Halted in his tracks, Nick stared out into oblivion.

Below, the front door gave way with a scream of shattered wood and metal, and Nick glimpsed something big, ape-like, blur past the foot of the stair with maniacal speed. What came next was instantaneous and expected. A sickly sweet giggle, then a scream, followed by a squelching snap, and then silence.

Trapped between a black hole and impending death, Nick stood and trembled. He had two options. The first was to go back downstairs and make a bolt for the door but risk being pulled apart by the beast in the kitchen, or fall into the oblivion that crept closer and closer towards him. In the end he chose neither and instead resigned himself to the blood stained step, wrapping his arms around his knees, hiding his terrified eyes within them. In the face of such odds and exhausted of mental reserves, Nick gave himself to despair, curled up foetus-like, where for just a moment he began to feel safe again, this ghost reality no longer holding meaning for him. Staring out from beneath his trembling arm, Nick watched the hulking shape of Jeremiah, the butcher of women, ascend the stairs, his insane grin corrupted with dirt and blood, his huge arms flexing responsively by his sides.

Nick felt a rush of cold air pass over his body as a hand of ice lay on his shoulder.

'*Can you feel the despair?*' Abaddon droned, not to Nick but to Jeremiah.

Nick just whimpered beneath Abaddon's icy grip. 'Please, let me go.'

'*Go?*' Abaddon said without the slightest hint of emotion. '*Tell me, Hesamuel, where would you go? Do you have the slightest idea where you are?*'

Nick remained silent, not wanting to hear the answer; wishing with all his heart that he could wake from this nightmare.

'*You are in the place that sleepers fear the most. You are in the devil's playground, Hesamuel. This is your avichi, this is your Hell.*' The word boomed and rattled off everything around them, sending ripples through the very darkness that surrounded them.

'This is a dream. It's all in my head. You're not real, none of you are!'

'But I am real, Hesamuel, and from the moment you close your eyes you are mine.'

'I've seen nothing!'

'Not that you remember, but you will. I give you this one opportunity. Join me and bear witness to the downfall of that old and rotting empire. Aid me in my purpose.'

'What?'

'Consider the possibilities, the rewards.'

'What are you talking about?'

With a bored resignation, Abaddon moved away and Jeremiah took his place grabbing Nick by his hair.

'I've been looking forward to this,' Jeremiah hissed, the stench of his voice filling Nick's throat with bile. Pain shot across the back of Nick's neck as an applied pressure threatened to separate his head from the rest of his body. 'Fucker! Do you know what real pain is? This isn't real pain.'

Jeremiah gripped Nick's arm and snapped it like a twig, flesh giving way to bone as the marrow splintered from his elbow to his wrist shredding through the skin to reveal its pearly blood-stained surface. Nick screamed, the agony burning through his body, the tears and snot of his suffering streaming into his wailing mouth.

'That's not pain,' Jeremiah continued. 'Pain is when I make you sit and watch as I drill your mother, your father, and your baby brother Andrew in the ass, and then when I'm done gut them like fish and choke them with their own intestines.'

Nick could feel bone grating against jagged bone as his forearm was twisted, the burning immense as his blood cascaded like a waterfall into the oblivion. Passing beyond screams, all that emanated from Nick's mouth was a high pitched whistling sound.

'If you will not join me, Hesamuel, then you have but one option. Take your own life. Kill yourself. Stop the agony before it begins because you should believe me when I say that what you have

experienced so far, like you, is nothing. End it now and save yourself an eternity of torture. Kill yourself, Hesamuel. Do it. Do it now!'

Nick's eyes snapped open into a glare of blinding light, his throat constricted.

'Nathan, he's coming round,' he heard Maureen's voice say from somewhere in the distance.

Something was jamming Nick's throat but he could not move or do anything to prevent it. Blinking against the bright light, his world was filled with asphyxiating chaos.

'Damn it, I think he's choking,' a male voice said.

'What? What's he choking on? Get him back under, his larynx is contracting,' Maureen ordered. 'Do it, do it now!'

Everything went dark.

The darkness was replaced by a clear blue sky where Nick was on his back in the grass choking, his eyes bulging under the pressure. On the other side of the prairie, he could see Jeremiah striding towards him, covered in the blood of every victim he had ever claimed, leaving behind him a trail of scorched grass.

Nick struggled to focus but before his vision became too distorted he managed to see Jeremiah reach down and grab an old, notched, wooden handle protruding at an angle from his thigh, pulling it loose to produce a large rusted meat cleaver which had been embedded in his own leg. Nick's face began to turn blue as his vision was all but gone. It could not end this way, it should not. There was only one thing left to do. He did not need to see; instinct was telling him that he knew the way, that he had done this thing before. Using the last of his reserves, Nick raised his body into a hunched stance and lurched towards the flowing water of the River.

Way off in the distance, just a mere speck on the horizon, a lone figure stood and cried out in agony as though he were right beside Nick pleading for him stop, but Nick was decided. Reaching the River's edge, he paused for only a second before toppling in, breaking the glassy surface and releasing his body, his mind, and his soul to the depths. Deeper he sank into its murky arms, giving himself to the safety and solitude of its emptiness; and the whole silent world screamed.

Chapter Eleven

Rubbing his tired eyes, Collins could feel the walls of his office closing in around him. How could he have been so wrong? Such a simple procedure and it had gone so terribly wrong. Had his own blind arrogance caused him to rush things? Or was Nick just not as strong as the physiotherapist had originally thought. Ever since his awakening she had been assessing Nick's physical progress, especially his swallowing. Everyone had noticed how the nasogastric tube that provided him with supplements had been irritating him. Most - more able bodied - patients tended to pull the tube out without help, unable to stand the nagging discomfort, but in Nick's weakened state it was an impossible task that only caused him further anguish. That was why Collins, with the physiotherapist's consent, gave the all clear to have the tube removed. It was such a simple procedure; you just dragged it out as quickly as possible and prayed that the patient did not cover you in vomit from the gag reflex. Collins had even taken the extra precaution of having Nick sedated to minimize any additional stress the procedure might cause his already fragile mind.

Leaning back in his green leather captain's chair feeling the cold hard padding push the centre of his back, he looked across the room at three small badminton trophies perched on top of the filing cabinet and tried hard, without success, to clear away any self-accusatory thoughts. Outside in the family room, the Howell's were waiting at his request. Mid-thought, his attention was diverted by the sound of a soft rapping at the door.

'Come in,' Collins said in a tone which sounded harder in his ear than he had intended.

The door crept open and Sarah sidled in holding a steaming cup of tea, trying not to burn her knuckles against the side of the cup.

'I thought you could do with one,' she said. Placing it on the coaster next to Collins's keyboard, she winced as her knuckles caught the side of the hot ceramic.

'Thank you.'

'I hope you don't mind me saying but, it's not your fault you know. We've all been observing him and we all thought it was time to remove the tube. You're not to blame.'

'Thank you, Sarah,' he said, giving her an appreciative smile even though he felt miserable and pressured inside. Of course it was his fault. That was the way the world worked. People needed someone to blame to make the sad futility of their lives easier to bear and the finger always pointed to the one at the top.

'Anyway,' she continued, 'I just thought you should know… that we're all behind you.'

There were no words to express the gratitude he felt for her kindness. However, as endearing as the sentiment was it had only left him feeling fraudulent and unworthy of their support.

Rubbing his temples, Collins thought back to the last time he had used the Glasgow Scale to test Nick's functional levels. The developmental manner in which Nick's sensations of vision, hearing, and touch were returning was slow at best, but a definite pattern had been emerging. Rebuilding a coma patient was like learning to play the piano. You began at first with a single note to which other notes were added over time until eventually a tune was formed. After a period of months you then moved on to more complicated, intricate tunes to create what could finally be recognised as music; the fingers becoming hardened and agile, seeming to glide across the once stifling keys. As it was, Nick's vision was good. Both his eyes moved in sequence, his pupils reacting normally, dilating in the dark and constricting to the light, and both his hearing and touch were perfect. His motor functions were weak, but Collins was in no doubt that over time, Nick could have once again become a self-sufficient member of society. He would have probably never played football again but he would certainly have become self-reliant, to an extent.

That was, of course, if Nick had not gone back into the coma.

Rising from his seat, Collins left the tea untouched and made his way out to the ward closing the office door behind him. Looking down the empty hall with a lonely sickness in his heart, the stillness was broken as Maureen flitted by carrying a tray of bloodied bandages.

Approximately an hour ago, Nick had regressed. He was stable and his vitals were sufficient, but the question of why still remained. Collins had not been present when the nasogastric tube was being removed but by all accounts the procedure had gone as normal. After all, it was hardly brain surgery. He had to stop stalling and give the Howells the bad news.

The corridor held an eerie calm as if the angel of death was keeping pace right beside him. Every so often, Collins would get the notion that no matter what miracles he performed, Death was constantly peaking over his shoulder, its sick and permanent grin leering at him in amusement knowing full well that he was wasting his time; that eventually Death came to us all. Rather than allow the idea to hamper him, Collins fed off it, using it to fuel his desire to excel, to stare right back into that hollow grinning face with a smile of triumph and contempt. Ultimately, Collins knew he was playing a game he could not win, but he would be damned if he would just lie back and allow it to be a one-sided match. Why should the cards always be stacked in the dealer's favour? If he could allow his players just one more chance to cheat Death, just one more chance at life, then good for them. Although the Reaper didn't have a grip on Nick yet, Collins could feel him waiting in the wings with open arms and a demon grin.

Not yet though, Collins thought. The game was not over yet.

Arriving at the door of the family room, he took a deep breath before entering. Janet was standing by the window staring out at the arable fields that stretched as far as the eye could see across the Lincolnshire flats, all the way to the east coast where holiday makers were playing without a care in the world. George was sat hunched by the radiator staring into space, a prisoner of his own thoughts. Collins closed the door and both looked at him without a saying word.

'Hi,' Collins said, taking a seat. He cupped his hands over his mouth and sighed. His stubble felt prickly against his palm. The silence prevailed, and when Collins cleared his throat the sound in his ears was deafening. 'Thanks for coming so quickly. There's no easy way to put this so I'll just come straight out with it. There have been some complications. I'm afraid that Nick's gone back into the coma.'

From the window, Janet stifled a gasp and turned away while George seemed to physically shrink. Collins stayed silent, unable to find words that could stop their suffering. There were none. Any attempts at a weak consolation would feel hollow and disrespectful. After all the misery they had endured and the long merciless months of waiting they deserved more than just a few simple words of condolence. They deserved the cold hard truth.

'We were removing his feed tube and while he was unconscious, Nick had some sort of seizure. We still don't know what caused it, but we're doing everything in our power to make him as comfortable as we can.'

'I don't understand. How could this have happened?' George asked. Janet remained motionless by the window.

'Like I said, we don't know,' Collins offered. 'The only thing I can think of is that Nick's awakening must have been a temporary reprieve; that something more sinister has been hiding in the background that could have manifested during his short time back with us. I think another scan may-'

'Is he going to die?' George asked, looking Collins in the eye.

Janet did not even react to the question. She just stared out the window showing no indication she was even listening. Held by George's stare, Collins became discomforted by its intensity and eventually looked away, unable to stand the pain which dug into his soul and filled him with guilt.

'At the moment your son is stable, but the next twenty-four hours are going to be critical. I have to tell you though his rate of decline is not good.' He paused. 'I really am sorry. Even if he was to recover now I couldn't guarantee his level of mobility.'

Without turning from the window it was now Janet's turn to speak.

'Are we talking vegetative?'

'Yes, what sort of disability are we talking about?' George added.

Collins shifted in his seat feeling the walls pressing ever nearer.

'If Nick wakes up, and at this stage that's a big if, of course we will do everything we can to help him function independently within society.'

'You didn't answer the question,' Janet said.

Collins mentally stumbled. 'Honestly, I don't know the answer to that. No-one could, not until he wakes up again.'

'And that may never happen,' George said, more as a statement than a question.

'As I said, the next twenty-four hours are critical. I know it's not what you want to hear right now but, we will just have to wait and see. I'm sorry, but at the moment that really is the best I can offer.'

'We know,' George said, understanding that despite everything, Collins was in an impossible position. 'We really do appreciate everything you've done for us. I... *we* know that you can only do your best.'

Collins smiled awkwardly then looked to Janet in anticipation of a response but she remained with her back to the room, not wanting the doctor to witness her grief.

'Is it all right for us to see him now?' she asked.

'Yes, yes of course,' Collins replied.

Janet's face was blank and cold, her eyes continuing their silent scream. It was like waking from a dream, a cruel, realistic dream where their hopes had taken form and the agonising wait that seemed so long had disappeared. But like a dream it had been a lie, a figment of the mind to tease and torment in the waking hours of dawn. The space in her heart where hope had once lived was now an empty husk where a woman called Janet Howell had once lived, dreaming, hoping that one day her son would return but the dream was over; all optimism gone. This was real life now, the life that she would have to accept and live with. It was time to return to the world again; after all, there was still Andrew to consider. For a long time she had been more than aware that both of them had neglected him terribly, prisoners of their own grief, and since the day of the accident any semblance of family had been placed on hold. It had not been fair on any of them, but especially Andrew. It was only now she realised that through her own selfishness he had been neglected, left to deal with the situation alone and it made her feel sick with shame.

'I think I'd like to see Nick now,' she said, facing them and collecting her handbag from the chair. 'Come on, George.'

Obediently, he stood to leave thanking Collins again for all of their efforts.

The walk to Nick's room was one of the longest of George's life. What happened next? Where exactly did they go from here, back to waiting and hoping and praying? What else was there?

And then it happened, the unthinkable; the one thing that no parent should ever think. For the first time throughout this entire five month ordeal George wished that Nick was dead. That on that fateful night the car which had ruined his body, and their lives, had done the job properly and finished him off. They would have still lost their son, but at least it would have been final. They would have known where they stood instead of being left in this limbo to wait and wonder if today was to be the day that their son would return or be lost forever. The more he thought about it the more he wanted it to be true. It seemed now the only logical resolution to this whole mess. At least then they would be able to grieve and rebuild their lives. Anxiety stirred deep inside his chest as the thought of Nick's death became ever more appealing. He just wanted it over with one way or the other; he wanted his life back.

As they entered his room, Nick lay motionless, the offending nasogastric tube back in place. His arms were limp by his sides, his chin tucked into his chest gathering folds of skin around his jowls. If it were not for the warmth of his body and the rhythmic beeping of the heart monitor anyone could have easily mistaken Nick for dead. George touched his hand just to be sure, and then quickly released it again as the warm horrible truth rushed back at him. Nick's breathing was shallow, his chest heaves hardly noticeable. Collins hung back in the doorway to keep his distance from the scene. Janet, however, needed the contact with her son. Bending low she kissed him, holding her lips tight against his skin, her eyes closed as she struggled with the emotions pulling her apart inside. He was her first born, her flesh and blood, and God how she missed him.

'Goodnight my baby,' she whispered, her lips brushing his skin. 'We love you so very much. Never forget that.'

A rogue tear fell upon his face and she quickly wiped it away using a tissue from her pocket, always the dutiful mother. Then, turning to face her husband, she gave him a tiny nod of acceptance. It was time to move on. What else could they do? For the first time in too long she looked at George as her husband and saw how terrible he looked, realising that she too was probably no better. It was tearing them apart. A line needed to be drawn and although they would never forget Nick she knew as well as George that the time had come to let go and start afresh, to be husband and wife again, as well as a mother and father to Andrew, their one remaining son. Moving to his side, she took George's hand and interlaced his fingers with hers. Any resentment she felt regarding his call to Amy felt pointless now.

'Come on, George,' she said, 'let's go home.'

George gave her an unsure yet sympathetic smile, enjoying the feel of her hand in his; still, after all these years. Nodding in agreement they both turned to Collins who was still observing them from the door.

'Thank you for everything,' Janet said. 'I know that you'll do everything necessary to keep Nick as comfortable as possible.'

'Of course, you can rely on it,' Collins said, sensing their calmness. A resolution had been made which he was now a part of. For the first time in nearly half a year the Howells seemed at peace. It did not always work this way, some parents just never knew when enough was enough, but at least this way was a lot healthier for all concerned. It was time for them to go home.

'I'll call you later when we know more,' Collins said, accepting their handshakes.

'We'll look forward to it,' George said, taking one last look at his son.

After watching the Howells walk hand in hand down the corridor, Collins returned to his office remembering the cup of tea waiting for him. Janet and George exited through the security doors; another unfortunate symbol of the age they now lived in. The elevator foyer was drenched in sunlight from a huge bank of windows that looked out across the Fens, and for that brief moment their spirits were lifted as if angels were guiding their step. Nick would never be forgotten, but an understanding had been reached, an acceptance. It filled them with an inner peace that neither had felt for far too long. George pressed the button and, as though the elevator had been waiting for them, the doors parted.

The car park was still busy. Janet took out the keys to her Honda runabout and unlocked the doors, the dull clunk of the locks popping simultaneously. The interior was stuffy, but after a few blasts of the air con the car soon cooled.

'You okay?' George asked, settling himself into the passenger seat.

'I'm not quite sure,' Janet said. 'I think so. It's just... oh, I don't know. I just don't know what I should be feeling right now. I know what I want to feel but it doesn't somehow seem right to. Does that make sense?'

'Yes, love, I think so. It's all right. Everything will work out for the best, it's got to. Why don't we just go home, hey?'

The journey was done in complete silence. No talking. No radio. Just the steady rhythm of the engine and the semi-muted world outside. Gradually, they nosed their way down the congested John Adams Way that served as the spinal column of Boston and the east coast's only link from north to south. It gave them the time they needed to think about the consequences of the morning's events. The closer to home they got, the heavier the reality of Nick's situation grew and turned their earlier feeling of relief into that old familiar numbness.

This was it; this was actually it. The promise of freedom from their cage of hurt and doubt was about to be fulfilled. The door was ajar and together they had to face whatever future that freedom had to offer. Maybe, in reality, that was why some people never really overcame the grief, the concept of moving on being more terrifying than the cage itself, the familiarity of pointless hope more comforting than having to face the truth and allow the world back in. Yet was not reality just a state of perception? Did we truly create our own reality, our own walls of containment according to the laws and sensibilities of whichever society and timeline we happened to be born into, or were the paths of our lives dictated to us from a higher power? These were George's thoughts as they trundled through the traffic. He had gone from feeling utter despair to acceptance and serenity in the space of no more than ten minutes and all because of an altered heart beat, a misfiring segment of the brain. With all of his heart he missed Nick but at the same time he wanted their life back; he wanted his home back, and although George wished more than anything for his family to be complete - the way things used to be before the accident - the circle had been broken forever. Nick, as they had known him, was gone.

Nick was gone.

Janet came to yet another stop in the traffic and as George stared out of the window he saw they had pulled up directly outside his old Grammar School. Nick had also attended the school, but things were very different now to how they had been back in George's day. The traditional school cap had been abandoned years ago and he could not believe how long the boys were allowed to grow their hair now. Back in his day anything over an inch on top earned you a whack across the head and detention. Of course, in today's society a teacher would find their career in ruins for just breathing in the wrong direction near a pupil, and to make matters worse the kids knew it. How the tables had turned. The world had changed in so many ways since George was a boy and maybe not necessarily for the better. But then, in some ways, it had. He remembered the torment he and his fellow classmates had received from rival schools because of those bloody caps. He may as well have worn a sign around his neck that screamed 'kick me!' Every night he had to cross the footbridge at the end of Rowley Road to get home, and every night he ran the gauntlet. Having been the only boy from his estate to go to the Grammar School, George had been instantly labelled an outcast, an infiltrator, a 'Grammar puff'. Friends he had grown up with now looked upon him with scorn and distrust. It had certainly toughened him up, though as the years passed by it seemed the less he remembered about those days. It was a funny thing that. Try as he might he could not remember one single face of the boys who had tormented him for so many years, or the emotions which had caused him so many sleepless nights. All that remained was the knowledge it had possibly happened a lifetime ago. Was that what would become of the memory of his son? No, he would never permit something as honest and precious as the memory of his firstborn to fall into the obscurity of time, he would never allow that to happen. They would celebrate him on his birthday, and lament him on the anniversary of his death and for all the times in between remember him with the same fondness and love with which he had filled their lives. Nick would not become just another child to die before his time.

After finally escaping the crawling traffic, George and Janet reached home to an audience of twitching curtains. For all of their interfering, the neighbours had been invaluable throughout the ordeal, especially when it had come to looking after Andrew when they both needed to be at the hospital. Even the miserable old nutcase from across the road, Mr Howard, having spent a lifetime being obstinate had stopped his usual torrent of unsociable behaviour in respect of their troubles. It was probably the most exciting thing to have happened to their little section of the world in years and it seemed that everyone wanted to be a part of it, or perhaps Janet and George were just being cynical about their good intentions. It was hard not to be cynical in the face of such adversity, but could that change now? With all hope gone, what did they have to lose?

Inside the house, Janet sat herself at the kitchen table while George went to the bathroom to empty his angry bladder. His new medication was helping but had not kicked in fully yet. Eventually, he joined her at the table.

'Kettle's on if you fancy a cup,' she said, standing up.

'Yeah,' he said.

The silence began again and George's insides burned with anticipation, needing to ask how she felt about it all. For all the years they had been married and the openness they shared the subject had reduced him to a scared old man. Why was he so worried, for God's sake? She was his wife. They should be able to discuss this like adults.

'So,' George began. He could feel his cheeks reddening. Janet let out a sigh and continued to make the tea without paying attention to him. Was he looking for some kind of admittance that she felt the same as him? To know that they had reached a point of no return and that enough was enough? That Nick was lost to them and would never return? Was he looking for her to say that it was time to pack things up now like a tired old circus and move on? Like George, she was a realist and all she wanted was to show the proper respect and be able to mourn the loss of her son in a proper and healthy manner but, despite what she may have felt in the hospital, was she truly prepared to let him go yet?

'Do you remember that time we went to Freiston Shore?' she asked, placing George's cup in front of him before leaning against the edge of the table to stare out the patio doors into the garden.

George took a moment to recall the memory.

'You remember,' she said turning to face him, 'when the kids were young. Andrew was still in nappies. We took Sheila and Graham's two with us and had a barbecue. It was Nick's ninth birthday.'

'Oh yeah! How could I forget? Nick slipped down that embankment and landed in a cow pat.'

'Right on his bum, bless him.'

'Ha, yeah. Stank like hell.'

'You wouldn't let him in the car so we had to strip him and put his jeans in the boot,' she continued.

'And then hung his Y-fronts from the car aerial to dry them out,' he cried. They both shook in fits of laughter at the memory of young Nick's underpants flapping in the breeze. It had been a perfect summer's evening as they weaved their way home in George's old Ford Sierra, down the narrow country lanes bordered on both sides by tall hedges, Nick's Spiderman underpants flying proudly above them.

'Do you remember that heap of mud and bricks at the back of the garden that he wouldn't let me clear?' George asked.

'How could I not, I was the one who had to wash his clothes. He'd spent hours playing in that thing with his Star Wars figures.'

'Thank God for the winter. I don't think I would have ever got that thing shifted. Do you think he ever believed that it had disappeared with the snow?'

'I don't know, he was always pretty clever,' she smiled with pride.

'Ha, and Lego. He used to live for that stuff. I think it's still up in the attic somewhere,' he said.

Another uncomfortable silence fell between them.

'Hang on. I've got it,' Janet continued. 'Rowdrawb.'

Tears began to fill George's eyes.

Rowdrawb; how could they ever forget rowdrawb?

Nick had been a toddler at the time, three and a half, maybe four. Every morning he would wake them up by climbing into bed and snuggling between them. It had been warm and full of love, and Nick was determined they should be awake with him. So, on one of these mornings, George had decided to teach him the game eye-spy. He'd started with something easy like curtains or some such, he couldn't remember exactly, and Nick's first attempt had gone well. Of course, they had tried not to get it straight away. But then after a while Nick came up with a real tester.

'I spy with my eedy beedy eye,' he chirped, 'Something beginning with ... rah!'

They scanned the room looking for possible answers.

'Radiator?'

'No,' Nick said, really pleased with himself.

'Robe?'

'No.'

'Radio.'

'No,' Nick giggled.

'R... R? What else begins with R?' George asked Janet.

They both looked around the room again, searching for clues. Eventually, George had to concede.

'I give up. What is it?'

'No, come on,' Nick said.

'I can't see anything else,' George said, hooking his arm round Nick's small frame.

'Look daddy, look!'

They both looked around again.

The Maelstrom

'We can't, darling,' Janet said. 'Come on, you tell us what it is?'

'Daddy, look!'

'We don't know. You've beaten us. You'll have to tell us,' George said giving Janet a puzzled look.

'ROWDRAWB!' he cried at the top of his voice, clapping to himself for being so clever.

'You what?' Janet said, looking to George and mouthing, 'What's a rowdrawb?'

George shrugged.

'There mummy, look, rowdrawb.' And as they followed the direction of his tiny finger their eyes were drawn towards the wardrobe in the far corner of the room. They both burst into fits of laughter.

'Why are you laughing?' Nick said.

'Oh bless your little heart,' Janet said, squeezing him and giving him a huge kiss on the head.

'What?' he repeated, looking at George. 'What is it, daddy?'

'That's a wardrobe, Nicky. Not a rowdrawb,' he explained. 'Bless you.'

'Humph,' Nick said, crossing his arms thoroughly put out for having his smartness corrected. 'I don't think so.'

'Don't worry,' Janet said, ruffling his soft hair, 'now you'll know for next time. Come here.'

And with that she scooped him away from George and into her loving arms.

'You're still mummy's clever little boy,' she cooed, snuggling closer into him. Nick giggled, and tried to push her away. 'I love you.'

Eventually, he gave in and returned her embrace. 'Love you too mummy,' he said, squeezing for all he was worth.

The coffee cup trembled in Janet's hand.

'What's going on, George? I just don't understand how I'm supposed to feel any more.'

George remained silent and stared at his own cup sat untouched on the table in front of him.

'I want to keep hoping but I just don't know if I can do it anymore. Are we supposed to?' she croaked. 'I'm sorry. It's been so long though, and he's gone back into the coma. I...'

George looked at Janet's tear-filled eyes reaching out for him. What she needed was her husband's reassurance that she was not a bad mother for thinking this way. Letting go was the hardest thing to do, yet even she accepted now that the truth had to be confronted, that it would only be a matter of time.

George reached across, taking hold of her hand to lower the shaking cup.

'Janet, I know that sometimes we can have our differences but I've always trusted you, and I've always believed in you. Now, this thing... this situation with Nick, it's made me think all sorts of things. It's made me doubt just about everything, my marriage, my faith, even my sanity. God knows, I haven't dealt with it in the best way but I see now, probably for the first time in a long time, that what's most important is all of this, the world we've built together, our home, our family. We're going to lose Nick. I accept that now. And I'm not going to say anything that hasn't already been said. If I could swap places with him I'd do it in a heartbeat, you know I would, but we can't change what's happened. And we still have Andrew to think about, and we still have each other.'

George squeezed her hand tighter.

'I love you so much Janet and I'm not going to let this break us. I'm not going to let this destroy what we have. The doctor's already said that we're going to have to be prepared for the worst and Andrew is going to need us when it happens. I'm not wishing it, God I'm not, but I think we both know that Collins is just being kind. He's not a stupid man.'

'No,' she replied, her eyes downcast. Tenderly, George touched her chin and raised her head so that their eyes met.

'We'll get through this. I miss him so much. He's my boy. But we will get through this.'

'And what if he makes it George, what if he doesn't die? What if he wakes up and everything's fine? We can be a proper family again.'

'Yes we can,' he whispered. 'I want nothing more than that, but that's what we said last time, remember?'

She remembered all right, the sight of Nick being sedated, his inability to speak or move, and the broken shell of her little boy in the body of a man she hardly recognised. Who knew what to think any more? She just wanted the world to go away; the whole damn dirty world. She was losing her little boy, and the whole world just carried on as if it meant nothing. Well it meant something to her; it meant everything to her. Finally she broke down and cried, sobbing her heart out like never before.

'It's all right, love,' George said. 'Everything will be all right.'

Chapter Twelve

In a place where time had no meaning, Abaddon sat cross-legged at the water's edge, *His* flowing coat fanned around *Him* across the ethereal grass, stained with dirt and blood as old as the Cosm, and a darkness that no light could penetrate; the darkness of pure evil. *His* mouth may have been grinning but *His* eyes, those terrible eyes, were devoid of humour. *His* skin was a hard crust, separated by a track of thorns that ran from *His* throat, up *His* face, and over the top of *His* bald pock marked head. Aeons of hate had deformed *Him* from the beautiful creature *He* had been at the time of *His* creation. *He* had hated for so long now *He* couldn't even remember what had sparked it, but what did that matter now? The swelling hate gave *Him* unlimited power, gave *Him* purpose. It did not matter that *He* was alone, that *He* was out of the light and sight of God. *He* had *His* hate, *His* distended angry friend that reminded *Him* what *He* was doing was right, that it was *His* purpose.

Still, Abaddon was not completely alone. Behind *Him* paced the looming figure of Jeremiah, his impatience driving him to distraction.

Abaddon ignored him keeping *His* eyes on the glassy surface waiting for a glimpse of Nick.

'I still don't see why I don't just go in there and fish him out. You promised me vengeance,' Jeremiah growled.

'*And you shall have it, but trust me you would not want to go in there.*'

Jeremiah sniffed with contempt and paced some more before finally stopping to take note of the scenery around them. The cloudless sky was a perfect blue, the flowing plains of grass a Technicolor green that was only broken by an oak tree in the distance, lush and full.

'What is this place?' he asked.

'You don't remember?'

Jeremiah looked around. 'I kinda remember something similar, in a dream maybe.'

Abaddon's smile widened. *He* found it good that even after all this time some things still managed to amuse *Him*; a sleeper's ignorance being one of them.

'This is The Border.'

Jeremiah remained blank.

'Below us is the gateway to Hell. Up there,' He said, nodding skyward *'is the place from where you take the greatest fall of all.'*

Jeremiah looked up at the pure blue sky and whistled. Then, ever so slowly, images started trickling back from a memory he wished he could forget. A recollection from long ago of standing on this very same prairie, thinking how idyllic it appeared, just before the hands took hold. Those grotesque gnarled hands that shot from the earth and dragged him down, deep into the bowels of his own personal hell. Jeremiah's had been the re-telling of every murder he had ever committed. This in itself was not the punishment because he actually enjoyed it, but it was the mocking realization which followed. The travesty which had been dealt to him at birth that he was and always would be a *man*, every murder reminding him that his most passionate desire - to be a woman - was nothing but a fantasy to be thrown at him in contempt of his depravity and sin. Envy was his Avichi; his personal hell.

Jeremiah looked at the ground with apprehension, half expecting those ghoulish hands to come grasping out; his black heart full of sadness and self-loathing.

Feeling Jeremiah's pain, Abaddon's smile became wicked. *He* had made an excellent choice of aide. Yes, this one would be very useful indeed.

'You know something, I don't even know your name,' Jeremiah said, pointing his rusty cleaver at the back of Abaddon's exposed head. 'I don't know a damn thing about you.'

Abaddon bowed *His* head in contemplation. Where to start? From the beginning? It would take a lifetime just to get started.

'*What would you like to know?* He asked.

'So, like, what *is* your name then?'

'*I have been called by many names. The sleepers once knew me as the King of the Grasshoppers.*'

'Grasshoppers? That doesn't exactly strike terror into the hearts of small children.'

Abaddon smiled. '*It was a long time ago, not that you would remember. You cannot even shed that pathetic sleeper existence of yours. Jeremiah Fleming? He is a figment. He does not exist. Why do you continue to hold on to that dream?*'

Jeremiah lowered his head and the weapon in his hand. 'It's my hell. To always be Jeremiah, to never forget my sins.'

'*And they talk of the evil that men do. To not know your true identity, now that is an evil indeed. Yet who am I to judge?*'

'So what's your hell then?' Jeremiah asked.

Silence fell as Abaddon considered the question. '*I have no hell.*'

'But we all…'

'*You will not question me again!*'

Jeremiah's eyes grew wide with fear.

'Yes of course. I shouldn't have pried.'

'*You will be silent and remain that way.*'

Jeremiah stood rigid and closed his mouth.

'*And now we shall wait.*'

* * *

A week passed by and Nick was still in the coma. It had been a week since George had last attended work, and what a relief it was for him to be back behind the wheel of his Dodge Calibre with the cruise control in charge. He glided at a steady seventy up the A1 to Doncaster ready to make his first call of the day. Being a representative of a shower manufacturer which aimed at the luxury end of the market, his job was made a lot easier with less come backs and complaints to deal with. In the past, he had been employed by less reputable firms that thought using cheaper components from abroad was the way for greater profits. The majority of his time had been spent chasing problems rather than sales leads which produced an adverse effect on his monthly figures, and made him look bad.

Slowing to negotiate a roundabout, George took the A630 into Doncaster. It was almost nine o'clock and the roads were busy with traffic. Eventually, he pulled to a stop outside the bathroom showroom and composed himself taking a mouthful of coffee from his travel mug. The front window was, as usual, a showpiece. To George's trained eye he could see at least fifteen grand's worth of product on display.

Locking the car, he entered the premises and was jumped out of his skin as a shower display sprang to life spraying water against the glass screen next to him.

'What do you reckon?' Jack, the owner, piped up from behind a tap display with a huge belly laugh, his accent thick Doncaster.

'Scared the bloody life out of me,' George said, regaining his composure. 'How about that?'

'But it made you notice though, right?' Jack said, grinning like the Cheshire Cat. 'It's rigged to a motion sensor. One of Michael's ideas.'

'Yeah, brilliant,' George said. 'Can I use your toilet, please? I just need to change my underpants.'

Jack laughed again before instructing his son, Michael, to put the kettle on. George loved coming here, it always cheered him up, which was exactly what he needed right now.

'So, how's business then?' he asked.

'Honest? Deadly, but I don't think I need to tell

you that. What's it like out there?'

'I don't think it's anything you're doing. It's the same for everyone, mate. The building trade seems to be a dirty word with the banks right now.'

'When's it gonna end though? It can't go on like this forever,' Jack said.

'Who knows mate, but you're right, the recession's got to end at some point or else we're all in the shit.'

'Come on; let's get that tea so we can drown our sorrows.'

'Sounds good.'

* * *

In the depths of the River, Nick felt calm and safe as he sank deeper into forgetfulness. Not only his memory, but his very soul was being systematically un-ravelled the longer he remained. Above him, the daylight that filtered down like a ghostly Jacob's ladder receded away. At least he was safe and at peace. No more pain, no more suffering, no more torment. Not that he could remember now anyway. The hurt was gone and Nick was filled with a lethargy that was dispelling his will to live, or even exist. Somewhere in the realms of time and space his body was lying useless in a hospital becoming weaker the deeper he sank. In the Cosm, Nick was dying, but at least here he was safe from the monsters above. Soon, they would be nothing more than a fading memory.

Then it happened.

A forgotten emotion kicked in from some far off place. The more worthless information he lost the less jumbled his mind became, his perceptions sharper. Nick had been here before. He remembered being chased. By what or by whom he could not be sure, but he remembered escaping to this very same place. And there had been a reason, a very important reason for staying alive but the answer was still beyond him. He had escaped to this place before… he had put himself into the coma to escape because he knew that his hunters would not follow, dare not. This was the place of final death. No more existence ever, in any shape or form. This was the eternal sleep. But he had to survive. He had to stay the course and get home. What he was doing was wrong, he could see that now. He had to get out of here but the more he struggled the deeper his body sank. The eternal sleep had taken hold.

* * *

Two hours and three risky teas later, George was shaking Jack's hand and thanking him for the display orders. Achieving the sale had given him a huge sense of worth and the quantity would be a good boost to his targets, proving to himself more than anything that he still had what it took.

'So we can expect to see the units by the end of the week then,' Jack said accompanying George to the door.

'Absolutely no problem at all, it'll be on your last drop,' George said, re-organising his folder.

'Great. It'll be good to get the showroom back to normal.'

For the first time in months, George felt genuinely lifted. His thoughts returned to Nick. He loved him so much, as much as any father could and more, but he was more convinced than ever now that life went on. Jack and Michael were proof that out in the world there really was happiness to be found, and it was time for him to return and embrace it once more. He was so sick and tired of the depression and the loneliness. Of being blind drunk in some pub while young locals, who were probably not even old enough to be there in the first place, laughed and jeered at him. Decked out in their knock-off jewellery and bad attitudes not one of them had ever thought to ask him why. Why he was always at the bar beating himself to death with a bottle of JD? Why he became so drunk that he would slip off his stool having to grasp the bar for support. His incapacitation made them smile and feel better about their own rotten worthless lives. In mocking him, their trivial, Jeremy Kyle lives did not seem that bad after all. Before them was living proof that there was always someone sadder and worse off than they were. So they jeered and cheered because it empowered them to ignore their own insecurities and faults. Well, George had had enough of being a public service. They would have to find some other source of amusement. Today was his retirement from that life.

Thanking Jack again for the order and giving Michael a wave, George tucked his folder under his arm and left the building, beaming with a sense of expectation.

Hanging his jacket in the rear of the car, George retook his seat in the front and noticed a bicycle shop across the road. They could all have new bikes and go out on rides together just like he and Janet had as young lovers when they used to cycle to remote country lakes where the insects hovered and weaved in the summer heat while George and Janet tried their best not to annoy the old men fishing and enjoying a tot of whiskey away from their wives. Janet would pack sandwiches and a fresh bottle of Corona lemonade straight off the cart, and they would waste the day without a care in the world. Where had those days gone?

Before striking the engine, George decided to check his phone for messages. He pressed the button and a female voice filled the car.

'You have... five new messages. To replay the messages please press...'

George pressed the required button without needing to hear the rest and leaned on the steering wheel.

'Hi mate, it's Nick from Crosier's. Need a favour on an urgent delivery. Can you give us a bell please, mate. Thanks. Bye.'

'To delete the message please press...'

George skipped to the next and found a message

from the anti-sales department, accounts.

'It's Pat. It says here you're going to Leeds, so pick up a cheque from Jenkins. Its three months late so if they don't let you have it tell them they're in court. And from now on, everything's cash on delivery only.'

Bloody accounts, he thought. Did they not realise that with the recession going on, everyone was in the same boat? They really needed to learn how to speak to people. Maybe then they would get a better response.

'To delete...'

'George, it's me.' He recognised Janet's voice straight away but it sounded strange, broken. 'There's been a call from the hospital. They're asking for us to go in.' A pause. 'There have been developments.' He could tell that she was trying not to cry. 'They want us down there so can you call me, please. I've got my phone on me so just call when you can. Bye.'

George stopped the messages and stared back out at the bicycle shop. Was this it? Oh God, was this really it? His mind went numb. He no longer knew what to think or feel. All he knew was that Jenkins and his cheque would have to wait. Right now, he needed to be with his family. Without a second thought, George kicked the car into action, pulled off the forecourt, and sped back towards the motorway.

* * *

Fuelled by his panic, Nick struggled against the swallowing depths trying desperately to swim upwards yet the more he fought the deeper he sank. The engulfing death turned ice cold stripping away his senses like the skins of an onion reducing him in size and validity. All memory of his life as Nicholas Howell was gone. Knowledge of his material body back in the hospital vanished into the abyss. The people he had known, the feelings of joy and pain, of bliss and suffering he had experienced were all gone together with his sight, smell, hearing, touch and taste. All that remained as a testament to him ever existing was base primeval instinct; that, and the knowledge that what he was doing was wrong. He should not be doing this. He should be staying true, staying the course. And with the disappearance of memory also went the knowledge of everything that had come to pass since his awakening. Neither Abaddon nor Jeremiah existed to him now as Nick became reduced to nothing but energy. It was at that precise moment his consciousness stopped its useless thrashings and submitted itself to the depths. Within its arms, Nick found peaceful rest, the overwhelming euphoria swaddling him like a new born baby. The coldness of death had left him now for he no longer had the body to feel it. Everything surrounding him was black and intangible as Nick felt himself becoming a part of the blackness.

I am... he thought. I am...

'Nicholas,' said a faint and distant voice.

Stopping his deliberations, Nick focussed his attention on the voice.

'Hear me,' the voice said again, becoming faint. Was someone trying to reach him? No, that was nonsense, who could be trying to reach him down here? No, he was fine just where he was. It was quiet here, so very quiet.

'Nicholas, hear me. You must not do this. You must return to me, Nicholas. We are important. You are important. Come to me, Nicholas. Come now.'

But Nick refused to listen, happy in his serene condition of wastefulness.

'We are dying. You do not have much time left, so please, I beg you. Come to me.'

A twang of far forgotten memory pulled within what was left of his being and he began to take more notice of what the voice was saying.

'Nicholas, we saw something that should never have been seen but now we know the truth we have to tell the others. If not then they will all continue to suffer. You must come to me.'

Why don't you just leave me alone? I don't know what you're talking about, and I like it here, he thought.

'I cannot leave, not without you. You must come to me. Do you not want to know why? I know you and I know your desire to learn the truth.'

Hearing the portentous words, Nick felt restless again but he liked it here. It was peaceful, safe. But then he felt the burning desire nestled in the soul of every living creature, the passion which flowed within and throughout the Cosm. The universal need to know the truth, to understand why, and with all gone to him now but instinct he was finding it harder and harder to resist his curiosity.

Why not?

Once the decision had been made, he did not even register how easy it was for him to raise from the blackness, especially after all his previous thrashings. It had been his own mortality which had dragged him down, yet with his ethereal body gone he no longer had the material need for survival. All that remained was a dreamy abandon and his hunger for the truth.

As he rose, Nick could feel himself getting heavier, more substantial, until the icy cold water tingled his reformed body and he became Nicholas Howell once more. Sight returned. Above him, the ghostly Jacob's ladder penetrated the murky water. With his nerve endings re-knitted he could feel tiny bubbles dance around him, tickling his skin as his ascent quickened, the water churning into a raging torrent that projected him to the surface.

Abaddon stared at the seemingly still surface; *His* renewed interest going unnoticed by Jeremiah who lounged on the grass behind his master, scraping dried blood from beneath his fingernails with the corner of his rusty blade. Abaddon, however, could swear that *He* had seen something stirring far below.

Abaddon shifted, staring deeper into the pool.

'What is it?' Jeremiah asked.

Ignoring him, Abaddon stared deeper into the water as bubbles began to break the surface and *His* eyes widened in expectation. Jeremiah moved to *His* side, transfixed as more tiny bubbles came to greet them.

'*I believe your waiting may be over,*' Abaddon replied.

The bubbles became more sporadic, intensifying in their rage, and the water crackled and blistered as if Poseidon himself was rising from the depths. Abaddon held his composure. Jeremiah though showed no reserve in his delight as his knuckles turned fever white around the hickory of his cleaver.

'Here we go,' Jeremiah snarled.

Nick's flailing body rocketed from the bubbling foam, soaring high over their heads before crashing onto the grass behind them. Standing over the broken figure sprawled out on the dirt, Jeremiah was bursting to sample Nick's flesh, to feel his warm sticky blood between his fingers. He looked from Abaddon to Nick then back again.

'*You may do with him what you will. He is all yours.*'

Insanity flashed across his eyes and Jeremiah turned toward Nick who was still groaning in pain. Abaddon just watched, and allowed his dry old lips to form a smile.

* * *

Janet's eyes were weak and bloodshot as she sat with Nick's hand in hers. The only movement from him was the barely perceptible rise and fall of his chest as the ventilator forced air into his lungs before drawing it back out again. Two hours had passed since Nick's body had lost the ability to breathe for itself. Hope was gone now. With each passing moment his heartbeat faded. The nursing staff had witnessed this scene a hundred times before but for Janet's sake wandered over every once in a while, more out of sympathy than anything else. They knew Nick's fight was over but Janet would need to realise it in her own time.

Standing dutifully behind her, Andrew placed his hand upon Janet's shoulder. She turned to find him offering her a coffee.

'One of the nurses made it for you, thought it might help, or something,' he said, trying not to wince as the heat radiating through the thin cardboard cup burned his fingers. With his dad still not here, Andrew needed to be strong for his mother, he needed to be the man of the house.

'Oh love, thank you,' Janet said, placing the cup on the floor and pulling him towards her. 'You are good to me. Do you want to come and sit with your brother for a bit? He would like that.'

'Yeah, sure,' Andrew replied. Taking a seat, he stared at Nick in fascination. He had never seen an actual dying person before. Sure, he had seen it plenty of times on TV and in films but that was different. This was real, and it was happening to him right now. There was no dramatic soundtrack, no moment catching close-ups. This was as real as it got to an eleven-year-old boy with nothing for comfort but the beeping of the machine and the barely audible weeping of his mother.

Two hours had passed since Janet had received Collins's phone call informing her of Nick's decline and so it had been two hours since she had left the message on George's answer machine. He had still not arrived and after his behaviour of late she wondered if he was likely to turn up at all. No, he had re-assured her things would be different now. He had promised her. So she sat and believed that he would turn up as soon as he could, yet at the same time a small part of her wished he wouldn't. The reality of Nick's condition was upon them now and she knew as soon as George arrived Collins would be asking them both the horrific question of whether or not he had their permission to allow Nick to die with dignity. Janet trembled at the very thought of it. Up until now she had not found the words to speak to Nick, instead finding comfort in just holding his hand. Yet now, in these final moments, she found her heart to speak.

'Hello, Nicky,' she whispered. Pulling his hand closer, pressing it to her stomach, her grief made all other words redundant. She wanted to shake him, wanted to slap him awake. Why was this happening? She broke down again and wept, her tears falling to the cold hard floor collecting in spots between her feet.

Placing his arm around her shoulder, Andrew hugged her tight.

'Why is this happening?' Janet whispered. 'He's not ready yet, he's just a boy. He hasn't lived yet. Don't take away my son, please.' Her tears came harder. 'It's just not right.'

Nick remained silent and still, his chest continuing to rise and fall in harmony with the ventilator's pump. It reminded her of Nick as a baby, of how she used to sit by his cot watching over him as he enjoyed the slumber of innocents, and while sitting there marvelling over the beauty she had brought into the world never once did she imagine she would be doing the exact same thing as he drew his final breath.

'It's all right, mum,' Andrew said between his own silent tears, his hardened pre-teen mind struggling to fight back the pain.

Pulling her trapped arm free from his embrace, she wrapped it around his small frame drawing him close.

'You do know what's going on here?' she said.

'Yes, I'm not a kid.'

'No, I mean really know. Nick's not well.'

'I know he's not, mum,' he said.

'And he's not going to get better.'

'I know,' he repeated, his voice full of sadness. 'He's going to die isn't he, mum?'

Janet composed herself.

'Yes,' she replied. 'Yes, he is. He tried so hard to fight but his body's just too weak. You do understand that don't you? He just can't fight any more.'

Andrew's tough exterior fell away and he began to cry harder than he had ever cried, his body shuddering within Janet's embrace.

'But why, mum? It's not fair. Why Nick? He's my brother. I don't want to lose my brother.'

Janet squeezed him, unable to offer any words that could make it better.

'I know, baby, I know. I don't want to lose him either but God wants him back.'

'Well he can't have him, it's not fair,' he repeated. But life was not that simple and not that easily bargained for. No amount of bad tempered 'it's not fairs' were going to let Andrew get his own way this time, no matter how much Janet wished it would. Trapped within her misery, there were no words to comfort him, so instead she left the door open, inviting him in to share the agony with her. She wanted so much to take it from him, to tell him everything would be fine. But it all seemed like an impossible lie she just could not voice. So instead, she clung to him with tear stained faces. God, she wished George was here.

* * *

Jeremiah's assault was brutal and swift. Pouncing with the ferocity of a wild animal he swiped the cleaver's blade opening Nick's heel like a gaping jaw, severing the tendon clean. It took a moment for his body to realise what had happened before the blood began to flow. The disorientation clouding Nick's thoughts swept aside as his world was engulfed with fire.

Taking a step back to admire his handiwork, Jeremiah watched with delight as Nick squirmed on the ground screaming, desperately grabbing at his butchered ankle. Jeremiah was going to enjoy this. Before the end, Nick would be begging for his very soul and as the dead have nothing but eternity, Jeremiah could take his time.

The agony was excruciating. Nick tightened himself into a ball clinging to the wound for dear life. He braced himself for the next blow but it never came. Jeremiah chuckled, which from his mouth sounded more like a growl.

'Please, no more,' Nick begged, his heart racing at the sight of his own blood.

Jeremiah felt disappointed at how easily Nick had broken. The second blow was delivered as deliberate and swift as the first. Jeremiah's face twisted into a mask of aggression as the rusted blade hacked deep into Nick's shoulder splintering bone, holding fast for a couple of seconds before Jeremiah worked it loose again flicking blood across his dirty overalls and the lush grass. Nick's screams were deafening and he dropped to the ground like a rag doll, his desiccated cries filling the air. With his face to the ground every panicked breath inhaled more choking dust.

'Help me,' Nick sobbed, hoping the mysterious speaker was still listening. 'Where are you? Please... help me.'

'I'm here, sweet cheeks,' Jeremiah sneered before sinking his boot into Nick's side. The force of impact flipped his body knocking the wind clean from him. Spread eagled on his back, Nick wrenched back his head to get air into his system before realising how, with his chin high and his neck exposed, the action must have appeared to his attacker.

Jeremiah's eyes glistened with intent. It was the moment of truth. He could take the killing strike right now but what would happen if he did? Would that be it, the end of his fun? Or would Nick return like the rest of the whores that visited him one after another. He hesitated. Afraid that once the decision was made this really would be the end. Jeremiah raised the cleaver high above his head.

Seeing his own blood dripping from the trembling blade, Nick gasped. He knew what was coming and, powerless to stop it, wondered too what would happen when the blow came. Would he die? Could you die in your dreams? He remembered dreams of falling, of the impact feeling real enough but without the pain. There had never been pain. This was very different though. In this dream he felt everything and while his wounds screamed he needed to remember it was only a dream. All he needed was control. That was when Nick realised he was reaching for air that did not exist, feeling pain through nerves that were not really there. No matter how damaged he thought his body to be, he had to remember that his real body was wasting away in a faraway place where genuine hurt existed. Surely this was all in his mind and with that being true then surely he could control its outcome? So, Nick stopped gasping and relaxed, ignoring Jeremiah's imminent attack. Then something amazing happened. It was like a switch being flicked inside his mind. Nick straightened his head and began to smile at Jeremiah, not in mocking but realisation. Jeremiah's raised hand faltered and he looked to Abaddon for guidance. That was the point when the grimacing angel suddenly realised his aide was losing control of the situation. Nick, or Hesamuel as he knew him, was becoming empowered.

'*Finish him*!' Abaddon called.

Turning back to his prey with a heaving growl, Jeremiah swung the cleaver at Nick's face.

But Nick remained calm, unflinching.

At Nick's command, the cleaver stopped just an inch from his nose, holding there as if suspended in time.

'Abaddon!' Jeremiah cried. 'What the fuck is happening?'

He tried applying more pressure but his hand refused to budge.

Nick moved from beneath the blade. It was now

Jeremiah's turn to be afraid as his movements were no longer his own. It was not until the cleaver was completely free from Nick's vicinity that Jeremiah regained control again and yet, at the same time, the strangest of things happened to him. Jeremiah found his hate was gone. His jealousy and the need to mutilate had left him, being replaced with a calm indifference he had never felt before. The sensation was bizarre yet uplifting as though a black cloud had been swept aside leaving him to bask in the warmth of the moment.

Climbing to his feet, Nick continued to smile at Jeremiah with compassion and Jeremiah found himself smiling back.

'*Finish him you fool!*' Abaddon roared. But Jeremiah was powerless to obey and simply continued to smile at Nick.

'I can't,' he said. 'What's wrong with me?'

Hearing the panic in Jeremiah's voice, Abaddon realised the murderer was no use to *Him* now. *He* needed a killer, a machine of death and in any other circumstance *He* would have had *His* puppet, but Nick had overpowered Jeremiah with a veil of enlightenment. *He* knew that as soon as Nick escaped that veil would be lifted and Jeremiah would return to his old brutal self but by then it would be too late, and that just would not do. That would not do at all. It was time for Abaddon to perform an act *He* had not done in over two thousand years since the days of Galilee; it was time for *Him* to spill blood again. Whatever happened, whatever the cost, Hesamuel could not be allowed to return to the Light. *His* original plan of making Nick insane enough to commit suicide, and therefore never being permitted entry to the Light again, had clearly failed. Yet while Hesamuel or Nick or whatever he wanted to call himself was in his sleeper state he was still vulnerable. While Nick was still unaware he could still be broken. *He* had to stop Hesamuel's return.

With blinding speed, Abaddon leapt at Nick, *His* razor-sharp talons outstretched and ready to do damage only inches from Nick's throat. *He* could imagine the soft flesh squeezing like jelly between *His* fingers. But Nick dodged the attack as he shot high into the air where he floated, suspended, all the time keeping his eyes on the monster below.

Abaddon's surety ebbed. Nick was preparing to wake. Staring up at him, Abaddon roared with a fury that shook the very air around them. In a wild frenzy, Nick searched the surrounding distance to locate his mysterious friend.

'Where are you?' he whispered. But the area was barren and empty. 'Come on, where are you?'

Again no reply was given, and in no time at all Abaddon was beside him, *His* long dark coat billowing out as though caught in a storm.

'You escaped me before, Hesamuel. I shall not make the same mistake twice.' Before Nick had time to react, Abaddon grabbed his butchered shoulder and sank his claws deep into the exposed muscle.

Nick screamed with the burn, lashing out with his free arm at Abaddon's unmoving face, at those piercing eyes that smouldered with malice and cruelty, but it was like punching solid granite.

Abaddon squeezed harder.

'Do you believe you can harm me?' He said amid the din of Nick's tortured screams. *'I am as old as time. I come from the beginning when the spark of creation was but an idea. I am the Locust King. I am Abaddon, Angel Guardian of the Abyss. I am the Destroyer. I am the end of all things.'*

Through Abaddon's fingers the anguish of every suffering soul, the agony of every betrayed lover, and the despair of every grieving mother flowed into Nick. Stabbing at his centre it coursed through his blood to the very edges of his aura, bringing with it unspeakable pain. Nick's eyes rolled to the back of his head as the darkness of eternity washed through him, wave after wave intensifying with each fresh pulse.

Suddenly, Nick became entranced by the image of a far off memory. It was the memory of his first meeting with Abaddon since his awakening from the coma, of the filthy bar with the mouldy glasses and the scarred woman. It was the remembered agony of Abaddon's icy grip, crippling yet nothing compared to the assault he was now being subjected to. Nick felt his spine begin to twist beneath the pressure. However, something strange had happened back in that bar. An emotion from deep within Nick had swelled to an unfathomable force which built in pressure, feeding off Abaddon's own hate.

Abaddon was an angel but somehow Nick had managed to turn *His* own power against *Him*, but how?

Like an insect being tortured by a child's flaming match, Nick's fingers and arms began to curl with bone crunching snaps as his body gnarled and twisted out of shape. It was but a taste of the horrors he would be subjected to and by the time Abaddon was finished with him, Nick's soul would be an unrecognisable shell of abandon and despair. Nick would plead for a death that never came and spend eternity in a constant state of change. Stories would be whispered in the deepest corners of the night about the one who had defied, and all would tremble at the very mention of Hesamuel's name, his suffering becoming the stuff of legends.

As Nick's limbs buckled beyond repair he could not even feel Abaddon's grip any more as he continued morphing into whatever nightmarish shapes the angel desired.

But the Light, oh the beautiful Light.

The knowledge came slowly at first, like a spark emanating from within the pain, a thread connecting Abaddon's consciousness to his own, and it was from this spark Nick discovered the strength to manipulate the pain. Mimicking the distortions of his own limbs, the energy began to twist and swell within him until, with a wrenching jerk his entire body stiffened and the power took hold. With a defiant roar the force left him repelling Abaddon's grip and spinning his attacker to the ground.

A silent witness, Jeremiah remained where he stood, not running to help his master; only looking on in fear and awe as Abaddon dusted himself before rising into the air again.

'*No more games!*' Abaddon roared, *His* anger spitting out through *His* burning eyes.

'Now, Nicholas!' called the long awaited voice. 'Come to me now. Our time has run out!'

Panic stricken, Nick spun around to locate the voice and saw in the distance the sweet sight of the lone figure on the horizon.

'Come on, Nicholas; do not let him catch you again!'

'Yes,' he spoke, and as though he had never been there Nick vanished leaving Jeremiah to wonder what the hell was going on.

As Nick's body cruised through the air at a blistering speed, the grassland beneath him flattened and swayed at his passing and the air became charged with the promise of revelation. Abaddon could not allow Hesamuel's return to happen, must not, and in a shot chased after Nick leaving Jeremiah to stand alone and watch as his master became nothing but a dark blip in the sky.

Nick dared not look back, all the time focusing his energy on the nearing figure and the closer he reached the faster he flew. With every passing moment he could feel his strength returning. Doors and chambers opened inside his mind as what seemed like a thousand baying voices clamoured at once for his attention, filling his thoughts with noise and empowerment. The closer he got the larger he felt, not physically but spiritually, and Nick could feel his mind calming, maturing into a passive state of understanding telling him that if he did not escape from Abaddon this time then he and countless others after him would suffer like never before.

Speeding above the luscious grassland, Nick chanced a look back, instantly regretting it as he saw the evil shape of his pursuer gaining, *His* long dark coat flapping wildly behind *Him*, *His* face a contorted mask of rage.

Nick had to reach the mystical figure. He needed to get there now, and then perhaps together they might stand a chance against Abaddon's bottomless well of strength. And with that thought Nick stopped dead. He was no longer flying but stood atop a cliff edge that was previously not there facing the owner of the voice. His eyes widened in disbelief.

'Who are you?' he asked. All of Nick's fear disappeared as the light emanating from the naked sexless being opposite him smiled over and through his body.

'Hello, Nicholas Howell,' it said. Its doll-like cherubic face mirrored his own just as Abaddon's black interpretation had back in Jeremiah's mirror, yet this time there was no fear, no darkness. Only love. It was pure and unconditional and radiated all about them.

'Who are you?' Nick repeated.

The being smiled with kindness.

'My name is Hesamuel, Nicholas. I'm here to tell you that we have done well and that it is now time for us to go home.'

'I don't understand? Am I dreaming?'

'No, you are not dreaming. I am. Life within the Cosm, the life that you have lived, the person that you are is my dream. Life is the dream of the soul. And now it is time for us to wake up.'

'Do you mean I'm going to die?' Nick asked without fear. How could he be afraid when stood amid such beauty?'

'Re-awaken,' Hesamuel corrected. 'In the Cosm, in the material world, yes your vessel will die but do not worry for the souls that are your family. They shall grieve you but when it is their time to re-awaken they will understand and grieve no more.'

Nick considered this and gave a small nod of acceptance.

'I think I understand now but please tell me, why are those monsters chasing me?'

Hesamuel smiled with beatific perfection. Michelangelo himself could not have captured such serenity.

'You have so many questions, Nicholas. It is time for us to wake up and for you to understand all. I am Hesamuel just as you are Hesamuel. We are one and the same person, yet you are the sleeper, you are my dream self. In the Cosm, what you see, I see, what you feel, I feel. You are my dream just as I am your reality and now it is time for us to re-unite and go home.'

'But what did I... what did we see that was so important?'

Hesamuel's smile faltered. 'It is now time for us to awaken.'

Stood on the cliff edge beneath the flawless sky, Hesamuel faced Nick with open arms as the light surrounding him embraced them both, once again reconciling the reality with the dream. Nick could feel his skin tingle. The solid sense of the ground beneath him disappeared as he felt himself begin to undo, the material of his body unravelling, giving itself to the light as his mind began to expand to the furthest reaches of time and space. The knowledge he was awakening to was boundless and the love that filled him was like none he had felt before. Not from his mother, or any relationship he had experienced while alive. This was pure white light, infinite happiness, and it was calling him home.

Chapter Thirteen

Having battled his way down the infuriatingly slow A52 back to Boston, George's head was a bag of nerves by the time he made it through the ward doors to Nick's bed. Just as they had been for the past two and half hours, Janet and Andrew kept their vigil, searching Nick's face for the slightest sign of movement as the monotonous beep of the life support machine signalled their failure and loss. Seeing his son like this again brought everything from that fateful night rushing back and made George stop short as he found himself unable to join them. Hearing his approach, Janet turned her tear stained face toward him and smiled with relief.

'Oh George, thank God you're here,' she said rising to meet him halfway. Throwing herself into his arms she squeezed him, and Andrew was quickly by their sides embracing them both.

'Dad,' he said. To George this simple word spoke volumes. Finally his time had come to be the father he knew he should be.

'What's been happening? How is he?' he asked Janet who looked down at Andrew still pressing his head against her thigh.

Janet chewed her bottom lip and shook her head.

'Okay, love. Okay,' George said, embracing her again.

'Parts of his brain have stopped responding. They've got him on a ventilator again,' she said, her voice trying to be strong but failing.

On the ventilator again.

That's how George had seen Nick the first time he had come to the hospital all those months ago. The dull beep of the machine, the artificial rise and fall of Nick's chest as the air was forced in, pushing the bad out. There had been the sight of the cannula in the back of his hand feeding his system with fluids, the tube up his nose, and the white plastic peg on the end of Nick's finger supplying the machine with his reassuring heartbeat. Back then though, Nick had looked an unrecognisable mess of blood and bruises. George had somehow managed to distance himself a little from the pain by pretending it was someone else. But seeing Nick now, seeing him healed and looking like his son again filled his heart with sorrow. He looked so peaceful. George began to weep, unable to contain his bottled emotions any longer, and Janet pulled him to her. But his body stiffened and the tears were sniffed back again. Today, he had to be the rock for her. He owed her.

'Is Dr Collins around? I'd like to speak to him, just to get the facts,' he said, wiping tears away with the corner of his palm.

'I'll come with you,' Janet said.

At that moment, Sarah walked past carrying a roll of translucent tubing.

'Excuse me, Sarah,' George said; almost afraid to raise his voice, 'I need to speak with Dr Collins.'

'Of course, he's in his office I think. You could try there,' she replied, and then in a more conspiratorial tone, 'would you like me to stay with Andrew while you're away?'

'Thank you,' George said before walking away.

'So, how are you doing?' Sarah asked Andrew as they both sat down next to Nick.

'All right,' he replied.

'Can I get you anything, a drink or some chocolate perhaps?'

'No ... Why is this happening?'

Sarah felt taken aback by the question and paused to form an adequate response.

'Your brother's body is very weak.'

'I know he's going to die,' Andrew said, 'but why?'

'Right,' she said, finding herself lost for words. What comfort could she offer a child who had already come to accept that his older brother was going to die? No child should have to sit and watch his own brother die and if she could have changed the outcome she would. But Sarah knew only too well that no-one lived forever. They had all tried their best with Nick but the time had to come when you just accepted the truth and moved on. With Nick that time had long since passed and unable to answer Andrew's question, she stood and kissed him on the top of the head.

'Would you like me to leave you for a while so that you can have some private time with your brother?'

Andrew nodded in response before leaving his head to hang in misery.

'Okay. Well look, I'm going to be working just up the corridor so if you want anything just come get me, all right?'

Andrew gave another unenthusiastic nod.

'Okay,' she whispered, and then left him to continue with her duties.

Alone with Nick, Andrew felt responsible for his brother's safe keeping while his parents were away. He wanted to talk too though. He wanted to talk to Nick, to tell him about the goal he had scored in Tuesday night's game against Haven High. To tell him about the way Sharon Carr who sat two desks away kept staring at him all the time, and how she and her friends giggled when they caught him looking back. Why were they laughing at him? What should he do? He wanted to know which trainers would look cool because mum and dad never knew about stuff like that. He wanted help with his art homework because Nick was brilliant at drawing. He wanted his brother back. But he could not find the words, so instead he spoke to God. In a conscious movement, Andrew clasped his hands between his legs, embarrassed that someone might see, then closed his eyes and prayed. That is how Sarah saw him through the door and she could not help but shed a tear.

George and Janet found Collins's office door ajar and George gave it the tiniest of knocks causing it to creak open further.

'Hello?' Collins called from his desk, his head buried in paperwork.

When they entered and saw him poring over a file of case notes, Janet gave a small cough. Looking up, Collins's eyes widened and he quickly stood to greet them.

'I am so sorry, I didn't realise it was you. Please, won't you both come in and take a seat. Can I get you anything, tea or coffee perhaps?'

'Thanks but we're fine,' Janet said, answering for the both of them.

'Right,' Collins trailed, retaking his own seat. Collins released a breath. 'I don't know what to say. I'm just so sorry this is happening.'

Both Janet and George were sitting poised and silent, hanging on his every word.

'Nick's retaining too much carbon dioxide for his body to handle. His cardiac output is winding down which is having an adverse effect on the amount of oxygen that's getting to his tissues.'

'What does that mean? Does that mean he's definitely going to die?' George asked, his stomach churning.

Collins paused and stared at them both. 'I'm afraid Nick's fight is over. I'm so sorry.'

Janet burst into tears while George closed his eyes.

There was a knock at the door and Maureen entered the room.

'Ah, Maureen,' Collins said, looking from her to the

Howells.

'I'm sorry for interrupting,' she said. George gave her a look of hopelessness while Janet tried to stop herself from crying.

Collins looked to Maureen for one last report. George turned at just the right moment to witness her give a single and deliberate shake of the head. Straightening his spine, George tightened his lips to quell his emotion.

'So there's nothing more you can do then?' he asked, trying to control his quivering voice.

'I'm sorry, George. There's just no more anyone can do. The ventilator is the only thing keeping him alive now.'

Janet burst into a fresh wave of tears and George held her close.

'You know what I am about to ask, don't you,' Collins said.

'There's absolutely nothing more that can be done?' George asked again.

'I'm sorry,' Collins replied.

The silence was excruciating, and then George found himself doing the hardest thing he had ever done. Twenty-one years ago he had held Nick's tiny palm on the end of his forefinger, thinking just how strong the grip of his soft podgy fingers were as his small, perfectly formed frame rested upon Janet's chest as she lay in the hospital bed. The labour had been long and tortuous for her. Her body had lost a lot of blood as Nick refused to come and George had been left battered from both fatigue and the sight of having to watch the woman he loved go through such an ordeal while being powerless to help. A specialist doctor had been brought in to prep for a C-section. George had been ordered to change into scrubs, and while he had been out of the room the midwife had pleaded with Janet to give it just one more push, and like that Nick was born; a perfectly healthy baby boy which they had created.

Everything else became insignificant. He was beautiful. He was the most perfect thing George had ever seen and it felt as though the slate of life had been wiped clean and was starting anew. They were no longer man and wife, they were a family. He envisioned days in the park kicking a football. He would teach Nick how to pencil draw just as his own father had done with him. They would go fishing, and he would make sure no matter what that if Nick ever had a problem George would always be there. He was going to be the best dad there ever was.

'All right,' George said as his eyes misted over and his heart brimmed with complete and utter failure.

Collins said nothing. Maureen exited the room to prepare.

'I'll let you have some time to yourselves. Please, just take as much time as you need,' Collins said, rising from his chair. 'I'm so sorry.'

Taking one last look at them, he left the room closing the door behind him.

Only now did George properly cry squeezing hold of Janet for all he was worth.

* * *

'It's time Nick, time to wake up and remember.'

* * *

Five Months Ago

'Are we drinking or are we sinking!' Nick yelled from behind the black graphite worktop of Sammy's Bar. The crowd called out his name, waving freshly dispensed notes from the ATM, all of them eager to be served with more over-priced cheap alcohol. The glittering atmosphere pulsed with the heavy beat of a Latino track that got the girls flirting and the lads flexing. It was Friday night, party night, and the Boston masses were out in force and ready to indulge themselves in one another. To Nick the crowd was just a blur of this year's pretty faces and manly stares; the next generation's coming of age. The girls adored him, and so did some of the men come to that, but all were there for one reason only, to get as pissed as their budget would allow and fall in love amid a haze of Alco-pop heaven; to meet the partner of their dreams and for a while feel important to at least one person. Nick viewed it as his personal duty to supply them with all the confidence they needed to fulfil their dreams and desires through the medium of alcohol, and they would love him for it. Tonight, he was their Messiah delivering the good news in good measures, filling them with the love of their God until stomach linings or empty wallets declared otherwise. After spending two years as a lowly glass collector mopping up the remnants of other people's dinners, Nick always hoped for the latter.

With a clever mix of beats the track changed to hip-hop making everyone who wasn't up and dancing rise from their seats and boogie where they stood. It also indicated to the staff that there was about thirty minutes left before last orders. Within all well organised businesses there were systems, the best always being the ones subtle enough to go unnoticed. For the staff of Sammy's it was genres. By the end of the evening whenever a particular musical genre was played they all knew which specific duties to perform be it re-stocking the fridges, sweeping the place for empty glasses, or just speeding up sales because time was running short. Hip-hop was a speeder. It got the crowd going, while also telling the bar staff to sell more and the glass collectors to get their backsides into gear unless they wanted to spend the whole night clearing up. Everything ran smoothly.

To Nick's right, half immersed in shadow, Amy was sipping on a Gatsby - Southern Comfort, lemonade and lime - deep in conversation with a muscular, ginger haired lad. They laughed at a shared joke, but Nick was not concerned. It was only Danny. They had met just over two years ago on a quiet night at the bar over a heated argument about the state of the British legal system. Nick had tried to make the point for reformation and the fact that everyone deserved the chance to change. Danny's opinion had been a little more pragmatic. All murderers, rapists, and paedophiles should be shot and burned, no exceptions. Why should the British taxpayer have to fork out to keep the scum alive? The fact that he was living on the dole in a state funded council house and did not pay taxes anyway conveniently escaped him at the time. While Nick did agree in the case of paedophiles, he argued what if the rape had been a story made up by a disgruntled ex or stalker, and what if the murder was in self-defence or a set up? After considering, Danny retorted that the death penalty should only be used if the person was convicted. Nick's replied that even innocents got railroaded though. They parried back and forth all evening until drink finally got the better of them and the fire of their argument burned itself out. Eventually, neither could be bothered and they conceded to shake hands, toast with a Budweiser, and move on to friendlier topics. Ever since that day they had remained the best of friends.

'Oi!' shouted a loud mouthed twenty-something from the opposite end of the bar, a young farmer type with too much money and not enough grace. Nick turned, feeling his exhaustion begin to show yet still managing to force a smile.

'Now then mate, what can I get you?' he said, sidling round his colleague, Becca, and her perfectly formed bottom; a girl who in Amy's opinion was far too attractive and flirtatious to be working with Nick. As he approached his customer it was impossible to ignore that everything about the man was slurred.

'I'll have a vodka and coke with a shot of tequila,' he blurted, reaching inside his trouser pocket for his tricky wallet which refused to come out.

'No problem. That'll be five twenty, please mate,' Nick said knowing full well that at this point he could have charged the drunk whatever he liked and got away with it.

Taking a short and a shot glass from beneath the bar Nick turned to the optics, making eye contact with Becca for just a little longer than was necessary. Giving him the slightest of smiles, she dropped her gaze. He had seen that look on more than one occasion from the punters across the bar and recognised its meaning instantly. Nick looked to Amy and saw her still deep in conversation with Danny. He looked back to Becca but she was no longer taking notice of him, now serving a couple of lads from the checked shirt brigade. Nick poured the tequila and pushed the short glass up to the optic nozzle, then returned to his own customer and passed the shot over.

Without even flinching, the man downed the tequila then daintily placed the glass back on the bar, screwing his face in disgust.

Please don't vomit, Nick thought.

The Coke was added to the second drink and quickly passed across to remove the acidic taste of the tequila.

'Ah, that's better,' the young man said, smacking his lips. 'Hey, come ere.'

Nick smiled inquisitively as the drunk waved him closer.

'Come ere,' he urged, dragging out the second word.

Leaning in, Nick was hit by the acrid stench of booze as the man's lips practically touched his ear, his breath hot on the side of Nick's neck.

'She so fancies you, you know,' he slurred.

'Who's that then?' Nick asked, needing to stand back.

'Come on, it's obvious; her. The blonde bit behind the bar,' he said nodding in Becca's direction with a conspiratorial wink. Nick turned his head to look at her before smiling back at the man.

'Yeah, yeah. Whatever.'

'No, seriously. I've been watching.'

I bet you have, Nick thought.

'Shit, I wish someone would look at me the way she's been lookin at you.'

'Well, how do you know they're not?' Nick offered.

'Ha, now you're just havin a laugh. Who the fuck would look at me?'

Nick scanned the bar and found what he was looking for.

'How about her over there?' he said, indicating to a lonely girl stood in the far corner twisting a plastic drinking straw between her fingers.

'Do me a favour. I might be pissed but I'm not fuckin desperate!'

'Whatever. It's just that I know for a fact that she's been watching you all night,' Nick lied. 'And I'm the sober one, remember?'

The man glanced at her for a second time.

'Really? Has she really?'

'Yep. I reckon all it would take is for you to go over and offer her a drink, and I tell you what,' Nick said leaning in again, 'you come back to me, I'll sort you out.'

Nick gave his own conspiratorial wink.

'Yeah? Cheers mate. She's really been lookin at me?'

'Seriously. Can't take her eyes off you.'

'Shit, right. Okay then, fuck it. Wish me luck.'

Nick stood back and winced as the vodka and coke was thrown down the hatch in one inning. Releasing the smallest of burps, the man smoothed himself down before straightening his shoulders and strutting over in what could only be described as an admirable attempt. With the amount of booze in this bloke's system he was going to need all the luck he could get. Nick just hoped that she was as drunk as he was.

Over he went, the greetings were made, and in a blind twist of fate the girl welcomed him with a smile.

Well what do you know, Nick thought, maybe there is a God after all.

Smiling at his handiwork, Nick looked again at Becca and then to Amy, who seemed to have finished her conversation and welcomed him with a smile, her beautiful eyes sparkling against the subdued lights. Nick smiled back then began wiping the bar, his eyes following the cloth, his mind buzzing with dangerous possibilities. He knew Becca liked him and the problem was if he was honest, there was a part of him that liked her back. Yet there was Amy. He loved Amy. They had been together since he was seventeen, over four years. Without Amy life just would not be the same. It would be like losing a limb and he was certain she felt the same. They had lost their virginity together. They had experienced their first nightclub together. They had taken their first holiday without parents together. They had studied for their A levels together. Just about everything new to them as young adults they had done together. Amy was more than just his girlfriend, she was his best friend. Then, about three months ago Becca had appeared on the scene. Sure, he had worked with beautiful women before – it's what drew in the punters - and the bar was awash with stunning girls all vying for his attention, but with Becca it was just different. He could not explain it. She just had this way about her which had captivated Nick from the start, and although it had been easy in the beginning to ignore, the more time he spent around her, the harder it was becoming to control his thoughts. He had even started thinking of her at night while lying alone in bed. It worried the hell out of him, and so he just kept his head down and scrubbed the bar for all he was worth.

'Hey, big bear.'

Nick looked up, pleased to find Amy's beautiful smile beaming toward him from across the bar.

'Hey, baby bear. How's your night been?' he asked, wiping his hands on his trousers before taking up hers.

'Okay, I guess. I've missed you. It's so unfair having to watch you being chatted up all night and not being able to touch you myself,' she purred.

'You know you're the only one for me,' Nick said. 'They know it too. You're not *still* jealous are you?'

'You wish,' Amy smiled.

Nick laughed and reached across the bar bringing their lips close enough to kiss.

'I love you,' he breathed.

'I love you too. I'm pretty tired though. I think I'll head off now.'

'Okay love, I shouldn't be too long. We're pretty much done now. Be about an hour or so, all right?'

'Cool.' Then she appeared nervous. 'Maybe we can talk some more, about… you know…'

'Yeah sure,' he offered. 'We can talk some more.'

Amy gave him an unsure smile.

'Cool. Well, I'll see you in a bit then. I'll leave the door unlocked.' They kissed, and then she was out the door and gone.

Nick sighed to himself. Two months ago, Amy had made the move to leave home and get her own place, a tidy second storey flat in Haven Hall that ran alongside the old Blackfriars Theatre on the main drag leading from the market place and not more than a two-minute walk from the bar. At first it was like a breath of fresh air to the relationship, a new chapter to be explored. They now had their own private space. No parents downstairs or in the room next-door. No hushed fumbling in the dark while the low murmur of the stereo disguised their sounds. At last they had the freedom to be as noisy and adventurous as they wanted without the fear of any embarrassing parental situations, and it was great. The only problem now was they had reached a crunch point. Amy had asked *the* question. Did he think it was time for them to take their relationship further, meaning Nick moving in on a permanent basis?

That was all well and good but Nick liked his life just the way it was. He had a certain amount of freedom to enjoy and a job he loved because it made him the centre of attention. He had a place to visit so he and Amy could be alone, but he also knew that he could leave again when he needed space to breathe. Moving in together was, of course the next natural progression in their relationship, and after the length of time they had been together Nick would have thought the idea should be a happy one. But the more he thought about it, the more anxious he became. Why though? What was he so afraid of?

He looked over at Becca who was crouched with a box of Budweiser between her legs as she restacked the refrigerators. Could his infatuation with her be just a knee jerk reaction to Amy's proposal? He had never thought of it that way before. Maybe that was it! As the realisation dawned, Nick needed to see Amy, to hold her and take in the smell of her hair, the softness of her skin, the warmth of her kisses, and then he would know.

'You're a fuckin star, do you know that,' came a voice from somewhere outside his thoughts.

Nick returned his focus to see the tequila-vodka man across the bar.

'That bird, she's well up for it,' he said a little too loudly, grinning from ear to ear. 'Better get me a medium white wine… for the lady.'

'Sure, no worries. One medium coming up.'

Last orders were called and the cleaning of the bar had been done with relative speed considering the carnage that had been left behind. All that remained to be cleaned were the sticky carpets which would be sorted by the ladies who worked the morning shift. There was nothing quite like the sugary smell of congealed cola and the boggy sensation on your feet as you had to forcibly remove your tread from the carpet. Nick hated to think what the alcohol was doing to his insides. He took two bottles of lager from the cooler and popped them into his jacket pocket.

In the main area of the bar, the doormen and staff were slouched around, supping on their well earned nightcaps. Despite the smoking ban, cigarettes were lit and collars were loosened. Nick made his way to the door.

'You off?' a burly doorman called who was swigging on a pint of cider.

'I'm gonna get an early one tonight, mate. Amy's waiting for me.'

'Ha, Nick's off for a shag!' the bouncer shouted which instigated mocking jeers. Becca only just managed a non-committal smile that went noticed by Nick.

'Ah, you lot are only jealous,' Nick said.

'Give her one from me,' called another doorman raising his bottle in salute.

'I'll make sure I do, Carl. I'll be thinking of you the whole time. See you all tomorrow,' Nick said, raising his hand in farewell.

'Night mate,' came the general reply mixed with the odd 'see ya' and just plain old 'night'.

Outside, the early morning air that flowed down the alley of Craythorne Lane held an icy chill. The only illumination came from a single street lamp which cast an eerie glow over everything. Looking down the alley and beyond, Nick could see drunken figures milling about, trying to outdo one another for a taxi ride home. Alongside the taxi rank was a string of betting shops, burger bars and late night kebab houses as well as another trendy fun pub where the majority of the local bad boys went. Behind those buildings ran the River Haven whose silt lined belly slid straight through the heart of Boston and out into the Wash. For some of the younger ones - and a few of the older ones too, come to that - the taxi rank became the local three in the morning fighting ground, which was why there was such a heavy police presence, Nick steered clear regardless. As he got closer to the rank, side stepping obligatory vomit, piss pools and discarded bottles, the atmosphere felt strange, like walking through a dream. Between the towering walls of the alley either side of him, Nick felt trapped as the relentless wind chilled through his shirt and jacket. He felt watched.

The moment Nick stepped from the alley, the wind disappeared and the lit marketplace welcomed him into its throng. With his head bowed so as not to catch the eye of any drunks from across the road, he moved past the watchful gaze of the police who were ready and waiting for the slightest sign of trouble.

Nick had noticed Becca's lack of enthusiasm over the doormen's jokes. She really did like him then. Why did life always have to be so complicated? Walking past an empty butcher's window he crossed the second alley that ran along the back of Sammy's where the drunks and fighters were tossed out, and past the old Shodfriars Hall where, high up in the rafters of the building, snooker balls clicked against one another amid a fog of illegal cigarette smoke and heavy betting. Should he confront Becca, put her straight? That was a stupid idea. Any confrontation would only be met with denial making him look arrogant. And besides, did he really want to just blow her off like that?

Nick's mind was buzzing with the noise of his thoughts. So much so that it blocked out the world around him and the sound of the approaching car that was ripping a path up the narrow one-way street on the other side of the Shodfriars building, the driver stupidly checking his Facebook page on his mobile phone because his need to stay connected really was *that* important. And it was in that split second, that Nick's entire world changed.

Without looking, Nick stepped from the curb to cross the short two metre stretch of road and became trapped in the glare of the anonymous headlights. His reactions froze with just enough time to register the terrified eyes of the driver whose arms went rigid against the steering wheel as the car ploughed into him. In one fluid motion, Nick's body was lifted from the road. The night air filled with the scream of brakes and the stench of burnt rubber. Life at the taxi rank came to a standstill as the innocent bystanders looked on in disbelief, their brains needing a moment to realise that what they were witnessing was true. Twisting midair, Nick smashed against the windscreen, his head shattering the glass with a sickening crunch and with no signs of stopping the car careened across the intersecting road, skidded across the drop curb on the other side squeezing between a set of wooden bollards before crashing head on into another parked vehicle. Nick was flung into the wall of the quayside, the only thing preventing him from falling into the ice cold river. There was another muffled crunch of something in his body breaking before he finally came to an uncoordinated stop on the gritty concrete.

At first there was silence, and then came the distant screams followed by the faint tramping of feet.

Beneath the pale moonlight, Nick's blood ran a shimmering black. He did not hear the taxi driver asking if he was okay. He did not hear the screaming girls being consoled by their shell-shocked boyfriends. He did not hear the wailing sirens of the two ambulances as they ground to a halt beside the carnage, or the police as they struggled to clear a path for the paramedics. He did not feel his vitals being checked before having his weight transferred to a collapsible gurney and into the back of the vehicle; the actions fluid and well rehearsed.

Further up the road, craning out her living-room window, Amy had heard the smash and was watching the scene with interest, following the ambulance as it sped past, and feeling sad for the poor soul inside. In the back of the racing vehicle, Nick was rapidly losing blood. His skull had been crushed and shards of splintered bone jutted out of his brain like a garden wall topped with broken glass. The paramedics first and foremost needed to stem, or at least slow the flowing blood, before it was too late. It was bad, really bad, and yet they laboured without the slightest sign of panic. Amid the chaos, Nick's entire world was black. Though he felt no pain, somewhere in a distant realm he could feel his body being tugged this way and that. He could feel every puncture, every cut as it happened but there was no pain to accompany it. Then he began to sink.

At first, Nick's head echoed with a soft buzzing noise similar to static as his life-force drained away, slowing down like an old clock until his body became lifeless and still. Then from nowhere there came an unfathomable surge of energy as Nick felt his consciousness rip free from the dead shell of his flesh like a huge fist being punched out through his chest. It was exhilarating and powerful, and Nick was overwhelmed with the sense of ultimate freedom. The blackness was suddenly replaced with the interior of the ambulance and Nick recognised his own body beneath him. He was not frightened by the sight, but sympathetic.

'Come on, mate,' the paramedic said to Nick's lifeless body. 'I think we've lost him. Yep, he's arresting. I'm going to start resuss.'

With a calm confidence, the paramedic took an Ambu-bag from one of the overhead compartments and, fitting it over Nick's face, pumped two breaths of air into his lungs, watching his chest ride and fall before checking his pulse again.

Nothing.

Cutting open Nick's shirt, the paramedic began a cardiac massage pumping down against his breastbone before administering more air into his system.

Nothing.

With a swift and practiced motion, the paramedic injected Nick with adrenaline and atropine but still there was nothing.

Nick viewed the activity with mild interest and found himself feeling oddly detached from any emotions or concern towards the condition of his body.

'Damn it. Come on, mate,' the paramedic said. He hooked the Ambu-bag to a rack above his head. 'I'm moving over to defib.'

Nick had seen enough. It was time to leave this place. The last thing he witnessed before leaving the ambulance was the paramedic giving his dead body a thump on the chest before applying gel to the electric paddles. Smiling, Nick left the ambulance and stepped out into the night sky.

From the rustling of the trees, Nick could tell there was wind in the air yet felt no cold. He recognised the street as Spilsby Road with its grand houses on both sides, elegantly illuminated by orange neon streetlights that gave off the same hue which had chilled him in Craythorne Lane yet now appeared tranquil and warm. Though his body was gone Nick felt more complete than ever, and as he looked down the empty street the trees and buildings obstructing his view became translucent like silk, allowing his vision to reach farther than would ever be humanly possible, piercing through with pinpoint clarity until it came to rest on the thing he searched for.

Amy.

With tremendous speed, Nick sped towards her passing through the material obstructions of the Cosm like smoke, hardly aware of their existence as the world rushed by. The action required no conscious decision, nor did he need to choose a direction in which to travel. He just knew that he was going to her and in an instant he was there, stood in the centre of *their* living-room, surrounded by the possessions of their life together.

Amy was still at the window watching the drama unfold in the street below. A fire engine pulled up and its crew leapt out to cut the unconscious driver from the wreckage. In her hand was the telephone which contained her excited yet concerned friend, Pippa.

'They're cutting the roof away now,' Amy said, stretching out further for a better look. 'No... it's too far away.'

Nick took his time to admire the room. In such a short space of time they had managed to fill the tiny space with so many memories and so much love. He thought back to their first night after receiving the keys. They had been so eager they slept on the living-room floor in sleeping bags, celebrating their new life together by candlelight with wine and strawberries picked that day. The rest of the night had been spent in passion and conversations of the adventure to come. Although the apartment was Amy's in name, they had chosen what little furniture they owned together with an old television set from Nick's parents. It had been such an exciting time. Nick hoped Amy would not mourn him for too long; she deserved nothing but happiness in her life.

As Amy watched the ambulance and fire crew transfer the unconscious driver from the decapitated wreckage, she saw the staff of Sammy's filter out the alley to see what all the fuss was about. Even from this distance she could make everyone out just by their shape or hairstyle. Then, something unsettling occurred to her. Nick was not with them. She stopped her update to Pippa and just watched in silence as a sickness began to grow in her stomach. She watched as Carl the bouncer, recognisable by his fat bald head, walked over to one of the policemen and chatted for what seemed like an age. After a few seconds of standing alone, he then hung his head and turned to the rest of the group. There was another moment of conversation, and then Amy registered the shockwave that rippled through the group as Becca's legs gave way beneath her and she collapsed, clasping her hands to her face in floods of tears.

'Hang on, Pippa. I'll have to call you back,' Amy said. 'No, I'll call you back.'

Amy hung up the phone and placed it on the floor. Where was Nick?

The longer she watched, the more the group seemed to crumble. Then, Amy's stomach churned as Carl and another thickset bouncer named Barry broke from the group, looked in her direction and started walking toward her building. And in that split second she knew.

Oh God, no. No, that couldn't be right, Amy thought, backing away from the window. Nick watched as she fell against the sofa. As she drew her knees to her chest wrapping her arms around them, Amy's forehead creased and her eyes darkened.

He was fine.

She rocked herself in an effort to hold back her reddening eyes.

Nick, where are you? Please, don't do this to me. Where are you?

Amy thought back to the racing ambulance and a wall collapsed within her.

Oh God no, please no. It's not Nick; it can't be. The tears came slowly, unsure.

Moving closer, Nick could feel the overwhelming conflict within her. She so wanted it to be someone else in that ambulance yet every part of her was telling her it was Nick, and as he stared into her beautiful hazel eyes he found himself filled with love and regret. He wanted so much to tell her that everything was good now. That she should not cry. He really was fine.

Amy heard a knock at the door but ignored it. She hugged her knees tighter and buried her chin.

The knock came again, heavier this time, more insistent. Nick looked to her and then to the door. Through it he could see the destroyed figures of Carl and Barry waiting to deliver the news, neither wanting to be there. Amy rocked herself, refusing to move. They knocked again, knowing that she was there.

'Amy?' Carl's deep voice called.

Please go to them, Amy, Nick thought. You shouldn't be alone right now.

Amy stopped her rocking and looked around the room in surprise. She had not heard Nick but something had touched her, touched her heart.

'Nick?' she said to the empty room.

Go to them.

Amy stood and stared around the room. 'Nick?' There came another knock at the door, louder this time, more insistent.

'Amy!'

Feeling her insides ache as the winds of change readied to blow her hopes and dreams to dust, Amy moved towards the door on unsteady legs. Nick had seen everything he needed here and left the room through the outer wall. There was just one more place he needed to go. The sight of the accident below no longer concerned him. He focussed his attention through the obstructions of the Cosm one last time and saw his family asleep in their beds.

Again, Nick sped through reality like a nimble fish and in an instant found himself in his old bedroom. It felt empty. The objects he had collected throughout his life which stood as a testament to the person he had once been meant nothing to him now. Their only purpose from this point on would be to serve as a shrine for those he left behind. Nick hoped he would be remembered as more than just a few worthless trinkets. In his heart he knew he would. The room was easy to leave.

Passing through the door without opening it, Nick

entered Andrew's bedroom. His brother was sound asleep beside the dim glow of his night light. Even after all these years, he was still afraid of the dark. Nick hovered close to Andrew's face.

Don't worry little mate, he thought. There's nothing to be afraid of. I'll always be watching you.

Andrew stirred and a tiny smile touched the corner of his mouth.

Sweet dreams, little mate.

Nick moved into his parent's room where he found them asleep in each other's arms like young lovers. Their faces appeared younger than their years and Nick could see within them the love that had sparked their life together so many years ago still burned as bright as ever.

'Thank you,' he whispered, looking down at them for the very last time. 'You have been the best parents anyone could have wished for. Every moment of my life has been a wonder and I thank you for sharing it with me. Take care of each other. I love you both.'

Just then the telephone started to ring downstairs and Janet began to stir.

Goodbye, Nick thought.

And he walked away.

All around him was the rushing sound of wind as the bedroom began to darken and fade. His last image of the material world was the sight of his sleeping parents still wrapped in the other's embrace until eventually all was black.

Silence fell all around and way off in the emptiness Nick saw a point of light accentuated by the surrounding blackness, piercing his curiosity like a spear, beckoning him to follow. All around, imp like whispers began to chatter and buzz like a swarm of gnats in the summer dusk but each time he tried to place them the whispers eluded him. Nick smiled, enjoying the sensation as the invisible beings played against his senses. He felt his consciousness begin to drift toward the light. Suddenly, immense exhilaration coursed through his soul as his body was thrust forward into the blackness. Far off in the distance, the point of light began to intensify blinding Nick with its brilliance until with one final burst of white he found himself on the plains of the Border, luscious green grass stretching as far as the eye could see, and before him stood Hesamuel.

Nick stared in awe and wonder at the shining being whose mere presence filled him with the sweetest serenity.

'Hello, Nick. I am Hesamuel.'

'Hello,' he replied. Hesamuel smiled and, for what seemed like hours, they just looked at each other like old friends reunited.

'Did you enjoy your life?' Hesamuel asked.

Nick's smile widened. 'Yes, yes I did. But why has it ended so soon?'

'Because that is the way we chose it. You have fulfilled all the tasks we set for you and I have learned so much from your experiences but now it is time for us to go home.'

Without question, Nick accepted what he was being told as the truth. Inside, he knew it to be true and was filled with an overwhelming sense of achievement that he had never experienced while being alive, as if the calm of the Light was shining upon him, overflowing his mind with joy and well-being. Accepting the truth, Nick fell into Hesamuel's open arms and wept with happiness. It felt like the most right thing he had ever known and with the release of his tears all the concerns of his previous life disappeared. He was going home.

Amid a haze of swirling stars and light, Nick's body unravelled, the molecules of his being melding with that of Hesamuel's as they became whole once again, filling Hesamuel with the joy and the pain of Nick's existence in the Cosm. As a slumbering onlooker from within, he had watched Nick's life through the years with envy, learning and philosophising over every tiny action and reaction to understand the deeper concepts and grow from the knowledge gained. Through the life Nick had lived for them both, Hesamuel had matured spiritually and was ready to elevate.

With the meld complete Hesamuel stood upon the plains whole once more and took in the expansive scenery. It was beautiful, there was no doubt of that, yet it was nothing compared to the plethora of textures and colours and smells and sensations of the Cosm. As always, he was really going to miss it. With mixed feelings, Hesamuel decided it was time to leave this place. From his outstretched hand the solidity of the scene around him began to sparkle at his fingertips before peeling away and ripping a black hole in the fabric of this constructed reality. Against the static charge of his skin more of the Border began to retreat from his shining body until a fissure large enough for him to step through was created, and so he did.

As soon as he stepped through, the tear behind him sealed shut and, floating in darkness, Hesamuel became transfixed by the beauty and splendour of the Maelstrom, an eternal darkness filled with the radiating songs of passing souls darting all around him, their numbers too great to comprehend, and far off in the distant dark, beyond the madness of the Maelstrom, was the Light. Some were going to sleep while others, like him, were waking again. Whichever, the travelling souls played round each other like moths in the moonlight, caressing one another with their warmth. To Hesamuel's eyes it was a beautiful sight and he submerged himself into the mêlée feeling his senses tingle with the proximity of his brothers and sisters, expectant of the dream about to be lived or of the journey home. It filled him with inspiration and comfort. Amid the chaotic dance, Hesamuel felt love, was consumed by it. He weaved his way through the ocean of light reaching ever closer to the point that was brightest. Like a beacon it called to him through the swirling mass, engulfing him, overwhelming him with the sole purpose of reaching home. Tearing through the ocean of souls passing up and over him, through and between, reaching ever nearer to the source, Hesamuel was consumed with the need to reconnect sweeping all else away. The closer he reached the blistering Light the more levels opened within him filling him with knowledge and power like never before.

Suddenly, Hesamuel's consciousness twitched.

An image left his mind just as quickly as it had entered, too fast for him to recognise. He pushed on further.

Again, his mind twitched and again an image vanished just as quickly leaving Hesamuel filled once more with the love that surrounded him, the warmth of the Light all about him now, his world consumed by its brilliance. Finally, he was home.

Wait.

This was not a voice speaking to him but his own conscience reaching beyond the Light for just a moment. What had that twitch been? At the very limit of the Light, Hesamuel paused, turning to face the swirling mass of nomadic souls. He could not be sure but something quite strange had touched him, something out of place. What had made his mind twitch like that? Perhaps it had been nothing. Still, curiosity got the better him. He was among friends here. He was in the radiance of the Light. What had he to fear?

Confident in this knowledge, Hesamuel moved away from the Light back into the throng of the Maelstrom, his vision blinded by the swarm as he ventured deeper without restraint or fear. Like playful children the souls whirled around him and every so often he would catch a glimpse of a face as they stopped to stare at him before zipping off again into the beautiful chaos. What had he felt? He moved deeper still into the clamour, until-

Hesamuel's mind twitched.

Just as before, the sensation came quickly and was gone again but it confirmed to him that there was definitely something not right. Hesamuel moved deeper still.

Another twitch came, stronger this time. What was it?

Hesamuel stopped to look around but was blinded by the storm of souls who seemed oblivious to what he was sensing. He moved deeper still.

An even stronger twitch assaulted his mind. He stopped. For the first time, Hesamuel felt unsafe; amazed that no-one else around him could sense what he was feeling. Whatever it was, he was close. Whether he had been noticed in return was uncertain but as he searched the golden mass he glimpsed the strangest of things. The indiscernible object had nearly passed him by but, through chance, he discovered a tiny pinprick of black which hung suspended against the writhing background, an unmoving blemish in the centre of such hopes and dreams. Hesamuel drifted closer, his eyes fixed on the anomaly for fear of losing it in the mêlée. With his hand outstretched, he reached toward it, hesitant. Just a hair breadth away, Hesamuel felt his life-force stir within him, the Cosm's equivalent to butterflies in his stomach. Perhaps it was nothing. Perhaps his fear was down to the thing being unknown rather than the object itself emanating any evil intentions. There was only one way to find out.

As his nerves reached a crescendo, Hesamuel took one last blind leap of faith hearing Amy's portentous words echoing inside his mind.

'What's the point of living if you don't actually live?'

With one final leap of abandon, Hesamuel swallowed his apprehension and touched the black spot, and everything went dark.

Chapter Fourteen

Hesamuel fell subdued as his own radiating light became extinguished by the dark leaving him stripped of warmth and naked. There was something *unnatural* about the darkness. It admitted no light. His senses were still sharp though and what he felt in the surrounding black was more than just hollow emptiness, it was pure dark, pure evil like he had never felt before. His body shivered beneath its weight and he could feel himself curling from within as if his very essence was folding in on itself to hide from what lurked in the gloom. Reaching out with his senses, Hesamuel searched the atmosphere. Pain flickered through his mind as the suffering of a billion screaming voices cried out from the dark. What was this place?

Hesamuel reached out again and his mind filled with rotten images of depravity, torture, and death. He gave a sharp intake of breath as pain racked his body infecting his being with foulness. Then, out of the darkness stepped two hideous creatures. One was the towering figure of Abaddon, his long coat stained with the suffering of eternity flapping at his ankles. The other was a stunted, hunched, monster whose deformities were so severe they verged on the ridiculous. Its lower jaw protruded further than the top exposing a ridge of rotten jagged teeth. The creature's flayed skin showed patches of raw bare cartilage, and its hunch was so cruel that the backs of its hands would have dragged the floor had there been one. The angel and the monster watched Hesamuel in silence.

'*Do you see his perfection?*' Abaddon asked the creature. '*Do you see how his spine is straight and true, his skin smooth and tight? Take a good look, for you will never be like this.*'

The creature appeared to sadden, letting its head

fall, and Hesamuel could not help but feel compassion.

'Depraved ones such as you could never be allowed to taste the world offered to such perfect souls as this. The Cosm is not for the likes of you. You are scum, a defiler of innocents, and rapist of the young. You deserve to burn for all eternity for the suffering you have inflicted on the defenceless sleepers subjected to your merciless acts of lust. You should be sodomised again and again for every soul you have violated.'

The creature bowed low and whined at Abaddon's feet. Hearing the monster's crimes, Hesamuel no longer felt pity for the wretch but revulsion, and Abaddon gave a distasteful smile.

'What do you think? Do you think she deserves another chance?' Abaddon asked, the slightest of grins touching *His* crusted humourless lips.

Hesamuel hesitated.

'I do not understand,' he replied.

'What is there not to understand? It is a simple question; could you give pity to this poor depraved defiler? Given the choice, would you allow this filth another chance to put right the wrongs of a previous life once lived or condemn her to an eternity of darkness?'

'Is that my choice to make?'

'Perhaps,' Abaddon said.

'Then no, I could not.'

'Hmm, it is interesting that you are so quick to deal out judgement when you live by a code based on redemption and the development of the soul. Each life lived to redeem and improve on a spiritual level. For a moment you felt pity for this miserable thing yet once you had heard her crimes you quickly rebelled against your heart's initial decision. All that time in the Cosm and you are still so quick to judge. Interesting.'

'Some things are unforgivable. To release her would only breed more anarchy and chaos.'

'But is that not the point of the Cosm? If it were a perfect world then how would you learn, how would you grow? Without the comparison of light and dark what examples would you draw from to

make the correct choice and follow the correct path to purity? Surely, this beast here deserves a second chance?

'No. If the Cosm was given over to chaos then it would collapse and come to an end. The Cosm would destroy itself. Some souls just delve too deep into the darkness to ever come back.'

Abaddon's smile widened as though Hesamuel had just struck upon a revelation. *He* was pleased to finally find a soul that understood his purpose.

'*Do you hear that? You are just too evil,*' Abaddon said to *His* grovelling companion. The creature stopped licking *His* feet and sniggered. A line of drool stretched from its cliff-edge jaw. '*Hmm... I think she quite enjoys being the way she is. Perhaps you are right; perhaps some souls are beyond saving. And Perhaps I should release her back into the Cosm? She could roam free once more and contribute to the rising chaos then maybe; just maybe, it would all come crashing down. Imagine that, Hesamuel.*'

'Who are you? What is happening here?' Hesamuel asked, his eyes flicking from Abaddon to the creature.

'*Who am I,*' *He* said in droll, lazy voice. '*What is going on? Hmm... Abaddon was the name given to me on the day of creation and it shall be the last name whispered on the day of Armageddon.*'

'Why am I here?'

'*You are being replaced.*'

Abaddon tapped his pet monster on the head. '*You may take your rightful place back in the Cosm now. Go on... off you go. Prove to me your worth.*'

With a menacing glare the beast rose from Abaddon's feet and examined Hesamuel with a curious eye as if deciding which part of him would be the tastiest.

Then, with lightning speed the beast struck, slamming into Hesamuel's chest with claws and teeth. Hesamuel's skin tore like wet tissue paper as they both tumbled into the consuming darkness, their struggling forms intertwined like sparring lovers, the beast attacking with uncontrollable savagery. Though the pain was unbearable, Hesamuel managed to grab the flailing meat grinder of a hand and with a sharp twist snapped the wrist clean so that each time the beast tried to strike her hand just flopped away. Releasing her grip from Hesamuel's back the beast howled in agony and grabbed her useless wrist in disbelief as she tried to focus through the pain and fear which had now subdued her bloodlust. Seeing his chance, Hesamuel struck thrusting his hand against the monster's chest, pushing his palm flat against her hairy skin. The beast's eyes widened as she experienced a moment of calm. Then, as realisation dawned, she started to thrash against his touch, trying to release his hold upon her.

But Hesamuel's hold was firm. His hand began to submerge into her chest past the layers of deformed skin and twisted ribcage until he finally touched the anguish within. One solitary tear fell from the creature's eye, coursing down her gnarled face before catching in the basin of her protruding jaw. Beneath the layers of filth and flesh, Hesamuel found her soul, her true soul. It felt dead and barren. As his fingers closed around its husk his heart overflowed with the sorrow of her regret and he felt a tear upon his own cheek that mirrored hers. Unable to bear the suffering any longer, Hesamuel clenched the dark force nestled inside and ripped it from her body. In a final imitation of life, the beast's lips parted as if drawing one final breath.

'Thank you,' she whispered, her wretched mouth barely able to form the words.

As her body fell to the darkness disappearing into its unremitting belly, exhausted, Hesamuel too fell backwards and hung suspended, his arms outstretched, and the dark force of her soul still pulsing in his hand until it finally evaporated like a whisper on the wind.

Abaddon simmered yet showed not one trace of emotion.

He glided over to Hesamuel's ravaged body and grabbed him by the top of the head so their faces were mere inches apart. Turning Hesamuel's head from side to side, Abaddon studied him. Without the energy left to speak let alone fight and his ruined chest raging with pain, Hesamuel just hung flaccid within the angel's grip.

'*You were supposed to die,*' Abaddon said. *His* breath was as dry and rotten as the grave. *He* released *His* grip leaving Hesamuel to float in the dark.

'*Since the beginning of time, the beginning of existence, I have been here. I was created by the Light to fill existence with evil. Without dark there can be no light. Like the Light, I am, and I will continue to fulfil my purpose long after you are gone until the Cosm rips itself apart in storms of hellfire and rivers of blood. And when all is done, the sleepers shall look to themselves and realise that all along they had the power to change things for the better if only they had the strength to believe in the concept of humanity. I have witnessed all since the beginning of time. Inside all of you is the capacity for murder and depravity. I did not put it there. It is just a question of knowing the right buttons to press.*'

'No...,' Hesamuel breathed. 'We would not do that. Create you to destroy everything we've built? Why? It makes no sense.'

'*Perhaps now you recognise your responsibility in all this. My existence is no accident. I was created for one purpose, as the embodiment of Evil and you are to blame, you all are.*'

Powerless to fight, Hesamuel was grabbed by the ankle and dragged into the darkness, unsure of which way was up or down. Moving further into the unknown, the lack of a solid association became claustrophobic pressing down on Hesamuel's will. As his head lolled from side to side, something flashed past this line of sight. He tried to look back but whatever it was had already disappeared into the darkness. He wanted to call out for help but the ability failed him, instead coming out as a feeble croak.

Abaddon remained silent.

Deeper they travelled until the emptiness was replaced by row upon row of iron cages stretching out in every direction as far as the eye could see. This was Abaddon's labyrinth, the treasure trove where *His* souls were kept. Each cage contained trapped and tormented souls that had once been filled with so much life yet were now reduced to grey hollow shells, crushed into submission by aeons of incarceration and darkness. They moved with a lethargic slouch, pacing their tiny eight by eight cells with no real purpose or reason while others sat motionless weeping with despair. The truly old ones just lay there as if dead and stared as Abaddon glided past with yet another victim.

'Help me,' Hesamuel pleaded, trying to cling to the bars that flitted past without success, his probing fingers peeling away lacking any real strength, his pleas falling on deaf ears of the already damned who just stared through lacklustre eyes. 'Please, help me.'

Abaddon continued *His* trek through the maze of hopelessness until they reached their destination. In the centre was one solitary open cage, empty and waiting.

'*Welcome to your new home, Hesamuel. You're going to be here for a very long time.*' Abaddon threw him into the cell. His damaged body hit the bars before falling to the dusty floor.

Then, without another word, Abaddon slammed the cell door shut and walked away.

The floor was cold and gritty against Hesamuel's face as he watched Abaddon's long dark coat sway about *His* ankles before disappearing into the darkness. Regretting his curiosity, Hesamuel closed his eyes and thought about the Light, the beautiful Light that had been so close. Why had he turned away? He was home! Why?

Hesamuel felt something tickle his hand which was resting between the bars but, lacking the strength to look he ignored it and just stared down the rows of cells at the point where Abaddon had vanished. Again, something tickled his hand as though he were being stroked.

'Hey!' a voice shouted from one of the other cages. 'Hey, you, get off him. Leave him alone!'

'But I can feel it. Can't you feel it? He is still radiating with the Maelstrom. It's been so long. Can't you feel it?' the other soul said from an adjacent cage desperate to touch Hesamuel's hand, itching for just a sample of the world they had left behind.

'Yes I can feel it, but I'm trying not to. What's the point? What's the point in torturing yourself with the memory? We'll never see it again, so... just leave him be.'

'Just a little touch, that's all I want. What's the harm in that?'

'It's not good for you. Why don't you just leave it be, this is our world now. Just leave it be.'

Though Hesamuel's chest still throbbed with pain, he managed to retract his hand from the bars.

'Hey there, pilgrim,' said a sullen voice from the cage to his left. 'Sorry about him. He hasn't been here that long. Hasn't had time to deal with the loss. I would tell you my name but I can't remember any more.'

'What is this place?' Hesamuel managed, still too weak to move.

'Lord knows, but I don't intend staying for very long!' said the other soul who had been trying to touch his hand. 'Do you have any news from the outside?'

'Outside?' Hesamuel asked.

'Ignore him,' the other said. 'I've learned to. I find it a lot easier that way.'

'But what is this place?' Hesamuel repeated.

'These are Abaddon's cages, on the edge of the Abyss. It's where he keeps us from returning home.'

'Why? I don't understand why he would do that. He told me that he had been created by the Light to bring about Armageddon. That can't be right can it? What about the legend of Satan?'

'Satan? Ha! Pilgrim, you have a lot to learn. Yeah, everyone goes on about Satan being the master of all evil in Hell causing pain and suffering with brimstone and fire and blah, blah, blah. Satan was merely the first angel to fall. That's all. Abaddon… well, he's a different matter. If that's what he told you then he wasn't lying. Angel's can't lie. He isn't trying to be evil; he *is* evil, evil incarnate. That's why we're here. Don't you realise?'

Hesamuel struggled to shake his head.

'That's what he does. Think about all the wars, and suffering, and the lies and the treachery; millennia's of pain and bloodshed.'

'But that's down to human nature, to sleepers trying to understand a better way. Eventually the balance is restored. The sleepers learn… *we* will learn a better way. That's why we travel to the Cosm, to make mistakes and learn by them without tainting the perfection of the Light. And when we return we come back better, stronger, more understanding souls.'

'I know that's the theory, but the balance won't be restored. It was never meant to be.'

'What do you mean?' Hesamuel asked.

'That's why you're here, that's why we're all here caged like animals. Through the sleepers is how he does it. From within the Maelstrom he steals the souls about to sleep, about to be born into the Cosm, and fills the new-born bodies with the damned, those who have long been banished; demons, murderers, destroyers, and when they are born their sleeping auras still radiate with the taint of the dark soul hidden within and from the inside they pick at the Cosm piece by piece spreading their evil, causing pain and suffering, infecting others with the stain of their own misery.'

'Some people are just born evil?' the stranger continued, 'never a truer word said. I have been trapped in this hole longer than I can remember, and it's because we know of his existence that none of us could ever be allowed to escape.'

Hesamuel thought about the history of the Cosm. Not just the wars and the political figures that caused them, but of the little things; of the way ordinary people acted towards each other. Lives full of precious days that should be treated as a gift but were instead consumed with lies and deceit. The total disregard which people showed the world bred from the decay spreading through the Cosm like a rampant virus left unchecked. The same decay which unleashed the selfish greed and lust of not only the rapists and the murderers and the paedophiles, but also the desires of ordinary people who were all the time being drawn deeper into the ever appealing darkness, being seduced by a way of life so full of promise yet delivering nothing but regret and a desperate yearning for a life once lived and lost. The Cosm was getting worse.

'But struggle is an integral part of the Cosm,' Hesamuel argued, 'what you are insinuating is just down to human nature. The way sleepers interact with each other, actions causing reactions. The very reason we dream is to recognise these mistakes and change ourselves for the better. That is the point.'

'True, strife is the lesson of the Cosm but Abaddon's influence is getting stronger, his methods more complex. Through aeons of sleep, monsters so atrocious they should never breathe the air of the Cosm again are being unleashed on a decadent world. Through aeons of hate and struggle, Abaddon has managed to create a silent army so destructive that I don't think he can be stopped, but do you want to hear the irony, pilgrim?'

Hesamuel used all his strength to look at his strange companion.

'Because we're all asleep within the Cosm no-one remembers the truth, and the only people who do come to realise are the ones who get ensnared in this desolate place hidden within the Maelstrom.' Reaching up to stretch his stooping back, the speaker leaned against the bars of his cage flexing forward. 'And as we've all discovered, no-one escapes, ever. So, no-one on the *outside*, as our insane friend over there calls it, knows anything about Abaddon, his purpose, or his influence, relying only on recycled dogma from old religions, ghost stories told to control the masses. And so the circus continues and the Cosm gets worse, and just as you proved it's all put down to human nature.'

The paradox of his imprisonment was more than Hesamuel could accept and resigned to the truth he rested his face back to the floor of his cage and closed his eyes to shut away the lunacy of the unknown speaker and the entire oppressive scene around him, finding refuge in his memories. The golden Maelstrom filled with love and imagination, and the radiating warmth of the Light and his craving for home. Yet, like a taunting phantasm the heat of the Light faded to ash and was replaced by the harsh reality of his prison. Why would the Light allow for this to happen?

In a place where time bore no meaning, Hesamuel opened his eyes again to find the insane soul's deadpan stare looking straight at him through the lattice-work of overlapping bars. How long he had been in this position was anyone's guess. Hesamuel returned the stare as he came to realise that in this place of nothingness what else was there to do but study one another.

'I don't remember the last time I was in the Cosm,' the insane soul said to anyone who would listen.

'Here we go again,' said the nameless pilgrim from his own cell.

'Shut up you!' he spat. 'As I was saying, I don't remember the last time I was in the Cosm. Tell me Hesamuel, what is it like now?'

'What would you like to know?' Hesamuel asked,

welcoming the interaction yet afraid of the longing those memories could produce.

'I don't know anything anymore. What form did you take? What was the name of your planet? Tell me the last thing you remember.'

Hesamuel thought back to Andrew and his parents, to Amy's tears.

But it was not real, not in the sense that the soul was thinking, not to the waking spirit. In the dimension of the sleeper, physical pain only served to harm the vehicle, not the traveller. The nameless pilgrim was right, what was the point in clinging to the memory of the Cosm when the memory of the Maelstrom and the Light was what was truly real. The Cosm was nothing but a dream, a testing ground. Even so, it was still a vital part of their existence because without it where would they learn to adapt and grow? Where could they make their mistakes without tainting the purity of the Light? That was the true meaning of Armageddon. If the Cosm no longer existed then the sleepers would become stagnant permitting apathy to seep into the Light, infecting it with its poisonous promise until the purity turned to chaos and fire. In his mind's eye, Hesamuel visualised the clarity of the Light begin to grey at the edges as an inky stain filtered its way in until the brilliant white was lost forever having no other way to go but darker. That was Abaddon's plan. That was Abaddon's purpose. Again, Hesamuel found himself asking the question, why? It made no sense that the Light, all powerful, would allow for this to happen and it filled him with frustration and anger.

'It makes no sense!' Hesamuel shouted.

The squabbling duo either side of him fell silent and stared at the unexpected and welcome change to their usual bombardment of insults.

'Absolutely!' the insane soul cried. 'None of it makes sense!'

'You don't even know what he's talking about so why don't you just shut up and let him say what he needs to say!' the nameless pilgrim yelled.

'Look you. I've just about had enough of your snide little comments. If I want to agree with what Hesamuel has to say then I will, just because you're too weak to hold the faith. I keep quiet-'

'Ha!'

'I keep quiet, I ignore the digs but it all comes down to faith. Tell me Hesamuel, what do you believe in? How far are you willing to go to hold the faith?'

'Leave him alone!' the nameless pilgrim said.

'Ah, shut up you worthless infidel. Call yourself a believer when all you want to do is curl up and forget. At least I'm trying to keep my sanity. I'm still trying to remember what home was like!'

'You actually think you're sane?'

'Enough!' Hesamuel shouted.

Both fell silent and looked at him with a mixture of fear and wonder; not because of his outburst but because of the way the bars to his cage creaked as he did it.

'What just happened?' asked the insane soul backing away to the rear of his cell.

'What did you do?' the nameless pilgrim asked.

'I... I don't know,' Hesamuel replied, staring at the motionless bars of his cage.

'Do it again.'

'I can't. I have no idea what I just did,' he said with the tiniest feeling of panic.

'You have to try!' the unnamed pilgrim cried. 'In all my time here I have never seen that before. Please, try.'

'Careful, he's starting to believe again,' the insane soul jibed.

'Be quiet you. Go on, Hesamuel, try.'

Staring at the bars, Hesamuel began to concentrate, to focus his mind on them but nothing happened.

To either side, the waiting souls stared in anticipation. Again, Hesamuel bent his thoughts towards the bars of his cage, staring at them with the intensity of a blast furnace. But still nothing happened. The nameless pilgrim sagged away into the shadows of his own cell while the insane soul remained bolt upright waiting for the miracle to come. This time, Hesamuel closed his eyes and began to visualise himself. In his head he saw himself sat in a lotus position, the angle of his vision floating around his imagined form, adding layer upon layer of detail to the scene as he tried to depict the smallest element. Then he began to imagine the hard cell floor beneath him, dark and dusty, and from it raised the bars of his cage like twisted shoots breaking through the crust of the stone floor, spiralling up in front of him and all around. Ensnared within their perverted columns, Hesamuel remained motionless, full of peace with his eyes closed while his mind's eye continued to circle around the evolving scene. Moving in closer, he could see the composition of the gnarled bars down to the finest atom, could feel Abaddon's evil throbbing within every fold of the metal as *His* oppressive strength writhed through its twisted heart. Hesamuel watched himself reach out towards the confines of his cell, caressing the bars with the healing love and forgiveness of the Light still residing within him, passing his hands up and around the cold structure as they began to soften and bend to his will, succumbing to the mercy that flowed from his body.

From the confines of their own prisons, the insane soul and the nameless pilgrim gawped in amazement as Hesamuel's cage began to disintegrate around him.

'Who is he?' the insane soul gasped, unable to contain his wonder. 'Is he an angel?'

The nameless pilgrim said nothing.

Within his mind, Hesamuel could feel the evil contained within the bars of the cage begin to infiltrate his own real body, trying to warp it to its own design. Yet the Light resting within his soul was still strong enough to withstand and shielded him from the dark until his mind glistened and found inner peace once more. Basking in the luminosity, Hesamuel felt the call of home and in his mind's eye saw a path to the portal streaking through the blackness like a golden thread, piercing through the invisible veil of darkness to the Maelstrom which would lead him back to the Light, that canvass of pure white light which tugged at the spark within him, beckoning him to return.

'Go!' the insane soul begged.

Hesamuel opened his eyes and bared witness to what he had done.

'He's right,' the nameless pilgrim seconded. 'Go while you still can. Return to the Light and pass on what you have seen. Get help. You cannot win this fight alone. Now, go!'

Bewildered and with his chest still ravaged from the attack, Hesamuel tested his legs as he searched the distance for Abaddon. It was only then that others around them began to wake from their lethargy and take notice. Some gave him a cursory glance while others stood in amazement, and the news of Hesamuel's miracle rippled through the infinite prison like a shockwave, each cell coming to life as the telling of the news spread further. At first it was a mere whisper, but soon the noise of their chatter rose to a deafening roar tearing through the darkness as the cages rattled with furious insurgence and the prisoners cheered in defiance as loud as their voices would carry.

The air became heavy and oppressive.

'He's coming. Go now!' the insane soul cried.

The longer Hesamuel hesitated, the darker the atmosphere became until row by row, the distant cells began to vanish into the engulfing blackness. Abaddon was coming.

'Go!'

Peering over the edge of his cell floor, Hesamuel stared down into the tumbling abyss that appeared dense enough to walk on if only he had the faith to try. Suddenly the air filled with a terrifying roar. Hesamuel gave himself to fate and launched into the void knowing he needed to put as much distance between Abaddon and himself as possible. Then he remembered the golden thread which his mind's eye had shown him, revealing the way home. With a burst of speed, Hesamuel thrust in that direction and hoped for the best.

Fuelled with furious anger, Abaddon erupted from the darkness, his clawed hands outstretched, his razor-sharp teeth bared in rage.

'*How?* He roared. '*How did you get out? No-one escapes, no-one!*'

Hesamuel hurtled through the black like a fearful comet, still trying to widen the distance between himself and Abaddon but failing with every passing moment. He was just a soul. Abaddon, however, swelled with the all-encompassing power and might of an angel, and his dark coat billowed out behind him like a relentless banshee as *He* drew ever near.

'*Where are you going, Hesamuel? There is nowhere else for you. This is my domain; my rules. All that is left for you is the suffering I will inflict upon your worthless soul. You shall never escape me.*'

Despite the crippling fear, Hesamuel kept his eyes closed blindly following the golden path inside his mind. If he could make it through then maybe he would stand a chance by losing the angel inside the Maelstrom. With every passing moment, Hesamuel could feel the portal getting closer.

But Abaddon felt it too and it was only now that *He* realised the direction in which Hesamuel was taking them. Was it foresight or luck that was taking him on this path? Whichever, it did not concern *Him*. There was no way he could allow this errant soul to re-enter the Light. If *His* purpose were ever to be known it would be the ruin of everything *He* existed for, the ruin of creation. He could never allow that to happen.

'I know your mind Hesamuel. You're heading for the portal aren't you?' *He* said with a wolfish grin, confident of his own prowess.

Hesamuel was sent spinning as a tremor of unseen force slammed into the small of his back just before Abaddon's talons sank into the top of his head sending fire through his body and malevolence pierce his soul, distorting it as though every part of him was being twisted and pulled inside out.

Together, they hurtled towards the portal.

Beneath Abaddon's grip, the dome of Hesamuel's skull felt like soft cardboard which if he so chose could be crushed with ease. But instead, with his free hand *He* reached towards the jet-black pinprick which subtly stood out from the rest of its dark surroundings, and with a thought tore it open to reveal the majestic blue and green of the Border instead. Hesamuel could do nothing but despair as the portal changed shape and the sickening sight ripped open. As they tumbled through the fissure into the crystal blue sky, Abaddon threw Hesamuel to the ground.

'Did you really think it would be that easy?'

But too afraid to move, and struggling to remain conscious, Abaddon's words were lost on him.

'No-one has ever broken free. Never! How did you do it?'

When no reply was given, Abaddon mistook Hesamuel's silence for a last vestige of resolve and crouched to whisper in his ear.

'Come now, you can tell me. How did you do it?'

But still, Hesamuel could not reply.

'Hmm… I do not like being made to look a fool. Tell me now or I will spend the rest of eternity torturing it out of you. I will make you so twisted and broken that even the worst from the very

depths of Hell shall weep at the sight of you. Now... tell me!'

But as Hesamuel's ears rang with noise, the angel's words still went unheard. With a roar of frustration, Abaddon kicked Hesamuel lifting him from the ground and flinging him across the grass to land in a cloud of dirt and confusion. Unable to react, Hesamuel accepted the blow and groaned. In one last effort, using all the strength he could muster, he began to slowly drag himself through the swaying grass, his blood soaked jaw broken and slack, his vision nothing but a misty blur. Abaddon stalked deliberately from behind and stared down at Hesamuel with contempt.

'I can do this for as long as you want. Just tell me how you escaped. Why put yourself through all of this unnecessary torment.'

It was not until Abaddon got closer that he saw Hesamuel's pendulous jaw swaying below his face.

'Ah, I see. Well it's no wonder you cannot reply, is it? Come. Let me fix that for you.'

Stamping down on the middle of Hesamuel's back, Abaddon crushed him into the ground before snatching him up to eye level, smiling as *He* shook Hesamuel's head making his jawbone wobble within the skin.

Taking hold of Hesamuel's jaw, Abaddon snapped it back into position. Hesamuel screamed in agony.

'That's better,' the angel said. Slipping his hand around the front of Hesamuel's throat, *He* squeezed. *'Now, tell me how you escaped.'*

'I... I'll... never... tell...' Hesamuel forced the weakest of smiles.

'I see.'

Quick as lightning, Abaddon struck Hesamuel in the chest sending him flying through the air. This time though, he was semi prepared but still ended up landing in an uncoordinated mess on the ground. Hesamuel knew this was a fight he could never win and was in no doubt Abaddon would spend the rest of eternity torturing him until the Maelstrom and the Light became nothing but myth.

That was when he saw it. Far off in the distance, Hesamuel's eye was distracted by a glimmer of light reflecting off what appeared to be a river. Instantly, and with a heavy heart, he recognised it for what it was. Given the choice, it now remained his only means of escape. He would have to go to the one place where even angels feared to tread.

The Final Death.

Hesamuel considered the souls trapped within Abaddon's hell and his promise to get help, to expose the unseen danger that was bent on destroying every living thing in existence. It had become his duty, his destiny. That was when he realised what he must do.

Closing his eyes and digging deep, Hesamuel stood tall and turned to face Abaddon.

'I know this is a fight I cannot win. You are stronger than me, more powerful, and I know that you can beat me and break my bones but even so, I tell you now that I shall never be afraid of you.'

Abaddon just stared, bemused by Hesamuel's bravery.

'Truly inspiring words. Such a shame only we are here to witness them. Allow me to reply. When I am done with you, your brothers and sisters will feel suffering like never before. Upon you I shall unleash my malice; upon them I shall unleash my wrath. And the Cosm will fall. Now come here!'

Abaddon sprung into the air, catapulting *Himself* at Hesamuel but this time he was ready and also took flight in the direction of the River. With every passing moment, Abaddon gained but this time Hesamuel had a plan. Possibly a suicidal one but it was a plan non-the-less. As the water came into view, Abaddon closed the gap reaching out to grab but Hesamuel ducked and plummeted like a stone towards the River. Confused, Abaddon stopped and watched as Hesamuel nosedived away burning a reckless path towards its glassy surface.

Surely he realised what he was doing? It had to be some sort of trick. Nothing else could explain such idiocy.

'*What are you doing, Hesamuel?*' Abaddon shouted down in confusion.

Ignoring Abaddon's calls, Hesamuel broke the water's surface and gave his body to its icy cradle.

Knowing better, Abaddon stopped just short of the ground and hung in the air.

'*What are you doing, Hesamuel?' Abaddon mused. 'Why have you given yourself to the Final Death? Surely you are not that cowardly? It makes no sense. This must be a trick. It must be.*'

Chapter Fifteen

Present Day

So it was now complete. With Hesamuel and Nick reunited once again, he remembered having risked the Final Death to escape Abaddon and in doing so placing himself into the Cosm's equivalent, coma; the only place where even angels feared to tread. Standing at the cliff edge, he gazed out across the plains searching for the dark angel.

With no more hesitation, Hesamuel held out his hand and summoned the portal to the Maelstrom feeling his anticipation stir as light sparked and crackled against his skin just as before. This time his urgency created a stronger reaction forcing the tear in reality to rip apart.

'*You shall never escape me!*' Abaddon roared. Hurtling from above, *He* slammed into Hesamuel propelling them both through the ragged fissure.

Together they tumbled through the dark toward the glow of the Maelstrom. As they plunged ever nearer, Hesamuel began to smile. Abaddon's anger suddenly turned to panic as *He* realised *His* mistake and the proximity of his unveiling.

Using all of *His* strength the angel stopped, and they hung together in a suspended embrace.

'*Clever, very clever. But not good enough. I warned that you would never escape me, no-one does. I am Abaddon the Destroyer, and you are mine.*'

Hesamuel tried to struggle but Abaddon's grip was solid. With no means of escape, Hesamuel journeyed within himself to regain his inner calm.

'Abaddon, do you remember when I told you that I would never be afraid of you? Well, I'm still here and I am still not afraid. My mind is clear now. I understand your true purpose, and mine. The question is, do you?'

Confused but unwilling to show it, Abaddon's anger flared and *He* squeezed with all the strength *He* could muster.

'Who are you to speak to me this way? I can crush the very light from your pathetic carcass!'

Feeling his body constrict beneath Abaddon's might, Hesamuel tried to strain against the pressure. But then, as his mind relaxed further, he found himself easing out a smile which only fuelled Abaddon's fury and the angel felt an emotion other than hate. Catching *Him* unawares, it was something *He* would have never thought possible, grabbing *Him* by throat like an invisible hand.

Still smiling, Hesamuel began to evaporate in *His* arms in a storm of twisting starlets that danced around the angel before disappearing leaving Abaddon bewildered. Lots of things confused *Him* regarding Hesamuel. He had escaped his cage. Had shown resilience to fear and, had evaded *Him* where no others had done before.

Floating in the darkness, staring at the distant lure of the Maelstrom swirling and playing in its eternal dance, Abaddon felt a terrible stirring inside *His* chest manifesting into something abhorrent. For the first time ever, Abaddon felt afraid.

On the Border, Jeremiah slouched on the grass at the River's edge intrigued by what secrets swam beneath its rippling surface. Had his soul been awake he would have known and understood its purpose, but he was still and forever would be Jeremiah and so, like so much else in his contained existence, the truth remained a mystery to him. Using his cleaver he poked at the water. Nothing happened at first, and then a terrifying force shot through the blade and up his arm threatening to pull him in. He fell back in panic realising his mistake as the blade dropped from his hand and disappeared into the murky depths.

'*I warned you to stay away*,' Abaddon said from behind.

Jeremiah turned with a start.

'What the fuck was that?' he cried.

Ignoring his question, Abaddon grabbed Jeremiah by the face and lifted him off the ground like a doll.

'*Have you outlived your usefulness?*'

Unable to reply, Jeremiah shook his head.

'*Can I still rely on you?*'

Jeremiah tried to nod.

As if hearing a far off call, Abaddon looked to the sky and closed *His* eyes, listening. A smile crept across *His* hard aged face. Abaddon looked at Jeremiah.

'*I have a very special errand for you. You are still useful, aren't you?*'

Again, Jeremiah tried to nod, his wide eyes peering through the gaps in Abaddon's fingers. The angel's grin widened.

'*Now we shall see, Hesamuel. Now we shall see.*'

Chapter Sixteen

At 2.47pm Nicholas Howell was pronounced dead.

Janet continued to hold Nick's hand long after he had passed feeling his skin turn cold until George persuaded her to leave. Andrew had just stood in silence with wide eyes, unable to stop staring at the body of his dead brother until he too was forced to leave by George.

Nick's suffering had dragged on for so long that George was more relieved right now than grieved. His son had finally been allowed the peaceful rest that should have been granted five months ago. Nick's soul was free and from its release they now stood a chance of a fresh start. Shielding their tears, they shuffled through the milling crowds in the hospital foyer, Janet clutching the bag containing Nick's possessions, and they left for home.

For the ward staff, life carried on as normal, Nick being just another tragedy of life's cruel drama. Just another job.

At the main desk, Collins was checking over the rest of the day's schedule while Maureen erased Nick's details from the white board. Neither spoke. Every patient he lost tugged upon his conscience and only time and experience had taught him that when the outcome did not go the way you hoped, there was nothing left but to accept it as fate and carry on. Without that belief he would have never found the heart to cope day in, day out.

Back in Nick's old room, Sarah and Nathan were performing the last offices in preparation for the removal of his body. The porters had been notified and would be along shortly to collect him. That was just how it went. Life carried on.

'You washing or drying?' Sarah asked, snapping on a pair of latex gloves.

'Drying please,' Nathan replied. 'I've washed enough cock for one day thanks.'

Sarah smirked and started cleaning Nick's ears.

Together they removed Nick's catheter, cannulas and the rest of the tubes exiting his body, dumping them into a bio-waste bag.

'You up to much tonight?' Nathan asked as he lifted Nick's head for Sarah to wipe the back of his neck.

'Not really,' she replied. 'Some of the girl's are going into town but to be honest I'm knackered, and I'm on an early tomorrow. You?'

'I was going to try the salsa class at the social but I'm covering for Jess tonight. Apparently she's got *another* hot date with some bloke she snogged in Sammy's last weekend.'

'What happened to the last one?' Sarah asked, looking up from her work. Nathan replied by waggling his little finger at her.

'No!' she said. 'But he was so big everywhere else.'

'Trying to compensate do you think?' he said with a smirk as he towelled Nick's chest. 'Personally, I would think he's a normal size; it's just that she's had that much cock her pelvic floor got left behind years ago.'

'Nathan, that's awful!' Sarah said trying to suppress her laughter. 'You bitch.'

'Hey, just telling as it is.'

Producing a fresh gown, Nathan rolled Nick's body while Sarah dressed him, nice and presentable, just as his mother would have wanted.

'So, have you then?' she asked.

'What, Jess? Do me a favour. She's hangin,' Nathan replied in disgust.

'Just asking,' Sarah said. She slipped a length of green canvass and two bed sheets beneath Nick's body.

'No. Never. She's a total ten pinter! She may get off with a lot of lads but in this town it's not difficult to go for quantity rather than quality. No, definitely not.'

'Okay, just asking. No need to get so defensive. Anyone would think you had something to hide. It's just that I heard this rumour…'

'Piss off.'

They both continued in silence with Sarah smiling to herself as she filled in the first of three death cards.

'All right, look,' Nathan said, stopping to look at her. 'Don't you dare breathe a word of this. Christmas party… last year.'

'You really don't have to tell me, you know,' Sarah said, trying not to laugh. 'Honestly.'

'You'd better not tell anyone.'

'Your secret's safe with me,' she said giving him a mock salute, still mindful not to let her gloved hand touch her skin.

Nathan gave her a stern look as he began wrapping Nick in the sheets like an Egyptian mummy before taping them down to prevent his handiwork unravelling on its journey to the morgue. Sarah wrote out the final two death cards. She taped one to the sheets and placed the other in the front pocket of her uniform.

'Right, glad that's over with,' Nathan said, pulling away his plastic apron and dumping it in the bio-waste.

'Do you still find this a bit creepy?' Sarah asked, doing the same.

'Nah, not really. Not anymore. It's just like they're sleeping. Fancy a coffee? My shout,' Nathan said, opening the door.

'Go on then. Twist my arm,' she replied.

They joined Maureen at the main desk. Collins had returned to his office to close Nick's file.

'Do you still take sugar?' Nathan asked.

'No,' Sarah replied, tapping her stomach. 'Got to

watch the calories.'

'Ooh, Nathan,' Maureen chipped in. 'I'll have a tea, please. Milk, two sugars,'

With a nod Nathan went to the staffroom. Sarah parked herself against the edge of the main desk.

'All done,' she said taking Nick's card from her pocket.

'Thank you,' Maureen said.

A moment of sombreness hung between them as the last record of Nick, a sad little piece of cardboard, sat like a desultory epitaph on the desk.

Is this how we all end up? Sarah thought, and let out a sigh.

'Hey guess what,' she said, desperate to break the mood.

'What?' Maureen asked as she studied a set of patient notes.

'It was true. You know, about Nathan and Jess.'

Straight away, Maureen stopped what she was doing and looked at her in shock.

'No!'

'Yup. At the Christmas party last year.'

'Little sods,' Maureen said. Her eyes were wide with glee.

Just as Sarah was about to continue, the hospital porters entered pushing their shrouded body wagon through the security doors. The simple gurney with its flat metallic sides still managed to fill Sarah with disquieting dread.

'Now then, sexy,' the younger said to Sarah with a thick cockney accent. 'And how are you today?'

'Hello, Geoff,' she replied in a bored tone. 'I'm fine thanks.'

'Good,' he said dragging the word out. 'You know, I reckon you get prettier every time I come up here.'

Sarah gave him short dry laugh and Maureen the

tiniest of looks.

'So, you've got another meat sack for us then. Where is he?'

'If you are referring to the deceased,' Maureen said, 'he is down the corridor in room seven.'

'Cheers, babe,' he said strolling off, winking to Sarah he passed.

'God, I hate cockneys,' Maureen said, not even trying to keep her voice down.

'Me too,' Sarah agreed, scowling at the back of Geoff's smug head as he swaggered away with his sidekick in tow. It would be worth kissing Geoff's colleague just to wipe that smarmy look off his annoying face.

Nathan returned with a tray of hot drinks and joined Sarah on the opposite side of the desk.

'If you both don't mind,' Maureen said, 'this is my work station, not a general dossing area.'

They both stood away, apologising.

'Nathan, I see on the roster that you're covering for Jess tonight,' Maureen said, taking a sip of her tea.

'Yeah well, I've got no plans and she said she'd return the favour,' he replied sensing a mocking hint in her tone.

'Oh, that's nice of her. An early Christmas present perhaps?' she quipped, smiling into her mug.

Nathan looked at Sarah who had found an interesting crack in ceiling. Nathan gave a nervous laugh before gulping his own coffee.

'You know what,' Geoff said as he made his way back up the corridor, 'you lot should change your jobs.'

'What are you talking about now?' Maureen asked.

'You lot should be comedians. I mean it, seriously. Ha ha, very funny.'

'What *are* you going on about?'

'The body? I'm up to my eyeballs today, all right, so come on. Or was this just a plan to get me up here, hey, sexy?'

Sarah gave him another disinterested laugh before stepping away.

'It's the room at the end,' said Nathan, pointing for effect.

'Yeah, the one with the open door,' Geoff indicated. 'That's where we went and unless he's done a Houdini then someone's pulling our leg.'

Sarah and Nathan looked at Maureen in confusion.

'This is ridiculous,' Maureen said. Barging past the porter she marched up the corridor. 'If this turns out to be a game of some sort I will be having very strong words with your manager. This is a ward you know.'

'Lead on McDuff,' Geoff piped from behind.

Entering the room, Maureen stopped dead.

'Nathan, Sarah,' she called.

Both the juniors rushed forward to be confronted with the sight. Strewn across the floor were the dishevelled sheets and death cards but no Nick.

'What the hell?' Nathan said.

'Would someone like to tell me what's going on?' Maureen ordered.

'Told you so,' Geoff said.

'Is this supposed to be your idea of a joke, you sick bastard?' Sarah scolded. She threw the covering off the porter's gurney to expose his lie but the cart was empty.

'Happy?'

'He was a person,' she continued, taking a step towards him. 'Don't you know the meaning of the word dignity?'

'Now hang on a minute,' he started.

Maureen crossed her arms and assessed the scene.

'You two, out,' she said to the porters. 'I need to have a private word with my staff.'

Geoff and his partner did as they were told and shuffled out closing the door behind them.

'Come on then,' Maureen said, expecting a speedy explanation.

'What? I have no idea what's going on. Seriously,' Nathan said as panic began to grow in his gut.

'He's telling the truth,' Sarah concurred. 'We prepped Nick up and left him here not two, three minutes ago. You saw us leave the room.'

'But still, there's no way even Geoff could've pulled off something as sick as this, or so quickly, Nathan reflected. 'It just doesn't make sense.'

'Okay, look,' Maureen addressed them. 'Yes, I did see you leave the room but I think that whatever little trick you've been concocting to fool the port-'

'Whoa!' Nathan interrupted.

'No way!' Sarah blurted. 'We're not lying here. What do you take us for? Do you really think that I would risk my career just to get one up on that dickhead?'

Sarah pointed her trembling finger at the door.

'Seriously, Maureen, we're not lying to you,' Nathan pleaded. 'I swear on my mother's life that we left him here wrapped and ready. I swear it.'

Maureen eyed them both, searching for the slightest hint of guilt and finding none. As a mother she had spent half a lifetime sniffing out ruses and though she agreed with Nathan that while there was not the time or the opportunity for Geoff to do anything that only left the two nurses standing before her.

'If I find out that either of you are lying to me not only will you both be out of here faster than your feet can carry you but I will personally make sure that neither of you work in this profession again. Is that understood?'

'I swear,' Sarah begged, close to tears as the three hard sleepless years it had taken her to get where she was flashed before her eyes. 'We're not lying, I swear.'

'She's right,' Nathan seconded, feeling his legs shake with adrenaline, terrified at the prospect of unemployment. 'Honestly this is nothing to do with us.'

Maureen eyed them. 'Okay, for now I'll believe you.'

Both were too shaken to show any relief.

'If I ever find out that you're trying to make a fool of me or the ward then my promise stands,' she continued.

'We'll get to the bottom of this, I swear,' Nathan promised.

'Yes we will,' Maureen said. She opened the door.

Geoff, who had been listening just beyond the door while his partner had stood at a respectable distance, sprang back as if nothing had happened.

'Right, you,' Nathan growled.

'Nathan,' Maureen warned. 'I shall take care of this thank you very much.'

Nathan moved aside so she could pass.

'All right then. Would one of you like to explain where my corpse has disappeared to?' she said lifting the corner of the sheet covering the wagon, taking another cursory glance inside.

'Hey, don't look at us,' Geoff said. 'We just got here.'

'Yes you have,' she said opening the door to her right. Inside, was an unconscious male newly returned from theatre but no sign of Nick. She moved to the door on her left and found it locked. The room was being used to house the diagnostic equipment and she carried the only key. She tried the next door along and then the next but again with no success. The further down the hall she went the more piqued her face became. Nathan and Sarah could feel themselves inwardly shrinking; their stomach's becoming tight balls of angst. As she approached the door nearest to the front desk Maureen did not even touch the handle. She turned, her face burning with anger at the two nurses shaking their heads at her with pleading eyes. Sarah was close to tears as she watched her nursing career dissolve.

Before Maureen got a chance to speak, Nathan stormed past her.

'I'm not having this,' he exclaimed. 'That body's got to be here somewhere, and when I find it Geoff, I'm going to give you such a fucking kicking.'

'Nathan!' Maureen said. 'I will not have that kind of behaviour on my ward.'

But he was too busy to listen, checking and re-checking all the doors, even searching behind drawn curtains, anywhere he could think of that could be used to hide a body. Sarah joined him by checking any of the areas he had not already searched. In desperation she even looked in the store cupboard but it was to no avail. Nick's body really had vanished.

As the commotion continued, Maureen scanned the ward making sure that Sarah and Nathan's odd behaviour was not upsetting the other patients and visitors.

With nowhere left to search they returned to the main desk more confused than ever, and afraid of Maureen's wrath.

'I just don't understand it,' Nathan said. Sarah stood by his side wondering how this nightmare could have happened. 'He's gone. We can't find Nick's body anywhere.'

'What do you mean, gone? Don't be so ridiculous,' Maureen said.

'Well we never took him,' Geoff said feeling the need to cover his own actions.

'He's not here I'm telling you,' Nathan continued. 'We checked the whole ward and he's not here.'

'But we performed the last office on him in that room, to the letter,' Sarah said.

'Did you two not take me seriously?' Maureen warned.

Nathan lost it, unable to contain his emotions any longer. 'Will you shut up for one minute and listen to us.

The body has gone.'

Maureen fell silent in shock and if not for the gravity of his statement she would have fired him on the spot.

'You swear to me that neither of you two have done anything?' Maureen said to the porters.

'Not us,' Geoff said, shaking his head.

Maureen marched off again in the direction of Collins's office and, managing to contain her own anxiety, knocked on the door entering without waiting. She found him by the window blowing on a hot cup of tea, just staring out at the world. Hearing the door he turned and smiled.

'You caught me,' he said turning back to the window. 'Damn shame about Nick wasn't it? I really thought we were making good progress with him.'

'Erm… yes, big shame. William, we have a problem.'

'Really? What's wrong?' he asked.

'I'm not quite sure how to say this. We seem to have …'

'It can't be that bad, Maureen? What's wrong?' Collins asked, concern entering his voice. He placed the cup on the desk.

'Well, it's to do with Nick. I honestly don't know how to tell you this. William, his body's disappeared.'

Stunned, Collins just stared at her, his expression unreadable.

'I'm sorry,' he began. 'How exactly do you mean… disappeared?'

'Just that. He's gone,' she replied. 'The junior nurses sorted him for transport and then came straight out to me. The porters arrived to take the body to the mortuary but it wasn't there.'

'A body doesn't just disappear.'

'That's what I said. Nathan and Sarah have searched the ward thoroughly and they swear to me that they have had nothing to do with this.'

'And you believe them?'

'I believe them. As for the porters, there simply wasn't the time for them to have done anything.'

'The porters? I don't understand. What have they got to do with this?'

'Nothing, it's just petty nonsense between the staff. William, this is serious.'

A tiny smile touched the corner of Collins's mouth. 'Are you playing a trick on me? What date is it?'

'Will, this is serious,' Maureen said. 'It's not a joke.'

Collins stared at her for a long time. Then all traces of humour fell from his face. 'But this is ridiculous. Bodies don't just disappear. Let me speak to them.'

'Yes, doctor,' Maureen said, following him into the ward.

The atmosphere between the nurses and porters had turned arctic, both sets eyeing each other with distrust.

'All right, what's going on then?' Collins said marching towards the group. 'I want to know exactly who is responsible for this... absurdity.'

'You'd better look at Tweedle Dum and Dee over there,' Geoff said pointedly. 'Don't look at us. We've only just got here.'

Collins looked at the two young nurses.

Nathan felt it his turn to speak. 'You need to keep your mouth shut before I do it for you.' Then to Collins, 'please doctor, we have no idea what's going on here. We prepped him, they came to fetch him, and he was gone. It just doesn't make sense but I swear on my career that I'm telling the truth.'

Sarah nodded in agreement and Collins struggled with what to say next.

'Right, you two with me,' Maureen said to Sarah and Nathan. 'We're going to search this ward again.'

Both complied and followed her.

'And be discreet,' she added.

As they walked away, Collins spoke with the porters who were idly slumped against the wall, the whole fiasco nothing but a huge inconvenience to their day.

'Hello guys,' he said.

They straightened themselves, still able to show a degree of respect.

'Doctor,' they greeted in unison.

'It looks as though we have ourselves a bit of a situation here, doesn't it?'

Both hummed in agreement.

'I'm sure I don't have to remind you that discretion is of the highest importance,' Collins said, throwing authoritative weight into his voice.

'Oh, of course, doctor,' Geoff said with a wink. 'Mum's the word, hey? You can rely on us. No probs.'

'I'm sure I can. This is a delicate situation but one I'm sure will be resolved soon enough.'

'No worries,' Geoff said smiling. 'Is there anything we can do to help?'

'I don't know? Is there anything you can do to help?'

The porters shifted uncomfortably.

Just then, Collins caught sight of Maureen at the far end of the corridor desperate for his attention.

'Excuse me for a moment,' he said to the porters. 'You've found the body?'

'Not exactly but there's something you should see. In any other circumstance I wouldn't normally worry, but well…'

'All right then, let's go take a look,' he said offering her to lead.

As they made their way through the ward, straight away Collins saw that the fire exit door was open. That door was never left open unless for scheduled maintenance and even then he would have been notified beforehand and someone would be stood for security. No work was being carried out today.

'Maureen,' he said, stopping at the open doorway. 'I want you to stay here.'

'Why?' she asked.

'In case the door closes. I don't want to get stuck out there.'

Maureen noticed a slight tell of uncertainty in his eyes.

'I'm coming with you,' she said. 'Nathan, can hold the door.'

'No,' Collins replied. 'I want you to stay here and wait for the others to return, please.'

Seeing his insistence, she agreed. Did he sense something she could not? Whatever it was, his decision was final. With a cocktail of anticipation and dread, Collins stepped through the door onto the steel balcony outside.

Instantly, he was hit by the abrupt change in temperature as the cold wind slapped across his face whipping his tie back over his shoulder. Out there, alone, he was reminded of just how much he hated heights. His fear had been compounded in his childhood by what should have been an innocent cable-car ride with his parents, God rest their souls, whilst on a family holiday in the Swiss Alps. The experience had terrified him and his vertigo had done nothing but escalate ever since. But despite his own anxieties, he was head of department and so carried the responsibility of leading by example.

Collins launched himself at the handrail, grabbing hold of it with both hands for dear life, keeping his eyes focussed onto the metal steps. Not daring to peek over the edge, he remained constantly aware of the distance between him and the ground. What the hell was he doing out here?

Even if he had looked down, what was he expecting to see, someone high tailing it across the car-park with a dead body over their shoulder? The idea was absurd.

If Nick's body had been stolen then it would more likely still be somewhere on the premises. But why? What possible reason could anyone have to steal his patient's body?

To his left was the stairwell leading up, and above him the underside to the next level. Slivers of daylight stabbed through the metal latticework. Without understanding why, something inside Collins told him to climb, that against all his instincts of self-preservation he needed to go up. Keeping his back against the outer wall of the building, he edged his way along the short balcony, the concrete pressing against the fabric of his clothing giving him a false sense of reassurance. As he reached the foot of the stairwell, Collins grabbed hold of the railing, but then a bout of dizziness spun his vision and he fell to the first step, the metal treads scraping his hand. Letting out a cry of shock, Collins hugged the pilasters of the railing, praying to any god that would listen to get him back inside.

'Will, are you all right?' Maureen called from the doorway. 'Let me go instead.'

'No, I'll be fine. Now please, just go back inside.'

Burning with embarrassment, Collins forced his nerves to calm and, releasing himself from the metal bars, climbed to the next level, never once looking down.

'What the hell are you doing out here, Will?' he said to himself. 'What the hell are you trying to prove?'

With his heart pounding, Collins stepped on to the next level and found it empty. For a second time, something inside him was telling him to continue.

The wind became more fierce adding to Collins's anxiety but having made it to the first level he found the next not so difficult to conquer and once up there, again found himself alone. Only one more set of steps remained and then he would be on the hospital roof.

His breathing became more laboured, his feet like lead. Just one more set of stairs. That was all. Just one more and then he could go back down to the safety of the ward with his head held high. Over and over again, he repeated it in his head with every footfall, counting the cold metallic steps leading to the roof. As he reached the top and his eye line broke the surface, he was greeted with the most beautiful sight he had ever seen.

The expansive sky was a brilliant blue. The wind continued to pummel him as if adding to the intensity of the moment. He had done it; he had reached the top and what an exquisite sensation it was. Thoughts of Nick's missing body were momentarily forgotten as an overwhelming sense of achievement filled him with new found courage. Laid out below were the flats of the Lincolnshire farmland stretching out to the coast in a fusion of green fields and ploughed earth. The year's wheat had already been harvested but he could still see swathes of yellow stubble where birds foraged for abandoned ears of corn. The view was astounding.

Collins gave the rooftop a cursory scan. The glare of the unhindered sun reflected off the steel air vents, stench pipes and satellite dishes. He stopped breathing. Through the jungle of metal and plastic Collins saw the outline of a man on the far side of the roof. Ducking behind an air vent, he peeked round the side to keep the person in view.

He was not trained for this type of situation. Collins knew his first action should have been to get straight back down and call security, but he couldn't. What if something happened while he was gone? For all Collins knew it could be a patient on suicide watch from 12A. Could this be the person who had stolen Nick's body? Collins prayed the body had not been tossed over the side. From this height the damage would be like a bug hitting a car windscreen. How could he explain that to Nick's family who had been through too much already?

As quietly as possible, Collins crept across the

stoned tarmac using the vents and dishes for cover. So far his presence had gone unnoticed but the closer he got the louder his shoes crunched against the grit. Reaching nearer, and without the blinding glare of the sun corrupting his view, Collins realised the man was naked and dangerously close to the edge, seeming to bask in the sun's glory, drawing in air like a convict smelling the sweet scent of freedom for the first time in years. Whoever he was, Collins had to get him back inside.

Now no more than fifteen metres away it was clear they were alone. Nick's body was nowhere to be seen.

'Hello!' Collins called across the windy space between them. 'Are you all right? You really shouldn't be up here you know!'

The naked man turned to look at the doctor and as he did the whole of Collins's reality came crashing down. From this moment on and for the rest of his life nothing would ever be the same again.

'Isn't it a beautiful day?' Nick said, smiling before turning back to look at the scenery.

Collins could not speak, could not move. Breathing became difficult. What the hell was happening?

Moving away from the edge, Nick went over to the petrified doctor, suddenly aware of his own nakedness.

'Where am I?' he said trying to cover himself with his hands. 'How did I get up here?'

As Nick approached, Collins staggered back and tripped over a protruding stench pipe. This was not real, this was not happening.

'Please help me,' Nick asked.

Collins strained to reply but still could not find the words.

'Please,' Nick begged. 'What's going on?'

Tripping over another obstruction, Collins's legs finally gave way and he toppled backwards, the grit of the tarmac scoring deep into his palms and elbows. He never once took his eyes away from Nick. His terrified, tear filled eyes, open wide in disbelief.

Chapter Seventeen

'So what do you think then?'

Standing outside the door of Nick's room, Maureen looked to Collins for an answer, for anything to explain what was happening? Together, they stared through the small pane of glass at a man who less than an hour ago had been dead. Now, that very same man was sitting on the end of his bed tucking into a lunch of roast beef as if he had not eaten in days. Collins just stared at him as he tried to make sense of it all before even attempting to offer a possible explanation.

The journey from the roof had been surreal. His fear of heights had vanished and when Collins re-emerged from the fire exit with the look of a man who had been to the edge of sanity, Maureen, Sarah and Nathan had rushed to his aid.

'William, what's wrong?' Maureen had asked. Ignoring her, Collins stared at the open door. That was when Maureen turned to the exit and her mouth dropped open in shock as the last person in the world she ever expected to see stepped through. Blocking out the sun's glare, Nick appeared naked as the day he was born.

Not a word was spoken, not a sound was heard save the distant beeping of the diagnostic machines. A mixture of terror and wonder filled their hearts and the more they stared the more uncomfortable Nick became with his naked state, shamefully trying to cover his manhood.

'Hi,' he said with embarrassment and confusion.

Terrified, Sarah drew in a sharp breath and backed away. Nathan grabbed her round the shoulders and pulled her close.

'No,' she whimpered, her voice rising in panic. 'This can't be right. Doctor, what's going on? What's going on?'

No-one went to Nick's aid, not even to offer him a blanket. They just stood and gawked as their perception of reality imploded. Nick's own fear escalated as Sarah began to cry. And no-one said a word.

* * *

Collins and Maureen continued to stare through the window at Nick.

'So what do you think then?' Maureen asked, unable to look through the window any longer.

'I have no idea,' Collins said, still wearing the same faraway look.

Sarah and Nathan had returned to their duties as best they could but was all the time staying close enough to Nick's room to witness any further developments. The porters had left with strict instructions of discretion.

In his room, Nick was enjoying the most delicious meal he had ever tasted, his mouth alive with every morsel. Yet as he satisfied his hunger he still had no idea where he was or more importantly, how he had come to be on that roof, and it scared him. He had been naked in front of all of those people! Christ, what had he been up to? Where were his parents? Where was Amy? There were so many questions but no-one was speaking to him, so he sat and he waited and ate his lunch. He had vague recollections of the room he was now in, unsettling flashbacks of pain and discomfort, and something else; something dark and elusive hiding in the back of his mind. But the harder he tried to place it the further away it felt. He ate another mouthful of potato.

Nick could see the doctor and nurse staring at him through the tiny pane of glass in the door and had so far chosen to ignore them. Swallowing back his food he had looked across to give them an unsure smile, but Collins and

Maureen had returned it with hard inquiring stares. What the hell had he done?

Nick went back to his lunch and did not look up again.

'You know, at some point someone's going to have to call his family,' Maureen said.

She was right of course; Nick's parents were going to have to be notified that their son was no longer dead. Even in Collins's mind the words sounded ridiculous. He knew if someone were to call him with the same news he would first think they were unwell and then recommend the nearest care facility. Yet here was the miracle on the other side of the door. A man who broke all the rules because not only was he alive but he could also walk and talk like a normal able bodied human being where before his... resurrection (?) he had hardly the strength to lift a beaker of water, or the brain capacity to utter an intelligible word let alone a complete sentence, and he was not only looking at a man who defied all the rules of medical science but also - if he could uncover the secret - the greatest discovery of all time, how to cheat death. Just imagine. For the first time since returning from the roof a tiny smile of ambition touched his lips.

Collins felt another presence other than Maureen's beside him.

'Dr. Collins,' said a clipped but delicate voice. He turned to look at the speaker. 'May I have a private word with you in your office, please?'

Standing beside him was the petite, manicured Ms Caroline Hopper, the hospital administrator. Somewhere in her forties, wearing a grey pinstriped jacket and figure hugging skirt that ended just above the knee with black leather boots, he could not decide whether she was trying to look like a professional business woman or a naughty teacher from a porn movie. Blessed with looks that belied her age, Collins used to find it difficult understanding why such a woman as beautiful and eloquently spoken as she had never married. If ever asked her answer would always be her career commitments but Collins thought there was more to it. Back when he was new in town after his first real transfer, a colleague had invited him to a dinner evening at the local college to help him widen his social circle, and he hated every minute of it. The entire event brimmed with self-importance and backslappers trying to outdo one another with nothing of any real importance to say. That was the first time, after his initial interview, that he had met Caroline Hopper on a social level and straight away she had impressed him. She knew exactly how to work the room. Her partner at the time had been a pleasant enough man called David who Collins had felt the most connection with. It turned out they both shared a passion for scuba diving and as a consequence of that evening arranged a few wreck dives together. Not long after though, David transferred to Edinburgh. While trying to chat with him across the dinner table, Collins became aware of Caroline's attempts to catch his eye in a way he knew he should not respond to. He remembered just how uncomfortable she had made him feel as she leant across absorbing his conversation with seductive interest. As the evening dragged on, her flirting became more intense. At one point, Collins had caught the contained anger in David's eye and from that point on made a conscious effort to include him in every conversation, much to Caroline's displeasure. Very quickly, Collins recognised her as a woman used to getting what she wanted from men naive enough to fall for her manipulative charms. He had met women like this before so was aware of the warning signs. When the evening had thankfully come to an end, Collins escaped to his car without so much as a by-your-leave and had reached the car park just in time to catch the tail end of an almighty argument between Caroline and David. Since that evening he made sure never to be left alone with the woman.

'Of course, Ms Hopper. Maureen, would you like to accompany us?'

'In private, if you don't mind, doctor,' Caroline said.

Trying his best to appear jovial, Collins motioned for her to lead the way and they both disappeared into his office.

'Close the door please,' she said, placing herself in the chair behind his desk. Collins obliged before turning to face her, connecting his hands behind his back. 'Please, sit won't you.'

'I prefer to stand if it's all the same, thank you,' he replied.

'Suit yourself. So, is it true?'

'I'm sorry. Is what true?'

'Come on, William. Let's not play games. I've got rumours of misdiagnosis and your department declaring patients dead when they're fit and healthy flying all over the hospital, so let's just get down to it shall we?'

Those damn porters, Collins thought.

'If you are referring to the patient, Nicholas Howell, there was no misdiagnosis. He was dead.'

'You watched him draw his final breath did you?' she asked, leaning forward to rest her elbows on his desk. Collins made a conscious effort to not instinctively glance down the open neck of her blouse.

'Well, no, not me personally but my staff are very capable of dealing with the situation. If, on the other hand, you're asking if I pronounced him then yes, I did.'

'Then you can't say that you saw him die.'

'I think you must have misheard me. I didn't see him die but I did pronounce him dead. My staff are very good at what they do, and we all know a dead body when we see one or else what would be the point of investing in all this very fine and expensive machinery. They are trained and qualified staff nurses. I don't need to hold their hands and wipe their noses,' he said feeling his temperature rise.

'Well I'm sorry, William but someone needs to re-evaluate their position. I don't think you fully comprehend the gravity of this situation. Do you have any idea about the legal ramifications?'

'*Legal* implications?' Collins repeated, pinching his lips together. 'I'm sorry Caroline but I think it's you that's failing to comprehend. Nicholas Howell died after slipping back into a coma. When he first awoke he was practically vegetative. After a few weeks he still had hardly any bodily control, limited vocal functions and only the barest awareness of his surroundings. He died, and yet now here he is sitting in that room walking and talking like you or me as if nothing has happened. For God's sake woman, will you just look at the facts for one moment?'

'Woman?' Caroline's eyes flared. 'Facts? The facts are that you pronounced a developing patient dead.'

'Look, this is confusing me just as much as anyone. We could be looking at the greatest medical phenomenon of all time and all you care about are law suits? Give me twenty-four hours to do some tests on him. Try and find out what's going on with him.'

'I beg your pardon? What the hell do you think this is? Do you have any idea of the storm this is going to create? No, you do not get twenty-four hours to perform tests. You don't even get one hour. What you will get is the opportunity to pick up this phone and contact his family.' She snatched up the receiver to emphasise her point, 'and explain to them why I shouldn't fire you here and now. In the meantime, I'm scheduled for a meeting with the hospital's legal team to find out what our position is and just how much damage we can expect to take. Christ, William, is it true that the juniors performed the last office on him?'

'Because he was dead!' Collins shouted.

'Well he bloody well should have been after that. It's lucky he didn't suffocate!'

'Why are you not listening to me?'

'Enough of this. Get on the phone and do as you're told. Thanks to you and your department I now have the day from hell,' she said, standing to leave.

Making her way around the desk, Caroline went for the door handle. Collins stopped her with a hand on the shoulder.

'No-one in my department has been negligent. We know our jobs.'

Caroline looked to where his hand was placed against the lapel of her jacket. To her childlike frame it looked huge.

'I would be very careful if I were you William,' she warned with an iciness that came easy to her. 'Given the circumstances of our meeting, and the fact that we are behind closed doors, who do you think a tribunal would believe in a harassment case?'

Struck with shock, Collins removed his hand, placing as much distance between them as he could. Damn it, this was exactly the reason he swore never to be alone with her and he had walked straight into it. She smiled at him.

'Now, be a good boy and get on the phone,' she said with an air of superiority before swishing out the door, slamming it closed behind her.

Collins stood motionless in shock. What the hell had just happened?

Moments later he emerged from his office like a man on a mission. If ever he needed a kick up the arse then this was it. Outside, Maureen, Sarah, and Nathan waited for him like a gaggle of street urchins, their faces expectant and fearful. Before any of them had an opportunity to speak, Collins took the lead.

'Where's Nick?'

'He's still in his room,' Maureen replied. 'What happened in there? What did she say?'

'I'll tell you all now so that you heard it from me first. Caroline Hopper is implying... no, actually she's not implying at all, she is openly accusing that either one or all of us have been negligent but I would say it's a safe bet she'll be gunning for me.'

They all erupted in protest knowing full well what they had seen and were still trying to come to terms with.

'All right, all right. *We* know the truth but that is not how she or the courts will view it,' he continued. 'Caroline has told me to call Nick's parents and explain the mistake we have made.'

'But this is utter crap,' Nathan objected.

'You don't have to tell me that,' Collins said. 'That's why I want you to call all the relevant departments and get as many tests done on him as possible. If this is to go legal we'll need as much ammunition as we can get. I don't know about you but I for one would like to know how a dead coma victim just wakes up and starts walking around. This is colossal and I am not about to let that witch destroy me or my department.'

'Right then,' Maureen barked. 'Nathan you call radiography. Sarah, get onto the path lab. I want full scans together with blood, saliva, and skin samples. Do *whatever* you have to do to make this happen. I don't think I need to remind you that all our jobs are on the line.'

'Yes ma'am,' the two juniors said in unison before rushing off.

As they disappeared, Maureen turned to Collins.

'William, I'll take care of the ward. I know its short notice but I'm sure I can organise some bank staff within the hour. Did something happen in there? Is everything okay?'

'I'm fine. Let's just make sure we get those samples before it's too late,' he said, grateful for her support.

'Do you think it already is?' Maureen asked.

For a moment their eyes met and Collins felt sure she understood their predicament all too well.

'Not daft are you,' he said with weak smile. 'I think you know as well as I that Caroline Hopper will do all she can to get her stories circulating first to save her own skin, even if it means sacrificing ours. All I want are those samples. In all my years I have never heard of, let alone seen, anything of this magnitude. No-one has. This is too wonderful a thing to let just walk out the door.'

'What are you saying?'

'Nothing, I… just ignore me. I think it is time for me to speak with my patient,' Collins said, and walked away.

Maureen watched him, worried and confused, as the reality of the day's events sank in. This was insane. The whole thing was like something from The Twilight Zone. This sort of thing never happened to real people; it was a late night movie at best. She had chosen a career in medicine because she not only felt a vocation to help people but because it was dependable. Science was solid and real. When a patient was ill you used the skills, the medicine, and the equipment at your disposal to nurse them back to health. There was no voodoo to medicine. It was about the precise implementation of drugs and practices applied at the right moment for the right condition. Medicine was real, tangible, and so there had to be a justifiable reason as to why this was happening.

Collins entered Nick's room and closed the door.

'Hello,' he said.

'Hello,' Nick replied.

'How are you feeling?'

'I feel fine… thank you,' Nick replied, finding new interest in the condition of his lunch giving it a cursory prod with his fork. 'I'm really sorry about the roof thing. I have no idea how I got up there. Have I caused much trouble?'

'Trouble?' Collins could no longer hold back his smile of excitement. 'No, Nick, you've caused no trouble at all.'

'It's just that I get the feeling I've done something wrong, you know. You all keep staring at me.'

'Nick, do you know who I am?'

Nick shook his head.

'Perhaps I should introduce myself,' he said, breaking the distance between them and offering Nick his hand. 'I am William Collins, but you can call me Will. I am a doctor here at the hospital, and this is my ward.'

Nick stared at him with fearful eyes before accepting his handshake.

Transfixed, Collins kept the shake going for longer than was comfortably necessary finding himself unable to let go, amazed by the warmth of Nick's skin, the human clamminess of his hand. Unsettled, Nick retrieved his hand and looked at him unsure.

'I'm sorry,' Collins said. 'I hate to have to rush you but time really is of the essence. Please tell me, what is the earliest thing you remember?'

For a moment, Nick just sat on the edge of the bed staring at the wall. Images of darkness and pain flashed into his mind. Of Abaddon's evil face and Jeremiah stalking across the grasslands wielding his rusty cleaver dripping with blood. Instantly, the images were gone just as quickly as they had appeared. Nick froze in shock at the vividness of the macabre impressions and the genuine terror they produced.

'What is it? Are you all right? What do you remember?'

'I... yes... I'm fine,' Nick replied.

'What did you see?'

'I'm not quite sure.'

'Please, take your time and try again,' Collins coerced.

Closing his eyes this time, Nick began to concentrate on summoning back the images and, steadily, more and more strange events filtered into his mind. 'It's dark.'

Collins watched, mesmerized, hanging on his every word, listening without a sound for fear of breaking the spell.

'It's night time. I'm walking down a street. I can see shops.'

'Do you know where you are?' Collins said, his voice teetering on a whisper.

Nick gasped and his eyes snapped open.

'Nick, what's wrong?' Collins cried. 'What did you see?'

Nick's breathing became trapped in his chest as his eyes began to water.

'It's all right,' Collins soothed, placing a reassuring hand on Nick's shoulder. 'Calm. It's all right. There, that's better, nice and calm. Now… tell me, what did you see?'

'Light. Blinding white light, and… pain. Something hitting me hard. Doctor, what happened to me?'

Collins could feel his own apprehension rising, and a tiny crack appeared in his professional veneer. Up until now his resolve had held strong, carrying him through the worst of this strange and unbelievable event but, sat here facing Nick, facing his overwhelming anguish, feeling his misery reach out for solace and answers, Collins's stoic facade began to falter. So, just as he had done before, Collins leaned forward with his hands clasped together and told Nick the whole sad and sorry truth of his condition, though this time purposefully omitting the section relating to his return from death.

When he was done the doctor straightened his posture and apologised. Nick stared into space absorbing the information.

'A car accident?'

'Yes,' Collins confirmed. 'You momentarily slipped away in the ambulance en route. The paramedics revived you, but you fell into a coma on the operating table.'

Nick exhaled, his mind going numb as he struggled to cope with the truth being spoken so bluntly.

'And I was gone for how long?'

'Five months.'

Nick cupped his mouth with his hands as he tried to remember the tiniest detail of anything relating to the accident. He remembered a blinding white light and the sensation of something striking every inch of his body all at the same time. Had the car headlights engulfed his vision? Could that have been the moment his life was ripped away? His thoughts moved to his family and his friends but most of all, Amy.

'What about my parents? They know I'm awake, don't they?'

Collins shifted uncomfortably.

'Yes, of course they do,' he lied as something cold and self preserving switched on inside him and his whole demeanour changed. 'I was talking to them only just this morning... by telephone. I'm surprised you don't remember. I think we should do some more tests on you just to make sure that everything is okay. It's better to be safe than sorry.'

'Well, of course. Whatever you say,' Nick agreed. 'I still can't remember how I got on the roof, and you say that you told me about my parents this morning? I don't remember any of it.'

'Don't worry. Your memory will come back eventually. All I want from you is to get as much rest as you can. Allowing things to worry you will only slow the healing process.'

Nick smiled with gratitude. 'I'll try my best.'

Just then there was a knock at the door. Through the small glass panel they could see Sarah's head bobbing about on the other side. Still trying to remain calm, Collins got the door for her and she entered carrying a tray of equipment. Straight away, Nick registered her nervousness, the way her eyes never left him for a second. Sarah placed the implements on the farthest edge of bed.

'Hello Nick,' she said, trying to steady the wobble in her voice.

'Hi,' he replied, looking from her to the doctor.

'I... I'm going to take some samples from you, if that's all right?' she asked, fumbling with one of the swab wrappers. Eventually, she managed to tear it open and pluck out the swab. 'Okay... could you just open your mouth for me, please?'

Watching her, Nick obliged tilting his head back. With a noticeable apprehension she reached inside his mouth and took a sample of saliva before placing the swab into a small plastic vial and screwing its tiny red cap in place. Marking the label with a fine black pen she placed the container on the tray, her movements slow and deliberate. Next she unwrapped one of the Vacutainers and looked at him fearfully. Nick stared at the quivering needle before looking to Collins who stepped in, gently relieving her of the device.

'It's all right nurse, I'll take over from here.'

'Yes... yes of course. I'm sorry.' Not looking back, she left the room, relieved to be away.

Nick remained on the bed, confused and unsettled.

'Is she all right?' he asked.

'I'm really sorry about that; must be first time nerves. Junior, you know. I'll take care of you.'

Nick fell silent as Collins snapped on a fresh set of latex gloves, wiggling his fingers for comfort.

'Have you ever given blood before?' he asked.

'I... don't remember,' Nick replied.

'Not to worry, it's quite painless, I can assure you. Would you prefer to remain sitting or lie down?'

'This is cool. I mean, sitting is fine.'

'Right then,' Collins said slipping a tourniquet around Nick's arm. Using the hand pump attached, Collins gave it a few blasts of air until the strap clenched tight. 'How does that feel?'

'Feels fine.'

'One more for luck then,' he said and gave the pump another squeeze.

Nick felt the band tighten.

'Could you just clench your fist open and closed for me? That's it. Right, I think we're ready.'

The vein in Nick's arm dilated and Collins massaged it with his thumb. Then he sterilised the area with a small pad.

'Ready?'

'Yup,' said Nick feeling the nerves in his stomach rise again at the sight of the tiny needle.

'You may feel a slight scratch. Just relax and this will all be over in no time.'

Nick exhaled and clenched his fist, turning his face away from the sight.

'Okay, just relax your hand for me. That's better. It's better for the blood flow.'

As the nurses tended to do all the manual hands on work it had been well over a year since Collins had even touched a needle but, with the confidence of his training, he inserted it smoothly. As soon as he saw the flashback of blood he levelled the needle off and advanced it a little further into the vein to stabilise its hold.

'Feeling all right?'

'Fine,' Nick replied, intensely aware of the thin shaft of metal penetrating his skin.

'Good good,' said Collins feeling his own confidence increase. Nick watched with morbid fascination as the small plastic vial began to fill with his own blood. It was dark and thick.

'Not afraid of plasters are you?' he asked with a grin. Nick gave a short laugh and smiled as his tension eased.

'Can I ask a question?' Nick asked.

'Of course you can,' Collins replied as he removed the vial of blood replacing it with another empty one.

'What's next? What I mean to say is, I feel fine but obviously there's my memory. Will I have to stay at the hospital or do you think it would be all right for me to go home?'

'Ah, well, what with your memory loss and the little incident with the roof today I think it would be best, for the time being, if you remained here with us. Just to be on the safe side, you understand. I'm certain your parents will be along soon anyway.' Sweat was beginning to dampen the collar of his shirt.

'Okay. I just wondered. That was all.'

'This must all be very confusing for you.'

'If I'm honest, I think I'll be a lot happier when I get to see my parents again. No offence.'

'None taken,' Collins said as the burden of his guilt became just that little bit heavier. 'It's completely understandable. Anyway, as I said, they should be along soon.'

Nick smiled eager to probe Collins about Amy but too embarrassed to ask. Instead he held his silence until the doctor finished his work then, with his tray of samples, left the room.

In the corridor, Collins went over to the main desk where the three nurses were waiting.

'Dr. Collins, I'm so sorry,' Sarah pleaded with tearful eyes.

'Please, don't worry. Under the circumstances I think anything can be forgiven today. You can make amends by taking these down to the path lab for me if you would.'

'Yes, of course. Right away,' Sarah said transferring the items into a sample bag and turning to leave, but before she got halfway up the corridor Collins called out her name.

'Yes doctor?'

'Stay with them. Do not let those samples out of your sight, and when you have the results I want everything including what's left of the samples returned here.'

'Yes doctor.'

Collins returned his attention to Maureen and Nathan. 'Right, what's the situation with radiology?'

'I've called in a couple of favours,' Nathan said seeming to enjoy the action. 'They're prepped and ready whenever we are. There's just one thing though.'

Collins remained silent waiting for Nathan to continue.

'They already knew about Nick. This thing is everywhere.'

'What? What were they saying exactly?'

'Not much but the inference is negligence,' he said.

'And what do you think?'

'I'm sorry, I don't understand the question? You know what I think. It's crap.'

'Then let's focus on that and do the best we can to figure out what's happening. This is our only chance.'

'Of course, doctor. Would you like me to take him down now?'

'Yes, right away, and I'm coming with you.'

'William... do you think that's wise?' Maureen interrupted. 'It's not really the norm is it? You would only attract more attention to yourself, and if Caroline Hopper ever found out we were doing this... well.'

Collins's shoulders dropped. He knew she was talking sense.

'Damn that woman. All right, Nathan, I'm putting all my faith in you. Nick returns here with no complications. Is that understood?'

'You can rely on me,' Nathan said.

'Go to it then.'

Unfolding a wheelchair, Nathan made his way to Nick's room. Collins and Maureen watched him in silence. They were concerned, not because it was Nathan, but because of the mounting pressure. If rumours of negligence were already spreading through the building mud tended to stick and despite every good deed that followed after this day a bad reputation was a hard thing to shake. Collins needed these results.

Nathan found Nick hunkered down on the opposite side of the bed with his back against the radiator and his head in his hands. From his blotchy cheeks and puffed up eyes it was clear to see he had been crying.

'All right, mate,' he said, without being too intrusive. 'Are you okay?'

'Why does everyone keep asking me that?' Nick replied, wiping his face using the corner of his sleeve.

'Look, I know you probably don't feel like doing this but, I've been told to take you down to radiology for scans; doctor's orders and all that.'

'Sorry, mate. Ignore me. He mentioned something about it.'

Nick's words fell away.

'Come on. Let me help you up. It doesn't take very long and it's completely painless.'

'Yeah, right, whatever. Let's just get it over with,' Nick said making to walk out the room.

'Whoa a minute,' Nathan stopped him at the door. 'Where are you going? You get to travel in style, mate.'

He patted the seat of the wheelchair and a tiny smile touched the corner of Nick's mouth.

'Look at it this way,' Nathan said as Nick lowered himself into the seat. 'At least you're still breathing.'

As Nick was wheeled up the corridor, Collins and Maureen watched them all the way to the security doors until they disappeared into the elevator foyer. Nick pressed the button then stared out of the windows at the world beyond wishing he could see his parents. From his low position in the chair, the ground was hidden but the sky was still as clear and perfect as it had been on the roof. Though the intense sunlight splintered against the glass he did not squint. He just closed his eyes and soaked in its glory.

The bell pinged, the elevator doors parted and they moved inside. The ride was bumpy. They entered the ground floor and Nathan wheeled Nick through a maze of corridors to radiology, pleased they had managed to arrive without incident or unwanted questions. So far so good.

Manoeuvring the chair, Nathan used his back to push open the double doors pulling Nick in with him.

'Morning,' Nathan called to the radiographer sat at his control desk tucking into his second lunch of the day.

With Nick present, the radiographer refrained from greeting Nathan with his usual 'morning, shit stick' instead plumbing for a safe 'hello'.

'Go on through while I get Bertha warmed up,' he said abandoning his BLT to tune the diagnostics.

Bertha was the newly installed MRI scanner, his pride and joy.

'Do you have any metal objects on you?' Nathan asked Nick, more as a formality than anything else.

Nick replied in the negative and was given a set of ear defenders.

'Gets a bit bangy in there but you'll be okay. I went in once. Fell asleep.'

Nick fitted the defenders into place and positioned himself on the table protruding from the mouth of the scanner like a huge tongue.

With Nick in place, Nathan left the room, appearing on the other side of the screen beside the radiographer.

'So, that's him then?'

Nathan refused to reply.

Suddenly, there was a squeal of feedback as the radiographer's voice filled the room.

'Hi Nick. How are you feeling?'

Nick raised his thumb in the direction of the window.

'Okay. In a minute the table will slide you into the scanner. While the scanner's operational I'll need you to stay as still as possible. If you start to feel claustrophobic just tilt your head back and look up. The end of the tube is open so you'll be able to see out into the room behind you. All right?'

Nick raised his thumb again and on that note heard a faint clicking sound. The table jolted and Nick was fed into the mouth of the machine. He closed his eyes and the process began.

Chapter Eighteen

Nick had spent the best part of an hour trapped inside the banging confines of the scanner, much longer than was usual but Collins had wanted him tested thoroughly. After the MRI, every inch of his body was bombarded with radiation particles from the X-ray machine before he was returned to his chair and left to sit alone in the empty corridor while Nathan and the radiographer chatted out of earshot.

Sat in his chair like a charlatan, Nick saw an elderly couple appear at the far end of the corridor. Though the woman was in obvious pain she held her dignity as her husband kept pace beside her, supporting her by the elbow when needed. Pride and an unwillingness to accept the truth of her situation prevented her from using a wheelchair and in the presence of such stoicism Nick felt an even bigger fraud. Shamefaced, he realised that physically he felt fine even despite the supposed injuries Collins had described to him. Despite all the fuss being made, Nick knew in his gut that there was nothing wrong with him. The old couple passed and he accidentally locked eyes with the old lady. To his astonishment, regardless of her pain, she still had the grit to smile at him. Nick smiled back then looked to his lap.

Nathan came back into the corridor. 'Right then, shall we get going?'

'Ready when you are,' Nick replied.

'Good. The doctor will be getting worried.' Nathan gripped the rubber handles of the chair and pushed Nick back towards the elevators.

Nick looked back towards the old couple who were now a little further down the corridor. The lady was searching for something in the bag she carried which had seen better days. Her husband tried to help but was batted away, the pain throbbing through her manifesting itself into irritation when she thought no-one was looking.

She should have this chair, not him, Nick thought.

Nick could feel his heckles rising, pumping him with the determination needed to fight past the awkwardness to speak his mind. 'Why?'

'Why what?' Nathan asked at the same time as offering a polite nod to a passerby.

'Why will the doctor be so worried about me? I mean, not being funny but I feel absolutely fine so why would he be worried?'

Nathan mentally stuttered. 'Well, you know, what with this morning and everything.'

'The roof thing? Yeah, don't remind me. I still can't remember getting up there,' Nick said, frustrated by his amnesia.

'Yeah,' Nathan said, still struggling to come to terms with the incident.

'It's just that even though there's load's I can't remember,' Nick continued. 'It's weird, like none of it actually happened. Everything around me just feels surreal. Apparently I died?'

Nathan stopped and looked down at the back of Nick's head.

'He told you?'

'Yes,' Nick said turning to look up at the nurse.

'I can't believe he told you. Please, tell me, what's it like?'

'What, dying? I don't know. I said I can't remember.'

'There must be something, like a tunnel of light or ... I don't know. Something?'

'Sorry, I don't remember. I can only just remember the accident and then the next thing I'm up on the roof freezing my nads... well, you know what I mean.'

They started moving forward again and when they reached the elevator the doors were already open and waiting. Nathan rushed them both inside before the doors had a chance to close again.

'So, you don't remember anything before you died then?'

The elevator began to move.

'I remember snippets, like flashes of memory but nothing I can put my finger on.' Nick's voice saddened.

'So you don't remember your treatment then?'

'In the ambulance? No, but by the sounds of it I wasn't in much shape then.'

'No, I mean here, in the hospital,' Nathan insisted.

The elevator came to a jolting stop and the doors parted.

'I don't understand. You asked me if I remembered anything about the period before I died.'

'Exactly, this morning, do you remember anything before this morning?'

Nick fell silent and it took Nathan a moment before the penny dropped. When it did, the impact of his mistake struck like an atom bomb. His career was over.

'This morning?' Nick asked. 'Why are you talking about this morning? Five months ago. I'm talking about five months ago... when I had my accident.'

'Of course, my mistake. Forget I said anything.'

'No, hang on. The doctor told me that I'd been in a coma for five months. He told me I died in the ambulance but they managed to bring me back.'

'That's right,' Nathan said, his eyes focussed dead ahead on the security doors of the ICU ward.

'So what are you talking about then? What happened this morning?'

Nathan remained silent. Though the chair was still moving Nick turned to face him.

'What happened this morning?' he persisted.

But Nathan ignored him, instead swiping his security pass against the scanner to activate the doors.

'Damn it, tell me! What happened this morning?'

Nathan looked down at him, unable to speak, his conscience struggling with whether or not to tell the truth but failing to find the words. Finally, he snapped. None of this bullshit mattered anymore. His career was over and he knew it. He could already hear Caroline Hopper churning the disciplinary cogs into motion and, together with Sarah's, his reputation was about to be destroyed. Two nurses who between them could not even recognise a dead patient from a live one then bagged and tagged him anyway? Who would employ them after that? They knew the truth, they all did, but given the apparent facts and the overwhelming evidence of a walking, talking, breathing Nick, only a madman would believe such insanity. With nothing left to lose and no regret Nathan decided to relieve himself of the secret's burden.

'I'm sorry, Nick,' he said, discovering a maturity that even surprised him.

'Just tell me. I know something's not right with me. Is there a chance I could die again?'

'You really don't remember, do you? You've been conscious for about two weeks, but until today could hardly speak or move. You were doing all right but then something happened, a physical decline, and your condition got worse until this morning you died. We tried our best but your body just couldn't cope anymore. Then a miracle happened. Sarah and I prepped your dead body for transport to the morgue but the next thing we knew you just disappeared. I mean vanished. We searched everywhere and then eventually Dr Collins found you on the roof, alive and completely back to normal. No scarring, nothing. No-one can explain it. It's a miracle.'

Nick just stared at him, his face shifting between

mockery and confusion. Nathan stared back with the eyes of the lost.

'But... that's impossible.'

'You don't need to tell me that.'

'What is this?'

'What? You think that I'm making it up? You think that I would risk three years of studies and a career just to wind you up?'

Nick went silent.

'So my family, my girlfriend, they all think I'm still dead?'

Nathan nodded. Nick sat back, beyond stunned. This was not happening, it couldn't be.

'This is some kind of joke, isn't it?' he asked.

'You fucking idiot, of course it's not. I'm sorry. I shouldn't have said that. I'm so sorry. Please, forgive me.'

Nick fell silent again.

'Please, I'm sorry,' Nathan continued. 'This is as serious as it gets. God knows what you must be thinking but I'll tell you now I'm scared shitless. I'm going to lose my job because of this.'

'What?'

Nathan just looked at him with a grim expression.

'Why? It's not your fault... is it?' Nick asked.

'No! It's nobody's fault. Like you said, it's just... completely impossible.'

'I need to get home,' Nick said. 'I've got to let my family know I'm all right.'

'You'd best speak to the doctor about that. It's not my decision to make.'

'It's not his either. I need to go home.' Nick made to stand.

'You need to sit down,' Nathan said clamping his hand down on Nick's shoulder. 'Don't fuck about. I'm already in enough trouble. Just see the doctor. He'll more than likely send you home anyway. Maybe I shouldn't have told you.'

Nick relaxed back down. 'Thanks for being honest with me anyway.'

'No problem,' Nathan said unsmiling. 'Just hold the door open for me will you.'

At the main desk, Collins was waiting to greet them giving Nathan an inquiring look. Nathan returned it with a nod which seemed a sufficient reply. During the short exchange, Nick studied Collins's face for the slightest signs of subterfuge. There was none. Outwardly, the doctor seemed calm, in control, yet unbeknownst to Nick his insides were a churning mess of angst. All of his thoughts were bent towards the outcome of the tests. He needed for them to prove something, anything that could save his career.

Back inside his room, Nick positioned himself on the end of the bed. Nathan wanted to say something more, words of comfort perhaps? In confessing to Nick he felt as though he now held a further obligation towards him.

He hovered in the doorway.

'Nick, there's something I need to say.'

Nick looked at him with tired eyes as the reality of what he had learned began to take its toll.

'I don't understand any of this,' Nathan continued, 'none of us do, but your family is still out there and I know that they miss you. Just remember that. What happened to you has happened for a reason, even if we don't understand it. Stay safe.'

Nathan then closed the door on his way out. In the years to come he would sit and think back to this day and wonder what exactly had made him say those words. At the time it had just seemed like the right thing to say, but after realising what he later came to know, what they all came to know, Nathan wished he could have taken it back.

Alone and afraid, Nick remained in deep confusion. Dead, alive, dead again and alive yet again and despite it all he had no memory whatsoever. All of his life he had been aware, had known what was going on within his own sphere of existence. His understanding of the world around him had meaning and solidity, and to some extent it had been safe, until now. Nothing would ever be the same again. There seemed to be no rules anymore, no law to the order of the world, and with no rules and no laws he realised he was now free to do exactly what he pleased. And right now he wanted nothing more than to see his family again. To let them know he was alive, waiting for them. They must know by now. The doctor must have informed them of the mistake, surely? Nick stared out of the window into the blue sky beyond and ached to be free.

Between Nick's return to his room and Collins entering again time appeared to drag and yet as he watched the door open he realised this would be his only chance to test the doctor's integrity.

'The scans went well I take it?' Collins asked, still battling to control the mounting pressure.

'Yep, not bad,' Nick replied.

'Good. We should have the results by the end of the day. Maybe then we can ascertain exactly what took place earlier.'

'That sounds great. Doctor...'

'Please, call me Will.'

'When will I see my parents? They still haven't been yet,' he asked, determined for his question to be answered.

'Well Nick, I... I don't know when they will choose to visit, I'm just the doctor.'

'But I've been here for five months now. Surely their visiting times must follow some sort of routine by now?'

'Well, yes, of course but... there are so many patients. I could not possibly keep track of the comings and goings of everyone that entered the ward.'

'So they might not even come today?'

'Maybe, maybe not. I really wouldn't know.'

'Well, do they normally come daily?'

'Nick, please, what is this all about? Are you feeling all right?'

'I *feel* fine. I would just really like to see my family, that's all.'

Collins felt his blood go cold. 'I'm sure they'll be along soon enough but, after all, it is the middle of the day. They'll have to be at work just like the rest of us, I should imagine.'

'You're right, of course, I should've thought of that.' Nick sat and pondered for a moment. 'Would you mind if I called them? Just to be able to hear their voices, it would mean so much.'

Collins panicked. Fobbing Nick off about visiting hours had been an insidious yet simple diversion but what excuse could he concoct for not allowing Nick a phone call? Even criminals got a phone call.

'It would really help if I could just hear their voices. I promise not to be too long.'

'Err... yes. I... let me see what I can do about that. We're not really supposed to use the ward phone for private calls but... leave it with me.'

'That's okay. If I could borrow some money I could use one of the payphones downstairs. Or borrow a mobile perhaps?'

'We're not really supposed to use mobile phones on the ward, and besides I would really like to see what the test results show first before we start letting you roam around the hospital on your own,' Collins said, desperate to punch his way from the corner he was pinned to. 'The last thing we want is for you to have another episode like this morning.'

Nick stared at the doctor with masked contempt, recognising his lie. Using a strained smile, Collins made his excuses and retreated back to the safety of his office slamming the door behind him. At the main desk, Maureen had been left to wonder what was going on.

Nick's mind was now set. Regardless of what excuses the doctor might create it was time for him to leave this place. As incredible as it was, if what Nathan had said was true then he needed to get home, to make his family aware he was alive and well. To find Amy and hold her once again, to feel the warmth of her kiss and absorb her sweet aroma. At worst, all that Nathan had divulged could just turn out to be a huge misunderstanding, and Nick's penance would be the embarrassment of returning to the ward. It was a price he was willing to pay as his insides burned with a feeling too strong to ignore. Clothed only in a hospital gown he realised it would be impossible to avoid suspicion but he had to try.

Rushing over to the door, Nick spied out of the small window looking down what he could see of the corridor, just managing a glimpse of the main desk. It was abandoned. Turning the handle, he paused one last time before slipping out of the room. Quietly, softly, he closed the door again and inched his way up the empty corridor keeping a watchful eye out for staff. No more than halfway down, he froze as Sarah appeared from behind a cubicle curtain. But, without seeing him, she turned in the opposite direction and disappeared into the booth next door.

Not wasting any more time, Nick reached the main desk and from there saw the security doors. He paused one final time to look at the ward that had been his home for the past five months yet which he had no memory of. It was easy to leave. With no more hesitation, Nick ran as hard as he could for the doors, the sight of his impending freedom filling his legs with momentum and, in one fluid motion he hit the doors, slapping the security button, and was through.

At the elevator, Nick bounced on his toes as

adrenaline coursed through him like a steam train. His eyes flicked from the metal doors of the elevator to the self closing security door and back again. As the security door clicked shut he heard the reassuring ping of the elevator bell. When the doors parted, Nick was confronted by a morbid looking family laden with magazines and treats from the shop downstairs. They stared at him with distrust but Nick's only concern was to get them out the way and him to safety. As they bustled clear of the elevator car, he practically fell over them to get through and as he pressed the ground floor button, throwing his back against the mirrored wall of the cabin in relief, the family just gawked at him until the doors slid shut. Feeling the motion of the cabin descend Nick exhaled with a smile of relief.

But it was short lived.

The elevator stopped at the first floor and a teenage girl decked out in makeup and gold joined him. Too busy texting, her thumbs moving at an incredible rate, she ignored him. The ground floor was reached in silence.

'Excuse me,' Nick said conscious not to appear threatening. She looked at him with a bored expression. 'Hi. I was wondering if you could help me, please.'

It took the girl a moment to reply.

'Erm… I don't know-'

'I… I need to call my parents but I've got no money,' he said smiling. Nick patted the gown against his thighs to accentuate his predicament.

The doors parted at the ground floor but neither moved. Nick looked out through the opening before returning to her, his eyes pleading for help. It took her a while but in the end she must have figured what could it hurt? For the sake of a few coins which she could easily spare, what business was it of hers who he wanted to call? What if the roles were reversed?

'Yeah, course,' she said reaching into her small brightly coloured handbag. 'Will a couple o quid do?'

'That would be great. Thank you so much, you've got no idea what this means to me.'

'No worries,' she said smiling and handing Nick the money. 'Hope it helps.'

As they left the elevator, Nick thanked her again and she walked off in the direction of the coffee shop smiling.

The phone booths were just a short walk from elevators and Nick was about to insert the first coin when a sickening realisation stopped him. What the hell was the number? All of his efforts had been for nothing, damn it. Nick was certain now that his escape must have been noticed, and doubly sure that they would be hurtling down as fast as the wind would carry them to stop him. If this escape was to work then he had to get away quickly, he had to follow through with the plan. Placing the handset back in its cradle, Nick left the booth with the two sweaty coins still clenched in his fist.

To his back was the gift shop, and to his left a salon with a poster model tossing her hair in the window. Next to that was the coffee shop where he could see his Good Samaritan greeting a friend, and beyond that was the main reception. Everything about the place was an intimidating gauntlet and like a lost child he staggered into the crowd. Nick had the main doors in view offering him the promise of freedom with every step. He was so close now he could taste it. His forehead beaded with sweat. Suddenly, a hand from behind rested on his shoulder.

'Hello love,' a soft female voice said. 'Are you all right?'

Nick turned to confront the nurse and his face drained of colour.

'Yeah, I'm fine thanks, just needed to stretch my legs. I've been cooped up in that ward for nearly a week now.'

'A week? What are you in for?' she asked,

concealing her professional suspicion, her hand moving from his shoulder to his forearm, still maintaining contact, still within easy grabbing distance.

'You know,' he whispered, nodding downwards, 'men's things.'

'Oh!' the nurse said in a whispered hush. Her hand dropped to her side in embarrassment. Then she winked. 'It's all right love; we've seen it all before.'

Nick gave her an uncomfortable smile and the nurse walked away. For a moment he just stood frozen as his heart pounded like a drum. Then, when she was a respectable distance away from him Nick turned and left the building.

Maureen was sat at the nurse's station when she buzzed the family in.

'Hello,' she said greeting the woman of the group with a smile. 'Can I help you?'

'Well, I don't know if it's anything to worry about but I think I just saw a patient get into the lift.'

'I beg your pardon; a patient from here?'

'I'm not sure. He *was* wearing a medical gown though. Pretty much barged past us. Nearly hurt my youngest.'

'I'm sorry about that. Could you just excuse me for one moment,' Maureen said, politely turning before marching up the corridor to Nick's room.

Without a pause she threw the door wide.

'Oh God, no,' she exclaimed and ran back down the corridor past the bewildered family and straight into Collins's office.

His head shot up with a start.

'He's gone,' Maureen cried through panting breath.

Collins sprang to his feet. 'What do you mean, gone?'

'He's gone, Will. A woman just saw him getting

into the elevator. He's gone!'

'No, no, no,' he said rushing from behind his desk and out the room. 'This cannot be happening! Why was no-one on the desk?'

'We do have other patients too you know,' she called after him.

Waiting at the desk, the woman watched Collins fly past to the security doors, barging through just as Nick had done. He slapped the elevator button repeatedly then paced back and forth across the foyer, all the while keeping his eye on the deathly slow floor counter as, bit by bit, the digital display counted down the elevator's progress.

On the third lap of his pacing, Collins happened to glance out the window. His pacing stopped. His beating heart sank. Below in car park was the figure of a gowned man running through the glistening maze of vehicles towards the main road.

'Nick, wait!' he shouted, pounding on the glass with all his might. Collins knew it was a useless gesture but what else could he do? 'Please, come back.'

The chill blew up his gown as Nick ran across the car park. The air was fresh and clean, adding to his heightened sense of freedom. The closer he came to the road the more he revelled in his success. Sharp stones dug into his naked soles but he did not care. He had done it. He really had done it.

Nick climbed the grassy embankment at the perimeter of the car park and onto the pavement. Passing cars rubbernecked him as they sped by but he ignored them instead concentrating on what he should do next. Then, like a sign of divinity the answer presented itself. No more than twenty metres away was a bus stop. Nick made his way over and waited beneath its canopy wrapping his arms around his body for warmth. The traffic passed by in a steady stream and stared at him like a circus freak. Thankfully it was not long until the beautiful sight of a blue and white bus came to a hissing stop at the curb. With another blast of hydraulics the door slid aside and the driver perched in his booth looked at him. Along the entire length of the bus Nick could see intrigued faces studying him. Those same eyes followed him as he stepped on board and asked for a single ticket.

The obese driver sat motionless, looking him up and down before coming to rest on his face. Nick turned to see every single passenger staring at him.

'Should you be on here, son?' the driver asked.

Nick's sense of freedom disappeared as his hope began to wane.

'Please, I just want to go home. I just want to be with my family where I belong. I'm not dangerous and I'm not ill. All I want is to get home. Please.'

The driver looked at him for a long time. Every passenger in the bus was silent beneath the weight of the moment, and the driver could feel their eyes pressing against the back of his skull. Nick placed his coins in the metal payment tray. The driver looked at them. It was a cautious hand that took the money and handed Nick his ticket. This *inconvenience* was eating into the driver's already tight schedule and besides, the last thing he wanted was to cause a scene. He was not going to die today for a poxy seven-fifty an hour.

'Thank you,' Nick said, and made his way to the back of the bus. While most people pretended to ignore him an old woman caught his eye and refused to let go. With an awkward embarrassment, Nick dropped his gaze and hurried past, finding a seat at the very back next to the window. Resting his head against the cool glass, he closed his eyes, and with a sigh of relief smiled.

The hydraulics hissed and the bus pulled away.

Every street corner held an unfamiliar turn and he absorbed his new surroundings like a child struggling to capture everything at a single glance. The bus continued its usual route in a town Nick had lived his entire life but now felt alien, and his lack of recognition terrified him. How was he to find home when any of the houses flitting by could be the one?

By now the bus was beginning to thin out and Nick was finding himself increasingly alone. They had just travelled along a short section of dual carriageway past a row of industrial buildings and through a jungle of traffic lights that did a fantastic job of slowing everything to a snail's pace. This steady crawl persisted all the way to a roundabout at the very end where road works were gouging a wound into the tarmac. Nick's worry deepened until the next set of crossroads sparked a memory.

The bus came to a halt. On Nick's left was a fish and chip shop. Its window displayed hand written posters advertising local events and bands he had never heard of. But it was across an adjacent pathway on the corner was a block of converted flats where his memories really began to flow. In Nick's memory though the building had been a pub called The Vine where Mrs. Fletcher, the lollipop lady, waited every morning without fail for the children to arrive. He could see the middle aged woman's luminous yellow jacket as plain as day. A boy and girl came running up to the path's edge, breathlessly bouncing on the curb while Mrs. Fletcher instructed them to wait. Coming up the rear, a woman was calling for them to stop as she tried to keep up with their younger, faster legs. Panting, she reached them, scolding the pair for running off like that. All of a sudden, Nick realised that the boy was him, no older than six or seven. The girl was his cousin, Natalie, always full of energy and eager to misbehave. The woman was his mother. Nick then found himself viewing the scene from a first person perspective, through the eyes of his six year old self.

Everything around him was so big; the buildings, the cars, and the people. The lights changed, the traffic halted and Mrs. Fletcher stepped onto the road. Nick felt a sharp pain engulf his arm as Natalie punched him before running across to the other side.

'Ow! Mum,' he heard himself whine in a dragged out childlike way.

'Go on, across the road,' Janet said ushering him along.

On the other side was a gents barbers called Malc's. Nick recalled his monthly visit with his mum, sitting in silence and waiting his turn while Radio 2 played out tunes from a wireless hidden somewhere at the front of the shop. The air within the salon was heavily scented with men's products. Nick had always found the smell familiar and reassuring. His hairstyle never changed. Trimmed on top, tapered up the back and sides, and feathered at the front. Just as his mother instructed. That had been the way of it all the way to being eleven years old until one day when he had been quietly waiting his turn as usual. It was no longer cool for his mum to be there and so, after much aggravation, Nick had finally convinced her that he was now old enough to go alone. In the cutting chair sat an older boy he recognised from school, so full of confidence. The way he carried himself, the way he talked; he was cool. Malc performed his duty while Nick secretly studied the boy, and as time passed by a strange emotion began to develop inside his belly, churning with rebellion. Ever since he could remember his mother had always told him what to ask for, what to say, but today he was alone and was going to do it his way. All he had to do was open his mouth and say a few simple words.

With his work complete, Malc whipped the gown aside and brushed away the clippings from the boy's neck and shoulders. The mirror was presented, and the boy smiled with satisfaction then stepped from the chair just in time to catch Nick watching from behind. A moment of awkwardness hung between them. Nick looked to the ground. The boy went to the counter, paid his bill and left.

Slamming the cash register shut, Malc came back into the belly of his shop. He was a squat, rotund man with piggy eyes and sausage fingers but a soft and kindly face.

'Right, Nick. You next?' he said, his voice peaking at the end of every sentence.

Full of angst, Nick placed himself into the wide leather chair, aching to be brave.

'What'll it be today?' the barber said, reaching around Nick's neck to fix the gown in place.

Nick's mouth tasted acidic. He could feel his cheeks burning with embarrassment. Malc just stared at him and waited for a reply. But the more he stared the more ridiculous and self-conscious Nick felt.

'Erm... could I... could I have what that boy before just had, please?' he asked imagining that just by voicing the question it would cause the world to crack open and expose his cowardice to the rest of the waiting customers who would turn on him en mass with laughter.

'What, Chris? Fancy a change, do ya? No Problem, you're the boss.' Malc plucked a freshly sterilised pair of scissors from his shirt pocket, and that was it. The old men by the window continued with their morning papers. The unseen radio played Jonny Cash without skipping a beat. Without his mother's permission, Nick had changed the course of his own existence, had made his own decision to change the monotony of his childlike appearance and the world just carried on as if nothing had happened. Nobody laughed, nobody batted an eyelid, and Nick learned a valuable lesson in confidence. For the first time in his life he felt like an adult. With his newfound sense of worth, Nick sat back and watched the transformation as the little boy that was, disappeared.

Back in the bus, Nick's mind became awash as images from his youth came flooding back in rapid succession one after another. Malc had since retired years ago, his hands no longer steady enough to control the blades, and his salon was now a tattoo parlour. At least Brian's fish and chip shop was still the same.

The hydraulics hissed and the bus began to move again. Nick rose from his seat and slapped his palms flat against the glass as the familiar sight of the crossroads crawled away. Could this be the area where he lived? They passed the flats that had once been a pub. He could see right down the adjoining street from where his infant self had come running, and the more he thought about his childhood the more the information came back to him. He remembered walking that street, turning left at the end and past a long stretch of prefabs, an entire avenue of them. That was it. That was his way home!

Running to the front of the bus, Nick vigorously pressed the stop button. The driver turned in his seat with an angry expression.

'All right son, I get the picture. All you had to do was ask.'

'Sorry. Can I get off, please?'

'Too bloody right,' the driver replied, releasing the doors.

'Thanks for this,' Nick said. 'You've saved me.'

Nick jumped from the bus and ran back towards the crossroads, the gritty path digging into his naked soles. Down Broadfield Lane, past the old folk's home to the end, he continued into Staniland Road, past the rows of prefabricated homes just as he had remembered, their elderly residents staring after him with intrigue. It was all coming back to him now. Nick took another left down Woodville Road, not caring about the strange looks he received. He made a right into Thornton Avenue past an unfamiliar newly built house, until he reached the very bottom where he came to a jogging stop.

His breathing heavy and his brow and back peppered with sweat, Nick saw his home for the first time in five months. This was where the memories were strongest. Filled with a sense of nostalgia, he walked the pavement seeing himself once more as a child playing with the old gang. When Wimbledon was in season the road became a tennis court and after that a football pitch. Adam and Leigh were the two brothers next-door, and there was Andrew Joyce from across the road who always asked every single person he met when their birthday was just so he could tell them their star sign. There had also been Paul and Steve. They were a lot older but still joined in when there was a game of footie to be had, or in the wintertime for snowball fights. This small stretch of road signified everything that had been good about his childhood and no matter what events had taken place after no-one would be able take those memories from him. Not even a coma.

As he approached the drive gates, Nick noticed his dad's car was missing. His mum's was parked in its usual spot just outside the front bay window. Every step filled him with a sense of homecoming. Ignoring the front door, Nick went down the side of the house. Only new visitors ever used the front door. To anyone else it was always backdoor entry and shoes off before you came in, regardless of the weather. Instinctively, Nick checked the soles of his feet. They were black with dirt and badly scratched but thankfully the marks were only superficial. Giving the soles of his feet a cursory brush down, Nick reached for the door handle and found his hand trembling. What was he going to say? What would they think? He suddenly felt uncomfortable in this place that should have been his home, as if entering the house of a stranger uninvited. That this was no longer his place or time.

Swallowing back his anxiety, Nick opened the door. Inside, the kitchen's warmth embraced him. The place was as spotless as he would have expected; everything clean and in its place with comforting regularity. Drifting down the hall from the living-room he could hear the war cries of a console game coupled with the clashing of weaponry.

Slowly, Nick opened the hallway door further and moved closer to the sound. Through the open living-room door, he saw Andrew's hunched figure, cross-legged in front of the TV. The flashing images of the game crowned the shape of his body like a Technicolor aura. Nick lingered in the doorway, happy to watch his brother's progress as his staff-wielding samurai avatar thrashed its opponents into submission.

'Hello little mate,' Nick said.

'Hi, Nick,' Andrew replied without thinking. Then, as though time had stopped, every muscle in his body tensed and he sat as still as the dead. The redundant samurai on the screen went down beneath a cascade of enemy blows. Too terrified to turn, Andrew listened with a heightened sense of awareness, convinced that he must have imagined it, that what he heard could not have been real. Andrew's vision returned to the screen and there in its reflection he saw the shadow of a man standing in the doorway behind him. Instant terror seized him. His frame began to tremble.

'Andy, please don't be scared. It's me, Nick.'

Too afraid to look, Andrew remained rigid as his brain tried in vain to convince his heart that the voice he was hearing was really Nick's.

'But you're dead,' he said.

'No, the doctors got it wrong, or else I wouldn't be here would I?'

'You might be dead but just don't realise it, like on that film. I saw you die. Mum asked me if I wanted to say goodbye to you. The machines said you were dead.'

'The machines got it wrong. I'm alive, Andrew, and I'm home.'

Andrew watched his brother's reflection in the screen and as Nick moved forward to touch his shoulder, to add solidity to his claim, he screamed in panic and propelled himself into the crescent of the bay window, cowering against the wall.

'Andy, please don't,' Nick cried, dropping to his knees in despair. 'It is me. Look, it's me.'

Nick reached out to touch his brother again. Andrew pressed himself even tighter against the wall. Seeing the terror in his brother's eyes, Nick moved back to give him space.

'How is this happening?'

'I don't know. A nurse at the hospital told me you all thought I was dead. I needed to get home to make sure that you knew it wasn't true.' Nick's eyes dropped to the carpet before returning to his petrified brother. 'I swear it's the truth, Andrew. I swear…'

Andrew stared at him in disbelief, at a brother that should be dead. Hunched up on the floor wearing nothing but a hospital gown, Nick had the appearance of a ghost. Could it be true though? Andrew remembered wishing with all his heart for God not to take his brother. Had God heard his prayer and allowed this one small grace? His breath caught in his chest with excitement and awe. 'This is really happening isn't it?'

'Yes,' Nick said, his eyes tired yet hopeful. 'No trick. How have you been?'

Andrew paused for a moment.

'All right,' he whispered, wiping the tears from his face.

'Good,' Nick whispered back. 'Mum and dad?'

'They're at the shop. Mum needed to get milk. They wanted me to go but I didn't want to. They'll be back soon.'

Nick's heart thumped with anticipation.

'How is this possible?' Andrew asked, wanting to touch Nick but still too afraid, his young mind having been exposed to too many dark images from the internet and horror films to think any other way. A huge part of Andrew's brain was still expecting Nick to transform into a flesh-eating zombie. How could this be real?

Unable to give a reasonable answer, Nick side stepped the question.

'So, what's this then?' he said nodding at the screen. 'New game?'

'Dad got it for me last week to try and cheer me up,' he replied, his eyes not leaving Nick's face for a second.

'Are you gonna show it to me then?'

Andrew relaxed a little and sidled his way over to the wireless controller lying belly up on the carpet.

'You're the captain of a Japanese army and you have to complete different missions. I've got to storm this castle but I can't get past the archers.'

'Can I have a go?' Nick asked crouching closer.

'If you want,' Andrew said passing Nick the controller. Nick took it with a smile and his little brother stared at his hand in wonder as it gripped the game pad and removed it from his grasp.

'Right then, what's the buttons?'

Andrew remained motionless and just stared at Nick. Then, with overwhelming emotion he launched himself at Nick, throwing his arms around his brother's shoulders, pressing his head against his neck.

Nick dropped the controller in surprise and returned the embrace.

'It's you! It really is you,' Andrew cried.

Nick hugged him closer, refusing to let go. 'It's me, little mate. I'm home and I'm never going anywhere else ever again. I promise.'

'Don't say that. You can't make a promise like that,' Andrew said.

'It's all right, mate. I'm not going anywhere.'

Andrew squeezed tighter then wiped more tears from his face. 'What are you going to tell mum and dad? They're going to freak.'

'I don't know. How about we forget that for now

and you tell me what these buttons do, hey?'

So, for the next twenty minutes Nick and Andrew sat together in front of the television punching, kicking and slashing their way to victory. Andrew was still in shock but playing together like this, focussing all of his attention on the game, was helping to loosen his nerves, to give him the time he needed to adjust. For Nick, it just felt good to be home again doing something normal. He knew that very soon everything would explode, so the most he made of this moment right now the better. His parents, and himself for that matter, would want to know what had gone wrong. How such a gigantic mistake could have been made? But those questions were for another time. For now, he was just happy to be in his own clothes again, and in his own living-room playing a game with a can of Coke, a bumper pack of bacon crisps and his little brother. Whilst Nick changed upstairs, Andrew had stood by the bedroom door and watched, afraid that if he took his eyes away for just a second his brother would disappear, that the whole event would have been nothing but the product of his wishful imagination.

Just above the din of the game they heard the sound of the backdoor being slammed. Nick looked to his brother.

'Can *I* tell them?' Andrew whispered.

'I don't think so mate, not this time.'

But it was too late. Before Nick had time to protest, Andrew was up, away and through the door.

'Mum! Dad! Come and look!' he was calling.

Janet was lifting the grocery bags onto the worktop. George was still outside clearing old chocolate wrappers from the driver's side door. 'Think of your heart,' Janet had scolded.

'Mum!' Andrew shouted.

At any other time she would have found his excitement endearing but now Nick was gone she felt dark inside as though something had been switched off inside her. There were no more smiles anymore. Her son was dead. 'What is it, poppet?' she asked.

Before she had even time to remove her coat, Andrew grabbed her by the hand and dragged her into the hall.

'You've got to come and see,' he cried.

'What? What is it? Can't it wait?'

'No, you've got to come and see now,' he urged dragging her into the hallway to the living-room, still terrified that unless they hurried Nick would no longer be there.

'Oh, what is it?' she said, beginning to get irritated now.

With one final surge, Andrew heaved her into the living-room, and Janet froze.

'Hi mum,' Nick said, stood in the centre of the room with an unsure smile.

Janet looked from Andrew to Nick. Then she turned away, struggling to accept the lie stood before her, looking anywhere so long as the focus of her attention was away from the unkind apparition of her dead son. But she could not help herself. She began to cry, snatching her hand away from Andrew to cover her mouth.

'Mum, its Nick. He's not dead. They got it wrong. The doctors got it wrong, mum.'

Backing away, her legs unsure of which direction to take, she stopped when the doorframe made contact with her back.

'He's telling the truth, mum,' Nick said. 'They got it wrong. This is really happening.'

'But I watched you die,' she croaked, her face streaked with makeup and tears. 'I stayed with you right until the end. I watched you die.'

'I can't explain it,' Nick tried. 'But… it's really me, mum.'

Nick held out his hand for her to touch and she looked at it as though it were something lethal. 'Mum, please, it's me.'

Janet opened her mouth to speak, and then closed it again. Words failed her. She pulled her own hands to her chest in a defensive action as her mind wrestled with the concept of what she was seeing. She looked from his hand to his face, that beautiful angelic face that she had kissed and stroked and marvelled over for twenty years and her heart began to falter, her defences crumbling as she gave herself to the insanity. Steadily, she reached out and felt the solidity of his hand.

'My God. How is this possible?'

'I don't know. I'm scared mum. Please...'

'Come here,' she said. Thrusting forward, Janet folded him into her embrace, squeezing with every ounce of strength she possessed, feeling the warmth of his body pressed against her own. 'My baby, it's you, it really is you.'

'I'm sorry, mum. I'm so sorry,' he said wrapping his arms around her.

'Shush now, it's not your fault, it's not your fault. Just... hug me. God, I've missed you. I love you so much.'

'I love you too,' Nick said, weeping. 'I'm so sorry.'

From the backdoor, George had entered with an armful of rubbish.

'Janet,' he called.

With reluctance, she pulled away, her face sodden with tears. 'Your dad, he's not going to believe this. George! Come here! You have to come here!'

'What's all the shouting about? What's going on?' he said as he dumped the rubbish in the bin and came through to the living-room.

'Hello, dad,' Nick said.

Nick?

George stood poised, confused. He looked to his wife then to his youngest son, before returning back to...

Nick? He tried to speak, but failed.

    Then, something in his mind finally snapped. Without a single word, unable to accept the truth of what was stood in their home; George turned away and left the room.

Chapter Nineteen

Trapped in thought, Collins sat at his meticulously ordered desk a picture of despair and ruin. From the other side, Maureen studied him with increasing concern as he accepted the realisation that his career was over. There would be no walking away from this. Not once Miss Hopper had sunk her perfectly manicured talons into him anyway. This was precisely the excuse she had been looking for all these years as payback for him not responding to her advances. The pettiness of her vendetta made him feel sick, yet the thing that galled him most was the knowledge that it was well within her power, her remit even, to try and help him if she wanted. The first thing Collins had done upon retreating to his office was tidy his desk to try and counterbalance the insanity raging around him. One blessing he could be thankful for at least was that he had managed to obtain the samples from Nick, even if it was instrumental to his downfall. Retrieving samples from a subject without their complete knowledge and consent was illegal. A patient always retained the right to give or withhold consent prior to any examination or treatment. The three components of any valid examination were competency, information and then consent, but how could Collins have told Nick that he had just risen from the dead? The fact still remained though that without these three requirements being fulfilled the Howell's would be well within their rights to file a civil action. It would be classed as an invasion of Nick's person and, with Caroline Hopper's input, would see Collins hung, drawn and quartered by every governing body who wished to become involved.

With his elbows on the desk, Collins cupped his

face and rubbed his eyes.

'This wasn't your fault, Will,' Maureen said. 'We all know what happened here today and we'll all say the same thing.'

Collins moved his fingers and looked at her. He wanted so much to share in her optimism, to believe that a silver lining awaited them at the end of all this but he would be a fool to ignore the frenzy which existed in today's legal and media system. Once the papers got hold of the story, his career would be over before the case even got to court.

Collins glanced at his watch.

'Please, William, speak to me. What are you thinking? Don't shut me out like this,' Maureen pleaded.

'What do you want me to say? That everything will be all right?'

Maureen lowered her gaze.

'You really want to know what I'm thinking. I wish I had taken Caroline's advice and just called his parents. I never thought I'd hear myself say that. It's too late now though isn't it; he could be anywhere.'

'We should inform the police. Get someone out there looking for him?'

'You're right,' he said, his words muffled as he dropped his face to his hands and exhaled through his palms. 'Although, I think he's probably made it home by now. I mean, have we had any reported sightings of a semi naked man wandering the streets of Boston wearing nothing but a hospital gown?'

'If you're trying to be facetious then don't. I came here to see if you're all right, not to be belittled.'

Collins flushed and gave her an apologetic look.

'I just thought we should at least call someone?' she continued.

'And I am sure that even if we don't we will hear soon enough,' he replied.

'Don't you even care anymore? One of our patients

The Maelstrom

is out there walking the streets, probably very afraid and in God knows what kind of danger, not only to himself but also possibly to others. What if he had an accident?'

'Then we would've heard by now. Maureen... it's over. Don't you get it? He shouldn't even be alive right now. I'd love nothing more than to continue trying to help, to have the opportunity to study his condition, find out why, but it's never going to happen. I'll be lucky if I am ever employed again after this.'

'So that's it then, it's all about you is it? What about the other patients out there? What about your ward?'

'After today it will not be my ward.'

Maureen glared at him in disbelief.

'Yes, well, today is not over yet and neither is my shift so if you don't mind I'm going to get on with helping the people who deserve it. I think I've taken as much self-pity as I can handle for one day thank you very much.'

Standing, Maureen opened the door and left. Without saying a word, Collins watched her go.

Outside, her heart pounded with anger. She paused to try and steady herself, and that's when she noticed how surreal the ward seemed to be. Still, she straightened her posture and regained control even taking time to smile at a passing couple. The rhythmic beeping of the heart monitors soothed her, calming her soul until her mind fell into step with its steady reassuring tone. Closing her eyes for a second, Maureen took one final moment to relax, and then continued on her way.

From the opposite end of the ward, Sarah approached and whispered to her. 'Mr. Thoroughgood in number four, his pressure's dropped dangerously low. I've been keeping an eye on him but I don't think he's going to last much longer.'

'Medication?'

'It's not effective anymore. We've been draining poison for the last six hours, but it just keeps coming. The only thing keeping him alive now is the ventilator. I really think Dr. Collins should have a word with his next of kin.'

Maureen looked in the direction of cubicle four. 'I'll take care of it. Don't you worry. You just carry on.'

'Well, actually it's time for me to go now. Second shift's here so we're just going to do hand-over and then I was going to head off if that's okay? I really need a drink, and some sleep.'

'Sarah, wait,' Maureen said, taking her to one side. 'Are you all right?'

'No, I'm not all right,' she said. 'I need to sleep.'

Maureen felt nothing but sympathy for her. Despite her own years of hardened experience, Nick's condition was like nothing anyone had ever seen before, outside of scriptures and fairytales. How were they expected to react given the circumstances? What were they supposed to do next? 'Will you be okay on your own tonight?'

'Not really, but what else can I do?'

'Look,' Maureen said, taking a pen from her breast pocket and a notepad from her side. 'Here's my home number. I knock off at seven-thirty so, if things get too bad, call me. I have a spare room you can use for as long as you need.'

'Oh, I don't think-'

'Seriously, I mean it.'

'Are you sure?' she said staring at Maureen with gratitude, struggling to contain her tears. 'Thank you, I'll bear that in mind.'

'Good girl. Now, go home and get yourself a shower. You'll feel a lot better for it.'

Sarah smiled with thanks, put the note in her pocket, and then walked away.

Maureen watched her for a moment, then went over to cubicle four and lifted the patient's notes from the foot of the bed. Flipping through the pages she studied the clipboard then the monitor.

'Hello Mr. Thoroughgood,' she said, not expecting a reply.

Maureen then replaced the clipboard and moved on to the next bed.

The last thirty minutes of the day was spent briefing the next shift before Nathan and Sarah left for home. In the foyer, they waited in silence for the elevator. Sarah stared out the window as she tried to come to terms with the uncomfortable sensation creeping around inside her. She really needed a drink.

The elevator arrived and Sarah pressed herself against the far wall in the claustrophobic space. The doors closed and they began their decent. Nathan stared at her, searching for a sign of understanding, of unity in the wake of the day's strange events. Nothing would ever be the same again.

With a light jolt, the cabin arrived at the ground floor but instead of exiting when the doors parted, they both hung back. Eventually, it was Nathan who was the first to speak.

'Would you like me to walk you back to yours?' he asked.

She looked into his hazel eyes.

'That would be nice. I'm down this way,' she replied indicating the corridor which led past the pathology lab. Through the Out Patients wing was the quickest route to the nurse's quarters at the rear of the hospital.

As they made their way down the corridor, the human traffic from Out Patients was beginning to thin as most of the consultants had already left for home. Sarah and Nathan walked without speaking, neither wanting the unnecessary babble of a pointless conversation. For now, it was just enough to have a kindred spirit close at hand, and as they strolled Sarah glanced at him and saw the confusion which had begun in the elevator but appeared to deepen with every step since then. For both of them the enormity, and reality, of the unbelievable events were finally sinking in, and neither wanted to be alone.

Through the next set of double doors, they entered the Out Patients waiting room where the last stragglers of the day were thumbing through out of date magazines to keep their nerves at bay. Crescent shaped booths lined either side of the main central isle that stretched all the way to the other set of double doors at the end. They passed an elderly lady sat alone, and Sarah avoided her gaze, not wanting to connect with the woman's searching eyes. Her pace quickened. Nathan quickened his own to keep up.

'Are you okay?' he asked.

'I just want to get out of here,' she replied.

'Sarah…'

But she ignored him. In truth she had no idea what she was feeling right now. All she knew was that the world she thought she knew had become an alien place that scared her. She needed to shut it away and collect her thoughts. Even in the huge open space of the waiting room she felt trapped and claustrophobic.

As they hurried through the reception, out into the open air of the drop-off point, Sarah found herself struggling for breath. She doubled over gulping back lungfull's of air. Nathan rubbed the centre of her back. This was probably the first physical contact they had ever shared. He felt nervous touching her, like holding a new partner's hand for the very first time.

'Come on, calm now. Breathe, slowly,' he spoke with the controlled tones of his training.

After a couple more gulps Sarah managed to find calm.

'Thanks,' she said straightening up, her face flushed pink, her eyes slightly watering. Nathan studied her.

'How're you now?' he asked.

'Fine, just a little shaken. God, I really don't know

what came over me.'

'I'm not sure it would be a good idea for you to be alone right now. Do you want me to sit with you for a bit?' Their eyes connected again and although Sarah felt overwhelmed with the events of the day, a day in which anything was possible, she suddenly felt uncomfortable with Nathan's proximity. In his eyes, she could see the same fear and exhaustion which she was trying so hard to suppress. Right now, the only thing she wanted was a bath and her bed, alone. She didn't want to think anymore about the craziness and, although something inside her wanted him to stay his presence would only serve as a reminder.

'No... thank you,' she said. 'Not right now. I just want to sleep. Anyway, you look as if you could do with an early night yourself.'

Nathan nodded. She touched the side of his arm with an awkward smile.

'No worries,' he half whispered. 'I'd better get going. You know where I am if you need me.'

'I do,' she said. 'Try and get some sleep.'

'You too.' Nathan sidled off to the car park to find his push-bike, hoping it was still in the same place he had left it this morning.

Sarah watched him walk away. Then, seeing him reach his old Raleigh, she turned and headed for home.

Although the entrance to the Out Patients department was quite a distance from the hospital's main reception, it was only a three hundred yard walk from the nurse's block. The utility road she was now on also served as the shoot through for the ambulance bay and incineration tower where all the hazardous bio-waste was disposed of. Consumed by her thoughts, she arrived at the bleak concrete tower block that was the nurses' quarters in no time. Its oppressive greyness loomed like a behemoth reaching for the sky which, although still a vivid hue of burning colours, was beginning to lose its brilliance with the retreating sun and only intensified her feelings of loneliness. Once inside, Sarah made her way up the stairs, and with every step planned her retreat from the world. She could already feel her mood soothing in anticipation of a long hot soak.

At the top of the staircase, she went through the fire door and fished around her pocket for the door key. The entire right hand side of the corridor was rowed with windows that allowed in the last of the day's light, creating wedges of shadow across the parade of apartment doors to her left.

That was when she saw him. Stood at the very end of the corridor was a man, his face hidden in shadow. He was watching her. Sarah stopped her search. Even when their eyes made a distant contact he did not move, did not flinch. No older than herself, he just stood and stared.

With her hand still in her pocket, Sarah's fingers brushed the key and with a feeling of unease she quickly inserted it into the Yale. Before entering, she looked again. He was still there, still watching. The back of her neck tingled as ice cold fingers played along her spine and vulnerability gnawed her insides.

Sarah hurried inside and with more force than was necessary spun round to slam the door. But before the Yale bolt connected with the latch, the full weight of the door was thrust back at her, smacking her in the face. Sarah flew back into the hallway of the apartment and as the door slammed against the wall, cracking the plaster, it bounced back to the frame again before finally coming to rest.

Sprawled on her back, gasping for breath, Sarah raised herself onto her elbows and stared at the inanimate door. Her already bruised face had gone numb again, but the shock had removed any capacity to scream, and her petrified eyes stared transfixed at the three by six panel of wood as fingers slowly curled around its edge and the door was pushed open. When the young man stepped into her apartment, Sarah was immediately drawn to his face, to his eyes, malevolent black eyes which glared down at her, shark-like, without pity or remorse. Finally, she screamed. He smiled. For an instant they were like statues, Sarah's vision seeing nothing but her attacker, her limbs locked with fear as the man studied his prey with admiration. Her mouth tasted foul and as she wiped her lips she found the back of her hand stained with blood. Again she screamed in the hope that someone, anyone, would hear her cries.

In one fluid motion, the man slammed the door shut and stalked toward her, his hands flexing into fists of anticipation. Sarah crawled backwards like a doomed fly caught in a spider's web and, seeing there was nowhere else for her to go, a grin of intent began to creep its way across the man's stubbly face. He took another step closer.

As she backed away the hem of her uniform rode up her hips. She reacted with horror when his gaze began to caress her milky thighs, admiring the dull white gusset of her panties. His eyes, those terrible black orbs, flared at the sight before moving on to the insinuation of a slender flat stomach beneath her taut uniform, sliding over breasts that were confined by the falsehood of her bra, watching them heave with delight. His grin widened.

Sarah flipped onto all fours giving the stranger a wondrous view of her rounded buttocks as she scuttled into the living area.

'Help!' Her lungs burned with the force. 'Please, somebody help me!'

Her cries went unheard though and only added impetus to the man's mounting aggression. He lurched forward snatching up a fist full of Sarah's hair, wrenching her backward and up to her feet. Reaching behind, she clawed at his hand and wrist, screaming for her life, trying desperately to keep her balance as she was dragged into the kitchen. His grip tightened and she could feel the agony of hair parting with scalp. Like a woman possessed, Sarah lashed out for all she was worth but every time she tried he always seemed just out of reach.

The man twisted another fistful of hair to cement his control. When Sarah screamed again he spun her round to face him, pinning both of her arms beside her body. Face to face with her attacker, clamped in the steel of his grip, Sarah's eyes went wide with terror, unable to focus on anything but his blank and merciless stare.

Her heart pounded and, as though she were a delicate rose, the man drew her close and started to breath in the scent of her hair and skin. He took his time to sample her diverse aromas of a hard day's work coupled with pure fear, absorbing lung full after lung full of the sweet smell that stirred within him a passion of desire. How he ached to be inside her. Their eyes locked once more and, almost immediately, Sarah stopped crying.

'Please,' she whispered. 'Don't hurt me, please, I'm begging you.'

Holding her firm, he once more allowed their eyes to connect.

'Make me beautiful,' he asked with an almost childlike voice.

For an instant, she just looked at him as she tried to understand the meaning of his question. Then, without realising he had already released one of her arms, she heard the sickening pop of her skin as the sting of cold steel was thrust into her belly. Sarah's body gave a small tremor and she looked down to see the man's fingers wrapped around the leather bound handle of a pristine hunting knife. At first there was no blood and Sarah stared at him in pain and confusion, wanting to ask 'why?' But when she pulled away the wound became unplugged and the front of her torn uniform began to stain.

'What have you done?' she whimpered, gripping her stomach with both hands as she toppled backwards to the floor.

But he did not reply. He just studied her in the final throws of her life as she struggled across the floor in a futile attempt to escape, bloodying the carpet in her wake.

Like being reunited with an old friend, the knife felt so natural in his hand, and his blood covered fingers toyed with the handle. How long had it been? How many years in the span of the Cosm had passed since the day he had last sampled a fresh kill? The ease at which the blade had slipped through her skin and muscle with just the slightest of resistance filled him with nostalgia and the longing of an age old dream. Tonight that longing would be satisfied.

With her hand outstretched, Sarah used every last vestige of strength to drag her dying body across the damp stained carpet, while her other still grasped the open wound despite the unbearable pain it caused. And then, in one final effort, one last stab of life, Sarah's entire body heaved forward and her face slammed into the carpet. There were no final words of parting, no momentous gestures of farewell. Without a sound, Sarah drew her final breath and died. The last sensation she would ever know of the Cosm would be the abrasive texture of a short pile carpet biting into the soft tissue of her tear stained cheek.

Save for the man's heaving breath, silence fell all around as the exhilaration of the kill coursed through his veins. Towering over Sarah's corpse, he rolled her over and brushed aside her hair to reveal her pallid, shocked expression; such a beautiful face. Bringing the knife towards her, angling its blade just along her jaw line, he stopped before making symbolic slashing motions just above her face. Not once did he make actual contact. Today would not be the same as before. That had been a life once lived in a Cosm which time had erased. Now was a different time, his time.

Laying the knife to one side, he scooped up Sarah's body to stare deep into her lifeless eyes. Then, with an unexpected majesty, he bent towards her hooking his arm beneath her head, drawing her closer so that their lips practically touched. Sarah's body still felt warm, just. With a final intake of breath, he closed his eyes and kissed her with a passion only lovers could share. The kiss was powerful and deep and even though it was not reciprocated he swelled with all the love a person could feel until their bodies fell as one to the blood soaked floor.

Not a sound was to be heard, not a movement was made. For what seemed like an age the pair just laid motionless in the crimson pool of her blood until, ever so slowly, something stirred. The man's back began to arch upwards and with what seemed to be an involuntary motion, he rolled over to one side.

Gasping, Sarah pushed the carcass of the dead man off her letting it roll to the floor where it fell unceremoniously. Once again, she gripped the wound in her belly and cried out in pain as she curled into a ball of hurt and disorientation. Eventually, her cries lessened and her body straightened so that she was now lying on her back staring up at the white painted ceiling.

She had to see, she had to know. Quickly, she leaped from the carpet in search of the bathroom. The mirror above the basin was tall and wide and told no lies. In total shock and amazement she looked at its reflective surface and touched her own face, not believing that which her own jet-black eyes were telling her. But she was no longer Sarah. Sarah's spirit would be, by now, somewhere on the Border waiting to be judged. Her body shuddered at the thought of those dark lacerated hands bursting from the soil. Her black eyes returned to the mirror. She could not believe it. It was a miracle. Then, bit by bit, her eyes darkened with remembrance and misery. Even with this new face, this new body, he could still not erase the memories of his previous existence. It was his curse; it was his gift, to always and forever be Jeremiah.

The Maelstrom

'I am beautiful,' he whispered.

Chapter Twenty

The next morning, Nick awoke refreshed and alert. After so much time away it felt strange to be back in his old bed, but as the morning light filtered through his curtains casting a charcoal hue across the room, it was just as he had always remembered. Stretching out his muscles, he yawned before snuggling back in to the warmth of his pillow, happy to be home. His mouth was stale with morning dehydration so he took a swig from the pint of water he always took to bed.

The memories of the previous day came back to plague him. There were so many unanswered questions. Considering what he had been told by Nathan, his family had reacted quite well, apart from his dad that is. George refused to accept what his eyes were seeing. He had stumbled in a daze to the bottom of the garden where he remained for the rest of the afternoon, slumped against the garden shed, too afraid to re-enter the house. All he kept thinking was that it must have been a dream. What other rational explanation could there be? Soon he would wake and his son would still be dead, and they would still have to face the morbid task of arranging his funeral. Transfixed beneath the afternoon sun, George steadily found calm. It was not until the sun had begun to wane that he decided to venture back into the house for no other reason than to prove Nick was gone.

Every step made his skin tingle and his palms clammy. Keeping to the path that wound like a serpent across the lawn, George could see no movement in the dining room through the patio doors. Once inside though, something about the kitchen seemed to have shifted. Physically, nothing was different but George's perception of what was now real had swung way over the boundaries of rational thinking. In the universe he now inhabited his dead son was alive somewhere in this house.

Janet was nowhere to be seen, yet was that not the nature of dreams? People came and went like smoke on the breeze. Regardless, he was now consumed with one singular purpose, to hold his son one last time before he too vanished into the void.

George found Nick on the sofa. Andrew was sat in the bay window, his eyes moving from Nick to George in a studious motion. Looking to his youngest son, George smiled with a faraway look before returning his attention to Nick.

'Hello, son,' he said.

'Hello dad. How have you been?'

'Not bad,' he replied. George placed his hand on Nick's shoulder to test the solidity of his son. The moment he felt flesh, his heart swelled with so much love and gratitude that his eyes began to well. His grip tightened with joy.

Without needing to be asked, Nick hugged his father squeezing as hard as he could, not letting go for a second.

'I'm sorry, I should've been there for you but I wasn't. I'm so sorry,' George said.

'Dad, don't. It wasn't your fault; none of this was your fault.'

George cried even harder before Nick had to pull away, the pressure of his father's embrace too much.

'I'm sorry,' George said, wiping the tears from his face and checking Nick for harm. 'I didn't hurt you, did I?'

'It's okay, dad. Everything will be okay now.'

George gave a tiny laugh. 'I know this isn't real, but please just allow me these few moments,' he begged throwing himself at Nick for another hug. This time though Nick held him back.

'I… I don't… dad, this is…'

'Just tell me one thing. I was a good dad to you, wasn't I? You had a happy childhood. I know I could be a bit harsh at times but please, tell me I was a good dad.'

'Yes. Yes, of course you were a good dad. You still are.'

Andrew sat stock still, taking it all in with a dazed silence. George smiled and gave a tiny nod of satisfaction.

'And you had a happy childhood, didn't you? Please, you have to tell me before it is too late.'

'Dad, what are you talking about? It's all right now. I'm back. I'm okay.'

'Son, I really wish that was true.'

'Dad?' Nick repeated. 'You have to listen to me.'

But George was on another level. He waited as though some esoteric truth were about to be imparted.

'I died…'

'I know son, I know,' George said, rubbing Nick's arm, 'and your mum and I miss you so much. So does Andrew.'

Nick looked at his brother who stared back with doleful eyes. 'Please, let me finish. Yes, I died but you're not dreaming, dad. This is really happening. The doctors got it wrong. Are you hearing me? They got it wrong.'

George just stared at Nick and blinked. His smile faltered as his mind battled with the concept between Nick's words and reality, still hopelessly clinging with every last vestige to what he considered to be real, refusing to descend into fantasy.

'You have no idea how much I want that to be true. You're my boy. I'd do anything to have you back, but I know that this is a dream.'

'No dad, this is real. I'm real.'

George's smile faltered even further and, with strange and distant eyes, he moved off into the kitchen.

Nick was left mortified. Andrew stood and took his

hand. Both like statues watching the empty door.

'I believe you,' Andrew said.

Nick heard the words but was too dumbstruck to acknowledge them. He wanted to chase his father, to grab him, to force him to see sense but would that only make matters worse? George was in shock but sooner or later he would have to accept that Nick was alive. If not then what else was there? This whole situation was just one big mess. Then the strangest realisation came to him. There had been no contact from the hospital; nothing. Surely, they would be looking for him by now? Surely they would have called? Had he been too hasty in his escape? Perhaps all of this would have sounded more convincing coming from Dr. Collins? But then what could be more acceptable than the solid hard truth of Nick standing before them with open arms?

He looked down at his brother. 'Thanks mate,' he said. 'I'm gonna go to my room for a bit.'

'Can I come?' Andrew begged. 'We can play Monopoly.'

Nick smiled. 'Of course you can, mate.'

In the master bedroom, Janet was organising Nick's clothes ready for washing. Even though they had been kept meticulous over the past five months her OCD had convinced her they were fusty and so decided to wash the lot again. Nothing would be too good for her son's homecoming. It also gave her time to think. She had seen George's reaction, begged for him to stay, but still he had walked out. Just as he always did. She felt so alone right now.

Outside her bedroom door, Nick had paused wanting so desperately to enter, to hold and be held by her. But instead he moved away, shutting his bedroom door behind him. Andrew was already on the bed unpacking the game, not completely oblivious to what was going on but wanting to give his brother as decent a homecoming as only he knew how. Playing together may have been a simple act but it was all he had to offer, just like the old days. And that was how they had spent the rest of the evening. Janet had listened to the comforting sounds of their laughter and allowed herself the tiniest of smiles. Life could finally get back to normal.

That had been yesterday and still there was no word from the hospital.

Sat in his bed, Nick made the decision to go back. All he had wanted was to be home, to prove to himself that his sanity was still intact, but now he could see his actions had been rash. His father was suffering and although Andrew appeared to be coping, maybe deep down it was just another form of shock. Nick had no idea; he was no expert. Yesterday he needed his family; today he needed answers.

The clock on his bedside table showed nine-thirty. Swinging his feet to the carpet, he got out of bed. His discarded clothes which had been left in a heap on the floor were now neatly folded on the chair next to his desk. He smiled at the thought of his mother stood over him, watching, and maybe even stroking his sleeping face. At least she accepted he was alive, that he was real.

The landing window let in the morning sun and from downstairs Nick could hear the spitting sound of grilled bacon. Bacon sandwiches with the rind left on, nice and crispy, oozing with brown sauce; his favourite. When he reached the bottom of the stairs, he saw his mother down the hall knelt by the oven prodding the sizzling meat with a spatula. For that instant he just stood and watched, his heart pounding in anticipation of her loving acceptance. Then she turned and saw him.

Nick's breath stopped as he waited, hoping that yesterday had not been a trick. He needed for at least one of his parents acceptance. With the spatula on her knee, its dull plastic edge glistening with hot grease, she stared at him and smiled.

'Mum,' Nick started but Janet stopped him.

'No... please. Don't say anything. Just let me look at you,' she said.

Moving towards him, Janet touched his face. Nick could feel the warmth of her palm tremble against his cheek and, cupping her hand, he pushed it flat against the side of his face so she had to believe, to know that he was real.

Janet gasped.

'How is this possible?'

'I don't know,' Nick whispered.

'Let's sit.'

Together, they moved into the dining area and took seats on opposite sides of the table.

'Would you like me to get you something to drink?' Nick asked, reaching for her hand across the table.

'No... no thank you, I'm fine.' Janet said.

'How's dad?'

'Your dad, yes. Yesterday, when I first saw you I thought I was... I thought I was going mad or dreaming or something. I just can't believe it. It's a miracle, a bloody fantastic miracle.' Janet squeezed his hand even tighter, needing to affirm that the Nick sat opposite her was still not some cruel joke. 'Don't worry about your dad. He just needs time, that's all. It's a big shock. We all had to accept that you were...'

But she could not say the word. She never wanted to speak that word again.

'But it's like he's gone mad.'

'I got a phone call last night... it was Maureen, from the hospital. She sounded as though she'd been drinking. She asked if I had seen you yet.'

'What did you tell her?'

Janet's eyes looked tired and old. 'I didn't know what to say at first; I mean this is insane, isn't it? But then I told her the truth, about you being here. Even when I said it, the words sounded stupid in my ears. All I kept thinking was that maybe she would think I was mad? But she just kept on apologising, saying how someone should've called us earlier. I don't understand what's happening, Nick.'

Just then, Andrew appeared. He had been in the hall listening, waiting for his own much needed answers. But before Nick had a chance to speak, Janet continued. 'You were… I never left your side; you have to know that. Even after you…'

Janet put a hand to her mouth but was unable to stop the tears. Both Nick and Andrew rushed to her side.

'It's okay,' Nick embraced and kissed the top of her head. 'It's all right.'

'I'm sorry,' she said. 'Look at me, I'm a mess.'

'No, no you're not. You're beautiful. Do you want a tissue? Andrew…'

Andrew snatched a fist full of kitchen roll and dabbed his mother's cheeks, his tenderness bringing a smile to Janet's face.

'Thanks love,' she said taking the tissues from him. 'I've got the two most handsome wonderful boys any mother could wish for.' She then directed the rest at Nick. 'I can't believe it. I still can't understand it?'

'Me neither,' he replied.

'Then we need to go back to the hospital and speak with Dr. Collins. See if he can tell us what's happening to you.'

'Before I left they did loads of tests on me.'

'What? How long have you been… awake for? How long have they known?'

'I don't know,' Nick replied. 'My memory's hazy. Things have been a bit weird.'

'That's all right. We'll find out,' Janet said, regaining some of her fiery resilience. When exactly would it have been deemed necessary by the powers that be to have informed them that their own flesh and blood, *her* first born, was still alive?

'Maybe the tests will show something?' he offered.

'Come on, get washed. We're going to the hospital.'

'Won't dad want to be there?' Nick asked.

'Best leave him for now, eh love? It's been a long night. We'll wake him later.'

But Nick understood her meaning, and even though George was still keeping his distance, Nick wanted to run up stairs, grab him and squeeze him with as much love as he could just to prove that everything was good now. The only thing stopping him was the fear of disappointment. Fear that the past twenty-four hours had been some huge cosmic joke and that just as his father believed his cold dead body was in a mortuary drawer. Yet he was here, he was breathing. He could feel the air fill his lungs as well, as the room's temperature on his skin. He could feel the weight of his own flesh and bones, the smoothness of his hair, and the oily coarseness of his fingertips. Nick, and the world he inhabited, was genuine. He was sure of it.

These thoughts plagued him all the way to the hospital as he stared at the passing world from the comfort of Janet's car. They made the journey alone, much to Andrew's annoyance. The radio was off and neither spoke, both consumed with their own thoughts. Janet was still angry at Collins for knowing of Nick's awakening and saying nothing and although her confrontational nature tended to get the better of her, despite her best efforts to contain it, all she was really interested in now was the truth. Eventually, Janet pulled into the hospital car park and found herself a space.

'You ready?' she said, terrified that if he chose to bolt she would be powerless to stop him.

'Yep,' he whispered. Nick's insides churned.

The morning chill had already ebbed and as they approached the hospital building both felt a detachment from the world as though their acceptance of the coming news no longer left them with anything more to lose.

The other visitors appeared to be staring at Nick like watchmen, questioning his every move. It reminded him of a time he had revisited a pub he and his old schoolmates would abscond to in the afternoons. They played pool and drank beer which, back in those days when it was all new and exciting, felt rebellious. The barman had known they were under age but served them anyway. After all, business was business. A few years later, out of curiosity, he had gone back to the pub to find it overrun with scumbags; druggies and their dealers, thieves and scrappers trying to make a name for themselves. Maybe they had always been there. Maybe between the mixture of alcohol and teenage intrigue, Nick and his friends had been oblivious to the darkness around them. But that night, when Nick stepped back in he was afraid. Where he had once been familiar, his face was now unknown and they eyed him like predators stalking their next meal. Nick could feel the weight of their stares bearing down on him. Genuinely afraid of being glassed for just catching the wrong person's eye, he had ordered a pint of lager just to save face, found a quiet corner and then bolted down half as casually as he could before leaving the rest for dead. Nick never went back again.

It was that same cold fear which touched him now and, while part of Nick needed answers the rest of him was terrified of the truth; and then there was Amy. When all of this was done he needed to find her, let her know he was alive. The more he thought of her the more he yearned. He needed to stay focussed.

In the elevator, Janet took his hand and smiled.

'You all right?' she asked.

Nick gave a tiny nod. 'What do you think he's going to say?'

'I don't know, love. Just leave the talking to me.'

'What if they're really angry about yesterday?'

'Don't you worry about that,' she said, giving his hand a squeeze. The label of his T-shirt was poking out the back of his neck. Always the dutiful mother she tucked it back in for him.

Nick tried to control the bile collecting in his stomach.

The elevator came to a stop and the doors parted. Janet was first to step out. Nick remained stock-still at the back of the compartment.

'Nick?'

'I don't know if I can do this.'

'But you have to,' she said. 'We're here now. Don't you want to know what happened?'

'Of course I do.'

Janet took him by the hand and gently coerced him from the elevator.

'It's okay to be scared,' she said, 'so am I.'

She pressed the transmitter button and the speaker crackled to life.

'Good morning,' spoke a female voice.

'Hello... it's Janet Howell.'

The intercom fell silent.

'I'm here with Nick.'

Instantly, the door lock buzzed and they made their way inside. Stood in the centre of the corridor to greet them was Maureen. At first she just seemed to watch in anticipation but then her excitement broke and she rushed forward.

'Welcome back, Nick,' she cried wanting to hug him just to be sure he was real. But she managed to contain herself, stopping her actions mid reach.

'Hi,' he said with an unsure smile.

'We've come to see the doctor,' Janet said, ushering Nick past her. 'I suppose he's been expecting us?'

'He'll be so pleased to see you. You have no idea

how worried we've all been.'

'I bet you have. Is he in his office?'

Maureen felt the sharp whip of Janet's words and shrank back in shame. 'Yes, he's free. I'll take you to him.'

Together, they made the short journey past the beds that had once been like a second home for them. Although Janet shared and understood the other visitor's pain, now that Nick was returned to her she was glad to be no longer sat there with them.

Maureen rapped at Collins's door then entered.

The doctor was by his desk sifting through a stack of papers. He looked up as if dazed.

'Nick?' Unable to believe his eyes, Collins rushed over to greet him, shaking his hand enthusiastically, refusing to let go. Collins guided him over to the nearest chair. Janet's eyes bored into him as he dropped to one knee, still refusing to release Nick's hand.

'Thank you so much for coming back.'

'It was mum's idea,' Nick replied, beginning to feel uncomfortable with the prolonged physical contact.

Collins turned to Janet and thanked her too.

'Don't thank me. You have no idea how thoroughly disgusted I am with you and your department. What kind of a place are you running here?'

Both Collins and Maureen hung their heads.

'When were you actually going to tell us? A day later? A week?'

'I'm sorry,' he said. 'There is no excuse. Nothing like this has ever happened before. I mean with Nick, and his… resurrection. It's just… a miracle. I have watched your family suffer. I wanted to be a hundred percent sure before causing you anymore anguish.'

'So that's it then, is it? You were trying to spare our feelings? We had a right to know! He just turned up unannounced. My husband thinks he's going mad, for God's sake. We thought our son was dead!'

Collins looked to the floor again, and then returned to the safety of his desk to retake his seat.

'I can understand how angry you must feel...'

'Oh I doubt that very much,' Janet countered.

'Mrs Howell ... Janet, please try and understand that none of us were prepared. There are no protocols for what happened with your son.'

Collins thought of Nick's body prepped and wrapped ready for the morgue, and his failure burned deep.

'We had no idea what was going on,' he said, 'we still don't. Like you, we all thought he was dead.'

'So you're saying you still don't know what caused this?' Nick asked with unease. 'But... you have to. You're the doctor. That's why we're here. I mean, if not you... then who?'

'Nick, I'm sorry. I don't know what to say.'

'Doctor, what's happening to me?'

Collins focussed, softly bringing his palms together on the desk as if in prayer.

'Yesterday, we performed every test we have on you to try and get to the bottom of this. You know this. We took bloods, urine, mouth swabs, MRI scans, a total body X-ray.'

'And?' Janet asked, thankfully naive to the fact that what they had done was illegal. Collins felt certain that her attitude would change when more investigations were made.

'Well you see, that's the problem,' the doctor continued. 'We couldn't find anything wrong with you, Nick. It's as though the accident never happened.'

'That's impossible,' Janet said. 'They must have shown something, surely?'

'Absolutely nothing. For want of a better way to describe it, he is as healthy as a new-born baby, which *is* impossible. There's no ageing of his organs, no contaminants in his blood. His liver and kidneys are spotless. His heart is as strong as an ox; but more importantly, the extensive brain damage Nick had suffered is gone. His twisted bones healed. Whatever happened to cause this, I would truly love to know because it really is as if he has been reborn,' Collins said, unable to contain his excitement any longer. 'You are a miracle.'

Nick and Janet stared at him in disbelief. Yet how could they not believe? Nick was here, living proof, alive and impossibly real, and more than anything, scared as hell.

Chapter Twenty-One

The curtains were drawn against the outside world. The room held the stench of death. In front of the bathroom mirror, concealed within the young body of the nurse he had murdered the evening before, the essence of Jeremiah stared back at the beautiful dead face he now controlled with eyes as black as his soul. Abaddon had given him a gift, and a task. The gift had been a portal back into the Cosm, to walk amongst the sleepers once again except this time aware, remembering everything; his previous life, the Avichi of his own personal hell, and the task he had been sent to perform.

The sensation of the knife in his hand as it passed into Sarah's flesh had sent shivers up his spine, like the good old days. This time though he had taken more than her face as his trophy. This time, utilising the power invested in him by Abaddon, he took her. He took her life and then he took her body.

Throughout the anguish of his sleeping years, and the twisted torment of his death, the only thing Jeremiah had ever desired was this one true wish; to be a woman. Yet at the point of his crossing from the body of the young man he had wrenched from the Cosm to Sarah's slender physique, apart from physical weakness, he still felt no different like an unseen force had sucked all of the energy from him. On the plus side though, he did feel more agile, supple.

After seeing himself for first time as a true woman, Jeremiah had spent the first hour of his metamorphosis coming to terms with his transformation and the rest of the evening posing and assessing his new form. Turning his head from side to side, noticing the delicate sway of his long blonde hair as it brushed against his face and tickled his cheeks. At first it had irritated him but after a while he came to enjoy its feathery touch. He tried brushing the hair aside like a shampoo model, twisting his profile in the mirror with exaggerated sensuality, continually watching himself from the corner of his eye. Every time Jeremiah tossed his hair he tried harder to be seductive, narrowing his eyes and sampling varying degrees of puckered lips just like Jayne Mansfield. From the noise of his own thoughts it was Jeremiah's voice which chuckled yet from Sarah's lips his thrill was emitted as a childish giggle. Jeremiah clasped his mouth. How wonderfully feminine he sounded. The moment was tainted though by the knowledge of his previous host decaying on the carpet in the hall.

The dead man's ankle taunted him through the open bathroom door and so Jeremiah slammed it shut. On the windowsill were candles streaked with globs of solidified wax that congealed into a hard pool at the base.

Jeremiah drew the blind closed and lit the candles using a book of matches from a nearby shelf. Then he ran a bath adding the oils Sarah kept by the basin. Cautiously, he submerged into the hot oily water and as it enveloped his stomach the knife wound in his belly filled with its boiling essence, the heat sliding inside his body causing his skin to tighten and sting. At first he struggled against the bizarre sensation but once he became accustomed to the rise in temperature he relaxed. All around him shadows of the candlelight danced back and forth across the walls and flickered as motes of dust sizzled in the flame. As his muscles loosened he sighed with contentment and closed his eyes.

For a while, Jeremiah lay perfectly still, enjoying the unaccustomed silence without fear that this momentary bliss would be replaced by more of the mocking desolation of his Avichi. Then, amid the sweaty steam and sensual warmth, intrigue crept into his mind. With virginal fear his hand began to wander.

From his flat toned stomach, Jeremiah's trembling hand stroked the centre of his torso up to the valley between his breasts where his searching fingers came upon a small taut nipple. He had never *properly* been with a woman before, had never known how it felt to touch another's body with permission and intimacy. As his fingertip gently probed the nipple he felt like a stranger in what was now his own body. Every curve was alien to him. Lying there in the candle light like a deviant and submissive all at the same time, his fingers caressed the underside of his breast travelling back up to the nipple which had tenderised in the heat. Unlike any man before he had the double pleasure of not only touching the breast but also knowing the pleasure of being touched at the same time. Spasms of excitement rippled through his body. He teased the nipple with feather light strokes until it went numb then, filled with desire and a teenager's eagerness he cupped the entire breast and gave it a good hard squeeze.

Jeremiah's chest filled with pain. Curled up in the confines of the bathtub, he cradled himself as though someone had just kicked him in the balls.

'Jesus Christ,' he whispered in agony, biting down on his lip. 'Fuck.'

Again, instead of his South American drawl, it had been the sweet tones of Sarah's voice that had expressed his pain.

'Ahhh,' he blurted, fascinated by the sound of his own voice.

'Hello,' he said. 'Ah, ah, ah. Hello. Me, me, me, me, meeee. Shit. Wow. Hello... hi. Hi, my name's...'

He could use it now. He would be able to interact as a real woman and at last use what for years he felt should have been his real name without fear of ridicule.

'Hi,' he said to the flickering ceiling. 'My name's Celine, I'm very pleased to meet you.'

After towelling himself down, and stepping over the dead man in the hall, Jeremiah moved into the bedroom to find something to wear. At the foot of the bed were two floor-to-ceiling mirrors attached to the sliding doors of Sarah's wardrobe. For a moment he just stood and admired his slender figure.

Thank God I'm not ugly, he thought.

Jeremiah twisted round to get a better look at his buttocks and was pleased with what he saw. He even gave a little girlie skip as he went to the drawers for panties, pulling out pair after pair of different coloured materials until he eventually found the ones for him. A sweet pair of black laced French knickers. He had never seen anything like them. The way the underside cut off at a horizontal line of daintily edged lace. Slipping them on, he stood before the mirror again with his hands on his hips and swayed from side to side admiring his round buttocks now cupped by the lace. For the first time in his life he felt sexy. The excitement within him spiralled like an inferno and he searched for more clothes. The next drawer down presented a selection of bras. Conscious of co-ordination he kept to the black ones settling on one with slim shoulder straps. Slipping his arms into the straps and trying to keep the cups positioned over his breasts, he reached behind for the clasp with absolutely no idea how he was supposed to fix them. Every time he tried, the bra just fell away, the straps slipping down to his elbows. He gave it one more attempt before removing the infuriating contraption. Holding the bra in both hands he thought about the best way to get the damn thing on. He toyed with the hooks, practised connecting and disconnecting them until his brain suddenly had a Eureka moment.

'You idiot.'

Holding one of the straps, Jeremiah threw the other around his torso catching it as it came around the other side and with a grin of achievement, hooked the two ends together across his stomach before feeding it round his middle so the cups were now at the front. After that he just slipped his arms into the straps and hoisted everything into position. It was not the most pleasurable experience he had ever known but at least he now looked the part.

Pushing the mirrored doors aside, Jeremiah revealed Sarah's heavily stocked wardrobe and stared in wonder at the sweet shop of designs. Rifling through the garments, brushing over blouses, jackets and skirts as well as tops of different colours and cuts, he found an elegant black dress. He lifted it from the rail. It felt weighty yet not in a heavy way. It was the weight of quality and he slipped it on closing the mirrored doors again to appraise the finished article. The first thing he noticed was how wearing the dress somehow made him want to straighten as though someone had strapped a rod to his back. It not only affected his posture but his entire attitude. Wearing the dress truly made him feel like a woman. He glided across the room feeling the soft material caress his body and had the strangest sensation of being naked. In trousers his legs had always been encased, but with his legs exposed beneath the dress, with skin brushing against skin, it made him feel self-conscious yet daring. With all that freedom down below it felt even stranger not having his male genitals swinging in the breeze. Finally, after all of the years of waiting, of ridicule and abuse, of even passing beyond the threshold of death and enduring the torments of Hell he was a woman, and it was time for the entire world to see who he really was.

Before he could entertain any selfish desires of his own though, Jeremiah had but one task to fulfil knowing that if he failed, the angel's sentence would be without mercy and *His* gift, so lovingly coveted, revoked. Looking in the mirror, dreaming of the wonders that gift could bring, he knew that to fail in so simple a task was not an option. Jeremiah would never return to that dark place again, even if it meant slaughtering every sleeper in this world. Finally, after decades of his bitter existence he had found his place and no-one was going to take it from him.

Positioning himself on the bed, Jeremiah spread his arms and legs wide like a black gowned snow angel and closed his eyes to block out all the background noise that filtered in from beyond the closed window. Mentally, he began to scan his body for muscle stress, concentrating to release all the tension from his forehead to his toes, sinking deeper into the soft duvet. All active thought was extinguished by imagining a piece of plain white paper to create a pure state of receptiveness. The more he relaxed the easier it was to clear his mind until eventually new, more fluid images began to appear. Though steady at first, their rapidity increased and the disjointed ramblings of the Cosm bombarded his brain. Millions of voices all scrabbled as one to be heard. Patiently, he allowed the chaos to flow over him, concentrating hard not to focus on any single individual, waiting as all the hopes and dreams, fears, despairs, joys and sorrows of the Cosm trampled his psyche in a relentless stampede powering through the eternity of time and space until at last, everything stopped.

'I see you,' he whispered.

Blinking against the daylight, Jeremiah opened his black eyes, disorientated as he lifted his sluggish body from the bed.

He removed the dress and rummaged through Sarah's wardrobe again for something more practical then, grabbing a set of Ray Ban's off the dresser to hide his demonic eyes, left the apartment while the image from his vision was still fresh inside his mind.

Chapter Twenty-Two

Janet and Nick returned home to find the house quiet and still. While his mother put the kettle on, Nick went into the dining area. Through the patio doors he could see his father stacking bricks in the garden. Heaving a spade that was nearly as big as he was, Andrew shovelled sand from a builder's sack onto a sheet of plywood laid down to protect the lawn. Watching them work together as father and son reminded Nick of the days when he and George had dug out the fishpond. He remembered the hard labour and his aching muscles afterwards, the agonising blister in the centre of his palm caused by friction from the spade handle, and how much he had just wanted to go and play with his friends. If only he had appreciated them for what they had been. Father and son together, sharing the tiny moments that passed in the blink of an eye yet would last in memory for eternity.

'Here you go, love,' Janet said, passing Nick a mug of tea. 'Mind, it's hot.'

'Thanks... How is he?' he asked.

Janet joined him at the patio doors. 'He's coming to terms.'

Nick paused.

'Is that true?' he asked.

Janet took a cautious sip of her coffee.

'I'm sorry for bringing this on you. I never meant for any of this to happen.'

'I know you didn't, love,' she said. 'Don't ever think that this is your fault. It was an accident. They happen to hundreds of people every day. It's not your fault.'

'But look at us, mum. Look at poor dad. He looks so old.'

'He's just tired, that's all. None of this has been easy for anyone. But you're back now and that's all that matters,' she said, wrapping herself around him from behind. 'My beautiful boy is back. I can remember when you were born; when I first held you in my arms. You were perfect. You came from inside me. I made you and you were perfect. Your dad was so proud, we both were. When you were about eighteen months you said your first word. It was dad or ad' as you said it then, but I'll never forget it. I don't have to tell you that it thrilled your dad, saying his name first.'

Nick smiled.

'We helped you take your first steps. I sat up with you every night teaching you to read so that when you started school you'd have a head start.'

'I think I can remember that,' he said as a remnant of the distant memory returned.

'Can you?' Janet smiled. 'Nick, both you and Andrew have brought so much happiness into our lives, in more ways than you'll ever know, and I don't want it to ever stop. This is what family is all about. We stick together and get through together. Your dad's in shock. He just needs time to adjust, that's all.'

'But what if he can't, what if he won't?'

'He will, I promise. He's your dad and he loves you more than life itself. Look, I've made him a cup of tea. Why don't you take it out to him, see if he needs some help?'

'All right, if you think it'll work,' Nick said, taking the cup.

Outside, the sun was baking and with every step Nick fought to level his anxiety. The tea in his hand slopped to the concrete so he stopped to compose himself then turned the corner into the garden. With a deep intake of breath, his heart thumping in his chest, Nick walked over to his father, purposefully leaving distance between them so as not to appear threatening to George's delicate condition.

Andrew stopped his shovelling and watched for a reaction from his father.

'Hello, dad,' Nick said.

George stopped what he was doing but was still unable to look at Nick.

'That for me?' he said noticing the mug in Nick's hand.

'Yeah, I thought you could do with a break.'

George stared at the mug as though it were something alien before taking it, unintentionally touching Nick's skin as he did so. Instantly, his eyes widened and a tear collected in the corner of his eye.

'So, what're you up to?' Nick asked, desperate to bring some normality to the situation.

'I'm ... erm, me and Andrew... we're building a wall,' George replied. 'Then I... thought about extending the rockery a bit more and maybe... take it up another level to try and... make the waterfall bigger.'

'Cool.' Cool? As soon as the word left his mouth Nick kicked himself. He looked at the weather worn ornamental frog spewing water from its mouth at the top of the miniature waterfall and remembered back to younger days when he had chosen it. Countless happy memories came flooding back to him filling more of the void that had lain empty until now.

'It'll only be a couple of feet high... nothing too big,' George continued, searching for words of his own. 'Your mum would go spare.'

When he felt the awkwardness begin to ebb, Nick dared a smile.

'Would you like a hand?'

'Are you sure you're up to it?' George asked.

'Absolutely.'

'Well... we could always do with another pair of hands. Come on, you can help me shift these bricks while Andrew shovels the sand.'

That was how the rest of the afternoon had been spent; a reticent yet proud father with his two sons working side by side, just how he had always imagined it to be. God only knew how it had happened but Nick really had come home. The son who worked beside him was no more of a lie than the solid red brick in his hand or the heat of the afternoon sun that caused his shirt to cling with sweat. Every so often, George would steal a sideways glance at the boys. Then sometimes it was just for the sake of looking, just because he could. Many times George had to compose himself to stop from bursting into tears of joy.

Even long after Andrew had got bored and disappeared indoors, George and Nick had continued filling the footings with concrete, neither wanting to stop in case the moment was lost forever. For Nick it was an apology for all the times he had refused to help his. For all those lost moments and memories they should have shared but never had.

For George, it was just good to have his boy back.

They drank lemonade while George shared a joke about a one legged nun that Nick must have heard a hundred times before yet, when his dad told it, was still just as funny as the first. Any strangeness that may have existed between them was gone. Now, he was home.

'Dinner's ready!' Andrew called from the patio door.

'Coming,' the two men shouted. They looked at each other with a smile.

'Thanks, dad,' Nick said, pulling off his work gloves.

'No, thank you. You've been a big help today,' George replied.

'You know what I mean.'

George placed the wheelbarrow down and took Nick by the shoulders pulling him close.

'Come here,' he said. Nick's chin hooked over

George's shoulder and he could feel his son hug him back. 'It's not often people get a second chance. I'm not going to waste a single minute of it. I don't understand any of this and I don't care. All that matters is that you're back. That's all that ever mattered.'

'I'm sorry, dad. I'm sorry all of this had to happen.'

'It's not your fault. We're all still here and that's what counts.'

Their eyes connected and Nick could have lost himself for an eternity in the pain George had stored up over the past five months. All of the pent up anger and frustration, the helplessness and self-loathing, it was all there reflected behind his kind and thankful eyes. It was his burden and his strength. 'Now then, come on. Buck up. Your mum's dinner's getting cold and you know what she's like.'

Nick gave a knowing smile.

'Come on,' George said, 'let's get cleaned up.'

Just then, Janet called out from the patio doors.

'Are you two coming? It'll be ruined.'

'On our way,' George called back. He threw his arm around Nick and they made their way indoors to the exquisite aroma of roasted pork.

'Something smells good,' Nick said.

'Shoes!' Janet cried as she transferred the serving dishes to the table.

Delighted with the normality of it all, Nick kicked his boots off at the door apologising as he entered. George followed suit.

'Doesn't change, does she?' Nick whispered.

'Nope,' George agreed.

'Andrew, keep stirring the gravy unless you want lumps. Come on you two; go wash your hands and faces, please.'

'Yes, mum,' they said trudging off to the utility room while Janet fussed over the cutlery. Just as Nick was leaving the kitchen she caught sight of his clothes.

'Look at the state of your jeans, they're filthy,' she clucked.

'Oh Janet, behave,' George said.

'Sorry, I'm fussing, aren't I? It's just so good to have you back.'

'It's good to be back mum,' Nick said, giving her a reassuring look.

Janet smiled, swelling with pride over the family she had produced, untouchable to the last. 'Come on; hurry up so we can get stuck in.'

Once everything was laid, they all took their usual positions at the table as though nothing had changed. Andrew was first to dive for the serving spoons.

'Wait,' Janet said, tapping his hand. 'Not yet.'

She took her time to look round the table at each of them. They were all smiling and happy just as she had always imagined. Finally, the homecoming she had dreamt of for five long months and it was every bit as fulfilling as she had pictured.

'I know we've never been religious or anything but I'd just like to say a few words before we eat. I've never been very good at this kind of thing but I wanted to, while we're all together, just say thank you to God for bringing Nick back to us. It's a miracle, and I want Him to know just how grateful we are. And the food, and everything we have here as a family.'

'But especially the food,' Andrew chipped in, 'and it's getting cold.'

They all laughed.

'That was a beautiful speech love,' George said, taking her hand across the table.

'Yeah, thanks mum,' Nick said, taking the other; together again at last.

The meal was just as delicious as it smelt and they ate until fit to burst. Under Janet's instructions they left the dishes, transferring to the living-room to slob out in front of the television just like old times. Loosening his belt and trouser button, George slid down onto the sofa next to Nick who found himself pinned between his parents. Janet cuddled into him, reassured by the warmth and solidity of his body. Andrew was on the floor by Janet's legs and, as a family, they tried to leave the horror of the last five months behind. No excitement, no drama. Just relaxing in front of the TV, losing themselves in someone else's story, safe in the knowledge that it was all just make believe. Except now, the Howells knew different. Now, they knew that horrendous things did happen to ordinary people. Of the life changing consequences a simple lapse in concentration could create. How the safety shrouding their unfairly short lives was so fragile, so precious, that to waste a single moment would be insane. Yet it was impossible to savour every moment of everyday with everyone you knew. In the end, the only thing that anyone could achieve was to make the most of the time given, no matter how short or insignificant; to live every day as though it might be the last; every second, every breath, every laugh, every tear, every heartbeat, and every kiss.

Every kiss.

Nick tried his best to concentrate on the show but, the more he tried to focus the more his thoughts turned to Amy. Somewhere out there she was going about her life completely unaware of his return. It had been easy in the beginning when he had no idea of her existence, no concept of the love they had shared. But now the knowledge saddened him to the core. For Nick, it was only yesterday. His thoughts and feelings were just as strong as they had ever been, and with each passing moment he could feel his anxiety mount. His need to see her, to touch her, to make her aware that he was all right, that he was back.

'Dad, I need to ask a favour,' Nick said.

Janet lifted her head from his chest and looked at

him.

'Of course, anything' George said, still engrossed in the show.

'Could I have a lift into town, please?'

'What?' George tore himself away from the screen.

'No,' Janet said without hesitation. 'What for?'

'Well… I haven't spoken to Amy yet. I should see her; let her know I'm all right.'

'But you've only just got home,' she continued. 'Spend some time with us and rest before you start thinking about anything else. Stay in tonight.'

'But, I've got to let her know. All I need is a lift. I'll stay an hour, max.'

George shifted uncomfortably.

'What… what is it?' Nick asked.

Janet stared at her husband, searching for help, for confirmation that the pain she was about to inflict on her son was necessary. George's eyes softened in agreement.

'Nick, there's something you should know.'

'Go on,' Nick said as Janet's unwanted dread began to work its way inside.

'Amy couldn't wait. She's with someone else now.'

Nick's stomach clenched as though the wind had been knocked clean from him. He looked to his father for a sign; anything to say it was a lie but could see in his eyes that it was true.

'Why are you saying this?'

'It's true,' George said.

'She told me herself,' Janet continued. Then she found herself doing something she thought never possible, she began to defend Amy. 'From the moment of the accident she stayed with you, every night for over two months. But then she started to lose hope. The doctors said you were gone, that it was only a matter of time. Nothing was changing, your condition wasn't changing. She had to let go.'

'You didn't stop though, you didn't let go.'

'That's different, I'm your mum. I'll never let go. But Amy couldn't do it anymore.'

Nick stared into her eyes, desperately trying to understand how it had all gone wrong, the tears welling in his own. How could she have abandoned him? Had she ever really loved him to have thrown away their life so easily?

He needed to get out of here, out of the room. Swallowing back his tears, Nick left for the refuge of his bedroom.

Downstairs, Janet remained on the sofa, full of guilt for the hurt she had caused but knowing it to be a necessary evil.

'Love, don't blame yourself,' George said. 'He had to be told at some point.'

But Janet stayed silent; aching with the pain Nick must be feeling right now.

'Come on, it'll be all right. He just needs time, you'll see.'

Chapter Twenty-Three

For a long time Nick stayed in his room, refusing to speak with anyone while he tried to accept the truth of what his mother had said. But no matter how hard he tried to rationalise it, his mind forced him to accept the sickening truth. He knew that if he could only see her again he would be able to change her mind, to make her see that all of her waiting would not have been in vain, that they could still be happy together. He had to try.

Nick went to the bathroom to freshen up. Janet was waiting for him at the top of the stairs.

'Nick, I'm sorry,' she began.

'Don't worry about it. You're only the messenger,' he said. 'Don't beat yourself up.'

'I know how much she meant to you, and how much this must hurt.'

'Means to me,' he corrected, unable to contain his anger. 'Yes it hurts, but I'm going to see her anyway.'

'But why?'

'Because I want her to know that I'm all right.'

'Nick…'

'Mum, just don't, okay. Don't argue with me on this. I'm going to see her whether you like it or not.'

'But I'm only thinking of you.'

'And that's really appreciated but I'm going anyway,' he said.

'All right. And what if she says no. What if she doesn't love you anymore?'

Nick leant on the wash basin and stared at the soapy water.

'Then at least I'll know I tried.'

Begrudgingly, Janet conceded. What else could he

do? Nick needed closure. He needed to know either way for his own sanity whether the love he and Amy had shared was truly dead or whether the slightest chance still existed that they might salvage something from this mess. Without it, how could he ever expect to move on and rebuild?

'One condition,' she said.

Nick turned to her. 'What's that then?'

'Your dad takes you and your dad picks you up, and no arguments.'

For a moment, Nick managed an appreciative smile.

'Thanks mum,' he said.

'I may not agree with you sometimes, but you're still my son,' she said with a hug. 'Go and do what you need to do. We'll still be here and ... no matter how it turns out tonight, don't forget that we love you. I don't ever want to lose you again.'

'You won't,' he said. 'I promise.'

Fifteen minutes later, Nick and George were on their way to Amy's. Nick's stomach cart wheeled with anticipation and his foot tapped repeatedly as adrenaline surged through his body.

'So, do you know what you're going to say?' George asked as he negotiated a turn.

'Not a clue,' Nick replied.

'Didn't think so. Just play it cool. No matter what happens, just remember to keep your self-respect.'

This was rich advice coming from a man who had spent the best part of five months at the bottom of a bottle, but Nick was still thankfully unaware.

'Don't worry, I will. I just need to know what's going on in her head. If there's nothing left then at least I'll know.'

'Right. You expect me to believe that?'

'I've got to try, dad. What else can I do?'

'Not a lot really, son. Women are a funny breed. Just play it cool, that's all I'll say.'

'Thanks, I will.'

Before too long, they pulled up opposite Amy's four storey apartment block. Nick could see her place was in darkness but then it was not dusk yet.

'Do you want me to wait?' George asked.

'No, it's okay. I don't know how long I'll be so you might as well go home. I'll call you later when I need picking up.'

'All right then. Just make sure you do though. Don't try walking or else your mum will kill us both.'

'Ha, I won't,' Nick said. He stepped from the car.

'Oh, and another thing,' George called before Nick had time to slam the door, 'if you do manage to get lucky at least call, just to let me know you're not coming home, all right.'

'Dad! Just get going will you? Bloody hell.'

George chuckled.

Smiling, Nick shut the door and watched George pull away. Alone on the pavement, he stared up at Amy's window and the place that had once been their home. What if this new boyfriend of hers had already moved in? Even though nerves were making him feel sick to his stomach, he needed to stay positive. Crossing the empty road, Nick made his way into the front entrance of the building. Nothing had changed. Everything was exactly as he remembered and yet it felt unfamiliar to him. He pressed the elevator button and recalled when he and George had carried a sofa up the fire escape nearly giving his poor dad a hernia. This building was as much a part of him as he was of it; so many memories, so many great moments.

On the second floor, Nick made his way to Amy's door feeling unprepared and scared to ring the bell. He tried to imagine how she would look now and prayed that her new boyfriend was not inside, not tonight. Tonight was for him, his chance to turn it all around and claim his life back.

Nick pushed the button. The doorbell chimed from somewhere inside. Searching for calm, he waited. For thirty seconds he waited without a sound from the other side. He pushed the button again, and again there was nothing. After all the nerves and build up, she was out. Nick exhaled and laughed as a weight lifted from his shoulders.

'Damn,' he said, resting his back against the wall, breathing heavily through a broad smile as the tension flowed away.

Wondering what to do next, he considered waiting for her return, but for all Nick knew she could be out for the night (with *him*) and the thought of spending the evening in a cold corridor like a lap dog while she was out there doing God knows what was not even worth entertaining. At the moment, Nick had no name or face to go by and so found it surprisingly easy to pretend Amy's new boyfriend did not really exist.

Then, an idea came to him. With renewed determination, Nick took the stairs and exited the building into the warm evening air. The sky was still faint as the remnants of the day fought to cling on. He needed something, anything, to prove that somewhere his old life still existed, that the sun had not yet set on everything he once held dear.

When he reached the market place, Nick was filled with a sense of homecoming as he passed the same old shops, unchanged by his time away. Ahead in the distance stood the eternal monument of St. Botolph's church, tall and proud, its two hundred and seventy-two foot tower keeping a vigilant watch over the town.

Suddenly, he stopped.

With his toes at the kerb, Nick stared down the narrow one-way street where the car that stole his life had struck him not a foot from where he now stood. He could still hear the screeching tyres, still see the world violently spin from view as he was sucked off his feet onto the car bonnet, still remember the pain. Nick's breathing quickened. Five months ago the air had been filled with the sound of screaming. Now there was only silence.

An approaching car slowed for a speed bump in the road and its passenger, a teenage girl, stared at him while her boyfriend tried in vain to save his oversized exhaust from the raised section. Nick held her gaze for only a second, and then moved on.

Down Craythorne Lane, he approached the main door of Sammy's and felt comforted by the music from inside drifting onto the street. Through the glass-block windows Nick could see the soft glow of lamp light and the blurred motion of people inside. He felt giddy to be walking back into the place, the hero returned, and the atmosphere embraced him like an old friend.

Above was the balcony from where people could observe the main gallery of the bar below. It was also the best vantage point for lads to peer down the girl's tops. The memories flooded back as the familiar sounds and smells enveloped him. The odour of furniture polish mixed with the faint tang of stale beer from the over abused carpets. The floor was quite springy tonight. Steve, the manager, must have shampooed the carpets recently. The walls were filled with memorabilia from the sixties and seventies; old posters, a signed Hendrix guitar (authenticity unsure) and other bits of tat that had been picked up along the way. To his left were tables filled with the young and the young at heart, while to his right was the bar. There were no doormen tonight. The idiots of the town only came out on a Friday and Saturday. Family may have been where Nick's heart lay but right here, in this place was where his life blood flowed, this place which had moulded him into the man he had become, for better or worse.

Moving to the end of the bar, Nick took a coin

from his pocket and tapped it on the counter. Steve and Becca were leant on the pumps chatting to some punters. He knew just how much it would irritate them.

'What's it take to get a drink around here?' he called as obnoxiously as he could.

Becca gave him a cursory glance, not even trying to disguise her contempt, before returning to her conversation. Nick rapped the bar again.

'Just keep doing that,' Becca called to him with stony eyes. Then, like a slap in the face, it hit her.

'Oh my God,' she whispered as her hand went to her mouth.

'What is it?' Steve asked, and then saw for himself. 'Nick?'

Becca raced from behind the bar and threw her arms around Nick planting her lips onto his. Her kiss was long and passionate and when he tried to pull away she clung on regardless. His fantasy about this moment, about the taste of her lips, the warmth of her body pressed against his, could not compare to the real thing. Finally releasing him, she pecked him once more on the lips before squeezing him tightly.

'Out of my way,' Steve said as his portly frame barged through to grab Nick, hugging him like a lost child. 'You're late. I'm docking your pay.'

Nick burst into laughter just as Steve did something which no human being had ever witnessed before from this mountain of a man. He began to cry.

'You daft bastard,' he wept, threatening to squeeze the very life from Nick. 'We thought you were dead.'

'Mate, that's lovely,' Nick wheezed, 'but I can't breathe.'

A roar of laughter and cheers erupted as Steve was told to man up.

'Ah, piss off you lot or else you're all barred,' he said, wiping his eyes as the crowd jeered him some more.

'Get this man a drink. Come on you rabble, make some room.'

Ploughing people aside with his mammoth arms, Steve took Nick over to one of the stools. 'Why didn't you tell us you were back? I would've done something. Organised a party, you know, got the old crowd in for ya.'

Becca placed a pint of lager on the bar for Nick.

'Thanks,' Nick smiled taking a long cool sip. It was like a little taste of heaven. 'To be honest I didn't know myself mate, kind of just happened. I went to see Amy but she's out.'

Steve gave him a sideways look. 'That's because she's here.'

Nick suddenly felt that old anxiety return and he placed his pint on the bar.

'Where?' he asked, searching the tables.

'Upstairs, Green Room,' Steve replied.

Nick stood to go but Steve held his arm.

'Wait, there's something you should know.'

'I know, I've heard.'

'About ...'

'Yes.'

'Oh, right,' Steve said. 'Well, he's here with her.'

'Oh… right,' Nick said. His enthusiasm sagged.

'Don't be mad with her, mate. She did her time and she waited. She was with you every night after the accident but thought you were gone; we all did. I shouldn't worry though,' he said brightening up, 'he's a total wanker. Do you want me to bar him?'

Nick gave a small laugh. 'No mate. If you barred every wanker from the place you'd have no customers.'

Steve grinned, pleased to have his old friend back. 'True.'

Taking one last gulp of beer, Nick patted his old boss on the shoulder and made his way up the stairs.

He was just about to step through the doorway to

the Green Room when he stopped. Directly beyond the door was the pool table taking centre stage with tables and chairs ringed around the outer edges of the room. He could see her sitting with three others, two men and her best friend, Pippa. She was happy, smiling, and for a second he contemplated just going back downstairs, finishing his beer and then calling his dad. But he loved her so much and the only reason Amy was there right now, with that man, was because she thought he was dead. It was time for her to see the truth.

Squaring his shoulders, Nick stepped into the room and positioned himself just short of the pool table. The music faded into obscurity and all he could see was her.

Amy had changed her hair. He liked it. It made her look more mature than he remembered. Still going unnoticed, he tried to guess which of the men his replacement was. Then, the blonde sat next to Amy took her hand and kissed it as if to remind anyone watching that she was his. Nick's jealousy flared and for an instant he wanted to rush over and rip her hand from his, to scrub it clean from the taint of his stinking lips; but he didn't.

Nick could see that everything was different now. He should not have come. He should have listened to his mother and stayed at home, enjoyed their company and then gone to bed, happy. There was still time for him to slip away unnoticed. He could leave Amy to her new life and never come back. After all, it had been his own stupid selfishness that had gotten him this far but now, faced with the irreversible truth, he wanted to run as far away as possible. To retain his memories of their history without the stain of *that* kiss, and of *his* face.

But it was too late. The conversation at the table stopped.

'You all right?' Simmo asked, wondering why his girlfriend could not stop staring at the man across the room. 'Amy?'

'Who's she looking at?' whispered the other man to Pippa.

'Jesus Christ,' Pippa exclaimed in shock, unable to believe what she saw. 'Nick?'

'Who?' Simmo said, looking from Pippa to Amy. 'Who's Nick?'

Amy rose from the table and slowly made her way over to the pool table forcing the two men playing to abandon their game and watch as Nick came to join her on the opposite side. When he stepped into the table light's glare, Amy gasped.

'Hey you,' Nick whispered.

That was all she needed. No other words could mean as much right now as those two simple words. When George had called and told her that Nick was awake she had been filled with so much confusion, and had gladly walked away to continue with her new life but all that was changed now. Seeing him here, how could she have been so foolish? Rushing around the table, Amy threw herself into Nick's arms and, remembering how it felt to be held by him, her emotions flooded back.

'I'm so sorry,' Nick said, squeezing her, kissing her head and face.

Amy clung to him as tight as she could. 'God, it's you. It's really you!'

'And I'm not going anywhere.'

'But how? The doctor's said…'

'We'll talk about it later.'

'Excuse me, but what the hell's going on?' Simmo said, rising from his seat. Pippa tried to hold him back but he shrugged her off.

'Oh God, Simmo,' Amy stammered. 'This… this is…'

'I'm Nick,' he interrupted, 'Amy's boyfriend.'

Amy looked at Nick with a mixture of horror and sadness over the life that had seemed so easy to leave behind.

'I'm sorry? Did I miss something?' Simmo exclaimed somewhat confused. 'Amy, what's he talking about?'

'Simmo, I think...' Pippa started but he cut her off.

'This has got nothing to do with you. Amy?'

The whole room went silent save for the background music that continued like an unwelcome guest, everyone's attention focussed on the drama, and Amy could feel all eyes trained on her.

'This is ... Nick, my... ex-boyfriend.'

Being labelled as *the ex* was like a kick in the guts. Simmo just looked at him with disdain.

'He seems to think differently. Is there something I should know?'

Amy shrank, feeling the burn.

'He was in an accident and spent a lot of time in hospital... in a coma... but, obviously, he's out now. This is the first time we've seen each other since the accident.'

'You never told me.'

'I couldn't. It was too painful. Can we talk about this later?' she pleaded.

The more words that came from Amy's mouth the more Nick's heart plummeted.

'And what about now?' Nick interrupted. 'Do you just want to ... forget about it? Forget about us?'

Amy just stared at him with teary eyes, unable to speak.

'Look mate, she's upset. Why don't you just go home and leave us in peace?' Simmo said.

'I'm not talking to you, I'm talking to Amy,' Nick said without looking at him.

'And you're clearly upsetting her so why don't you...'

'Why don't you just shut up and mind your own business,' Nick said, ready to step it up a gear.

'You what?' Simmo countered.

'You've known her for all of what… five minutes? Amy and I have history, years of it, so why don't you fuck off and let us sort this out alone.'

'Well, it didn't take a lot for her to forget you in a hurry. Maybe she was just waiting for the right opportunity?'

'You cheeky bastard,' Nick growled, lunging for Simmo's smug grin.

'Nick, no!' Amy cried, throwing herself in his path. 'Just stop it, both of you. Neither of you own me. I make my own decisions!'

'Amy, I'm sorry,' Nick said backing away; angry for losing control. 'I never meant…'

'Nick, just don't, alright,' she said waving him off.

Simmo stepped back with a grin of satisfaction, thinking he had gained the upper hand for not losing his temper first.

'Come on babe,' he said slipping his arm round Amy's waist, 'let's go home.'

'No, I'm going to *my* home, alone. I need time to think.'

'Amy?' Simmo started.

'No! I'll speak to you … both tomorrow.' Amy rushed from the bar full of embarrassment and confusion. Giving both Nick and Simmo a look of contempt, Pippa quickly followed leaving them to stand redundant in her wake.

The two men just stared at each other with equal hatred, and then Nick followed suit and made his way downstairs.

Whispers of the confrontation had already filtered down and Becca came to him, but Nick ignored them all. The place suddenly felt claustrophobic and rotten, and he needed to get out. He needed to be home again, in the safety of his bedroom where he should have stayed all along. Damn his stupid pride.

Without saying goodbye, Nick left the bar for the very last time, unaware that he would never see any of them again. And as he powered his way down Craythorne Lane towards the marketplace he failed to notice the figure of a woman emerge from the shadows behind him.

Chapter Twenty-Four

Both Janet and George were startled from their semi-conscious state on the sofa by Nick slamming the back door. It took them a moment to realise what was happening until Janet saw him flash past the living-room door and stamp his way up stairs. Ever since Nick had left the house earlier she had anticipated this and had spent the evening formulating scenarios of how best to comfort her son on his return. At the foot of the stairs, she just managed to snatch a glimpse of him as he disappeared into his room.

'Nick,' she called up after him. 'I thought we agreed that your dad was going to pick you up?'

The only reply she received was the slamming of his bedroom door.

'Looks like you were right,' George said.

'I should go up there.'

'No love, leave him until the morning.'

'But he's upset. He needs me.'

'He needs his privacy. Nick's not going anywhere and he's a grown up now. Speak to him in the morning.'

With a heavy heart and one final glance up the staircase, Janet returned with George to the sofa.

In the darkness, Nick played the events over and over in his mind and got angrier with every re-run. It had taken hours for him to find peace in sleep. Then, in the early hours of the morning he woke again with a wretched feeling of betrayal. How could she have done this to him?

Somewhere in the darkness, Nick sensed movement and he froze, forgetting all thoughts of Amy. His widening eyes gradually became accustomed and started to feel ridiculous, convinced that his strained mind must be playing tricks on him again until the spectral image of a woman on the end of his bed emerged through the gloom. Nick shot back, pressing himself flat against the wall like a trapped animal.

Hidden in the confines of Sarah's dead body, Jeremiah stared at Nick with all the time in the world.

'What's going on?' Nick stammered. 'Who are you?'

Nick could just make out the slightest of smiles touch the woman's lips.

'Hello Hesamuel,' Jeremiah spoke with Sarah's dulcet tones.

'I ... I don't ... Do I know you?'

Jeremiah's smile widened.

'You're from the hospital. But, what are you doing in my room?'

Ever so slowly, Jeremiah crept up the bed like a stalking panther until they were practically nose to nose, so tantalizingly close. He imagined running his ice cold fingers across Nick's chest, his warm blood drenching Jeremiah's decaying skin, his mounting desire pulsing with blissful agony within his female groin.

Jeremiah leaned in and brushed Nick's ear with ice cold lips. 'I've been looking for you.'

'Your name's Sarah. You're one of the nurses who took care of me. I remember you. But how did you get in? What are you doing here?'

'Well now, that's the question isn't it,' Jeremiah said.

Something glinted in the corner of Nick's eye and that was when he saw the carving knife on the duvet. Jeremiah picked it up and placed it on the bedspread between them.

'What's that for?' Nick asked. His voice barely a whisper as every muscle in his body locked with fear.

'To get your attention,' Jeremiah replied. 'Why don't we call it insurance?'

'For what?'

'I'd like to make you a deal.'

'What ... kind of deal?'

'Abaddon sent me to destroy you ...'

Nick began to panic. 'Look please, I don't ...'

'Hush. Please, let me finish,' Jeremiah urged. 'As I was saying, not that you'll understand what the hell I'm talking about, but I've been given this wonderful gift, and all I have to do is destroy you but before I do that I have another option for you to consider and, believe me, if you value the brief time that you have here you'll listen real good.'

'But I don't know anyone called Abaddon. You've got the wrong person, I swear. I've only just got out of hospital. I've been in a coma for five months. You know this. You took care of me. You've got the wrong person.'

'Ha, I know all about it. Now, I want you to think back real hard. I want you to remember when we met on the Border.'

'What?'

'Just concentrate. Trust me, everything depends on it.'

Nick broke into a sweat as his eyes darted from Sarah's face to the knife.

'You touched me, Hesamuel, and I felt whole again. You took away my pain; you took away the darkness in my soul and helped me remember how it felt to be one with the Light again. My deal is this. Do it again, for good. Take away the darkness. If you can do this for me then I swear on my sweet mother's grave - and I loved my mother - no harm will come to you, from me anyway.'

Nick's mouth turned arid, stunned by just how mad this woman really was. Breaking into their home and putting herself on his bed proved her conviction, but listening to the craziness coming from her mouth only assured Nick that if he did not think fast he was as good as dead. Suddenly, Nick thought of his parents.

'Where's my family?'

'They're safe. For now, this is between you and me.'

'For now?'

'Can you do it?' Jeremiah urged, gripping the knife handle.

'Yes, yes I can do it,' Nick lied wondering what the hell to do next. 'Just put the knife away, you don't need that anymore.'

That was when Jeremiah knew Nick was lying. He had heard the whines of enough pleading victims to know they would say just about anything to get him and the weapon as far away from them as possible just to stay alive. Jeremiah knew; it was his vocation. No-one ever escaped and no-one survived. That had been Abaddon's reason for choosing him. The Cosm was nothing but a testing ground and through a life once lived he had learned to kill and love it, savouring all of its finer moments until in the end murder became almost predictable.

Jeremiah hung his head in disappointment. It had been foolish for him to think that Nick would remember any of it while his soul still slept inside his living body. This was not over though. There would be another time, another chance for him to follow his own agenda. Jeremiah now had all the time in the world. However, right now was Abaddon's time, Abaddon's plan.

Nick watched in silence, his eyes flitting once more from Sarah's face to the blade, and without warning her head snapped up, piercing him with a stare so malevolent that Nick knew this was the end.

'Please!' Nick shouted, feeling tears of desperation filling his eyes. 'Please don't. I can help you... let me try!'

'I'm sorry, you had your chance. Maybe we'll meet

again ... in another life.'

'Wait!'

But it was too late. When the blow came it was swift and accurate from a lifetime of practice. At first there was pain, then darkness, and then nothing.

The End of Book One

ABOUT THE AUTHOR

Matthew Barnes lives in Boston, Lincolnshire with his partner, Dawn, and their two cats, Bert and Ernie who are a constant source of distraction and amusement in equal measures.

Made in the USA
Charleston, SC
13 April 2013